Enthusiastic praise for America's
newest thrill-master,
WILL STAEGER
and
PUBLIC ENEMY

"An unusual mixing of humor and suspense.
If Carl Hiaasen wrote a James Bond adventure,
it might be something like *Public Enemy*—
funny and scary and slightly larger than life."
Connecticut Post

"Cooper is a hero for our cynical age,
and Staeger gets it all dead right.
Say hello to a major new talent."
James Siegel, bestselling author of *Derailed*

"Excellent . . . hold-your-breath action
and a chilling outcome as real as today's headlines
. . . a spy novel for our times."
Madison County Herald (MS)

"For avid fans of the first book, this one's a must-read,
and those who skipped the first
should give it a shot, too."
Booklist

"Will Staeger and his unique brand of
adrenalized lyricism are gonna be around
for years to come."
Gregg Hurwitz, bestselling author of *Last Shot*

Books by Will Staeger

PUBLIC ENEMY
PAINKILLER

WILL STAEGER

public enemy

HARPER

An Imprint of HarperCollinsPublishers

This is a work of fiction. Names, characters, places, and incidents are products of the author's imagination or are used fictitiously and are not to be construed as real. Any resemblance to actual events, locales, organizations, or persons, living or dead, is entirely coincidental.

HARPER

An Imprint of HarperCollins*Publishers*
10 East 53rd Street
New York, New York 10022-5299

Copyright © 2006 by William H. Staeger, Jr.
ISBN: 978-0-06-076590-3
ISBN-10: 0-06-076590-9

First Harper paperback printing: May 2007
First William Morrow hardcover printing: July 2006

HarperCollins® and Harper® are trademarks of HarperCollins Publishers.

Printed in the United States of America

Visit Harper paperbacks on the World Wide Web at
www.harpercollins.com

10 9 8 7 6 5 4 3 2 1

for Sophie and Brick

He pressed the button and the cacophony began. The big door descended, wheels running noisily along the twin metal tracks, and then it was over, and he stood in silence, and darkness. He thought of releasing his grip on the handle of the coffee mug he held; he knew the ceramic mug would shatter, the lukewarm coffee pooling on the concrete floor, never to be swept clean. But he didn't drop the mug. Instead, he made his way in the semidarkness to the light switch, and in a few seconds the ceiling-mounted rack of fluorescent bulbs bathed the garage in a diffused moon lime glow.

A black Chevy Blazer occupied one side of the garage. Along the opposite wall were rows of fertilizer bags, stacked nearly to the ceiling. Beside the fertilizer stood bags of grass seed and topsoil; two dozen red, five-gallon fuel canisters were pushed against the bags.

The man approached the workbench at the back of the garage. He used pliers, a Phillips-head screwdriver, and a soldering gun to secure a series of contents within seven crimped lengths of narrow brass pipe. This took him about twenty minutes. When he finished, he set the seven devices in a neat line on the bench.

What he did next would have horrified his wife, but not for the reason he supposed it should have. Armed with a fishing knife, he sliced open each of the bags of fertilizer and, one by one, emptied their contents into the cargo space in the rear of the Blazer. He ignored the bags of topsoil and grass seed. When he had filled the back end of the SUV nearly to its ceiling, he removed a stepladder from its hook on the wall, stood it beside the Blazer's passenger-side door, and proceeded to pour the remaining complement of fertilizer through the sunroof, burying the leather seats his wife had demanded they include as an option in three feet of ammonium nitrate pellets.

He closed the rear doors and made sure each of the side doors was sealed. Then, mimicking his transfer of the fertilizer bags, he carried each of the five-gallon canisters of fuel from its place against the wall, up the stepladder, and, obscenely, poured each container's fuel in through the Blazer's sunroof. The garage soon reeked of diesel fumes.

He took the lengths of crimped brass pipe, reached in through the sunroof, and dispersed the devices evenly throughout the vehicle. From his perch on the stepladder, he reached into his pocket and depressed the appropriate button on the Blazer's car-alarm remote; the sunroof closed and the parking lights flashed once, the doors locking noisily.

He came into his kitchen, where he noticed a plastic fire engine parked beneath the kitchen table. He took the toy from under the table and returned it to the playroom.

The kitchen stairwell took him into the basement. Once there, he opened the top door of the aging refrigerator-freezer reserved for soft drinks and beer. From his pocket came the trusty Phillips-head screwdriver, which he used to remove ten screws at the base of the freezer. When he had the screws out, he reached beneath the edge of the panel he'd just unfastened and removed a metal storage container the size of a shoe box. He used a combination to open the container's lock and opened its lid to reveal fourteen glass vials, each plugged with a wax-sealed cork.

He pocketed a pair of the vials, resealed the container, and returned it to its hidden compartment.

In the kitchen, he ran warm water over the vials in the sink until the cold fluid became less viscous. Vials repocketed, he returned to the garage; at the workbench, he broke the seal of the first of the vials and removed its cork, revealing the gelatinous, deeply blue contents within. He stood, nearly motionless, observing the reflection made by the fluorescent lighting on the surface of the fluid. He had thought through this part upward of ten thousand times, inevitably drawing the same conclusion he drew again now.

He had no choice.

Seizing the vial in his right hand, he lifted the tiny container to his lips, threw his head back, and consumed the flavorless fluid in a single swallow. He set the vial back on the workbench and stood still for nearly five minutes while his stomach grumbled noisily, objecting to the offensive drink it was forced to digest. He left the second vial in his pocket.

From an open cardboard box on the workbench he removed the last of the day's devices: a tiny black box with a green flip switch. While approximately the same size as the car-alarm remote, it was nonetheless simpler in both design and purpose.

Using the stepladder, he climbed onto the Blazer's roof and stretched out, facedown, on the cool surface of the vehicle's skin. In his right hand was the black-box remote. He looked at it, then readied his thumb beside the flip switch.

Electing not to engage in further doubt or debate, he pushed the switch against its housing and closed his eyes.

He thought to himself in the instant before his death that he would be the first martyr of his kind. Perhaps nobody would know it; perhaps nobody would open, or understand, his message-in-a-bottle. Perhaps when the truth emerged, if it ever did, his wife and son would come to understand; perhaps not. No matter. He knew he was acting piously, and that his actions were just, and necessary.

At that point his thoughts ended abruptly as, along with

the Blazer and the majority of the house enveloping it, the man's body was dispersed in a sudden, crude, foul-smelling eruption of fire, black soot, and enflamed fragments which, in their violent fury, flattened nearly two square blocks of the suburban housing development in which the man and his family had once owned their home.

Powell Keeler III, Po to his friends, was following the sloping curvature of the Lesser Antilles in the 150' Trinity motor yacht that was not his own. Po had taken his time since setting out from the Caracas Yacht Club four days prior; he'd been clear enough with his client, an old high school acquaintance and owner of the Trinity. They'd come to an agreement, Po taking the gig on one condition:

There wasn't any rush.

His client needed somebody to sail the Trinity back home to Florida, a return leg on which the client, following his family's six-week cruise through the Caribbean, did not care to use the boat. Having caught wind of this predicament, Po, bonded yacht transporter as he happened to be, offered his services as a favor—such favor being predicated upon his old buddy's fronting him fuel money, a token fee, and sufficient cash to cover one month's premium on the bond Po held as a condition of his transport license.

Once his old pal acquiesced, Po headed down to Venezuela posthaste.

Standing now at the helm, Po eased the yacht along its northwesterly course from a point some ten miles due east of

Virgin Gorda. It was early, with the first orange crescent of sun an angry harelip on the black horizon. Seas were calm. Po had elected to navigate around the British Virgins, looking to avoid its endless supply of reefs and shallows on his way to the evening rendezvous he hoped to share with the bikini-clad babes known to cluster at the main swimming pool of the Atlantis resort on Paradise Island in the Bahamas.

The Trinity was loaded with dual Furuno FR2115/6 radar units, which Po had taught himself how to use a few jobs back. This meant, among other things, that Po understood perfectly well what the instruments were now telling him.

Four vessels, one of them significantly bigger than the Trinity, loomed directly in his path. The fleet was camped out five miles to the north, with the two smallest boats on his screen closer than the others. The yacht's radar had also detected an airborne object that wasn't flying particularly fast, located halfway between the Trinity and the fleet.

A helicopter.

It had been five minutes since Po had spied another high-altitude speck in the brightening sky. Based on what he'd been able to see, Po had a pretty good idea what kind of plane it was, and this, in turn, gave him a pretty good idea what the fleet of boats and their helicopter escort were all about.

The "speck" was a P-3 Orion surveillance aircraft. Having detected his early morning departure from Anguilla, the plane's occupants had tracked his subsequent route and, extrapolating, assumed the worst—as might be expected from the Coast Guard's regional antidrug task force fleet. The fleet's assigned duty was to intercept, impound, or destroy the seemingly endless supply of "go-fast" racing boats bound for Florida or alternate points north. On a typical day, upward of three go-fasts—super-high-speed racing machines with their cargo bays retrofitted to haul upward of two tons of coke—took their shot at the continental United States from the general vicinity of the Greater and Lesser Antilles.

On average, the Coast Guard was going two-for-three, season-to-date.

Po was well versed on how to deal with such drug-interdiction efforts, misguided though they were in coming after him. The problem—over and above the secret cargo he had agreed to cart up to Naples in the hold of the Trinity—was if you let the Coast Guard snatch you in international waters, you were pretty much doomed, since the Department of Homeland Security claimed to possess the right to impound and destroy any "suspicious" boat in such waters, whether or not such boat was shown to be holding contraband. The preference, upon seizure, was to immediately destroy the boat. By taking out vessels, the task force reduced the pool of drug-running ships it had to battle; plus, scuttling ships relieved the task force of the time it took to cart the impounded vessels to San Juan or Miami, where seized boats were broken into their base parts and prepped for federal auction.

Po toggled the radar display and the zoomed-in perspective on the monitor revealed that one of the smaller boats had kicked into gear and was now approaching the Trinity at speed.

He saw that the helicopter too had set its sights on him.

Gunning the yacht's throttle, Po gave the wheel a quarter-turn to port, making a steep turn out of the open waters of the Atlantic into the territorial reign of the British Virgin Islands. Without probable cause, drug-interdiction etiquette dictated that in NATO-ally territorial waters—the BVIs, Martinique, or Montserrat, for example—Coast Guard officers could only board and inspect a vessel with its captain's permission. Even then it was mostly a waste of time, since the Coast Guard held no official power of arrest in the sovereign territory of another nation. In NATO-ally territorial waters, the task force simply preferred to pin down the offending vessel and summon the local authorities for arrest and impound.

Sporting the benefit of a two-mile cushion between the

Trinity and the chase boat, Po zipped down the middle of the Sir Francis Drake Channel, aiming for the friendly confines of Road Harbor—the bay abutting Road Town, Tortola, capital city of the British Virgins.

It seemed to Po that the early-to-rise local populace and overwhelming presence of tourists on the most populous island in the BVIs would at least lessen the likelihood that the Coast Guard task force would fuck with him.

When the first of a pair of 22' Coast Guard "OTH" chase boats, accompanied by the aerial support of its teammate, an MH-68A "Stingray" helicopter, met up with Po Keeler and his client's yacht, it happened just inside the rocky spit that shielded Road Harbor from the rolling swells of the channel. The encounter that followed might have proceeded in a perfectly civil manner were it not for the condition a second client of Po's had imposed upon him as part of the shipment of the eight large cargo crates currently stacked in the hold of the Trinity.

The cargo was to be accompanied on the journey from Caracas to the yacht's home port in Naples, Florida, by two men, whom Po's secondary client referred to as "security personnel." The security personnel possessed, according to the secondary client, all required documentation and approvals—in other words, while they were Venezuelan, and spoke no English, their passports were ostensibly stamped with a U.S. Department of State authorization number that would clear them through customs. The client assured Po the "security personnel" would stay out of his way on the trip, and in fact were instructed to leave him entirely alone. They brought their own provisions, promised to remain in the vicinity of their cabins, and agreed never to leave the boat.

Po frequently accepted money in exchange for hauling illicit shipments during his licensed transport gigs, and in so doing stood by a strict set of rules: no drugs, no guns, and no explosives. And while he had never before agreed to cart "security personnel" along for the ride, the Venezuelan who became his secondary client was paying big money—and his cargo, whatever it was, otherwise complied with Po's rules. Thus, despite his misgivings, and largely influenced by the hefty cash advance, Po agreed to the deal, watching as the eight crates and two accompanying "security personnel" were loaded into the Trinity's hold from the pier at the Caracas Yacht Club. The two men skulked aboard without so much as looking at him, and hadn't made a peep since.

A squat, rubber-hulled speedboat featuring a deck-mounted turret gun and little else, the OTH, named for how fast it could get itself "over the horizon," had four soldiers aboard for its approach. One manned the deck gun, aiming it in the general direction of Po Keeler; two stood on the yacht's side of the OTH, hands held near their firearms like a pair of cowboys set for a Wild West draw. The fourth spoke into a handheld microphone that broadcast his voice over a set of loudspeakers Po observed to be mounted on bow and stern.

"This is the U.S. Coast Guard District Seven task force!" the agent said. The sharp treble tone of the agent's voice over the OTH's loudspeakers pierced Po's ears, audible despite the roar from the Stingray helicopter hovering behind the yacht. "Request permission to board your vessel!"

The Stingray banked slightly against a gust of wind.

Po descended the steps that led from the cabin to the deck of the yacht. Keeping his arms stretched away from his body, he brought his right hand to his forehead in a salute, made a two-fisted thumbs-up gesture, and waved the task force agents aboard.

As two soldiers from the OTH prepared to board the Trinity, Po turned slightly to the side. This allowed him to see something the soldiers could not. When Po saw it, an ulcerous burn that had been coagulating in the vicinity of his heart—establishing itself the minute the "security personnel" had skulked aboard his boat—sank suddenly into his gut and exploded.

With only their jet black hair visible to begin with, the head of first one, then both of the Venezuelan skulkers emerged from the hatch Po knew to access the engine room. As the men rose from their hiding places, Po observed each to be armed with weapons appearing both bulky and slim— bulky enough to be of military grade, slim enough to have been stowed in the suitcases the fucks had toted aboard the boat.

Po made the instantaneous decision to abandon ship.

In two leaping bounds, he reached the polished chrome railing at the bow of the Trinity, planted a foot on its gleaming edge, and propelled himself outward and down.

And while he intended it only as a survival measure, Po's dash-and-splash maneuver also served to distract both the Coast Guard gunners—the soldier manning the OTH's deck gun and a second in the helicopter—in a way that gave the Venezuelan gunmen all that they would need to accomplish their intentions.

With the Uzis they'd stowed in disassembled form in their suitcases, the men took aim at the deck of the OTH and threw down, strafing much of the chase boat's rubber hull with their poor aim but nonetheless managing to dispatch all four of its crew before a single bullet was fired upon them in return.

The pointless nature of this proactive salvo was illustrated in abrupt fashion as the machine gunner aboard the Stingray helicopter, only momentarily distracted by Po's dive, let loose on the Venezuelans with his .50-caliber gun. In guilt-ridden overcompensation for his failure to properly defend the agents aboard the OTH, the machine gunner continued to pummel the bodies of his targets with round upon round of shells long after both men had died, riddling the rear, then the midsection, then the whole length of the Trinity, shouting obscenities at the offending gunmen as he went. Sparks flew, then smoke spewed, and finally the entire stern of the Trinity erupted in a blast wave of orange flames. Roiling black clouds followed the explosion into the Caribbean sky as flames licked skyward, reaching twenty or thirty yards above the deck of the yacht.

It wasn't until this pyrotechnics display had been all but consummated that the machine gunner remembered and took aim on the man who'd dived overboard.

By then, however, the pilot of the helicopter had begun screaming at the machine gunner through his radio headset to cease fire. When the gunner did not comply with his order, the pilot pulled the Stingray out of the fray. By the time the machine gunner finally relented, both he and the pilot could plainly see that Po Keeler's outstretched arms were raised skyward in hapless surrender. He was treading water almost directly beneath the helicopter, head mostly submerged, sputtering and gasping as he sought to reach his hands as high in the air as possible to indicate his innocence.

Keeler began a frantic dog paddle for the hull of the OTH chase boat. He held one arm aloft as he pulled himself aboard with the other, maintaining his one-armed gesture of surrender throughout. At length he managed to turn himself around and plant his rear end on the gunwale, where he proceeded to raise his other arm and drop his head in relief and disgust.

At that point the task force commander followed the protocol he'd been instructed to heed in cases of armed conflict within foreign territorial waters. Following a cryptic update from the pilot of the Stingray, the commander hooked himself into a satellite phone line from the bridge of the task force's main cutter and dialed the man he knew to be the head of law enforcement operations for Road Town.

The Coast Guard's designated liaison for any such drug-interdiction activities inside the borders of the British Virgin Islands was the longtime head of the Royal Virgin Islands Police Force and newly elected chief minister of the BVIs. He was a man who, despite his elevated status as chief minister, still went by the nickname he'd bestowed upon himself during a time when he'd held a more junior position on the force.

The full name of the task force's designated liaison was Roy Emerson Gillespie, but those who'd met him—and even a few who hadn't—knew to call the man by his preferred, self-appointed nickname: Cap'n Roy.

Cooper studied his opponent. Prescription sunglasses keeping anybody from reading his eyes, long-sleeved silk shirt somehow made to look like a polyester blend, a single, curling tendril of smoke rising all day and all night from the cigarette he kept clasped in his hand—Cooper didn't recall his taking a single drag on the cigarette in forty hours at the table, and yet that tendril of smoke remained, rising endlessly from the season ticket the man's yellow-nailed fingers kept for themselves at the edge of the felt.

There was never once a change in the expression on the man's face, only a mild wince that never eased, as though he'd had prosthetic makeup applied before assuming his position at the table. Earlier, Cooper had noted the resemblance to photographs he remembered seeing on the back of Tom Clancy novels; as the battle wore on, he began to wonder whether the man cleaning his clock for twelve straight hours might actually have been the best-selling author, before writing this off as a delusional endeavor enacted by his fatigued, inebriated mind.

Of all the skill-free competitors who'd made it through to the eight qualifying tables—a roster loaded with Russian mob bosses, CEOs both current and deposed, even a head of state—Cooper just had to get stuck with this clandestine four-time World Series of Poker champion bluffing him out of the building from behind his Tom Clancy prosthetics. With maybe eighty percent of the paid-in-full bozos taking Fidel up on his offer—comped charter jet, free digs aboard the converted cruise liner, and an endless supply of brown-skinned hookers, all in exchange for a one-time $250,000 entry fee—just to *blow* their money . . .

They had worked more or less together in picking off the other competitors at their table for the first twelve-hour session, but once the amateurs were dispensed with, Clancy had begun working him over like a speed bag. He did so most notably on three separate intentional busted bluffs, where the prosthetic Clancy had made a relatively large wager on dog-shit hole cards, losing as though it was becoming a habit, careful each time to "accidentally" reveal his cards rather than just cede the hand. Cooper knew what he was up to—*Look, buddy: when I bet big, I'm always bluffing*—but his knowledge held no value as the momentum began to shift, his piles shriveling like a scrotum in ice water. He felt as though he was watching a train wreck develop, the way he figured you'd feel when parked on the tracks inside a stalled, locked car, that blinding, Cyclops headlight of the train making its relentless approach.

All of which had set the stage perfectly for the moment in which he was now mired.

Head-to-head, the winner moving on to the finals—loser headed home two-fifty large in the hole. Forty hours of this hard-earned semifinal round culminating in the largest pot Cooper had ever seen, every color of chip imaginable covering every square inch of the felt. Clancy had just taken Cooper's ten-thousand-dollar softball of a last-round raise and bumped him another two hundred grand. Clancy, of course, wasn't risking all of *his* chips: the bastard still had maybe four hundred grand stacked beside the cigarette hand, and knew perfectly well his raise was enough to force Cooper all-in. Engineered to psychological perfection, no less: Cooper had been losing consistently for a couple hours now, and Clancy knew Cooper had become starved for a win, tempted to gamble on Clancy holding another of those dog-shit hands he'd let him see so many times in a row.

Cooper suspected Clancy was holding a high pair, a good place to be in a game of Texas Hold 'Em featuring three face cards out there on the flop. Meaning it had come to this: Cooper could hold on to his remaining eighty-some thousand in chips—cling to this crumbling cliff he'd been trying in vain to prop up—or roll the dice, as it were, and give his opponent the chance to put him out of his misery. His pair of sixes in the hole had a snowball's chance in Havana of winning the hand, but if he didn't play for the steal, he'd be out of chips in another thirty minutes anyway.

Cooper pushed the last of his chips into the gargantuan pot, pointed a finger and lowered his thumb to indicate a trigger-pull in the direction of his opponent, and eyed the backs of Clancy's pair of cards. Over they came, and Cooper took in the colorful pair of kings, meaning Clancy was full of kings over jacks, and that the tendril of smoke and prosthetic mask were headed for the final table and a shot at the five-million-dollar championship prize, while Cooper, with his deadly two pair, was headed home around two hundred and fifty-two thousand lighter than when he'd stepped off the porch of his bungalow five days back.

For the hell of it, as the man raked in the enormous pile of chips, Cooper examined his opponent's expression one last time, checking for any outward sign of satisfaction, pleasure, vengeance, or thrill. He found none—only the unchanging prosthetic wince.

The tendril rising.

Cooper left.

He took a three-hour catnap in the morning sun, going without a lounge chair, just laying himself out on a towel by the lone functioning pool. Wearing nothing but a pair of green

Tommy Bahama shorts decorated with palm trees, he passed out until he felt alert enough to get behind the wheel of his Apache—point his racing boat east and try to stay awake while it took him home.

Cooper had more of a dark weathering to him than a tan, his shoulders a deep brown, precancerous wasteland of bone-dry skin, the rest of him a few notches lighter but just as worn. His black hair was streaked with more gray of late, though the gray was hard to see now that he'd started chopping his mane a little shorter. For any of the competitors wandering past on the deck, it was hard to place his age: could have been forty, could have been sixty, depending on the angle. When he opened his eyes, one thing that could be seen was that W. Cooper, as he was known, was a man who'd checked out a couple decades back.

He'd lost at this poker tourney the year before too, at the inaugural launch. That made a cool half million he'd blown in thirteen months, but he wasn't ready to count it as a loss just yet: play in this thing six, seven times and he figured he'd be able to pull out a win, putting him, considering the advertised payout, somewhere around three-point-five million ahead. All that had to happen for this to play out was a little luck—and for Fidel Castro to remain alive.

Once he'd caught wind of Castro's private game, he knew he wanted in, but as a so-called employee of one of Fidel's least favorite institutions, landing an invite involved certain evident challenges. For the chance to even get a *look* at the sordid cast of competitors certain to be invited to Castro's personal cash-stash fund-raiser, though, Cooper figured it would have been worth whatever measures it took to secure a ticket in. He found what he needed on a highly classified list of Agency assets in the Greater Antilles, reading the name, four or five down from his own, of a Cuban national holding a position on Fidel's personal security detail.

Cooper made a few phone calls and discovered that somebody in Langley had, at the Cuban's request, arranged for the defection of his second cousin, once removed, who happened to be one of the country's top pitching prospects. Upon his defection, the pitcher had succeeded in signing a three-year, $6-million contract with the Florida Marlins. Cooper thinking at the time he dug this up that the three-year contract put the kid about 5,999,999 bucks ahead of what he would have earned during an entire career playing ball in his homeland, the only money he'd make back home being the second job the Revolution required him to hold.

Cooper pulled a string or two, got the Cuban security officer's phone number, and went ahead and had the man pile atop his debt-to-America-related assignments the addition of the name W. Cooper, with the address of a post office box in the British Virgin Islands, to the list of invites to Fidel's inaugural game. One particularly heavy bag of U.S. currency later—*small bills preferred*, the invite said—and Cooper was doing battle with some of the richest men ever to cheat on their wives, the competitors doing so by way of a seemingly endless supply of Cuban call girls provided by Fidel between the marathon sessions of Texas Hold 'Em. Castro held the event aboard a refurbished cruise liner, which Cooper heard from a fellow competitor had fallen victim to repeated instances of Legionnaires' disease before its big-name corporate cruise company had decommissioned the vessel and dumped it for free on whoever was interested in signing a waiver clearing the company of any residual liability.

By Cooper's count, in that first year of holding the game, Che's old buddy Fidel had managed to land forty-two takers, which, after the nominal cost of refurbishing the cruise liner, transporting the guests to the event, and buying their food, drink, and women, the last surviving symbol of all things revolutionary had pocketed five million good old-fashioned American dollars of his own, above and beyond the winner-take-all five million dollar purse.

Duly rested, Cooper abandoned his poolside slumber on the deck of the cruise ship and cleaned out his cabin. He threw on a tank top, slipped into his new choice of flip-flops—Reefs—and got one of Fidel's charges to ferry him over to his Apache. He fired up the boat's twin MerCruiser 850-horsepower 572-CID blowers and immediately slammed the throttle all ahead full, shooting for the best time the 41' Apache could muster for zero to sixty knots on its way out of the otherwise tranquil Havana Bay.

The trip back to his home turf, which he preferred to make using a route running south of Puerto Rico rather than north, took him just over three hours. It put him in dire need of another nap, Cooper swinging out of the Sir Francis Drake Channel and into the Conch Bay Beach Club lagoon, a shallow bay wrapped in white sand, palm trees, and what had once been the best snorkeling, pound for pound, in the Caribbean. The preponderance of visiting tourists had eroded the pristine quality of the aquatic scenery somewhat.

Normally, he might have found it interesting that a pair of U.S. Coast Guard cutters were parked across the channel from the club. This was something he had seen before, but only once. Today, however, the only thing that interested him in the slightest was a drool-ridden snooze fest.

He splashed down in the Apache's skiff and rode over to the beach club dock. He stepped out of the boat without tying it off, leaving that for Ronnie, the club's errand boy, to handle. Cooper knowing Ronnie would need to flee, midtask, from his lunchtime table-bussing duties in the Conch Bay Beach Club Bar & Grill to do it—and if Ronnie couldn't get there in time, Cooper would be more than willing to delay his nap for a few minutes to stand and watch the putz swim out and retrieve the boat from the open bay. It might even be that the resident barracudas would grow agitated at the errand boy's presence, and bite him.

Cooper planted his feet on solid ground for the first time in six days at ten till two in the afternoon, the oppressive Caribbean sun beating down on him through the humid soup that passed for air. He had fantasized about this moment for days, the fantasy largely responsible for keeping him awake during the latter portions of the head-to-head battle with his prosthetic-faced opponent. He had pondered, considered, even salivated at the prospect of a tall glass of Maker's Mark on the rocks, a swordfish sandwich, basket of conch fritters, and a bare minimum of eighteen consecutive hours of sleep.

Because of this, Cooper did his best to ignore the additional presence—coinciding with the cutters across the channel—of the 24' Royal Virgin Islands Police Force patrol boat parked against the last piling of the beach club dock.

Reclined on the pilot's seat was a cop wearing the RVIPF's standard Marine Base getup—royal blue polo shirt, beige khaki shorts, black-and-white-checkered cap with a glossy bill. The cop resembled a running back in the prime of his career—thick, muscular thighs, tree trunks for arms, and an abdomen flat as a board. He also exuded, by nature, an infectious optimism, one of the reasons Cooper liked him. His name was Riley, and Cooper didn't bother to greet him. He knew that his presence inevitably meant that the cop's annoying superior officer, the chief of police and newly elected chief minister, wanted to see him.

Cooper strolled through the restaurant, the place crowded today for lunch, ducked behind the thatched-roof bar, and poured himself a pint glass of Maker's Mark over very little ice. The local kid working the bar continued making the drinks he'd already been making without so much as a glance in Cooper's direction.

Cooper took a moment to pull a long sip from the bourbon. Observing the glass to be emptied by a third, he served himself a refill, seized a menu from the stack behind the bar, opened it to the lunch options, swiped the pen from the breast pocket of the bartender's T-shirt, encircled the swordfish sandwich and conch fritter selections, wrote COOPER across the bottom in two-inch block letters, set it on the counter in front of the bartender, thrust a finger upon it, told the bartender, "Tell Ronnie," then took his glass of bourbon and headed out of the restaurant.

Discovering that along with Riley, the patrol boat, and the cutters, he was also going to have to try to ignore the chatty buzz at the normally peaceful bar, Cooper kicked off his Reefs and trekked barefoot through the sharp-stoned garden path mainly just to prove that he could. Passing a series of freshly painted, breezily designed two-unit structures equipped with air conditioners and colorful flourishes of blossomed flowers, he ducked past one last palm frond to the last in the set of bungalows. On this very last of the buildings, bungalow nine, a board had been nailed into the concrete foundation on the corner nearest the garden. Positioned at shoulder height, the sign's style and placement reinforced the message its words delivered:

KEEP OUT.

Cooper ascended the stairs of his weather-beaten bungalow, came in through the unlocked door, and plunked himself upon the frayed armchair in the middle of the room's main living space. A bed, a table, an ottoman at the foot of the armchair, a kitchenette with a portable fridge, and a mostly outdoor shower-and-toilet stall were all that defined the place. Cooper took in none of it, putting back most of the bourbon, holding one of the ice cubes in his mouth, and leaning his head back against the chair's soft headrest. A faint hint of hope formed in his head, a final conscious thought.

It might just be I got away with it. Maybe, just maybe, I can sleep.

Giving in to sheer, unadulterated bliss, Cooper lost consciousness before the ice cube melted on his tongue.

4

The knock on the jalousie panes of his front door, and the deep voice that came in the wake of the knock, pulled Cooper abruptly out of paradise.

"Somebody order some food, mon?"

Cooper didn't need to hear the *mon* to know it wasn't Ronnie, the soccer-playing Englishman and dutiful errand boy, standing on his porch with the swordfish sandwich. He could smell the sandwich through the door. He could smell the side dish he'd ordered along with it too. The voice went on.

"Ladies in the kitchen make it up nice 'round here. Something special 'bout these conch fritters."

Cooper's rumbling stomach nearly shook him from the chair.

"Go home, Riley," he said. His own voice sounded sludgy and deep to him, ridden with the sleep he wanted so badly to return to.

"Swordfish still piping hot," Riley said outside the door. "Gonna cool off, I leave it waitin' for you on the porch."

Thinking he would just consume the food and let Riley have his say before dispatching with him, Cooper said, "Fine."

He had a pretty good idea how to get Riley to skedaddle.

Riley pushed open the door and came in supporting the tray of food one-handed, the solid-bodied cop looking like a practiced waiter. As little as Cooper knew Chief Minister Roy Gillespie to allocate to police salaries, he figured Riley was moonlighting somewhere—but probably not in the food-service industry.

Cooper took the tray and started in on the sandwich. After he'd inhaled a good chunk of it, he looked up from his lunch.

"Whatever it is you want," he said, "you've got until I finish this food to give it to me."

Riley nodded pleasantly.

"Cap'n Roy looking to see you, mon," he said. "We had ourselves a little excitement in the harbor this mornin'. Maybe you heard, maybe not, just comin' in now."

Cooper temporarily neglected the last remaining corner of the sandwich while he laid waste to the conch fritters, making sure to dip each gob in the spicy Thousand Island sauce.

"Yeah?" he said, mouth full.

"Yeah, mon—Coast Guard task force take somebody out, and hard," Riley said, "but they not quick enough on the draw this time. Multiple casualties, mon."

Cooper sipped the ice water Ronnie had been kind enough to add to his order. "Sounds exciting," he said.

"Uh-huh, well, way these things work, we seize the vessel, the contraband, everything. Any drugs, we hand 'em over to the Coast Guard. Anything else, we keep."

"And?" Cooper polished off the remaining corner of the sandwich and popped the last two conch fritters in his mouth.

"And Cap'n Roy askin' me to come get you. Says he thinkin' maybe you be willin' to help with some o' the more complicated matters."

Cooper placed his tray on the ottoman, moving his Power-Book and its portable printer aside with the lip of the tray as he set it down. He lifted the glass of ice water again, drained it, and set the glass back on the tray. Then he reclined in his armchair, assuming almost precisely the same position in which he'd recently fallen asleep.

It was time to get Riley to skedaddle.

"Riley," he said, "for all intents and purposes, I haven't slept in six days. Plus, the only thing I managed to accomplish in the process of this sleep deprivation was to lose two hundred and fifty thousand bucks. Actually it came closer to two fifty-two, counting fuel and incidentals. Ordinarily, Lieutenant, I wouldn't trouble you with such matters. The reason I mention it now, however, is so that when you return from this friendly visit and report back to our esteemed chief minister, you'll be able to explain my position entirely clearly."

Cooper had closed his eyes. Riley waited, but Cooper offered no further comment.

Finally Riley said, "And what that position be?"

One eye popped open. "My position, Lieutenant, is that the only way you're going to get me out of this chair for the next forty-eight hours is if Minister Roy is willing to pay me around two hundred and fifty thousand bucks to do it. Two fifty-two, to be precise."

Cooper shut both eyes again. He quickly began to feel the trickling onset of sleep, but the return of bliss slowed when he sensed Riley hadn't left. He opened his eyes to find the lieutenant still standing there. In fact, not only had Riley not left—the man had a grin plastered across his face.

"When he ask me to come visit," Riley said, "Cap'n Roy tell me somethin' like this: 'Tell him this time, we make it worth his while.'"

"Riley," Cooper said, "I don't even think Roy knows what two hundred and fifty thousand *looks* like. Strike that—no doubt he's seized that much and more from anybody with a busted taillight giving him the chance to do it. But we both know he'd never give a penny of it to anybody. So skedaddle."

Riley held his grin.

Cooper said, "What the hell is so funny?"

"Probably be true," Riley said, "that this is the kind of thing fall outside my area of expertise, mon. But still, with what I seen today, it seem to me there be a lot more than two-fifty to go around."

Trying in vain to keep up the fight now that his skedaddle strategy had backfired, Cooper dropped his head to wrestle with his predicament. First, he remained skeptical there was in fact that much money at stake. Second, he couldn't think of any good reason he should help Roy do whatever it was Roy needed help doing. The last time he'd helped Roy out, what followed hadn't exactly been a tea party. And third, as Cooper knew quite well, the more Roy was paying, the more questionable the task would turn out to be.

Cooper mused that he *could* think of a few things the money he'd just lost might come in handy for, were he to find a way of recovering it. Assuming, of course, that Riley's assessment was correct, and that Roy was actually good for it.

Christ.

"I'm tired, Lieutenant," Cooper said.

Riley's smile grew one notch wider and he issued a clap that resounded through Cooper's sluggish skull like a crazed pinball.

"I'll do the drivin', mon," Riley said. "You can sleep on the way over."

As he steered Cooper past the Coast Guard cutter anchored outside the entrance to Road Harbor, Riley tossed a jovial salute to the sentry standing guard at the stern.

The sentry didn't bother acknowledging him.

Cooper observed the attack helicopter parked on the cutter's helipad, rotors spinning. The chopper made a lot of noise, which made Cooper notice the unusual preponderance of noise as a whole. Except for semidaily cruise ship dockings and the regular arrivals of the turboprop commuter planes delivering tourists to Beef Island, Road Harbor was normally a peaceful place. But not today.

Coming around the breakwater—a place where Riley had made a grim discovery a year and a half ago—Cooper caught his first view of the mayhem at the root of all the noise pollution. That was the only word for it, *mayhem*— Cooper never having seen such bustling activity or having heard such noise here in nineteen years as a neighbor.

Roy's Marine Base fleet was out in force—actually in its entirety, Cooper counting all five boats including Riley's, the other four buzzing around the harbor in what Cooper had come to recognize as Cap'n Roy's way of assuming control of a crime scene: every cop on the scene remained active, but if you looked closely, you would notice none of them was accomplishing a thing. The volunteer salvage team was deployed in full SCUBA gear, most of them busy on the pa- trol boat decks, a couple of them swimming in the bay. The city's fireboat was spraying a geyser of water, the 40' tug po- sitioned the farthest possible distance from its target so as to allow for the most glorious possible arc of seawater, even though whatever fire had been raging had long since been doused.

The target of the fire hose was a custom luxury yacht Cooper pegged at 140-plus feet, the word *Seahawk* posted on its side in tall, cursive, sterling silver letters. The yacht's stern had burned down to a charred stump, and was still warm enough to be steaming under the deluge from Roy's tug. A second, smaller boat, an open-deck rubber-hulled deal featur- ing the familiar red-and-white Coast Guard paint scheme, was lashed to the Marine Base pier ahead of the yacht, and displayed no apparent damage. Cooper recognized it as one of the task force chase boats he'd seen from time to time, and knew it to be capable of speeds in excess of sixty knots. Fat chance that boat had of catching his Apache, at least not when he had the MerCruisers tuned—knob the fuel aerator over to its richest mix and he'd leave that chase boat in the dust.

Riley took the long way around, circling the harbor on his approach. Cooper guessed that Roy had instructed him to do this—make sure he caught the full scope of the mayhem—so he ignored the intended view and instead took in the passing shoreline. They swung past the empty cruise ship berth, eased along Road Town's main waterfront district: a pastel rainbow of shops, the new ferry terminal, one pair of strip malls, then all of it giving way, up and back, to half-constructed buildings and rougher lots on the slopes of the town's two hills.

Unwatched tour concluded, Riley brought them into the harbor's bigger marina. He passed the series of lime-and-red storage buildings lining its eastern edge, approached then passed under the fountain of water spraying from the fireboat, then finally pulled the patrol boat alongside the only available stretch of dock space. The dock fronted a grouping of aluminum-sided structures Roy had succeeded in getting everybody to call the Marine Base.

It was only after they'd parked that Cooper encountered the first sign that Roy might not have dispatched Riley solely to roust him from slumber.

Three upstanding members of Roy's regular militia—meaning non–Marine Base men, cops wearing long pants and patent-leather shoes—stood guard before the closed doors of a building called the Barn, a storage facility in which the lesser-ranked Marine Base cops normally housed the department's heavy marine equipment. Cooper took the presence of the regular RVIPF cops as a sign—since, first, in looking back, he couldn't remember their having guarded anything, ever, and second, because today they also happened to be armed.

In the British tradition, RVIPF cops typically did not carry.

The lanky West Indian who always seemed to be busy with something or other on the Marine Base pier took the patrol boat's bow line from Riley, secured it to a tack, and went back to his business. It appeared to Cooper that the guy was gutting a fish on one of the wide planks of the dock.

Looking forward to getting home, Cooper didn't wait for Riley to lead the way and instead leaped onto the dock, stern line in hand. He tied the line off, stuffed his hands in the pockets of his swim trunks, and, after a glance over the shoulder of the fisherman to confirm that it was, indeed, a fish he was slicing open, headed inland solo.

In a matter of seconds there appeared, strutting toward him from the Marine Base headquarters building, a man with the stiffest spine Cooper had ever known. Like the director of a big-budget action film deigning to greet the studio representative visiting the set of his picture, Cap'n Roy Gillespie, apparently having decided to lose his three-piece chief minister suit and reoutfit himself in full police-chief regalia for the occasion, reached out for a handshake as they met a few yards from the dock. Cooper rudely kept his hands lodged deep in the pockets of his swim trunks.

Cap'n Roy wore a pressed white polo shirt, sharply creased gray slacks, the same shiny cap with the checkered band that Riley wore, and a set of gleaming patent-leather shoes. Cooper marveled yet again at how these guys could consistently wear slacks in the humid ninety-degree heat without emitting sweat from a single visible pore.

They stood in the midst of a gravel parking lot currently occupied by more police and civilian vehicles than Cooper remembered ever having seen anywhere in the islands. Roy remained undeterred by Cooper's rebuff; his smile gleamed so pearly white it made his deeply black skin appear almost blue.

" 'Ey, mon," he said, "if it isn't the spy-a-de-island, come by to see us down the Marine Base way." The words flew from his mouth like the lyrics to a reggae track.

"Normally it'd be a pleasure, Roy," Cooper said. He always avoided using Roy's self-proclaimed nickname. "But today isn't really the best day."

"We under high alert, mon. State of emergency."

"I see that."

Roy motioned for Cooper to follow as he started toward the Barn.

"Got something I'm thinking you maybe wanna see, mon," he said with a wink.

Cooper followed him across the gravel. He elected not to bite on Roy's joke—this was exactly what Roy had said the last time Cooper had been asked to help the RVIPF out of a bind.

"This time," Cooper said, "I'm encouraged by the approach you instructed Lieutenant Riley to take."

"Yeah?"

"Yep—primarily because Riley seemed confident my demand for a fee in the amount of two hundred and fifty-two thousand U.S. dollars would be met."

Roy returned the salute from the guard at the main door to the Barn, unlocked the padlock himself, and opened one of the big double doors to which the padlock had been affixed.

"This time 'round," he said, "money be the whole point."

Cooper followed him inside and Cap'n Roy didn't say another word.

Cooper figured Roy was waiting for Cooper's eyes to adjust—that was what Cooper was waiting for—and when they did, Cooper beheld the sight that had injected the Royal Virgin Islands Police Force with such fiscal optimism, and the reason Roy had clammed up.

It seemed the stash the chief minister was holding inside the Barn spoke for itself.

Set out as though for auction, or maybe to photograph—lit, as it was, by police spotlights rigged to function as museum-style lighting—there stood a collection of various objects, some massive, some miniscule, but every single one of them appearing to be made of solid gold. The collection filled the Barn, a building Cooper had once seen host a full-court basketball game. It looked to Cooper like the second coming of the King Tutankhamen exhibit, a display he remembered observing in relative awe as a child.

He quickly counted seventy smaller objects—busts, heads, vases, an egg—along with a dozen full-body statues, three room-size tapestries, and nine boxes of varying sizes. Pretty much every one of the objects depicted, in one form or another, exotic figures wearing bejeweled robes, or warriors in full headdress. Cooper sensed a sort of recognition, a familiarity, with the faces depicted by the figures—and then, when his eyes had adjusted well enough to make out the features of the individual faces, a sudden anger swelled in his throat.

The surge made him want to yell, to scream out a string of obscenities and brutally trash the display Roy and his boys had so carefully arranged.

He swallowed back the odd impulse, wondering whether he might have just gone insane, whether it was in this one moment that he had finally lost it, crossing over the line of lunacy: *Goddamn statues, I'll kill you, who am I, I'm hearing voices, WHO AM I?* But then, as quickly as it had come, Cooper's bout with madness retreated.

He had a fleeting sense of the source. It had to do with the familiarity he'd felt before the swell of rage had come—he *knew* the faces on the idols on display in the room, or at least descendants of the people portrayed by them. The high, thick peaks of the cheekbones, the slope of the forehead, the teardrop orbs of the eyes . . . it had been people with faces something like these who had once imprisoned and tortured him, and who continued to torment him even today, by way of a recycling nightmare circuit that rarely neglected to make its overnight visit. .

There you have it—you've just racially profiled a bunch of gold statues.

Walking around the building to examine the artifacts with a more rational eye, Cooper guessed the faces portrayed in the works were Central American Indian—similar, though not identical, to the faces of his one-time captors. He pegged the look of these faces as a pure ethnic strain of what had appeared in his captors as one watered-down dose among many.

The full collection of artifacts was in mint condition, polished to a degree rivaled only by Roy's shoes. Eight large, opened wooden crates stood in one of the back corners of the Barn with cardboard spaghetti and other padding paraphernalia strewn about them. In seeing this, Cooper was reminded of what he'd read about that old King Tut haul: anybody foolish enough to dig up somebody's sacred burial ornaments, plus anybody foolish enough to come into contact with them down the line, was said to be subject to a curse. With death generally befalling those who caught it.

Cooper considered he wasn't exactly in a death-curse kind of mood—and that meant it was time to call off whatever Roy had in mind for his latest in a long line of bullshit stunts. The chief minister could keep whatever money he was offering, and recruit somebody else to handle whatever questionable task Cooper had been ferried over to undertake.

"Catch," Roy said from behind him.

Cooper turned and instinctively caught the foot-high idol Cap'n Roy had just tossed him. As Cooper began to object, Roy threw him a second, smaller statuette—and then a vase. Half-juggling those he'd already caught, Cooper snatched each from the air as they came before realizing what he'd just done.

Great—whatever curse has befallen the robbers of this tomb's bounty now rests squarely on your own shoulders.

"Seem to me," Roy said, flashing his pearly whites, "you find the right buyer, that ought to add up to two-fifty large. Maybe even two fifty-two."

Cooper examined the goods he held in his hands. The dull *clunk* resulting from contact between the sculptures confirmed that they were, in fact, solid, and they certainly looked like gold to him.

Thinking, *Well, you've already got the damn curse,* he looked over at Roy.

"I'd put these three at one seventy-five, tops," he said.

After standing expressionless for a moment, Roy nodded sharply, reached down to retrieve an ornately carved gold box, then tossed this too in Cooper's direction. Cooper caught it in the crook of his elbow.

Roy said, "There you go, mon," appearing pleased enough to worry Cooper to the extreme.

Cooper nodded.

"Which begs the question," he said, "of what it is you're paying me to do."

"Yeah, mon." Roy found a canvas bag at the base of the wall nearest him, came over to Cooper, and held it open while Cooper deposited the idols, vase, and box within. Roy zipped the bag shut and handed it to him.

"Come on down to the office," he said, starting out of the Barn, "and we talk about that."

After a few steps through blinding sunshine, Cap'n Roy led him into the Marine Base headquarters, a single-floor boathouse Roy had remodeled into a reception-cum-squad room, complete with hallway, holding cell, interrogation room, unisex restroom, and, mainly, a massive corner office for himself. Roy's personal office featured, among other luxuries, a vast expanse of windows affording him an entirely unobstructed view of the bay. He rarely used it now, but still retained it solely for his own use.

Roy removed his cap, reclined in the chair behind his desk, and placed both hands behind his head. From this seat, he could see much of his kingdom. Cooper took the assigned guest chair, a wooden creaker he assumed Roy had rescued from the town dump. From *his* seat Cooper could see nothing but Roy and the series of marine steering wheels and anchors affixed to the wall behind.

The idols *clunk*ed inside the bag as Cooper set it on the floor.

"Coast Guard task force come with them heavy guns, but no jurisdiction," Cap'n Roy said. His eyes were on the harbor. "Anytime your boys come into the BVIs, rule says the drug war need to live slow for a bit."

"My boys?"

"And yet," Roy said, "once in a while, it seem some unavoidable circumstance result in a fracas like the one we seen today. This happen, mon, and it put us in a gray zone. And that about where we be now: one big, fat gray zone."

Cooper knew this to be Roy's favorite sort of zone.

"Homeland Security, they okay with us keepin' the boat. Better for us to do the disposin', you see. But they prefer the contraband, of course, remain wit' the U.S. of A. Sometime back, in an unrelated matter, we hold a little discussion 'bout this and come to a compromise: drugs or weapons, we hand 'em over. Anything else, and that contraband be confiscated—public property of the BVIs, mon. Belongin' to the islanders."

Cooper saw no need to speak.

"Still, we like to keep your boys playin' by the rules, and sometime that take some encouragement. And this time, we got ourselves a bit o' leverage. It seems there one survivin' smuggler, and we got the man in custody—right here in the building."

"That so."

"Yeah, mon, and the Coast Guard want him. Our position be, Coast Guard take the boat and we keep the loot—only then we consider handin' over the smuggler. Sure you can see my reasonin'—that boat worth nothing to me, burned half to a crisp. Them artifacts, well, that be another story."

"When you say the boat's worth nothing to you," Cooper said, "it's the public property of the British Virgin Islands 'you,' correct?"

"Oh, yeah, mon, nothin' but."

"Just clarifying the rules of the gray zone."

"And ain't that nice of you, mon. You know, it turn out, after a bit o' interrogation, this smuggler tell me the contraband *you* just took fifteen percent of is one shipment among many in a pipeline of antiquities flowin' south to north. He takes a few transport deals, stays out of it other than that."

"Out of curiosity," Cooper said, "you planning on telling me anytime soon what it is you want me to do?"

Roy, smiling, made a sweeping gesture toward the sprawling, sunlit view of Road Town. "Take a look—lovely place, ain't it? Yeah, mon."

Cooper refused to turn. "Had a look on the way in," he said. "I've had a thousand looks on a thousand ways in."

"Movin' back from the water, though, it get worse, eh, mon? Roads gettin' some potholes, people hungry too. Conditions not be the best among the entire population."

Cooper yawned.

"Seem to me," Roy said, "somebody knowin' the kind of people you know might be capable o' findin' us a fence, or a buyer—maybe one willin' to pony up top dollar for the native treasure trove you just finished pillagin'. Nobody need be tellin' you how far that money'd go toward helpin' us rebuild our strugglin' little village by the sea."

Cooper felt the urge to ask Roy a question—*Native treasure trove of which natives?*—but he let it go, since there would have been no rational way that Roy could have known the answer. Plus, it was an answer Cooper wondered why he felt curious enough to ask about at all.

Leave it alone, he heard himself think.

"Took you long enough," Cooper said, "to get to that nifty little word."

Roy grinned. " 'Fence'?"

"Yeah," Cooper said. "Fence."

Cap'n Roy stood, replaced his cap, and flipped open a Nextel phone.

"Come on down," he said into it, "and take Cooper back to the beach."

Cooper snuck a look out the window. The fireboat was easing off on its dousing of the yacht with its arcing spray, the geyser from the fire hose going limp. The SCUBA divers were climbing out of their boat onto the Marine Base dock. The show, it seemed, was winding to a close.

"Any interest," Roy said, "in seein' the smuggler? I'm set to sit down with 'im again, see if there's anythin' else useful he know might be good for me to know too."

Cooper lifted the heavy bag of idols, hearing the *clunk* again as he picked it up.

"I'll pass," he said.

"Riley give you some photos for the road. We snapped every little thing in the treasure trove. Got 'em from every angle—eBay-ready, mon," he said.

Cooper, standing, saw that Riley now stood in the doorway down the end of the hall.

He looked down at his sack of contraband. *I could take this with me and decide later.* Give Chief Minister Roy a call from his bungalow, tell him he'd be taking a pass on the fencing assignment, and ship the pirated goods back by way of the Lieutenant Riley shuttle. Or, if the mood struck, he could make a few calls, toss his bag of goodies in for a commission fee, and call himself even on his poker losses.

Deciding he was too thick with lethargy to undertake any brash decision making just yet—*Always good,* he thought, *to keep your options open*—he heaved the sack over his shoulder.

Without so much as shaking hands or otherwise offering Cap'n Roy any form of farewell, Cooper left the chief minister's office, ambled down the hallway, and out past Riley into the blinding sun. He held his free thumb up and out as he passed Riley. Hitching a ride.

Riley followed him down to the dock.

5

The next morning, at six—after he'd had only fifteen and one-half hours of sleep—one of the goats residing on the old man's private residence behind the club woke Cooper up. This was a daily problem. The goats worked like a combination rooster and alarm clock, alternating only due to weather—in rain, they didn't make any noise until seven; if the sun came out, they were whining away from six o'clock on. They'd always stop after thirty minutes or so, and Cooper had never quite been able to figure out why they performed their rooster imitation in the first place. Somewhere along the line he satisfied himself with the theory that each morning, one of the goats became convinced today was the big day—that somebody would open the gate and let him wander off the old man's property and down to the beach.

The snorkeling ain't what it used to be here, kid, he wanted to tell this morning's goat. Too many boats been mooring here too many years. There's something wrong with the coral, so stay up where that old farmer feeds you apples, where you eat the shrubs on the hill, or whatever it is you do when you're not pulling alarm clock duty.

He made a pit stop for a cup of black coffee at the beachfront veranda, where Ronnie was already up, slicing melons for the guests who'd bought the meal plan. They usually started coming down from their bungalows around seven-fifteen. Cooper sat in one of the chairs and kicked his feet up on the railing, from which spot he watched the sea as it shifted from gray to blue. Parts of the lagoon soon turned a bright shade of turquoise, a color you only found in the waters of the Caribbean and maybe a scant few other exotic locales.

Across the channel, where Tortola hunched, and off to his left—St. John—he could see places where the sun, rising behind him, had begun to pummel the islands with its rays. As with most mornings, Cooper felt as though he were staring at a postcard. He'd grown accustomed, but never tired, of the view.

"What did you do with the bucket," he asked Ronnie without looking at him.

Ronnie continued with his slicing. He was working on a honeydew melon.

"Used it the day before yesterday on the ferry," he said. "Think I put it behind the kitchen."

Cooper nodded, still examining the view, then polished off his coffee and stood. Ronnie had a look at him: Cooper wore an old blue swimsuit, no shirt, and his swimming goggles, which he'd wrapped around his neck. There were enough old scars on his torso to make his skin resemble a tie-dyed shirt.

"Gettin' to work this morning, then, are you, mate?" Ronnie said.

Cooper grunted as he set the coffee cup on one of the trays Ronnie would use to bus the breakfast tables once the guests came.

"Yes, I am," he said.

When Cooper cleaned his boat, he cleaned every inch. For the all-important scrubbing beneath the waterline, he liked to dive in with the swim goggles and a sponge, mopping off accumulated grime, all the while counting off the seconds to test how long he could hold his breath underwater. Due to many years of skin diving on deeper and deeper wrecks around the islands, he'd recently been able to set his personal best, managing to count to one hundred and ninety-four: three minutes and fourteen seconds without coming up for air. Having sucked down the prosthetic-faced Clancy's secondhand smoke for a few days, though, Cooper didn't hold out much hope of breaking any records.

He took his dinghy out to the Apache and brought the big racing boat in to the dock. The dock didn't fill up until eleven-thirty or twelve, when all the visiting yacht-charter types came over from their catamarans aboard a fleet of identical-looking gray Zodiacs, mostly to sample the club's cooking, made famous by Rosie, Odessa, and Dennise, the three well-fed West Indian women who'd been working their culinary artistry there for years.

Cooper flipped the bumpers over the edge and pulled against the dock, gunning the throttle then killing it—let the boat coast into position, no bullshit reverse-forward-reverse throttle work needed here. As the Apache lolled against the side of the dock, squeezing the bumpers, Cooper tossed one line to the dock, came around to the bow to grab the other line, leaped to the dock with it, tied it off, then strolled to the stern and secured that line. He already had the bucket out on the dock, and a hose too, which he'd stretched from the spigot behind the kitchen.

Inside the bucket were his implements of destruction: the tools, towels, and solvents he used to clean his boat. The five-hour boat-cleaning job was something he could have paid one of the local kids, or even Ronnie to do, but he didn't trust anyone but himself to do it properly, or at least that was what he told himself. In truth, he had discovered it was as good a way to confront his demons as any. A kind of self-controlled therapy session.

Unlike the nightmares.

He did the work every sixty days or so, not because the Apache needed it, but because he did. He would always need the work; it would never go away. It would always stay with him, and that was why he was here, killing the pain, in one of the only places in the world where he'd thought there might be enough natural painkillers to salve any wound. But not his; his never left. It always needed fresh treatment, another dose of medication to ease the pain. A prescription to help escape the episode of his life that had brought him here—accomplished by way of skin diving, drinking, dope smoking, fucking, sunbathing, poker playing, and six or seven thousand other idle pursuits the British Virgin Islands and its environs had to offer.

But sometimes it took facing the music—and when he knew he'd need to play the tune, he preferred to do it while cleaning his boat.

The twelve-man team descended on the palace under the cover of night. They came by way of a high-altitude drop, released into the jet stream miles east of the target, the plane inaudible from the palace grounds. They came to earth silently, invisibly, the soft pads of their specialized boots ballet shoes in the choreography that followed.

It was sickeningly easy. They slaughtered the small army of sentries in seconds, aware of precisely where each guard was posted, the position of the dictator's defenders matching the satellite images each man on Cooper's team had studied relentlessly before taking the plunge into the night sky. It was too easy, Cooper soon coming to the nauseating realization that no leader of any country, of any size, could possibly be taken down so simply, with so little resistance.

Even so, they executed the prime minister in his bed while he slept, the silent spits from Cooper's muted assault rifle ending the prime minister's reign as planned—planned, Cooper came to learn, by a desk jockey aspiring to a spymaster's seat on the hallowed seventh floor of the CIA headquarters building in Langley, Virginia. The desk jockey,

*though, had grossly underestimated the influence and savvy
of the minister of defense overseeing the palace guard. So
poor was the desk jockey's intelligence, in fact, that he'd
been fully ignorant of the defense minister's ability to catch
wind of the mission Cooper's team had been deployed to accomplish. Cooper supposed he, or somebody on the squad at
least, should have considered the possibility too. But what
the hell, he came to think, did we know back then? We were
stupid goons, riding on adrenaline, raiding the palace of an
evil dictator, an ally of the Soviet empire America intended
to vanquish.*

*As the last breath passed from the lips of the sleeping dic-
tator, a second wave of soldiers in the prime minister's guard
rose from hiding places throughout the palace and dispatched with eleven of the twelve members of Cooper's goon
squad in the span of sixteen seconds. Fleeing the palace by
way of a hall behind the first-floor kitchen, Cooper found
himself surrounded—undiscovered in the initial trap wave
but doomed to certain capture. He was hopelessly outnum-
bered, finding a guard lurking behind every door, window, or
passage, Cooper creeping along in his vain search for a way
out of the palace and into the jungle beyond. But he found no
such means of escape, and instead hid in a janitor's closet,
hoping to remain in his hiding spot until they'd forgotten
him, or decided they'd counted wrong—that they'd taken
down the whole invasion team. It worked for a few hours, but
they knew he was around, Cooper hearing the search as they
worked through the nooks and crannies of the palace, approaching the kitchen, the hallway, and finally his precious
closet. He decided the best chance at anything was surrender, so when he heard them in the kitchen he eased open the
closet door, reached his hands out past its knob, and pushed
his gun into the hall with his padded shoe.*

*He'd never been able to determine why they hadn't just
killed him. He supposed their anger needed a symbol, a puny
enemy to attack, and as the sole survivor of the assassina-*

tion squad, he gave them that. He learned much later that the minister of defense had publicly decried the terrible tragedy of the loss of the nation's leader, then declared martial law and announced the appointment of himself as prime minister for the length of the late leader's term. He'd promptly locked up or killed the senior members of the opposition party who might otherwise have defeated him in an election.

He also locked up the sole surviving member of the assassination squad that had assisted him in his rise to the throne.

As many times as it was possible to take a human being there, they took him to the brink of death. The very limits of pain and blood loss. On a rotating cycle—following a few days of isolation and continued starvation—they would walk him to a torture chamber in the depths of a seventeenth-century dungeon he supposed he had some Spanish explorer to thank for. They would strap him to a chair. The chair had no seat, and Cooper, fully naked, his balls exposed through the bottom of the empty chair, would be whipped—strafed. Torn. The whip had something on it, not nails but something like them. Sharp. Grating.

They whipped his penis, his nuts, and ass, the same every time, doing it until he bled a puddle, and they thought he might be dead. Each time, the clouds of pain would lead him to a serene, peaceful state, the cliff edge of death. After it was determined he had survived yet again, they would throw him back in the prison cell, one of a few dozen subterranean rooms in the subterranean facility. They would come back and check a couple of days later to see whether he had died. Seeing his chest bobbing slowly, they would give him just enough food—usually in the form of a crusted tortilla chunk—for him to notice he was dying of starvation.

Enough to get him through to the next session.

After too many cycles to count—when he sensed death's tendrils becoming more permanently present, like the prosthetic Clancy's tendril of smoke from his uninhaled cigarette—Cooper vowed to make whatever pathetic move he could muster the next time they came. With what little he had left, he would take them.

And when he did, he would kill them all.

Cooper remoored the Apache about ten minutes
ahead of the first Zodiacful of lunch guests. He came back in
on the skiff, tying it to one of the tacks on the dock, and
headed back to bungalow nine. As he had hoped, there was a
ham-and-cheese sandwich and some ice water waiting for
him on the table beside his kitchenette. He opened the
room's tiny fridge and found a fresh six-pack of Budweiser
too—*Good work, Ronnie, you putz,* he thought. Planting
himself in the chair at the table in the kitchenette, Cooper put
away the water, three beers, and the sandwich, watching people come over for lunch from their very expensive sailboats
moored in the bay. He could see out through the jalousie
panes of his kitchen window, louvered open as they were on
the other side of the screen designed to keep out the bugs.

When he was through with the sandwich, he looked over
at the built-in shelving behind his reading chair. He'd been
attempting to ignore the presence of the foot-high statue
he'd put there, but the more effort he put into ignoring it, the
more he noticed the thing.

Upon his return from Tortola, he'd taken the idol out of
the canvas sack and set it on the shelf. He'd thought at the

time that it would look good in his room, which made him
think the gold stash might not carry a curse with it after all.
Maybe the idol—or whatever, he thought, you call one of
these things—was a good-luck charm. A sentry, standing
guard, warding off evil spirits. At least he could give the theory a shot: test out the idol's spiritual powers by seeing
whether it kept Cap'n Roy from calling, or Lieutenant Riley
from returning to bring him to the good chief minister.
Maybe the idol had already caused Ronnie to bring the sandwich for him.

Either way, Ronnie must have wondered what the fucking
thing was—this shining golden idol planted on the top shelf
of his otherwise Spartan room, the only chunk of decor in
the entire bungalow, not counting the pair of conch shells
he'd moved aside to make room for it.

He popped his fourth beer and took a thick slug of it as he
came over and sat in his reading chair. As always, he found
the first taste of the beer to be disappointingly lukewarm.
The refrigerators in the bungalows ran on propane; they
were meant to keep a half gallon of milk from spoiling, or a
dozen eggs cool, so guests could make their own breakfasts
if they wanted. The little fridges wouldn't keep beer or soda
cold enough unless you remembered to take out the ice
cubes from the freezer box and put the beverages in their
place. Ronnie never did it that way when he brought something over, and Cooper never thought ahead—he wanted a
beer when he wanted it, never thinking to put the second, or
even the third, in the freezer while he drank the first. *Be nice,
now that I'm on the fourth bottle, to be sipping an ice-cold
brew.* He drank some more of the lukewarm beer anyway.

He thought about the smuggled artifacts Cap'n Roy had
asked him to unload. Contrary to Roy's supposition, he
knew next to nothing about the business of art theft, and
couldn't think of anybody from his list, at least not offhand,
whom he might impel to assist in the fencing of a batch of
stolen *objets d'art*—assuming, which he figured it was safe
to assume, they were in fact stolen. Had to have been stolen

from somewhere—and it could be that Cap'n Roy knew by now where they'd been stolen from, considering Roy was holding the last surviving smuggler in his brand-new Marine Base holding cell. Finishing the fourth Bud, Cooper thought a little about Cap'n Roy's offer to join him for the interrogation of the smuggler. Maybe, if he was going to figure out what these goods were worth and how to unload them for the highest price, it wasn't a bad idea to take him up on the invite.

The problem, as Cooper understood it, with modern-day art theft was that most major works were accounted for, so when you did steal them, your only real recourse for profit lay in the insurance payoff. Swipe it and give it back, and you could find yourself a nice chunk of change, maybe ten percent of the thing's appraised value. Plus, along with the money, the insurance company agrees not to press charges.

Cooper figuring this meant the only way anybody was going to make any real money on art theft in this day and age was by finding something new—Indiana Jones style. He assumed it still happened, and wondered whether Cap'n Roy's newfound stash represented the fruits of such tomb raiding. A roomful of gold, buried for centuries, uncovered by an earthquake—or maybe a backhoe excavating a stretch of rain forest so a parking structure could be laid down in its place.

Too bad these raiders picked the wrong route north.

Cooper thought of somebody it might make sense to call. The somebody he was thinking of could probably at least tell him what these things were—where they came from, who made them, and when. He could take Lieutenant Riley's pictures, a couple items from his loot bag, and—if nothing else—determine through this person whether Cap'n Roy had seized somebody's private collection, looted from the owner's Beverly Hills mansion, or whether the goods had been pillaged from a two-thousand-year-old burial site.

He wasn't sure he wanted to call anybody at all, or do anything whatsoever, but he was starting to develop a fondness for the idol watching over his bungalow. He decided, from the look of the thing, that it was a she—the bust of an Aztec priestess, or Mayan she-monk, or whatever the hell it was the Mayans or Aztecs had preferred to call their female religious leaders. This golden priestess delivered here by fate—to keep him safe from intruders, hurricanes, and cold beer.

He rose, retrieved and opened lukewarm Bud number five, and came over to examine the idol at close range. When he did, something bothered him about her. It came as a kind of flutter in his upper gut—a familiar sensation, or at least a sensation of seeing something familiar. It wasn't anything like the racial-profiling rage he'd felt earlier, but was instead a form of *déjà vu*—only not quite, at least not in the strictest sense of recalling that he'd been here before. As he stood near the shelf and sipped his beer, he realized the *déjà vu* stemmed from what he was *hearing,* rather than feeling.

He'd just heard a quiet call for help—a request for an assist.

From a statue.

He knew he ought simply to conclude that he'd spent too many years alone, that such imaginings were not a sign of good health. Plus, it might just have been the barley and hops talking. Still, in hearing the call for help from the twelve-inch Mayan priestess, Cooper was suddenly faced with the notion that his second case as detective-to-the-dead had just come knocking at his door.

'Ey, Cooper, cawed the priestess, her accent oddly misplaced in an islander's lilt, *we hear you're pretty good with dead folks. Friend of ours, in fact, tell us you help him find peace in the ever after . . . and we thinkin' you maybe wanna help us too. Something wrong need rightin', Cooper, and you know what? You might just be the man for the job.*

Cooper tossed his latest empty bottle in the kitchen wastebasket. He had a few things he wanted to do this afternoon—swim a few loops around Conch Bay's shrinking coral reef, jog up and down the beach, maybe throw back some Pusser's shots while toking on a joint at the end of the beach club dock just to see whether he could freak out a few of the incoming dinner patrons. But instead of doing any of these things, Cooper lifted his satellite phone from the table where he kept his laptop. He dialed the number for the chief minister's office, and told the receptionist, whom he knew and who knew him, that he was looking to speak to Roy.

The receptionist found the chief minister in short order.

"Yeah, mon," Cap'n Roy said when he picked up. "You find some rich bastard interested in doin' some interior design for his mansion, thinkin' maybe our little treasure trove do the trick?"

Cooper ignored the question.

"You still have your smuggler in custody?" he asked.

"Captain o' the good ship *Seahawk*? Marine Base be fillin' up after a night of good times in town last night, so we still got him, yeah, but he up in the big house now."

"Ours, though, I take it," Cooper said. "You haven't given him back to the Coast Guard."

He was double-checking that Cap'n Roy was talking about the prison on the north side of Tortola, which the prior chief minister had arranged to have built at a cost of $33 million before being sent there himself for extorting ten mill off the top.

"Before you comin' down to see what he has to say? Not a chance."

If there was something Cooper despised most, being predictable was it.

He asked for and memorized the vitals on the smuggler, said, "Get me a pass and a room," then hung up on the honorable chief minister.

He'd drag a couple answers out of Mr. *Seahawk,* call on the other person he'd thought of, and go ahead and unload Cap'n Roy's personal King Tut exhibit at full freight. The faster he got it done, the faster he'd be two fifty-two to the good—and the faster he'd have Cap'n Roy out of his hair.

He was already thinking he might have some difficulty parting with the priestess, though—he was growing attached to the idea of keeping her as a good-luck charm on the shelf of his room.

"Don't go getting any ideas," he said to the idol on the shelf, grabbed the last lukewarm Budweiser from the propane-fueled fridge, found a clean T-shirt, and went to take his scrubbed-and-buffed Apache out for a spin to Road Town.

7

The idea of Tortola's having a prison was akin to building a second Louisiana Superdome on the moon. The permanent resident population of the island fell somewhere in the range of twenty thousand people, with another ten thousand or so planted around the other islands in the chain. This sort of population usually rated a town jail at best, but since the esteemed leaders of the local government saw the BVIs as a semi-sovereign nation destined someday for independence, it only made sense that such a place should have its own prison. They ordered one up that could house 110 inmates.

When he came in through the main entrance, Cooper noted—as he had the first three times he'd been here—there was no razor wire on the chain-link fence rimming the property. He asked the RVIPF guard at the front desk how many overnight guests they had staying here this week.

"Fourteen," the guard said, "includin' the smuggler come in this mornin'."

Cooper knew these guys loved to use the word *smuggler*. The word was an important element in the RVIPF's basic training regimen—Roy handed to each new trainee a boxed DVD set featuring every episode of the *Miami Vice* television series, on which such trainees were quizzed incessantly. Accordingly, Cap'n Roy's troops reveled in anything even close to a drug bust.

Cooper told the guard he was here to see the very smuggler he'd just mentioned. The guard nodded, took his ID, and started in wordlessly on some paperwork behind the counter. Cooper knew three of the remaining thirteen inmates to be a set of Colombians Roy and Riley had caught a year ago toting a catamaran full of cocaine bricks, the idiots moored right in the main Road Town marina with their stash. The drug runners had offered the waitress working the dockside restaurant a baggie of uncut coke as payment for their sixty-eight-dollar tab, not including tip. The waitress, who happened to be Riley's niece, had made a call from behind the bar, prompting Cap'n Roy and his boys to come on down to the restaurant and haul in the patrons before the Colombians had finished their cappuccinos. By Cooper's count of the penitentiary population, with the three Colombians, the deposed former chief minister, and Cap'n Roy's new smuggler catch, this meant there were nine local convicts, up here on the hill doing hard time in the Caribbean sunshine between the three square meals a day and free cigarettes they got as part of the sentence. This being at least twice what any local job got you.

Those hotel room tax dollars hard at work.

The guard buzzed him in, where he was met by another. The second guard took him down a shiny hallway with recessed overhead halogen lighting. Midway down the hallway, the guard peered into a small window, which was built into a door. Satisfied, he waved, and another, unseen guard—Cooper thinking it was probably the guy at the front desk again—flipped a switch and the door unlocked itself. The guard pulled it open and gestured that Cooper was welcome to go in ahead of him.

Cooper took him up on the invitation and came in to face the seated figure of Powell Keeler III, nickname Po, legal resident of Southampton, New York, date of birth June 14,

1962. All this per the bio dictated to him over the phone by Cap'n Roy, Cooper thinking the Hamptons made sense for somebody who captained boats for a living, something the chief minister told him "Po" had insisted was the case.

Po Keeler sat opposite a countertop built into a wall that cut the room in half. A large rectangular hole in the wall was covered only by half with a Plexiglas shield, so that an inmate could easily climb over the shield whenever he saw fit. Holes had been pressed through the section of Plexiglas so that any sound waves that didn't make it through the opening one foot above could pass freely through the Plexiglas shield at face level. Cooper thinking maybe he'd invite the prison's architect out to the Conch Bay Beach Club, where they could have him install a furnace and forced-air heat to combat the ninety-degree temperatures.

Keeler himself, Cooper observed, was tan enough to pass for a professional yacht charter captain. He had the general appearance of a New England WASP but with too much sinew. The wisp of hair at his forehead seemed too long, the skin on his neck a little too riddled with age spots—the sort of blemishes that bond traders, stuck inside all week making their money, didn't get. And Keeler looked sloppy: among other features, Cooper could see that one of his nostrils displayed a short crescent of snot crust. Biff from Connecticut wouldn't allow something like that to be seen, even while incarcerated.

Cooper pegged Keeler immediately for the upper-crust equivalent of a belonger, the BVI term for noncitizens who, after a period of living in the islands, were granted limited rights of citizenship. Po Keeler hung out with the wealthy, but didn't quite fit the mold. A belonger. Cooper also thought he might have seen Keeler around somewhere; as many tourists came to visit the West Indies, those who made a living in its marinas were few, and you could always tell the type.

Cooper flashed Keeler one of his fake ID cards, going with an FBI laminate this time. On the cab ride over, he'd stuffed it into the part of his wallet that flipped easily out and back.

"Got some questions for you, Po," he said. "Hope I'm not interrupting anything you had going out in the yard. They put a pool in out there yet?"

Keeler flipped his hand limply.

"Whatever," he said.

They were both seated now, on opposite sides of the half-ass Plexiglas shield.

"Why don't you tell me what happened here," Cooper said.

Keeler looked at him for a minute.

Then he said, "Who the fuck are you?"

"Po," Cooper said, "maybe I should climb over this bull-shit divider and beat your ass until you're lying on that million-dollar linoleum floor in a pool of your own blood and a busted-up face. Maybe then I talk to one of the guards, have him bring in whoever it is he tells me's the randiest, longest-dicked rapist in the joint, then go out and fire up a Cohiba while he pulls an Abu Ghraib on whatever virgin ori-fices he's able to find on that lily-white temple of yours. Be honest, I think a guy they've got in here now, name of Big Boy Basil, could use the exercise. He is one fat, stinking lummox of a man."

Keeler looked at him for a while, not really reacting, maybe watching to see whether Cooper was planning on making a move, or maybe whether Cooper was going to break out laughing at the joke, if in fact it turned out to be a joke. After his moment of study, Keeler shrugged and said, "Hell, I'll tell you the same thing I told the police chief. 'Cap'n' somebody, man called himself."

"Cap'n Roy."

"Whatever. Like I laid out for him, I'm down here doin' what I do. I transport yachts once in a while. If somebody needs it, you know. I charge a nominal fee, let them handle the insurance, and deliver it home from wherever they left it, or maybe vice versa."

Cooper noticed Keeler performed a kind of involuntary

nod—a short jerk of his head down and to the left—at the conclusion of every sentence. It looked as though his sub-conscious mind was unable to hide his pride at completing the full sentence each time he pulled off this amazing feat.

"This time around," he said, "I'm taking that Trinity back to its home in Naples. West coast of Florida. *Was*. Fuck. Owner of the boat just took his family through the ABCs, on down to Caracas."

Cooper translated: the ABCs were Aruba, Bonaire, and Curaçao, down at the base of the Antilles chain.

"You start in Caracas?" Cooper said.

"Yeah. Near to it, anyway. La Guaira."

"That where you picked up the load too?"

Keeler studied him again before answering.

"Yeah," he said. "That's where I caught it. I don't mind telling you guys. Told 'Cap'n' what's-his-name too—Rudy, or whatever—in the spirit of cooperation. Because I want to get out of here, ya know? But I've been meaning to ask: is anybody going to give me a phone call around here? I need to call my attorney, all right? Nobody has given me my call."

Cooper shook his head, trying to avoid smiling as he spoke.

"That's in the good ol' U.S. of A. where you get your call. They don't give 'em out 'round here. Pay phones are for shit anyway—you're trying to call a lawyer in the U.S., you can forget it. Never make it through. But," he said, "in the spirit of cooperation, I'll see what I can do."

Keeler doffed one of his involuntary nods and said, "Whatever. Look, I take some money on the side. Ship a few things people need shipped on my transport runs. People know I do it, so word gets around, you know? So I'll get a call, maybe a visit—like this time, guy coming down the dock in the marina before I leave. You know? So anyway, if I can, I take a few boxes along for the ride. Make a few extra bucks for my trouble. I'm strict on my rules: no drugs, no firearms. I know my way around with the Coast Guard task force teams, you know, how to steer clear. They don't give a shit about anything but drugs and guns."

"Usually," Cooper said. "Usually you know how to steer clear."

"Fuck me. I knew it was a mistake the minute I did it. This time, the guy on the dock I told you about was offering thirty grand up front plus twenty more on delivery. Eight crates, he says. Eight crates and two guys who come along with the crates."

"Fifty grand? Sounds like a little more than the going rate."

"It is. All the more reason to pass on a bullshit deal I never should have taken. Truth is, I figured the two guys who came along for the ride were part of the cargo. Maybe even the whole thing. I was wrong."

"What do you mean?"

"Guy shows me the letter they had from the State Department, looked legit, which he said would satisfy any customs officer, allow these guys safe passage. Said they'd pass any inspection. I figured at the time that the extra money was for the stowaways, you know? That the shipper, he was making something up about what he was shipping, the part that these guys had to come along with, when the deal was, they had something up their sleeve with these two guys and they needed to bring 'em into the U.S. aboard my ride."

"Like they were terrorists maybe, then."

"Well, yeah, but—" Keeler stopped and kind of froze, looking as though this was the first time he'd actually considered the scenario: Po Keeler the stooge, Cooper thought, delivering al-Qaeda operatives into the belly of the beast for a few grand cash money. "No, look," Keeler said, "that wasn't what it was. What it was wasn't much better, though, was it? Not for me. *Fuck me*—how did I know these assholes had guns in their suitcases? These punks were like those mariachis in that fucking Antonio Banderas movie."

"Must have missed that one," Cooper said.

Keeler shrugged.

"Quit bullshitting me, Keeler. Where'd you get the crap in the crates?"

Keeler made a noise that sounded like a cross between a laugh and a cough. Cooper supposed he intended it as a grunt.

"All that gold and shit?" he said. "Man, I told you already. And I didn't know anything about what was in the crates until that buddy of yours showed me the pictures he'd taken."

"Buddy?"

"Whatever. Look, I don't ask any questions. Except two. Like an airline ticket agent, you know? Same two questions all the time. Only mine are, 'Any drugs?' 'Any guns?' Otherwise, I go as low as half up front, rest on delivery, cash only, negotiable rates. Got a friend in Mustique with a dog comes and sniffs out any drugs—guns too. That dog smells anything, I dump the load in the deep blue sea. Otherwise I stay out of it."

"Who was supposed to make the pickup in Naples?"

"Deal was, somebody will come down to the boat. Whoever it is shows up, he gives me the twenty grand, he gets the crates. Pretty standard deal. No names, no numbers."

"So anybody who shows up at your destination with the right amount of cash can take possession of the goods?"

Keeler shrugged. "Their rules, their problem. Not mine. Anyway, I don't want to know any more than that. Know what I mean?"

"Who made the deal with you in Venezuela? The guy who came down the dock."

Keeler didn't say anything for a second or two. Instead, he looked Cooper in the eye. Maybe, Cooper thought, Keeler was acknowledging that Cooper had found his way to the one piece of information he actually had to offer. Keeler was obviously a schemer—kind of guy who could always work his way out of a scrape—and Cooper had the feeling Keeler was sizing him up. Calculating how Cooper might be of use in getting him out of this bind, now that Keeler was about to give up the only worthwhile piece of information he had to give.

"The guy in Venezuela is somebody I've talked to a couple times," Keeler said. "He made a few of my deals. Makes 'em for another guy—his boss. Bastard isn't making any more of my deals, though. Motherfucker. But let me ask you something."

Cooper waited.

"That card you flashed me. Your wallet. Said you were FBI."

"Yup," Cooper said.

"But you aren't. FBI, I mean."

"Nope."

Cooper watched the schemer at work.

"You aren't part of the local constabulary—that part's easy. Still," Keeler said, "he *is* a buddy of yours. Isn't he? The police chief, or minister or whatever. Cap'n Rudy."

"Everybody pretty much knows everybody else 'round here, Po," Cooper said. "And it's Roy."

"Okay—buddy, acquaintance, whatever, I don't give a fuck. Here's where I *do* give a fuck: you have any idea whether that bastard's planning on turning me over? Extraditing me. Giving me up to the Coast Guard, or whoever."

Cooper said, "If you're asking whether I've got some inside scoop on the chief minister's intentions, the answer is no. If he has any intentions at all."

"It's better for me if he doesn't," Keeler said. "See, here's how it works. Local country holds me, right? Then down the road, sets me free. Far as the Coast Guard, the rest of the U.S. law enforcement organizations are concerned, I never even hit the radar. Nobody files shit, so they forget about me, and I'm all set." He nodded. "Your buddy extradites me, though, and I get brought up on charges. Maybe some bullshit terrorist charge, way you mentioned it could seem like. Besides anything else, you know what that means for me? Means nobody's insurance pays out. Not mine; not the guy owns the boat. Not a red cent. Means I'm out of business."

Cooper watched him.

"So anyhow," Keeler said, "I'm thinking I might have a friend or two, might be able to help your buddy out. Maybe even the guy owns the Trinity. Give your buddy a few things he's looking to get. Maybe slip a few zeroes into his numbered account in, what, the Caymans, maybe?"

"You met him," Cooper said, "right?"

"Yeah, sure."

"He strike you as the kind of guy be opposed to a proposition like that?"

"No."

"There you go."

Keeler looked at him, Cooper thinking the man was probably trying to decide precisely what he had meant by *There you go.*

"On the other hand," Cooper said, "the good chief minister tends to listen when I offer advice. And if I don't hear in the next thirty seconds or so who it was came down that dock in La Guaira, my next stop will be the civic center, where I'll drop by Roy's office and recommend he extradite you ASAP."

Another involuntary nod came quickly from Keeler.

"The guy in Venezuela," he said. "He said he came 'on behalf of Ernesto Borrego.' "

Cooper took this in. The name didn't mean anything to him.

"Actually he didn't say 'Borrego,' " Keeler said. "He called him by his nickname—El Oso Blanco, I think it was. Or maybe El Oso Polar—I can never remember which."

Cooper didn't need Keeler's translation of what followed.

"You name the language," Keeler said, "but anyway, they call him 'The Polar Bear.' Good luck reaching the guy who came down to the dock—I'll give you his pager, but he was a messenger, nothing more. You want to know who arranged this thing, it's Ernesto Borrego—the Polar Bear, or whatever the fuck. I've worked with his people before. He's into a lot of shit down there."

Keeler gave Cooper the messenger's pager number, and

Cooper stored the digits in the part of his brain the many years of bourbon hadn't yet destroyed.

"What about in Naples," Cooper said. "Anybody there?"

Keeler shook his head.

"No," he said, "only Borrego. That fuck. And you don't need to pull any Abu Ghraib shit on me, man. That's all I know."

"Catch," Cooper said, and tossed his boxy little satellite phone over the top of the Plexiglas shield. Keeler caught it, regarded the thing, then looked at him.

"Your phone call," Cooper said.

Keeler didn't waste any time. He punched out a number, waited for the assistant to get his lawyer, then ran through a half dozen issues without worrying whether Cooper was listening in. Then he broke the connection and threw the phone back over the shield.

Cooper caught it, stood, and knocked on the hallway door. Within four or five minutes the door *chunk*ed open and the guard who had brought him to the room showed up to escort him out.

He turned to Keeler.

"Live slow," he said.

Just before the door closed behind him, he heard Keeler say, "Whatever," and then the door was locked down again and Cooper headed back out into the sunshine.

8

Forty seconds after Julie Laramie showed up for work, she was asked to leave. This was not an uncommon event, since her boss, the newly appointed deputy director of intelligence, had carefully fostered his reputation as a combination absentminded professor and introvert and, befitting his reputation, routinely "forgot" he'd been asked to participate in certain meetings. Malcolm Rader's senior staff—of which Laramie was the ranking member—got to do the honors.

Laramie had booted up her desktop but not yet sat down when Rader shuffled into her brand-new private office and handed her a slip of paper. He offered an apology for the late notice, then asked her to attend a meeting at the address written on the slip:

101 INDEPENDENCE AVE, WESTON ROOM (3C)

"Senate-mandated interagency intel session," he said. Laramie knew there to be plenty of this sort of meeting in the aftermath of the findings of the 9/11 Commission.

And that brought her to now—grumbling at Rader's

feigned absentmindedness from the confines of her car. By not telling her about the meeting the night before, he'd already made her nearly an hour late.

From the C Street exit off I-395 she made her way to First, inferring that 101 Independence meant the corner of First. She drove past her destination twice without seeing it, repeatedly scanning the numbers on the block of historical buildings along one side of Independence Avenue until she realized why the address had sounded familiar: because she'd been here before. Turning her glance from one side of the street to the larger building across the way, she observed where Rader had sent her. Staring at Laramie in its full-block glory—*While you,* she thought, *search fruitlessly for some office building that doesn't exist*—stood the massive building with the address of *101 Independence Avenue.*

It was one of three similar structures that, when taken together, were more commonly known as the Library of Congress.

She felt a swell of disquiet as she found a distant on-street parking spot for her Volvo. Tugging at the parking brake, she saw that it was almost ten-fifteen—*seventy-five minutes late.* It took her another six minutes to make her way through the entrance of the James Madison Building and exhaust her own resources in the vain search for a sign suggesting the whereabouts of the Weston Room.

At that point she gave up and approached one of the information desks in the lobby, where a middle-aged male librarian was camped out behind the counter.

"Any chance," Laramie said, "there's a place called the Weston Room within a couple miles of here?"

She offered the message slip as a visual aid, and though she smiled as she did it, Laramie had lost all interest in pleasantries. She was more interested in taking some Extra-Strength Tylenol, or perhaps eating some breakfast, which she'd skipped in order to make it to her office at a reasonable time following a longer-than-usual morning run. In the wake of her battle with fellow commuters on I-395, she'd begun to wonder whether somebody at the Starbucks that marked the starting point on her jogs had decided to torture her with decaf.

Her head was killing her.

The librarian smiled flatly, his eyes dead and unpleasant behind the lines that creased his face when he smiled. He pointed to the great arching hallway to Laramie's right.

"There's a stairwell past the Madison tablets at the end of the hall," he said. "Take it to the third floor—that's the '3' in the '3C' on your note. Then you're going to follow the signs to the screening room, which you will pass on your way to the stacks on the C Street side of the building—'C.' When you get to the back corner of the floor, you'll need to look around, since there isn't a sign except right beside the door. The plaque there will tell you you've reached the right place. The Weston Reading Room." He returned the message slip with another courtesy smile.

"It's only a little over a mile," he said.

Laramie would have appreciated the joke had it not been for her growing hunger problem. She thanked the man with the skin-deep smile, started across the lobby, then thought of something and came back.

"One more thing," she said. "Has anyone else asked for directions to the Weston Room today?"

The librarian thought for a moment before shaking his head no.

"What about, um, normally? Is it ever booked by outside groups for meetings?"

"Don't think so," he said.

She thought about his answers on her way down the hall, and after a climb up two flights of stairs and ten minutes of stack wandering, spotted the librarian's promise of a plaque beside a door. She decided she was literally approaching a mile, or more, from the lobby, but there it was nonetheless— a brass plaque with the words WESTON READING ROOM tacked onto the wall beside the open arch of a doorway. According to her watch, she was now almost ninety minutes late.

Laramie came over to the doorway and stood out of the line of vision of anyone who might be in the room. She listened for a moment and heard nothing—no voices; no shuffling of papers.

She decided there was no conceivable way some "Senate-mandated inter-agency intel session" was currently taking place in the Weston Room. She considered that Malcolm Rader would not willingly, or even unwittingly, send her into some kind of trap; she couldn't even think what form of trap would be set in the Weston Room anyway, outside of the evident sex-crime potential found in the quiet corners of any huge library. And Laramie—along with the pepper spray buried in her purse, anyway—could handle herself.

No—Laramie decided Rader had known exactly where, and for what purpose, he was sending her, and this meant a couple of things. First, it meant there was somebody in the Weston Room waiting for her—provided the person, whoever it was, had been willing to stick around for upward of two hours beyond the designated meeting time. Second, she thought, whoever's in there is somebody Rader—*your boss*—answers to.

Meaning she should probably go ahead and take the meeting.

She stepped through the arch to see that the Weston Reading Room was a collection of hardwood reading tables enveloped by Italian Renaissance decor, approximately the size of a squash court and dominated by the presence of four immensely tall stained-glass windows that lined one of its walls. About half of the room's lamps, all standing on the reading tables—of which Laramie counted twelve—were lit. The room looked to her like an inspiring, if stiff, place to engage in study. But more than anything, it looked to her like the perfect place to hold a quiet meeting nobody would know was taking place.

She figured this for the reason a man she recognized was seated at one of the tables at the far end of the room. He was facing the stained-glass windows, but Laramie had a good angle on his profile, and if you happened to work for the Central Intelligence Agency, which Laramie did, it was particularly easy to recognize a man like the one seated at the table in the Weston Reading Room. Among other reasons, the walls of the Agency's headquarters building in Langley, Virginia, were lined with portraits of the men who'd held the job this man had only recently been compelled to vacate. Laramie had also met with him once or twice.

It had been about a year since the man had left his portrait-related post, a forced resignation attributable equally to the corrupt practices of his late deputy director and the fatal dose of satellite intelligence Laramie herself had stumbled across and then proceeded to ram up the hierarchy's tail end.

Laramie detected the scents of coffee—and food. She saw that the man she'd been sent to meet with was chewing a bite of the sandwich he held in his hand; as Laramie watched, he set the sandwich down and took a sip from the unmistakable white cardboard cup, the single green word that may as well, for Laramie, have said *oasis* instead of *Starbucks*. On the table across from the man sat an unopened bag, along with a second cardboard cup of coffee.

Deciding things were looking up, Laramie approached the table beside the stained-glass windows for her breakfast meeting with Lou Ebbers, the former head of the CIA.

Ebbers stood. He wasn't smiling, but on the other hand he wasn't frowning either. He offered a hand and Laramie shook it. She was starting in on an apology when she thought better of it—hadn't the meeting she'd been told to show up for never really existed in the first place?

"Morning, Lou," she said.

"Afternoon," Ebbers said in his trademark North Carolina lilt. "Took the liberty of picking out a sandwich for you. Coffee's got skim milk and Equal, way I'm told you like it."

Forgoing the chance to reply to his jab at her tardiness,

Laramie came around the table, set her bag on the floor, and took the seat across from him, which she figured was what he wanted her to do. She took two long gulps of coffee; as Ebbers sat back down, she opened the brown paper sack and withdrew the sandwich within. It was turkey, lettuce, and tomato on a croissant, the same selection she always had them make for her in the CIA commissary.

Once she'd eaten half of the sandwich, Laramie said, "This does not appear to be a 'Senate-mandated interagency intel session.' "

Ebbers sipped his coffee.

"Doesn't, does it," he said. Laramie smelled caramel and wondered whether Ebbers, like Rader, preferred the sissy drinks from the Starbucks menu.

Ebbers said, "You familiar with the post I took when the president accepted my resignation?"

Laramie thought for a moment.

"You're at the Pentagon, I think," she said. "But I can't recall anything more specific than that."

"Deputy secretary for Domestic Law Enforcement Agency Interface, Defense Intelligence Agency," he said. "I also hold the concurrent post of special assistant to the national security advisor."

Laramie nodded. She knew that positions like the former DCI's involved such unintelligible titles for a reason: nobody could ever remember them, therefore no one had any idea what persons with such titles did. She assumed the "special assistant" part of his job reflected more accurately his stature and role. Lou Ebbers, it seemed, was an unaccountable sort of person.

Ebbers eyed a set of three newspapers stacked on the corner of their table.

"Startin' with the paper at the top," he said, "take a look. Page D1. Column six."

Laramie pulled the first of the papers over. It was the Southwest Florida *News-Press*, D being the Local & State section. The paper was dated just over five weeks ago. She saw the headline of the story Ebbers had pointed out. It said, BURST GAS MAIN KILLS 12.

Ebbers sipped at his coffee again; since it appeared he was waiting for her to do so, Laramie read the article. It was a pretty basic story, a longer version of the headline: an explosion had destroyed a block of homes in a rural housing development located near the center of the state, forty miles east of Fort Myers and about two hours from Miami. The development community, called Emerald Lakes, had been built in an unincorporated portion of Hendry County near a town called LaBelle; it was mentioned in the story that the development had gone bankrupt five years prior, after fewer than five of the two hundred housing units had been sold. A real estate firm called Superior Home Manufacturing Ltd. had acquired Emerald Lakes out of bankruptcy and subsequently managed to find buyers for approximately half the homes in the community. The article reported forty injuries as a result of the blast, none serious, in addition to the twelve deaths. A local sheriff was quoted as stating unequivocally that the incident "was in no way terrorism related." He also said that the management company, Superior Home Manufacturing, did not appear to be at fault.

"Next paper in the stack," Ebbers said when he could see she'd finished. "Feature headline."

Laramie plucked newspaper number two from the pile, also the *News-Press,* dated three weeks after the first. It was a longer piece:

DEADLY FLU LEADS TO QUARANTINE
LaBelle (Wednesday)—The death toll from the influenza epidemic that has plagued LaBelle, in Hendry County, has risen to 93, leading authorities to quarantine a portion of the county. Residents of LaBelle had already been stricken recently by a gas main explosion that claimed 12 lives and injured 40 in a housing de-

velopment in nearby unincorporated Hendry County. In a prepared statement, Hendry County Sheriff Morris Haden said, "All surviving residents of LaBelle have now been admitted to two local hospitals. The grounds of the hospitals and large portions of the town itself have been quarantined so as to halt the spread of this highly contagious and deadly flu virus."

No one has been allowed in or out past the quarantine demarcations during the past 48 hours, Sheriff Haden said, except approved medical and law enforcement personnel. Since the quarantine, Sheriff Haden said there have been no new documented cases outside of the quarantine zone, making him "cautiously optimistic" that the quarantine is working effectively.

Authorities have been troubled by the rapid spread of the devastating flu, which is said to be an altogether different strain than the avian, or "H5N1" flu virus experts have predicted could escalate into a global pandemic. Despite its differences from the avian flu, to date, there has yet to be a documented case where a victim afflicted by the LaBelle influenza virus has survived. Officials from the U.S. Centers for Disease Control (CDC), now working on-site in LaBelle and at local hospitals, confirmed that the spread of the flu appears to have slowed or even halted.

(CONTINUED ON PAGE A7)

Laramie turned to the indicated page and finished reading, finding only one additional interesting fact: an official at the CDC had issued a statement indicating that no evidence had been discovered linking the flu outbreak to the gas main explosion three weeks prior.

"One more," Ebbers said. He pointed to the last paper in the pile and told her to turn to page A2.

In one of what she assumed were many follow-up articles

to the prior quarantine piece, the last in Ebbers's series of exhibits, published yesterday, confirmed the successful quarantine of the localized flu epidemic. Thirty-two additional victims had died, raising the total casualty count to 125, but the more recent victims had already contracted the virus at the time of the quarantine and there had been no further reported infections. The article echoed the concerns expressed by authorities in the prior article, stating that all victims who contracted the virus had in fact died from its rapidly progressing symptoms, which were said to be the same as in other flu cases but far more severe. There was another reference to the LaBelle flu breakout being a unique strain, rather than the mutated form of H5N1 experts were wary might develop soon.

Concluding she ought to read newspapers more often and shake her addiction to the heroin of cable television news, Laramie deposited the third newspaper on the other two, drank most of the rest of her coffee, set the cup on the table, and folded her hands in front of her. She felt awkward in a specific way she couldn't place.

"Be interested," Ebbers said, "in hearing what you think."

It suddenly occurred to Laramie the reason she was feeling uncomfortable: it seemed she had stumbled into a job interview. In realizing this, she found it difficult to determine how she was expected to act—what she was supposed to say. Sure, Ebbers had summoned her by way of Malcolm Rader, and appeared to be interviewing her—but for what position, she had no idea.

Makes for a tough interview.

"First of all," she said, "I suppose I'd hazard a guess there's a higher likelihood than the Centers for Disease Control admits that the gas main explosion and the flu epidemic were linked."

Ebbers watched her but didn't interject.

"And if there is, in fact, some kind of connection," she said, "then it could also follow that the sheriff was slightly premature in dismissing the possibility that the explosion was an act of terrorism. I'd guess, therefore, that's why he specifically came out and said so. But anybody you show these three articles to—at least anyone in our line of work—would draw the same conclusions, I think."

"Possibly," Ebbers said.

Laramie shifted in her chair, which still didn't help her figure out what to do with her hands. After a while, when Ebbers hadn't said anything further, Laramie locked them together on the surface of the table.

"If you'd like me to assess potential culpability," she said, "based on the theory it's an act of terrorism and the blast and virus are connected, then I'm going to need to ask a lot of questions."

"All right."

Laramie wasn't sure whether he'd meant, *All right, then go ahead and ask the questions,* but considering that for the second time in as many minutes, Ebbers said nothing further, Laramie figured it was safe to conclude he wanted her to proceed.

She was, after all, in a job interview.

"Did the explosion actually have anything to do with a burst gas main?" she said. "If not, what was the nature of the explosion? Where did it originate? What were the materials used to cause the blast? Was it a crude car bomb, or sophisticated plastic explosive charge? Remote detonation or suicide bomber? If suicide, who was driving the car? Who owned it?"

Ebbers remained silent and unexpressive, so Laramie went on.

"If the flu epidemic was tied to the explosion, what was the connection? Did the bomb release some kind of toxin that results in flu-like symptoms? If it's actually the flu, what strain of influenza is this? New? Old? If old, where else has this severe an outbreak occurred before? Were studies done on that outbreak and samples of the virus stored at a lab? Who had access to that lab? Or is it really the first true outbreak of mutated H5N1? I suppose I could continue."

Ebbers said, "As you know, the independent counsel

lauded your efforts in the Mango Cay matter. We agree with the counsel's assessment."

Since it was hard to miss, Laramie noted Ebbers's use of the word *we*. She knew better than to ask.

"Thank you," she said.

"What we found most compelling," Ebbers said, "was your allegiance. Even when both your job security and explicit orders from your superiors countermanded that allegiance, you remained impervious to influence from outside or above, and concentrated solely on shutting down what you perceived to be an intended act of deadly force by an enemy of the state. Also it did not appear that you required much in the way of supervision in the course of getting the job done."

Laramie wasn't sure what to say, so she didn't say anything.

Ebbers reached into the interior breast pocket of his suit and came out with a stapled document of something in the order of fifty pages. It was creased down the middle from the way he'd stored it in his pocket.

"One of your classes at Northwestern was an independent study project," he said.

Laramie had to think about this for a moment, mainly since she'd taken two such courses. In each, she'd been required to generate a limited version of a thesis but, other than regular meetings with the designated professor, you didn't have to attend class to get credits for the courses. Some chose the electives out of laziness. Laramie had taken hers for two reasons: first, she'd wanted to explore a pair of topics that no available courses covered; and, mostly, she'd seen it as an opportunity to spend a little more time with a professor named Eddie Rothgeb. Which in retrospect had been a very bad idea.

"Actually I took two," she said. "Junior and senior years."

Ebbers flattened the photocopied document on the table before him and Laramie could plainly see the cover page she'd printed for her senior independent study paper. The former DCI turned the cover and flipped through the first few pages of the report, which she recalled being fifty-seven pages in length. At the time, her longest report of any kind.

As Ebbers began leafing through some of the pages, Laramie could see that the copy Ebbers had brought with him had various sections underlined, highlighted, even boxed. Handwritten and typed notes bled from the margins across the original text, and at the top of each page was a stamp. The only word she could make out on the stamp was CRYPTOCLEARANCE. There was a hyphen followed by a number at the tail end of the word, but from across the table she couldn't make out the number. The number, she knew, would indicate the level of clearance required to gain access to the document, and while she might not have been able to see the number, the odd fact remained that Laramie's fifty-seven-page undergraduate independent study paper appeared to have been classified at one of the nine highest levels of secrecy in the American government.

The higher the number that followed, the fewer the number of people who were allowed to see it: while CRYPTO-CLEARANCE-1 might have meant that every member of the Senate Select Committee on Intelligence, the president's cabinet, and three or four tiers of CIA, NSA, and FBI senior staff had access, CRYPTOCLEARANCE-9 was supposed to mean that maybe eight to ten people on earth made the cut.

Laramie felt the twirl of butterflies in her stomach as she thought she caught the numeral 6 on one of the stamp marks. This seemed impossible, or at the very least disturbingly strange. Then Ebbers turned the page and she realized it was not a 6 at all—because, as was rather obvious, she was reading upside down.

What?

Laramie attempted to freeze her brain for a moment. Stop it from reacting and point it, instead, in the direction of her paper. She preferred to do this by a method recommended to her by her father; he'd told her about it during one of his drunken fits, if she recalled correctly, but it had stuck. He'd recommended she count to three in the famous childhood manner—by then, he told her, you'd better be able to figure out what to do.

One-Mississippi.

She thought of the topic she had written about. She thought about the case she had made, how and what she'd spelled out in the paper.

Two-Mississippi.

As she considered what was in the report, and what it could mean that it was highly classified and in the hands of a senior intelligence bureaucrat with a mysterious and forgettable job title, the butterflies in her stomach condensed to a heavy, concentrated mass that sank toward her legs.

Three.

She decided to wait to hear what Ebbers had to say about the paper before jumping to any conclusions. She felt the sinking mass ease, and lift—after all, it was almost impossible, even ludicrous, to think what she was considering might be the case—

"What's most interesting," Ebbers said, glancing through her report, "is that you wrote this five months prior to 9/11."

The way he looked at the pages, Laramie could tell he wasn't reading. That he'd seen it before and knew it well.

"Terrorism," Laramie said, mainly to buy some time, "wasn't, um, exactly a new phenomenon, even then, of course." She immediately felt foolish for saying this. "There are obviously more than a few mistakes in there, sir, as—well, as I'm sure you know."

Ebbers smiled a tight-lipped smile.

"Fewer than you might think," he said.

He refolded the document along its crease and put it back in his pocket.

"A car service will pick you up from your hotel room tomorrow after an early wake-up call. You will be taking a morning flight out of Dulles. A bag has been packed for you and will be delivered to you at your destination in Florida. Your own car will be returned to your condominium and the keys will be waiting for you on the kitchen counter—right where you always leave them—upon your return."

Laramie said, "Is this an open-ended trip?"

"I'll get to that," he said. "It's important no one from your professional or personal life knows where you're going. We'll watch the hotel and your condo during the next forty-eight hours and monitor the activities of some of the people you encounter as a matter of routine. Some will understand you to have called in sick."

Laramie stared, not ready to appreciate the irony of calling in sick in order to investigate a strange flu epidemic.

"A tour guide will greet you on arrival and transport you to the operations center. During this investigation, your guide will arrange for all necessary logistics. You will meet with the principals heading the investigation to date. There is, as you might expect, a multijurisdictional pig fuck of special agents-in-charge, case officers, Homeland Security officials, CDC scientists, doctors, local authorities, even diplomats and politicians waist-deep in the mud puddle. Talk to any and all such personnel as you see fit. You will have access to all the documents these people have seen or generated; have a look at these too. Do whatever it is you prefer to do in the course of your assignment, Miss Laramie, but one way or the other, I'll need you to recommend to me how we should go about finding the culprits and shutting them down. I'll need a report from you on this topic seventy-two hours from the time you arrive in Florida."

Ebbers scratched his chin.

"Meaning," he said, "I want you to get in there and figure out what the fuck is going on, and once you're there, you've got three days to do it."

Laramie looked around the table but could find only the uneaten half of the sandwich, the empty cups, the sandwich bags, the newspapers, and the reading lamp, but no apparent hint as to what was going on here. She knew this much: Ebbers had shown her the copy of her independent study paper only so she could see that he had it—perhaps see the *stamps* on it. This meant he was telling her something; she knew that too. But he certainly couldn't have been telling her what she *thought* he was telling her.

Except that he just had—hadn't he?

Laramie tried to get a grip and think through the circumstances from a practical point of view. In a few seconds, she'd thought of some things.

"Um," she said, "taking the part I believe I understand from this, I should say that I find it unlikely the—well, let's say the special agent-in-charge working this thing for the Bureau gets a call. From me. 'I'd like to talk to you about the case. Everything you know. What you think happened here, and why.' Let's be honest, he won't exactly be forthcoming—"

"He'll talk to you. And so will everybody else."

Laramie blinked.

"In its way, the investigation is now ours," Ebbers said. "You are now working for us. Your guide will give you the rest."

There it was again—*ours. Us.* She looked at him, and he looked back at her in silence. She wasn't going to ask the questions she wanted to ask. She could tell that if she asked, at least directly, he wouldn't answer. At least not directly. Maybe she didn't need to ask; maybe she already knew.

"One more question," Laramie said.

"Go ahead."

"I recognize that you wouldn't tell me anyway, but if I don't ask the question I'll wonder whether I should have. I can't *not* ask the question."

Ebbers inclined his head.

"Is this an exercise?" Laramie said.

Ebbers thought for a moment.

"A fair question," he said. "You ask, I presume, because you haven't heard of any organization of the sort that has just 'borrowed' you. Also because you hadn't previously studied, and so are only vaguely familiar with, the news coverage of the Florida incidents. And so on."

"Yes."

Lou Ebbers smiled.

"I would like you to treat this as though it is not," he said.

Ebbers stood, drained his coffee, gathered the newspapers, tucked them under an arm, crumpled his sandwich bag, removed the plastic lid from the coffee, stuffed the crumpled bag in the coffee cup, closed it, and proffered a two-finger salute.

"Good luck," he said, and walked out, leaving Laramie alone with the remaining half of her turkey sandwich and the empty Starbucks cup.

Because Cooper refused to fly American Eagle, he rode his Apache to St. Thomas, where he'd discovered by way of a few clicks that a direct flight ran to Dallas twice a day—American Airlines, no Eagle. He connected to Austin and was picked up outside the baggage claim by a stork-legged, humongous-breasted woman who was already giggling when Cooper saw her leap out of her Mercedes. She was already giggling, he supposed, because she was always giggling. She had bee-stung lips, long black hair lopped off into bangs, and big, round eyes with creases in the wings that made her look as if she were smiling even when she wasn't, which, from Cooper's three-day, hands-on experiential episode, wasn't often. She was a tenured professor of archaeology at the University of Texas at Austin, though this wasn't how Cooper knew her: he knew her as one of three women chartering a trimaran out of Tortola during a "ladies' week out," a six-day trip bopping around the snorkeling and watering holes of the Virgin Islands.

The Conch Bay Beach Club Bar & Grill had been a natural stop on the tour, but after the planned one-night stay, Susannah had convinced her two friends to leave her at the club for the last few days of her trip, while they caroused about the rest of the Virgins and retrieved her on their return to Road Town.

It seemed Cooper had triggered the release of a hormone from a long-dormant gland; despite Susannah's admitting, over their first drink, to going without sexual activity for six years running, Cooper seemed to remember nineteen as the number of times they had managed to copulate in the succeeding seventy-two hours. Susannah had handed him her card on her exit walk out the dock—flipping it over, tapping him on the ass, kissing him on the cheek, and waving so-long as Cooper read the inscription she'd written on the back of the card: *If you ever want to try that again, you call me right away, Island Man!*

Seeing as how the federal government had already handed Minister Roy his share of expense and inconvenience by way of the Coast Guard's antics, Cooper decided he'd charge the first class airfare for the trip to Austin on his Agency expense account. Take a pound of flesh out of Uncle Sam's hide: a $1,600 penalty for causing a temporary disruption of paradise.

Cooper came to the States twice a year at most. When he came, he tried to limit the extent of his travels to somewhere around a thousand-mile radius from Conch Bay. This pretty much meant Florida, though he was occasionally willing to stretch and hit a spot along the Gulf of Mexico or, on the rare occasion when it became necessary, Washington. Normally he stayed away from points in between. Normally, he stayed away, period.

He'd called Susannah and asked whether she would be the right person to speak with about sourcing and dating a collection of apparent Central or South American native artifacts. Susannah had squealed with glee and answered in the affirmative. Cooper thinking that it wasn't a bad thing, getting that kind of response, particularly with him calling for the first time since their three-day tryst eleven months back.

Susannah drove them through Austin in her circa early

eighties 450 SEL, the car spewing toxic diesel exhaust as it puttered along Sixth Street, Susannah chattering the whole way about Austin's music scene and the film festival they held there in the spring. When they hit the campus, Susannah pointed out a few passing landmarks before slipping into her reserved space in one of the faculty lots.

"We're here," she said through a toothy grin, "Island Man."

Cooper had a dive bag containing the pictures Riley had given him and a change of clothes for a one-night stay—along with his canvas bag of loot, which had required the Secret Service ID card he'd been trying out lately to get him through Houston customs without causing a four-alarm panic. He'd told the U.S. Customs supervisor he was part of a National Security Council task force, and that the artifacts were seized contraband. He provided a phone number and the name of a deputy secretary in the State Department in case the customs supervisor saw fit to delay him unnecessarily and verify what he'd just been told. The guy didn't place a verification call on the spot; Cooper assumed he dialed the number as soon as Cooper left the customs wing in the airport, but remained in view of the closed-circuit cameras. Cooper knew the call would yield the proper verification.

They came into the E.P. Schoch building, home of the department of archaeology, and Cooper saw that it looked pretty much like every other graduate school building he'd seen—classroom doors, bulletin boards, semigloss concrete floors, a lot of natural light, and a few fluorescent fixtures that added little to the illumination equation. Susannah took him to the basement, unlocked a door that said LAB 14 on an orange plaque, reached in, flipped on a bank of lights, and exposed a room that looked like Cooper expected a place called LAB 14 to look: a series of long soapstone countertops populated with microscopes, racks of tools and flasks, textbooks, and the usual implements of note taking and calculation.

He swung his bags onto the teaching slab, an island built perpendicular to the counters meant for the students. Susannah went behind the island, opened a drawer, and came out with some glasses, brushes, and a series of tools Cooper couldn't identify.

Then she put the glasses on and dropped them down her nose in a way that made her look a little older, though considerably more appealing.

"Whattaya got for me?" she said.

Cooper opened his two bags, stacked the pictures in front of her, and stood the three gold objects on the counter behind the pictures. He'd left the priestess idol on his shelf to ward off evil spirits like Cap'n Roy and Ronnie while he was gone.

"The pictures are of the whole set," he said. "There's literally a boatload of these things, some the size of the real deals here, some bigger than this table, some a lot smaller than what I brought."

"Okay."

"I'd like to know from what period they originate. What region, tribe, whatever, too. If they're real, that is. Presuming that's something you can determine. I want to know mainly so I can figure out what they're worth and who would want to buy them. I suppose if you can answer my last two questions, I don't really care about the others."

Susannah began her examination of the pictures. After the first few, she started making little "hm" and "mmph" sounds while she looked them over. Following something like three rounds of such noises, she said, still looking at the photographs, "Did you steal these, Island Man? Or am I not supposed to ask."

Cooper admired the way she asked the question: jovial and deferential, giving him the chance to shoot down what she was implying, but still asking the question. He found a stool and pulled it under him.

"You're not supposed to ask," he said.

She took some closer looks at selected shots with a magnifying glass, moving it around, leaning down and peering through it. As she leaned forward, Cooper noticed, and remembered, the sheer, unadulterated size of her breasts. They were drooping loosely inside the cotton summer dress she wore. Susannah dressed like a Jimi Hendrix fan from the sixties, all the way down to the Birkenstocks; keeping bangs in the front, on this particular week she'd twisted the rest of her hair into a French braid that ran to the top of her ass. If he remembered correctly, she'd claimed to be in her late thirties when he'd met her. She could easily pass for early thirties, at least from the right angle—more than he could say for himself, from any angle whatsoever.

Susannah eyed him after pulling up from one of her magnifying-glass looks.

"You can have them if you like," she said.

She refocused on her work, taking a look at the originals he'd lined up on the countertop, lifting the gold box, turning it upside down and around, running her finger across one of the symbols inscribed on its base. She set it back down, picked up, examined, and returned the other two originals, then came back at the box, taking it and heading to the back corner of the room, where some microscope-looking pieces of equipment were clustered on a stretch of countertop beneath a periodic table of the elements on the wall.

"You ever take a walk around the campus here?" she asked him from the corner, not bothering to look up from whatever she had begun working on.

"Here?" Cooper said. "No."

"You'll like it. Some of the finest-looking coeds anywhere in the country. Probably in the world. Blows *me* away sometimes."

Cooper realized she was asking him to skedaddle.

"How long do you need?"

"Probably take me two hours. You'll be able to take your collection home with you, but it'll take a couple days to get results on some of the tests I'll do. Even before you leave, though, I should be able to answer most of your questions."

She continued to work on whatever it was she was working on.

Cooper stood, paused, almost said something, decided not

to, shrugged, and took his leave of LAB 14, destined for a stroll around the campus of the University of Texas.

Cooper had worn pressed beige khaki shorts, a white polo shirt with stitched monotone patterns of tropical flowers, and a dressier pair of Reefs—brown leather with a buckle—to help him clear the customs check. It was warm in Austin, but not BVI warm, so he felt a little chill strolling from one quad to the next. He didn't give a shit about the University of Texas coeds, and instead decided he'd use the two hours to get a dose of exercise. The dressy Reefs, which he'd almost never worn, weren't as comfortable as his other pair, but he managed to avoid any blistering on his stroll, Cooper choosing a course he figured would take him on the widest possible loop around the campus.

On the return leg he checked a directory and found his way to the university's main library, called the Flawn Academic Center. He ducked into the air-conditioned building, feeling the icy chill on his sweaty arms, and found the periodicals archive without asking for help. On a card beside each monitor, the workstations in the archive displayed a list of the periodicals the UT system was able to search, dating back to 1994. He found the system didn't require a password for use, so he plugged in three keywords as a string, and in a little under a minute the system returned just under three dozen hits. He scanned the headlines, chose nine articles that appeared relevant to his intentions, and punched the Print icon for each article. It took him a few minutes to find the printer the workstations delivered to, but when he did, Cooper walked around behind a vacant librarian's counter and snatched the pages he'd printed off the device. He then made his way to the big study room he'd seen near the front entrance and sat down to read.

Each of the articles covered a slightly different angle on the same political scandal. With a pencil and a few slips of notepaper, he took down a few lines of notes, mostly pertaining to a pair of names that either recurred in or, in some cases, were the subjects of the articles he'd printed. When he was finished reading, he tossed the articles in a wastebasket, pocketed the two slips of notepaper he'd filled, and walked back outside to complete his exercise loop.

"You on island time?"

Cooper checked his watch for the first time that day. It had been four and one-half hours since he'd left the lab.

"Live slow, mon," he said.

Susannah, who had been reading a thick, well-worn book while perched on one of the stools, set down the book and stood.

"I'm finished with what you wanted me to do," she said. "So what do you say? You want to see the bats?"

"Excuse me?"

"The bats. Come on. I'll show you. You've never seen anything like this. And when we're finished, maybe you can bat me around for a while."

She giggled and made for the door.

Cooper gathered his dive bag and canvas sack, discovering that she'd already replaced the photos and artifacts and zipped them up inside the bags. He came over to her by the door. Susannah's hand rested on the light switch; she had long fingers and strong hands. While he stood there, his chest brushed against one pillowy breast; he could hear her breathing too, the two of them standing in the doorway where the sounds they made were bounced back at them by the doorjamb.

His flight back to St. Thomas wasn't until nine-fifteen to-morrow morning.

"Whatever the hell you're talking about with the bats," he said, "let's do it."

She flipped off the lights, locked the door, started toward the stairs, then spun, ran at him, leaped into the air, wrapped her legs around his waist, and emitted a high-pitched squeal that Cooper decided was Susannah's version of a rebel yell.

10

Riley was at the Conch Bay dock again, reclined in his seat in the patrol boat, goddamn cap pulled down over his eyes as though he'd motored over for no better reason than to have a nap. Coming into the lagoon, Cooper switched over to the dinghy and cut a mean stripe past a couple of SCUBA students on his way to the pier. This time he didn't waste any effort on the game of get-the-cop-to-skedaddle it had turned out he was pretty shitty at playing. Instead, he tied off his boat and punched the sole of one of his sandals against the side of Riley's boat. It made a satisfying *thuk,* as though he might have succeeded in dislodging a piece of the boat's chrome trim from the hull.

"What now?" he said.

Riley poked up the brim of his hat.

"Smuggler," he said, "turn up dead."

It took Cooper a couple seconds.

"Po Keeler, you mean," he said.

"Yeah, mon."

"Clearly you're operating under the flawed assumption that I give two shits."

Riley didn't say anything.

"It happen inside?"

"No."

Cooper nodded. "You let him out, then."

"Yesterday noon."

"When did he 'turn up'?"

" 'Bout seven A.M. today."

Cooper thought about the deal Po Keeler had been wanting to make with Cap'n Roy. He thought that he could connect some dots were the mood to strike. Not that the mood had hit, but it was easy enough: *Busted smuggler bribes top local law enforcement official; top local law enforcement official releases smuggler from prison; busted smuggler turns up dead.* Coincidence wasn't being too friendly with Cap'n Roy Gillespie.

It occurred to Cooper that Cap'n Roy might have recorded the conversation he'd held with Keeler—probably had—almost beyond a doubt, he decided. Meaning it might be that Riley was here on a public relations mission—that he'd come to smooth out the suspicious wrinkles on the otherwise starched-and-pressed bribery-and-murder scheme Cap'n Roy had conducted before realizing he should check the prison tapes. At which point he learned that Keeler had vetted his payoff idea with Cooper before taking his shot with Cap'n Roy.

"So what do you want, Riley?" Cooper said. "Actually, let's skip the theatrics: what is it our esteemed chief minister is too busy to come and ask me in person?"

Riley surprised Cooper by actually answering his question.

"Look pretty bad on Cap'n Roy," he said, "if that smuggler's body turn up and people find out about it. People like the Coast Guard, even—especially them, since Cap'n Roy just finished arrangin' the man's release. He asked me to bring you up to the pine scrub, where we found him, and that's about all he said to do or say. But you and I both know the chief minister's thinkin' 'bout a favor you did for him some time back. Thinkin' maybe you be up for pullin' something 'bout the same, one more time around."

"Christ," Cooper said.

"Yeah, mon," Riley said.

"Maybe I should put up a sign on my bungalow: 'Cooper's Disposal Service.' Why wrap a body in a rug and take it down to the local dump when you've got me hanging around? A one-man dead-body transfer station."

Riley kind of shrugged with his head. There wasn't, Cooper supposed, much for him to add.

"What do you think, Riley?"

When Riley didn't say anything for a moment, Cooper said, "And don't waste my time with the Royal Virgin Islands Police Force party line. A lot of Roy's predecessors, fellow superior officers of yours, have done worse. His being a cop, especially a BVI cop, doesn't put him beyond reproach in the slightest—so don't give me a whitewash. I want to know what you think."

"Yeah," Riley said after looking at Cooper for a while. "You right about that—some done worse."

Cooper waited.

"And I know you're saying if he did it, well then, you're out," Riley said. "You know—if that be the case, you don't want the first part of it. But if it's seeming like he didn't do it, then, yeah, mon, maybe you might come by and lend a hand."

"'Might,'" Cooper said, "being the key word. Go on, Lieutenant."

Riley aimed his eyes right at Cooper's, and Cooper saw some hardness in them—accepting the challenge he'd just been offered by Cooper's use of his rank—and a softness too, maybe something in there showing that Riley was a little disappointed in his boss, whether in what the man had done, or in the way he'd handled it.

When he was finished looking at Cooper with those couple of things in his eyes, Riley shook his head.

"No, mon. No way."

Cooper kept looking back at him.

"Either way," Cooper said, "Minister Roy is getting himself in pretty deep."

After another little while of looking at him, Riley gave Cooper a nod.

"Power to the people," Riley said.

Cooper stood still for a moment, thinking he was liking Lieutenant Riley more and more, and wondering, among other things, how the hell he would succeed in convincing the medical examiner of the city of Charlotte Amalie, USVI—even though the man happened to be on his list of fully extortable targets—to toss the second clandestine homicide victim in as many years into the incinerator without that coroner asking anybody in the government that employed him for permission to do it.

Then he climbed back into his dinghy, unlashed its line, and fired up the Evinrude for another big-wake ride past the unsuspecting SCUBA pupils on the way back to his Apache.

"Let's see what you've got," he said to Riley, "in that shit bucket you call a patrol boat. I'll handle my own transportation this time."

The afternoon was sticky and dank, one of those overcast days that stunted your attitude and made your skin crawl— the heat, a sopping humidity, and no sun breaking through the whole day long. Made you wonder why people came or lived here—made you notice all the grunge and grit, the streets behind the hotels, the rummies looking for a quarter, the squalid neighborhoods beginning to overtake the streets currently under the reign of the luxury resorts.

Two hundred feet up a pine-forested hill behind an inlet called Hurricane Hole, Cooper surveyed the very dead body of the belonger-to-the-rich, Po Keeler. Amid a sea of pine needles, ferns, and seemingly misplaced desert scrub, Keeler, with his too-gritty tan and unkempt hair, was splayed out, kind of folded up and bent unnaturally, as though he'd been thrown or rolled here. The stand of pines in which Keeler lay was strewn with plastic bottles, a KFC bucket, some crinkled waxed-paper wrappers, and, farther up the hill, a white plastic garbage bag that had once been packed full but appeared to have been ripped open and raided since, Cooper thinking probably by the black squirrels that usually got into everything.

Above the plastic garbage bag, the hill grew rapidly steep, until, another hundred feet up, Cooper could see the railing of a turn in the road that passed by on its path to the prison.

He knew Keeler looked as if he'd been tossed here because he had. The turn in the road above was known locally as the Dump, a spot where locals who'd fallen behind on their monthly garbage payments came by after dark and flipped a Hefty sack or two out the window as they made the hairpin turn and kept going. Anything with food in it, in fact just about everything at all was torn to shreds and mostly removed by the local wildlife; once or twice a week, somebody from Roy's posse or the parks and recreation squad came in here with an ATV and raked up the remains.

The rake job on today's remains would be a little more labor intensive.

Cooper and Riley had moored in Hurricane Hole, called that because that's what it was: a small, murky bay somebody once dredged out of the pine scrub, the place where anybody who motored over fast enough to win the first-come, first-serve rule stored their boats during stormy weather. Two of Cap'n Roy's Marine Base cops had been waiting for them, sporting the force's single, fat-wheeled ATV, which they'd parked in a way that blocked the view of the body from the turn in the road. When Cooper showed up after the climb up from Hurricane Hole, the Marine Base cops had removed the camouflage-green tarp they'd previously laid over the body, so that Cooper could get a look.

Cooper saw enough to determine, for what it was worth, that Keeler had been capped at least twice: there was a bloody mess on the front of his polo shirt and a jagged little hole in his forehead. The aim of the shot that had tagged him in the forehead appeared notably precise. Makes it pretty easy, Cooper thought, to conclude that it had been a professional who'd aced the once-bonded yacht-transport man.

"I've seen all I need to see," he said, and nodded in the general direction of the guys leaning against the ATV before heading back down the hill. Riley came uphill past him and threw off a salute on his way by. Cooper knew Riley would get the Marine Base boys to wrap up the body with the tarp; they'd then carry it down the hill and load it aboard his Apache.

Cooper's Disposal Service.

He didn't return Riley's salute on his way back down to Hurricane Hole.

11

It was closing in on eight-fifteen when Cooper made it back to Conch Bay, the tarp-mummified body of Po Keeler freshly sloughed off to Cooper's man at the Charlotte Amalie morgue, the Apache's deck hosed clean of the body's blood and scent. It had only taken a few grand and the usual unveiled threats to convince the expatriate former plastic surgeon to agree to lighting up a special session in the kiln, but even the mere act of holding a conversation with Eugene Little, M.D., made Cooper want to shower off. Toss a little corpse-incineration into the mix, the possible though unlikely murderous impropriety of Cap'n Roy, plus the afternoon visit to the garbage-strewn bend called the Dump, and Cooper was feeling ripe for a full-body chlorine wipe. Thinking he ought to grab the nearest bleach rag from Ronnie's arsenal of busboy tools and scrub till he bled—hell, even then, he'd probably still feel the grime clogging his pores.

Every time—every goddamn time he went along with one of Cap'n Roy's under-the-radar sewage-treatment schemes, it seemed he came out looking, and feeling, dirtier than the sewage itself.

He double-parked his dinghy alongside the most ostentatious Zodiac he could find, every tack taken tonight by the capacity dinner crowd. Balling his T-shirt around his Reefs, he hucked the assembly to the dock, dove off his boat into the lagoon, and started in on a crawl headed away from shore. He swam hard for a long while, poking his head above the surface every fifty strokes or so to ensure he wasn't about to get run over by a cruise ship, but otherwise pushing his head into the ocean and swimming blindly, satisfyingly, in the dark, out to sea. At the point when his chest cavity had become a full-time vacuum, sucking for more oxygen than the atmosphere had to offer, Cooper stopped, treading water, and turned to see where he'd wound up. The fear that always came next, he found exhilarating.

The current in the Sir Francis Drake Channel was deadly—fast, strong, and deceptive enough so that if you didn't pay attention, it'd take you all the way around the point and into the open Atlantic. Do it at night and it got worse—it was easy to slip past a rock, or another of the small islands to the east, and lose your angle on the lights that could show you where you were.

He could see the telltale yellow incandescence of the Conch Bay Beach Club, but only barely, and it wasn't straight behind him anymore—looked to be a good two miles east of him now. At least he hadn't passed behind Peter Island, which could have put him out to sea for good. Still, the current was strong tonight, strong enough so he'd be hard-pressed to make it back. Probably, he thought, feeling the rush of fear he'd come out here to feel, if you're lucky and strong, it'll be two, maybe three A.M. by the time you drag your ass back to the bay, and the way you'll be splashing through your last mile, I'd put the odds around fifty-fifty some tiger shark gnaws off a chunk of your thigh before you get there.

Cooper knew that the worst part of it was the pace: you didn't swim hard enough for the first two hours, you wound up too discouraged to make it back. You'd look up, nearly dead from the workout, only to find you hadn't gained an inch relative to the landfall you were trying to make. Twice, out on these swims, he'd been forced to succumb to Mother Nature—give up, drift for a while, keep an eye out for lights and swim toward them like a maniac once he spotted them. The first time, a friendly shift in the current brought him back to a beach on the opposite side of Tortola just after four in the morning; on his second flubbed effort, he was picked up by a deep-sea fishing charter off of St. Thomas around dawn.

Tonight, it was a hard haul, but he made enough headway early on to fend off the discouragement factor, and no sharks made an evident play for him. Just shy of two-thirty, he looked up from his slow-motion, straight-armed windmill crawl to see that he'd just about run his head up into the Conch Bay ferry they kept moored ten yards from the dock.

He kept his stroke on autopilot until he felt the sandy bottom rub up against his knees, stood shakily, headed back out on the dock, retrieved his T-shirt and flip-flops, and made directly for the sack. There was nobody around, and only the dim yellow safety lights were lit, as he shuffled through the kitchen and garden to bungalow nine. Lacking the energy to peel off his wet swim trunks, he simply left them on and toppled into bed.

Sometime shortly thereafter, as Cooper began to feel the creeping pull of sleep, his ears were pierced by the single most aggravating noise he remembered hearing. Lost in the initial moments of unconsciousness, he must have missed the short chortle that signaled an incoming fax on the HP all-in-one he kept hooked to his mobile sat phone console, but he didn't miss the rest of it: the ink-jet housing grinding along its plastic strip, the creaking rollers contorting the paper through its designated route, the cartridge whining and whirring as it shot the page with thousands of pinpricks of black ink. Worse still—at least for Cooper in his fatigued post-swim state— was the length of the document ink-jetting itself to fruition. He kept thinking the racket would end with each succeeding page, but then the goddamned machine would suck another sheet into its maw and grind out another round of noise. Cooper counted fourteen pages before the racket ceased.

Thinking, after ten minutes of staring at the fan attached to his ceiling, that he could always sleep in—at least so long as the goat-of-the-day wasn't going nuts—he flopped his legs out of bed, took the two steps into the middle of his room, and snagged the document from the printer. He flipped on the light and sat in his reading chair, loudly pushing the wires and other paraphernalia out of the way as he kicked his ankles up on the ottoman and sat back to read.

The cover page, otherwise blank, contained the ink-jet-transmitted version of five words written in Professor Susannah Grant's looping cursive script. It said:

To: Island Man
From: Me

Cooper tossed the cover page on the floor and started in on the other thirteen, where he found Susannah to be true to her word: she'd promised her analysis of the artifacts within forty-eight hours of their lab session, even delivered eight hours early. Cooper hadn't necessarily expected a three A.M. transmission, but all the better. His swim had just about cleansed him, and the sooner he found a buyer and unloaded the merchandise, the sooner he'd be free and clear of Cap'n Roy's filth. Cooper thinking if Susannah's fax gave him enough to go on, he might just be able to place a call in the morning, set up an exchange, and be done with it. Done with the artifacts, done with the incinerated body of Po Keeler, and done with Cap'n Roy.

It occurred to him there was the issue of who had killed Keeler—Cooper assuming, begrudgingly, that Roy hadn't. He decided he would cross that bridge when he came to it. If ever.

He read that Susannah had concluded the artifacts belonged to some Central American native tradition, likely Mayan from what she called the Decadent period—date of origin, mid-nineteenth or early twentieth century, which sounded odd to him. She deemed them authentic, with a total value she called "difficult to estimate," though she referenced a similar, smaller collection that had been auctioned through Christie's in 1998 for an average winning bid of $1.24 million per piece. Assuming full authentication, a comparable perceived value, and a few years of appreciation, Susannah estimated that the auction-house value of Cap'n Roy's stash would fall between sixty and eighty million bucks.

She spelled out the likelihood of the potential geographic origin of the gold used in the artifacts—somewhere along the continental spine connecting North and South America. She bolstered the gold-origin data with a cultural analysis of the images depicted in the collection. Most of what was depicted on the pieces, she said, fit the cultural, religious, and societal norms of "original" Mayan civilizations—in other words, those whose artifacts might have dated a millennium earlier than 150 years ago. Nonetheless she insisted the artifact-dating results were reliable, and speculated as to one possible explanation: the creators of Cap'n Roy's stash of artifacts currently lived, or, some 150 years ago *had* lived in some remote locale, comprising one of what was generally estimated to be at least a few hundred "isolated remnant civilizations" found in mountainous, jungle, or otherwise treacherous or inaccessible regions of Central America.

Susannah wrote that she suspected this "remnant civilization" was "in all likelihood now lost," since she had been unable to find anything relating to the existence of a contemporary tribe or cultural group currently practicing the sort of lifestyle depicted in the carvings and sculptures in the collection. Also, she wrote, such a group would be "unlikely to part amicably" with such burial artifacts as these. They were too sacred.

Cooper noted with an internal twinge that Susannah had narrowed her estimate on the whereabouts of the artifacts' origin to a region encompassing the lower midsection of Central America. She'd boxed out an area on a map, including within her marked box parts of Honduras, Nicaragua, and Guatemala. Staring at the rectangle of black ink Susannah had marked on the map, Cooper felt a vague, echoing thump, as though a muscle in his heart had decided to expunge its contents prematurely.

Cooper didn't exactly keep this part of the world on his list of favorite places to visit.

Sitting there in his reading chair, the one light in his bungalow shining down from its nook in the ceiling fan, he gave some thought to Professor Susannah Grant. He thought about her mostly to stop himself from thinking about some other things he didn't want to think about—but thinking about her didn't offer much help.

After their afternoon in the lab, she'd taken him for a ride in her coupe and shown him one of Austin's claims to fame—North America's largest colony of Mexican free-tailed bats, all residing beneath a single bridge called the Congress Avenue Bridge. The bats headed out for the night's insect hunt, in a dizzyingly endless stream, from beneath the bridge, beginning around dusk. Cooper found it odd but impressive. Afterward, she'd insisted on visiting him in his room at the Hyatt, but after a mere ninety minutes of remembrance, he'd sent her home early, Cooper regretting the whole trip upon the first brush of skin. Thinking that sometimes you just knew you'd made a wrong turn—time to head back.

She didn't take the early dismissal particularly well, but despite her dour mood at last glimpse, Professor Grant had delivered.

Cooper didn't like what the analysis was telling him about the people who belonged to the artifacts—or had, once. He didn't like what it meant about the plea for help he was now certain he'd heard the golden-idol priestess on the shelf demand of him. And he didn't like something else about all of this—particularly if Cap'n Roy *hadn't* been the one to ace the belonger-to-the-rich.

Cooper tossed the fax onto the cement floor of his bungalow. It made a loud slapping sound—to Cooper, a perfect noise, an exclamation point on this episode of his life. He stood, shrugged his shoulders, rolled his head around to loosen the kinks in his neck, reached over to flip off the light, took the two blind steps he'd taken a few million times before—usually drunk—and fell back into bed. Thinking, as he imagined the muck and grime slipping from his body, that Susannah's map, and what existed within it, didn't matter for shit. Thinking that he'd heard all he needed to hear, and that the end was therefore near.

Cap'n Roy's stash was worth as much as Roy had hoped, maybe considerably more—one large shitload of dollars. With one, or maybe two phone calls tops, Cooper held no doubt he'd be able to find somebody to take the goods off Cap'n Roy's pesky little hands—a *fence*—and be done with it.

Done with the artifacts—and done with Cap'n Roy.

For good.

12

Laramie arrived in the freshly built Southwest Florida International Airport terminal and followed the signs to the exit. Hoofing it past the baggage claim, she wondered whether they'd had somebody on the flight, or sent somebody to keep an eye on the gate. Somebody who'd tell the guide, whoever the guide was, that she was here.

Less than a minute after she stepped out into the humid heat, a Jeep Grand Cherokee nosed into the crosswalk stripes nearest her. The Jeep's passenger-side window zipped down, and when nobody else on the sidewalk made a rush for the car, Laramie stepped to the curb and leaned down for a look inside. She saw behind the wheel a man in a corduroy baseball cap pulled low on his forehead. The color of the hat was a muted pastel falling somewhere between pink and orange. He wore a clean white T-shirt and worn blue jeans, his skin a sunbaked version of what looked to Laramie like Mexican heritage. There was a subtle athleticism and wear and tear to the man—he looked, Laramie thought, like a migrant farm worker who'd come to own the farm.

"Welcome to Fort Myers," he said, speaking across the seat through the open passenger-side window.

Laramie nodded, bag still strapped over her shoulder.

"Ever been here before?"

Laramie looked around. "Florida? Yes. Fort Myers? No."

"Old people, golf courses, a few beaches, one hell of a lot of oranges, and a lot less swamp than there used to be. Hop in."

Laramie decided not to be a nervous Nellie—there was no reason to think the farm-owner sitting behind the wheel was anyone but the "tour guide" sent by Ebbers. She opened the door, tossed in her bag, and climbed in.

The guide eased off the brake and the Grand Cherokee slipped out into the traffic loop.

"Drive's about an hour," he said, eyes on the road. "More than enough to bring you up to speed. Not that there's much to talk about yet. Not that's been figured out, anyway."

Laramie watched the airport's landscaped palm beds switch over to pines and ponds as they moved off airport property and climbed a ramp to I-75 North.

"So what exactly are we talking about, then?" she said.

Her guide looked over at her.

"We're talking about a 'flight school clue,'" he said.

Laramie thought she understood but asked him to clarify anyway.

"Somebody made a mistake," he said. "Blew himself up a little ahead of schedule with the ammonium nitrate car bomb he'd put together in his garage. Blew up his house while he was at it, and dispersed, in the process, a miniscule percentage of the airborne filovirus serum he'd been storing in his basement freezer. When we say 'flight school clue,' we're saying what you think we're saying. We feel we have in our suicide bomber today's equivalent of the clue left by the 9/11 hijackers, which was fumbled, when they enrolled in various flight schools to learn how to fly a 767 into a skyscraper."

Laramie noticed his use of the term *we,* her "tour guide" deploying the word in the same way Ebbers had. Except, that was, when he'd referenced the 9/11 flight school clue being missed.

"Key difference being," he said, "is if our bomber had succeeded in dispersing the whole batch of the pathogen he was keeping, a lot more thousands of people than took the hit in 2001 would be dead already. With more on the way."

"Who was he?"

"Name was Benjamin Achar." The guide pronounced the *ch* as though it were a *k*. "However, based on his Social Security number, Mr. Achar appears to have resurrected himself from a case of SIDS he came down with thirty-six years ago."

"As in sudden infant death syndrome?"

"One and the same."

The guide flipped on his blinker, changed lanes to pass a semi, turned off the blinker, and slid past the rig.

Laramie looked out the front windshield as they exited the turnpike at State Road 80. Once they left Fort Myers behind, SR-80 became somewhat more barren, the strip malls and golf communities on either side of the highway switching over to pine barrens and driving ranges, then orange groves—lots of them.

"You're saying he was a sleeper, then," Laramie said. "A deep cover terrorist."

"That's the theory."

"Working for who?"

The guide smiled a compact, tight-lipped grin.

"Believe that's why I was told to pick you up at the airport."

"We don't know," Laramie said.

"Nope."

The highway lost its extra lanes and narrowed to one lane in each direction. Laramie thought about the things he was telling her. She considered thirty or forty questions she could ask, then thought that it would probably be a busy seventy-two hours between now and the time she'd need to give her findings to Ebbers, and that maybe the better idea would be to play it by ear.

They passed through the city of LaBelle, followed by an endless residential development called Port LaBelle—each looking utterly bereft of activity—and then Laramie saw a sign indicating he'd turned them onto State Road 833 South. Orange groves and a patchwork of other farms gave way to some very small homes in terrible disrepair, followed by a roadside trinket shop, gas station, and short bridge. The bridge took them over a narrow stripe of water, the skinny waterway straight as a canal, stretching to the horizon in both directions. Over the bridge a stretch of swamp came, then more pine trees.

A berm blocked the swamp water from the pines; the trees looked emaciated, bereft of green outside of the occasional branch or needle. The stretch of trees didn't last long. At its back end, rapidly approaching, Laramie could see the identical roofs of a number of houses.

The guide slowed the Jeep. Ahead of them stood a set of orange pylons and two Florida Highway Patrol cruisers parked lengthwise across the road. The guide lowered his window as the state trooper standing against the hood of the nearest cruiser approached, hand resting lazily on his firearm. Her guide pulled what looked to Laramie like a pair of credentials from a pocket on the door—the kind of credentials VIPs wore at sports events, clipped to a lanyard you could keep around your neck. The trooper took the credentials, peered inside the Jeep for a look at Laramie, then, wordlessly, retreated to his cruiser, withdrew a clipboard, copied some information to the sheet on the clipboard, replaced the clipboard in his cruiser, and returned the guide's credentials.

A second trooper roamed over from his own cruiser to move one of the orange pylons out of the way, and the first trooper waved them through.

The guide turned into the entrance of the housing development that was home to the stretch of identical tile roofs Laramie had spotted from the pine forest. The entrance boasted a sign with raised green letters nailed into a beige slab of what looked to Laramie like plywood: in a glorious burst of optimism, the sign announced that the name of the housing development was **EMERALD LAKES**. Laramie couldn't see any water along the road. She wondered if maybe they'd find the lakes inside the development.

As the guide negotiated the simple street grid, Laramie observed that no one was home. They passed duplexes first, then single-family homes, the uniformity of the structures alarming. There were no cars in the driveways, no lawn mowers running, no sprinklers in operation; nobody tinkered with anything in a garage, watered a lawn, or walked a dog. They were driving through a dead town.

The guide turned a corner onto a street called Gem Road, at least according to the bent-over street sign on the corner. As they made the turn, Laramie was confronted by at least one reason behind the apparent evacuation: on both sides of the street, starting about fifty yards in, the homes had been leveled. In the searing white-hot sunshine, Laramie thought immediately of Iraq: it looked, albeit in abbreviated fashion, like a war zone. Some twenty homes on each side of the road had been reduced to rubble, the concrete foundations holding firm in jagged chunks, the remainder of what had once been walls and roofs strewn across Gem Road and the surrounding real estate. A vehicular path had been cleared down the middle of the street, but squat cliffs of rubble otherwise ruled the day.

He parked near a shallow crater midway through the damage.

"Ground zero," he said. "You can get out and sweat for a while if you like, but you can probably see all you need to see from here."

Laramie said, "I'll go take a look," unlatched the door, and stepped into the soupy heat.

She was hit by a scent she couldn't place, something between fern and marijuana, and wondered whether it was the fragrance of the swamp on which they'd built the neighborhood, steaming its way to the surface through the crater now that the buildings on its surface had been blown away—or just some cleaning agent they'd used on the blast site.

She poked around the edge of the crater. Among other

revelations, the exposed strata of the six-foot cliff edge of the crater's interior outed the development's contractor as a cheapskate—there was no more than an inch of asphalt forming the roadbed, without a single chunk of gravel to facilitate drainage. She wondered idly whether sinkholes the size of garbage trucks might eventually have appeared, with or without explosion.

There was little else of note to observe, though Laramie had long since discovered it was difficult to determine what would turn out to be of interest in such situations—especially if nobody was telling you much about any of it to begin with. Something she *could* tell was that the blast had unleashed its wrath mostly horizontally. The crater that marked ground zero from the explosion was relatively shallow, only a little deeper than Laramie was tall, occupying a space that would logically seem to have been the garage of one of the homes along the street. Other than to carve out a crater of this depth, the explosion's effects had refused to go deep, instead taking out a football field's worth of homes in all directions. Not a single wall remained standing for the length of the street.

She walked around the edge of the crater and examined the remnants of the foundation of the "ground zero" house. Chunks of the structure still stood, reaching somewhere around mid-basement before the cheap cinder blocks had been torn from their spadework, sheared like wool from the sheep of the first layer of foundation. It was oddly quiet. Laramie heard only the sounds of her muffled footsteps in the rubble and the distant roar of the air conditioner at work beneath the hood of the Jeep.

She saw shards of burnt metal, orbs of rock and cinder block, and reddish dust strewn everywhere. The dust seemed to be shifting, maybe blowing in the breeze, only there wasn't really a breeze, just the thick, still, ugly heat. She felt a sharp, stinging pain on her leg, looked down, and frantically whacked away at her ankles—realizing it wasn't dust, but *ants*. Millions of them. Fire ants, or red ants, or whatever kind of ant was red and bit you. The bites hurt like hell, Laramie suddenly feeling as though she'd joined the cast of a straight-to-video horror flick—a helpless *femme fatale* stranded in a Martian landscape populated by deadly, if unrealistic creatures. She had the overwhelming sense of nature commencing the process of taking back the land.

Turning back toward the street, she felt a twinge of embarrassment—the rookie, having a look at the site, getting chomped by the resident critters in front of her new boss. By the time she came around the crater, though, the shame had moved out of the way to make room for the shot of anger that took its place.

She opened the door of the Grand Cherokee, planted herself within the chilled confines of the car's interior, and jutted her chin in the direction of her taupe-skinned host.

"You could have told me about the ants," she said.

A smirk creased the lines of his face beneath the baseball cap.

"They get you?"

"They got me."

He shrugged.

"Sorry about that. Ready for tour stop number two?"

"Depends," she said.

"The ants haven't taken over task force headquarters, if that's what you mean," he said. "At least not yet."

13

Fourteen agents—special, investigative, and other-wise—sat around eight rectangular tables somebody had arranged in a square. The makeshift war room occupied a gym-size space that until a month ago had composed the cocktail lounge of the Motor 8 Luxury Motel, a one-story lodge nestled between mobile home parks along one of the endless supply of seemingly identical two-lane highways Laramie now understood to crisscross the state. The $38-a-night establishment had been adopted as the operational headquarters for the multijurisdictional pig fuck to which Ebbers had alerted her—and her guide had then delivered her.

As they'd pulled into the motel lot, Laramie wondered how the country's law enforcement community had managed to survive before the creation of SUVs, since it was evident that the Emerald Lakes incident had resulted in, among other things, an invasion of black-on-black Suburbans, Envoys, and Expeditions, with no window left untinted.

Inside the former cocktail lounge, the task force's biweekly powwow came to order. A man stood near the L formed by a pair of the tables and cleared his throat. He looked about fifty, and projected a demeanor befitting a Fortune 500 exec more so than a G-man; the charcoal suit he wore caused Laramie to realize there wasn't anybody in here outside of her guide who wasn't suited up. This made her note further that there appeared to be no representative of the local constabulary present, not unless some sheriff's deputy or other had elected to abide by the feds' dress code in order to gain an invite.

"Let's get it rolling," Head Fed said. The murmur of conversation and shuffling of paper relented. "Bill, you want to start? One second—" He extended an arm in Laramie's direction. Laramie noticed that his eyes shifted, a bit uncomfortably, to take in her guide, who leaned against the bar along the side of the room, well back from the proceedings. "Give a warm welcome to the newest member of the task force."

He did not give her name. Laramie's guide had recommended she not identify herself personally to any of the task force members; perhaps the Head Fed had been given similar instructions.

"Our new friend is here on behalf of the president. Special investigator." Laramie blinked and tried to avoid stealing a glance in the direction of her guide. Neither he—nor Ebbers before him—had described her assignment the way the Head Fed just had. "She'll be debriefing some of you over the next forty-eight hours. Make yourself available. Bill."

A man who Laramie presumed to be Bill jammed a pen behind an ear and stood a few seats to her right. He carried fifteen or twenty pounds more than the anonymous Head Fed and stood about three inches shorter, but he was suited up and clean-cut just like everybody else in the room.

"Couple of you haven't been here for a while—welcome back to the Motor 8." From behind his ear he drew, then uncapped his pen, which looked to be a dry-erase marker. "With some of the task force out of the loop of late and due to the presence of our new friend, Sid asked that I take it from the top." He extricated himself from the table-and-chairs setup and approached the white board hanging on the wall behind his seat.

"We pretty much all know what we've got," he said, "and what happened, but I like using this goddamn board, so nobody fuck with me while I do it." He uncapped the dry-erase marker to a muted chuckle or two. In the upper-left corner of the board, he drew a circle, then wrote *Emerald Lakes* in the middle of the circle. Underneath the circle, he wrote, *Achar*. He then drew a series of outward-fanning lines that made the circle look like a child's depiction of the sun.

"So the perp," Bill said, " 'Benny' Achar, as his wife calls him, blows his Chevy Blazer sky high with a fertilizer bomb he put together in his garage, living, as he was, in the formerly bankrupt though lovely community of Emerald Lakes. Still haven't found the lakes—any of you spot one, let me know and I'll draw it on the board here." Bill composed a trio of arrows running from his sunshine illustration toward the middle of the board, where he drew a box. He filled the interior of the box with the words *LaBelle (125)*. "Turns out Achar," he said, "in detonating himself and the neighborhood, has earned the honor of being the first terrorist to detonate a 'bio-dirty bomb' within the borders of the United States. Benny's dispersal of our mystery pathogen"—he wrote *Pathogen X* across the three arrows—"results, as you know, in the publicly referenced outbreak of a wicked flu, killing a hundred and twenty-five residents of Hendry County before our quarantine puts on the brakes."

Alongside *Pathogen X* he drew an = sign and the words *Filovirus (new)*.

"Wasn't the flu, of course," he said, "but a heretofore unencountered strain of filovirus, similar to Marburg, only more potent, possessing, as it seems to possess, the added quality of airborne transmission. You sneeze, you give this thing to whoever you sneeze on, which is not the case with the known filovirus strains. This one flies." He drew a makeshift set of wings around the words *Filovirus (new)*, then drew an arrow from his *LaBelle (125)* square pointing toward the left edge of the board, where he wrote and underlined the word *Filo*.

"Also infects animals and people without prejudice one way or the other, and is transmittable from one to the other, much like the oft-discussed potential avian flu mutation. Sadie will give you more on the filo," he said, "but let's hit the perp first."

Beside his original *Achar* sunshine illustration, Bill wrote and underlined *Perp*. Beneath the underlined heading, he wrote *SSN, Mobile, Bonita Springs, Wife & Son, Seattle, LaBelle,* and *1995–1996.* Yawns came from at least two of the agents seated at the table.

"Benny's married—Janine—with an eight-year-old son—Carter. Achar's prior residence was in a similar housing development outside of Bonita Springs, Florida, where he lived when he met his wife. Got married in 1998. She's from Seattle—or, more accurately, Kent, sort of a 'Seattle-adjacent' locality. The newlyweds moved into the home in Emerald Lakes just prior to Carter's birth. Achar was employed by UPS—drove the truck. Had the job since 1997. Convenient job, as we know. And speaking of dates, the real Benjamin Achar was born in Mobile, Alabama, on February 4, 1969, where he also died, only much more tragically, at eleven months of age. Cause of death, sudden infant death syndrome. We've got nothing on the 'current' Achar prior to February 1995." He pointed to one of two women, not including Laramie, seated at the table. "Mary has some more on our perp."

"Mary," came a voice, which Laramie determined to be the Head Fed giving Mary her cue.

Mary, who wore a black jacket over a puffy white blouse, stayed in her seat. To Laramie she looked about the way you might expect an FBI profiler to look: pallid, sagging skin beneath the eyes, mildly inhibited. She cleared her throat before speaking.

"The current Benjamin James Achar is of diluted Hispanic origin," she said, "with strong Caucasoid features.

Based on photographs, we can make the call that he's of Central or South American heritage. From our access to home videos and so forth, it's clear Achar did not have a foreign accent. Actually he sounded exactly like someone born in Mobile and relocated to Bonita Springs is supposed to sound. So if he's a sleeper as we postulate, he could have come from Colombia, or Chile, and had extensive language training, or he might just as easily have been born in Nebraska, or adopted in Mississippi, and simply happens to have had parents of Central or South American descent—maybe a John Walker type, living here and joining the other side, whatever the other side might be. Beyond this, the news flash on my profile of Achar is that there is none. Not the serial-killing kind, or any other sort that would point us anywhere significant."

Laramie noted the way Mary referred to both Achar and the wife: she called them by name, as though Mary knew each of them personally. The word *perp* did not appear to be in Mary's vocabulary. Something occurred to Laramie about the way Mary was seeing Achar—something involving the sympathetic angle of it—but she lost the thought as quickly as it came.

"He was a blue-collar guy," Mary said. "Spent most of his time after work with his son or out in the yard with the lawn mower. From all accounts, good husband to Janine, understanding guy, loved by his in-laws. No evident visits to the Bonita Springs or LaBelle strip joints, no massage parlor girlfriends, no odd, telltale hobbies or habits he was keeping from Janine. In short, Benjamin Achar was no Scott Peterson, with some secret life he was keeping on the side." Mary scratched her head just behind the ear. "There are two points about this otherwise unexciting news I'd like to emphasize. One, it may be worthwhile for you to pay attention to the fact that Achar was not of Middle Eastern descent or of the, uh, Muslim persuasion. And two, though this is just a hunch of sorts—I found him too well put together. Almost to an unrealistic extent."

The Head Fed, whom Laramie assumed Bill had meant when he'd used the name Sid, spoke up.

"Explain that," he said.

Mary turned to face him. "I'm certain I was prejudiced by knowing, in advance, that he had stolen somebody else's identity, but regardless, I found too few flaws in the picture. Even the best man, or woman for that matter, has a flaw. Even you, Sid."

Nobody laughed at Mary's attempt at humor. Sid smiled but didn't seem to mean it.

"In the case of somebody like Achar, it'd be normal to find, upon digging through the things you only find in the course of a criminal investigation, that he drinks too much, surfs Internet porn sites after his wife hits the sack, was said to have struck his wife at a party—whatever. In Achar, we've found no such flaw. Only the stereotype to a T: drove the Blazer, leased a Nissan Altima his wife preferred to use, had four grand on three credit cards, built mostly from purchases at The Home Depot and Best Buy. No evident problem with authority figures at the job, no substance-abuse issues— nothing. It's as though he climbed into a blue-collar Halloween costume but didn't notice that a few pieces of the costume were missing."

When Mary added nothing further for a few consecutive seconds, Bill gave her an inquiring look and got a nod in reply.

"That's it," she said.

"Don't skip over Mary's first point," Bill said, addressing the group again. "Achar was not of Middle Eastern descent, and he isn't a Muslim extremist. Welcome to post-9/11–post-Iraq. We have the list of hostile regimes and most-wanted terrorist financiers compiled by the intelligence reps on the task force, and obviously some of them are from Central or South America. Point being, however, it appears Mr. bin-Laden may have lost his perennial ranking as public enemy number one."

Beneath his *Perp* heading, Bill wrote *Open Road #1*, followed by another three words: *Identity, Heritage, Affiliation.* Then he circled the whole line.

"Anyway, this is what we're calling 'open road number one' in our investigation," he said. "The identity, heritage, and affiliation of our perp all remain a question mark. We don't have the answers on this guy prior to ninety-five, and we need to find them. Once we do, we ought to be able to determine who's behind him, and therefore what the new kids on the block, whoever they happen to be, might have in store for us. Sorry to say that outside of Mary's scoop and the records of his whereabouts dating back to 1995, we've got nothing more on Achar since our last session. Oh, there is one update."

He underlined the spot where he'd written *Wife & Son* earlier.

"Not exactly a breakthrough," he said, "more the opposite. On the wife, we've assumed he had to have shared something critical with her, something real. Pre-costume, I guess you might say. So we're still holding her, been cycling interrogators through, going after everything there is to go after with her. She's given us a lot on the current Benjamin Achar, but unless she's real good, it does not appear he told her anything. That she had any idea. We're just about ready to make the official call that Janine Achar, maiden name Marino, does not herself appear to be a sleeper. The background check on her is done, we've got a real history on her and her family. No legal troubles—one episode of shoplifting in college. Realty license with Century 21, last commission March of 2005, for fifteen hundred bucks—soccer mom, folks, with Italian-American roots going back for at least a few generations. So we're about ready to make the call that she isn't good for it."

He shrugged, took the dry-erase marker, and beneath his earlier underlined heading of *Filo,* Bill wrote the words *Organic/Synthetic, Source,* and *The Plan.* He drew another circle, this time around *The Plan.*

Bill gestured toward the second woman in the room, a black-rooted blonde with her hair cut short.

"Sadie," came Sid's voice.

Sadie stood and Bill returned to his seat. Sadie was taller than most of the men in the room and, like most of the others, looked a little haggard around the eyes.

"Achar's pathogen is a combination of microscopic synthetic materials and a heretofore undocumented filovirus that was clearly genetically engineered," she said. The woman spoke with the sort of assuredness Laramie could tell, from just one speech, that Mary the profiler wished she too possessed. "It's more complicated than this, but here's how it's designed to work: no ordinary microorganism, including known strains of filovirus or even the 'new' strain contained in Achar's serum, could possibly survive the direct impact or heat of a fertilizer-bomb explosion. In other words, ordinarily it would be impossible to effectively detonate a 'bio-dirty' bomb—the 'bomb' portion of the act of destruction would destroy the biological component. In English: the explosion would kill the virus."

Sadie went on.

"The 'Marburg-2' pathogen Achar dispersed was different. I would call it both frightening and technologically staggering. In studying undetonated portions of Achar's serum, we've learned that uniform-size colonies of the filovirus have been coated with a microscopic polymer sheath. Porous enough to allow the filo to survive within, yet capable of absorbing the shock of a massive impact and temperatures in excess of eight hundred degrees Fahrenheit. In our tests, upon impact or burning, a significant percentage of the sheaths—over fifty percent—disintegrate, but only *after* absorbing enough of the shock to allow the filo housed within to survive. The other fifty percent of the sheaths caught fire, or suffered a degree of damage that killed the filo colonies within.

"Final note on the technical specs," she said. "The Marburg-2 filo appears to be capable of surviving for an indefinite hibernation period when stored at temperatures approaching zero degrees Celsius. Achar was storing it between his freezer and fridge, judging from what we were able to pull from the wreckage—that'd coincide with the right temperature range. This quality is similar to but slightly more hardy than a 'normal' flu or filovirus."

Sadie reached down and punched the space bar on the notebook computer she'd been keeping on her section of table. The sound of a tiny whirring fan kicked in and a large blue square of light faded into view along the wall behind Sid. Images that Laramie assumed were shots of individual "filo" cells—or whatever, she thought, you call a single virus—cycled through a slide show on the wall as Sadie spoke.

"Once released from the sheathing, what we've got is a genuine filovirus, not a chemical agent. As Bill covered, it is airborne—you can catch it from a sneeze, not just a blood transfusion. We've never seen this before. Also it can pass from animal to human or human to human. It does have a short infectious period, so early quarantining, as we accomplished here, should remain effective. We're working around the clock to test various antivirals for effectiveness, but don't hold your breath. Filos are fierce, maybe the single most resistant and fastest-acting viral agent known to man, and this one's the fastest we've seen. Forty-eight hours, infection to death. Breakdown of all internal organs, gruesome hemorrhaging—we've been through all this, I just want to emphasize that our lab efforts aren't likely to deliver overnight results."

The filo slide show ended and the screen returned to its prior blue state.

"We're recommending continued stockpiling of Tamiflu and Relenza, over and above what's already under way in anticipation of the avian flu mutation. These antivirals appear to reduce the infectious period. The best hope for an actual vaccine, however remote, will come from the source of a similar outbreak—if the initial human outbreak of a similar filo took place in Zaire, for instance, there may be somebody there who survived it, or carried it into the community to begin with, without incurring the symptoms. We find out why that host survived and we've got a starting point. Again, don't get your hopes up—no such filo vaccine has been found yet."

Sadie hit a key on her laptop and a map of the world appeared on the wall, decorated by thirteen red dots positioned on various continents.

"Working from a canvas of the past one hundred years, we've tracked thirteen localized outbreaks involving similar symptoms and acquisition rates. Four of our thirteen cases have taken place in the past decade. The closest match is an extremely localized outbreak of Marburg in rural Guatemala—seven patients and a medical staff of four, including two Peace Corps volunteers, died at a medical outpost of symptoms as close to those found here as we've been able to identify. 1983."

A male agent raised his hand. "Where'd we get the description of the symptoms?" he said.

Laramie had a pretty good idea he was CIA just by looking at him.

"One of the Peace Corps volunteers kept a journal," Sadie said. To Laramie her gravelly voice was starting to run out of fuel. "Copies of the journal made their way back to CDC about ten years ago. We have doctors on-site, but again, don't get your hopes up. The trail is cold."

The CIA man, Laramie observed, didn't nod, offer thanks, or otherwise acknowledge the response to his question. Sadie, who didn't seem to mind, whacked away at the keys of her laptop and caused a map of the United States to appear on the wall where the blue square had been. Sadie motioned to Bill, who stood again. Laramie took the opportunity to steal a glance at her guide, and found him missing. The doorjamb he'd been leaning against was empty. She did a slow swivel and checked around the rim of the room; no cigar. It seemed he'd flown the coop.

"To the plan, then," Bill said. "Here's where we are on this: our guy fucked up. Achar blew himself up before he had positioned all the virus serum in the correct spot. Maybe he made a mistake with whatever fertilizer and fuel he was storing in his garage, maybe it just blew up on its own when he wasn't ready for it—but don't forget the wife and son. They left town to see the wife's parents in San Diego on the same day Achar blew himself up, and she's admitted he booked the trip for her. So for this reason we think he meant to do it on the day he did it, he just got it wrong. He set off the blast prematurely, and the result of the mistake is he failed to disperse even ten percent of the filo he was keeping in the basement."

Bill paced in front of the image of the map.

"We need to assume Achar wasn't operating alone, if only due to the sophistication and quantity of the virus. Under this assumption, Sadie has calculated the potential intended effect on the American populace."

Laramie glanced again at the doorjamb her guide had abandoned, and something caught her eye. On the floor, where he'd been standing, was a black Tumi travel bag. Laramie knew it was a Tumi because it was hers—the bag Ebbers told her they'd pack and deliver here.

Sadie came up with a remote control about the size of a business card. As she strolled to a spot beside the image on the wall, expanding circles began illustrating themselves on the wall from an epicenter in Florida Laramie assumed to be Emerald Lakes.

"If Achar doesn't make his mistake," Sadie said, "and instead gets his entire batch of serum dispersed, then just over two hundred times the amount that got airborne would have been up for grabs." Animated, wavy lines appeared on the map and spread from the initial area covered by the expanding circles until the circles reached the greater Miami-Dade County area, which began to blink. A number appeared near ground zero—125—then zeroes began fading in at the number's back end, so that 125 became 1,250, then 12,500, then 125,000, then 1,250,000 with a question mark beside it.

"With immediate exposure to this large an airborne filo sample," Sadie said, "it's our estimate that nearly ten thousand people would have been infected in the same period it took the hundred and twenty-five to come down with the disease in our real-world case. Infections would have occurred over a wider area, making quarantine efforts initially less effective. If the filo had reached Miami or Fort Myers, it might have spread at a rate that could easily have resulted in a hundred thousand deaths or more. Our conclusion is that Miami was ultimately the perp's target. His mistake in detonating the bomb when he did resulted in a stunted spread of the filo that prevented it from reaching the urban center he had hoped to strike."

A second expanding-circle illustration began in Washington state, east of Seattle. The same expansion, followed by the animated wavy lines pushing north, south, east, and west, played out across the Pacific Northwest. A third sequence illustrated itself in the Chicago area, a fourth in Texas, and a fifth in the northeast, near Boston.

"We've modeled ten sleepers detonating similar devices, and releasing a full dose of filo with no preestablished quarantine measures to slow the spread of the fever." More expanding circles faded into view on the map, in the heartland, Rocky Mountains, then Manhattan. "You should know there is the potential effect, assuming there are other sleepers in this network, of ten to fifteen million casualties. Add to this the threat of overlap—meaning," she said, "if two or more of the bio-dirty detonations occur within the same prequarantine period—say, forty-eight hours—you could see double the number of deaths, or triple, or worse. The effect would be a nullification of any quarantines. A 'piggybacking' rate-of-infection effect would likely activate a series of 'perfect filo storms,' or super-plague zones, where, within such areas, all are exposed, and no life is spared."

Hurricane-like shapes visually connected three of the initial virus zones into three ominous-looking and extremely wide swaths of territory on the map. Casualty numbers beside the affected plague zones shifted from hundreds of thousands to tens of millions, then froze. Finally the image on the wall dissolved back to blue. Sadie closed her laptop and the blue square disappeared from the wall. She returned to her seat.

Sid stood.

"Who sent the filo to him?" he said. "How'd it get delivered? The perp's profession presents both a problem and an opportunity, since every package with which Achar was associated should have had a tracking number. Bill's group is working from lists of shipments Achar picked up, delivered, or otherwise handled. It's a big list with no apparent connections to illegal medical labs or terrorist organizations."

Sid came around the table to the place where Bill was seated. He reached over Bill's shoulder, took hold of the dry-erase marker Bill had employed, went to the board, and drew a long arrow from each of the words Bill had circled. Sid's arrows all led to the same place at the bottom of the board, where he wrote and double-underlined *Public Enemy #1*.

"We are assuming Achar wasn't acting alone. He was just early, and ineffective. Why was he early? Why did he go maverick?"

Beneath his *Public Enemy #1* line, Sid wrote, *Time = Public Enemy #2*. Laramie thought briefly of the idea that had shown itself, then escaped her earlier—an idea that had to do with Achar, his wife and son, and Mary's take on them—but then the idea, whatever it was, retreated again into the abyss.

"What if there are nine, or eleven, or thirteen others out there, and they're laying low for, what, another two weeks? A month? We don't find out who they are, where they are, and who's giving the orders before whenever it is they're planning their D-Day, then Bill, you can kiss your wife goodbye. Sadie, your brother, and your nephew—hemorrhaged out in an emergency ward. Bob—those five rugrats of yours—they'll die first."

He encircled the batch of words he'd just written on the board.

"Public enemies number one and two. Session over."

14

Cooper watched the landing lights approach, then
flare, then douse as the ATR 72-500 cargo plane punched
down on the longer runway of Terrance B. Lettsome International Airport. The blank-skinned turboprop charter wheeled
into its assigned stall and the engines eased. As instructed,
the pilot kept the props whirling. The bridge to Beef Island
was sealed off for the night under the guise of midnight repair work—if he leaned back a notch, Cooper could just see
the spinning kaleidoscope of blue and white emanating from
the Mitsubishi minivan cruiser parked lengthwise across the
bridge. They had the airport to themselves.

It was a clear, hot night. Cap'n Roy stood beside Cooper
on the tarmac, out of uniform for the first time Cooper remembered seeing. Might, Cooper thought, be decked out in
the khakis and sandals you'd see anybody else wearing, but
the man doesn't look one inch less the chief minister. Didn't
matter what you wore—keep a look like that on your face
and you could forget going casual.

Riley came out of the terminal behind them with a lanky
patrol officer named Tim. The last time Cooper encountered
him, the skinny young cop had been carrying a body bag

down the Marine Base dock to Cooper's Apache. It gave Cooper a creepy sort of feeling—he wondered whether Tim's presence might bring bad luck. It certainly had last time.

Behind the plane now, Riley took hold of the handle beneath the cargo door at the back of the plane's fuselage. He pulled open the big door, unfolding then locking its ramp in place. Cooper watched as a bulky, tanned, short-sleeved arm appeared from inside the plane. The thick man connected to the arm peered down at Riley and Tim, then at Cooper and Roy. Satisfied, at least by Cooper's take, that the passengers aboard the plane hadn't been duped into some form of bust, the guy ducked back inside, then reappeared behind a much smaller man, whom he followed down the stairs.

Cooper knew the smaller man—had summoned him, in fact. When he spotted Cooper, the smaller man stopped, turned, and gestured for his handy-dandy thug to return to the plane. The bigger man climbed back inside, then came out again carrying two overstuffed black canvas bags. The smaller man ignored Cap'n Roy's presence and came directly across the tarmac to Cooper.

"Give you the benefit of the doubt," the man said.

Cooper nodded and motioned to Cap'n Roy. The bigger man took the hint and slogged his way over to Cap'n Roy through the torpid heat and handed the chief minister the two bags. Showing little sign of effort, Cap'n Roy took and set them down, unzipped one, reached in, dug around, then zipped it closed—Cooper catching a glimpse of the sea of U.S. currency within as he did it—before doing the same with the second bag.

Cap'n Roy then waved to Riley, who had retreated back near the customs area in the terminal.

"Good enough," Cooper said to the small man. "We're in business."

Because of the ATR 72-500's engines, he had to say it loud.

The smaller man retreated to the plane with his thug, dug out a cigarette, and had a smoke while he waited, solo, in the wash of the whirling turboprops.

Riley and Tim returned at speed aboard a forklift and a three-car luggage train. The forklift held two reassembled wooden crates, cut down by half to fit the plane's cargo hold, and the luggage train spilled over with maybe four dozen pieces of baggage. Working quickly, though not without evident strain, Cap'n Roy's minions loaded the semidisguised contraband aboard the plane, Cooper finding the ordinary-luggage thing amusing—first, because he knew the seemingly typical bags Riley and Tim were hefting around happened to be stuffed with solid gold, and at two-hundred-plus pounds each, were highly likely to do some lower-back damage to this rookie team of baggage handlers. Marveling at the sheer number of bags, he also wondered where the hell they'd got all the damn things—it was as though Cap'n Roy had been seizing a few Samsonites a day for months on end, eagerly awaiting the day when eight crates of stolen Mayan artifacts would arrive in Road Harbor aboard a flame-scarred yacht.

The smaller man and his thug checked each bag and both crates before Riley and Tim loaded them aboard. The thug held a clipboard, which the smaller man took from him and wrote upon following his examination of each bag. It looked to Cooper as though he didn't trust the bigger man to get it right.

Twenty-nine minutes after the plane had pulled in, the last garment bag was stuffed into the belly of the plane. Without another wasted gesture, the smaller man climbed the plane's stairwell; the thug followed and closed the door behind them. Riley leaped aboard the luggage train and sped back to the terminal, Tim following in hot pursuit with the forklift.

The propellers rose in pitch and threw down against the humidity in their distinctive, baritone wail, and then the ATR 72-500 was taxiing away from the terminal and off into the darkness. Cooper counted a hundred and twenty-five seconds before the plane sped into view again, appearing in the splash of light from the terminal, nosing up and shooting from the runway and into the night.

He counted another nine seconds before the plane could

no longer be seen, swallowed whole by the deep black of the Caribbean night. Cooper heard Cap'n Roy make a *cluck-cluck* sound of some sort, and as he turned, he found himself forced to field another toss from the chief minister.

This time Cap'n Roy was throwing a few bricks of cash at him.

He caught the money, shoved most of it in the pockets of his swim trunks, and, offering no parting gesture whatsoever, started back for the terminal. He had made it about halfway there when a stinging sensation pricked him in the corner of his eye. He waved it off, intending to shoo away whatever bug had stung him, then realized it hadn't been a bug at all. Instead, turning his head in the direction of the source, he realized it had been a visual sting—a sharp burst of light in the distance which, in the time it took him to turn, had already expanded into a blinding cotton ball of orange. He found the lack of noise accompanying the ballooning burst of light odd, since what he was seeing came with the one-word translation of *explosion*—

At which point the sound waves came along, and the out-of-sync *crack* and bass-toned *voom* completed the translation.

Once it had sunk in, Cooper let his eyes fall to Cap'n Roy, who had stopped, bent over the two bags, frozen in the motion of lifting them from the tarmac.

Cap'n Roy stared at Cooper, and Cooper stared back at Cap'n Roy.

While it seemed a bit of a stretch—a stupid set of acts, were Roy to have committed them—Cooper's game of connect-the-dots matching Cap'n Roy up with the murder of Po Keeler, and now the detonation of the plane, remained too easy to play. He took the theory for one last spin. Had Roy gone completely off the deep end? Offed the yacht transporter or had him offed, and then, deciding he'd got away with that, gone ahead and blown the plane out of the sky, post-exchange, post-sale, that plane going up in a ball of flame that took out the people inside too—the only people besides himself and Roy's own band of merry men who might otherwise identify the corrupt Virgin Islands cop who'd sold the stash of gold?

Staring at the chief minister, Cooper considered it would also be logical for Cap'n Roy to experience a moment of hesitation and suspect *him*. He knew, though, that once Cap'n Roy considered things, the good chief minister would conclude there was nothing in it for him—as he, unfortunately, found himself concluding with regard to Cap'n Roy. There were much easier ways for Roy to keep things quiet— plus, Roy wasn't a cold-blooded killer, at least not according to Cooper's experience with the man.

Cooper looked at the bags in Cap'n Roy's hands. In case Roy couldn't see his eyes in the darkness, he jutted his chin in the direction of the bags.

"Be good to get that money out of here," he said to the chief minister.

Cap'n Roy held his eyes.

"Where this money goin'," he said, "nobody be findin' it anytime soon."

Cooper, still looking at him, turned his shoulders, kind of pivoting at the hip until he had himself squared up with the islands' top cop.

"We need to get something straight," he said.

Cap'n Roy watched him.

"If you had anything to do with this," Cooper said, "even indirectly, I will find out. Understand, I chewed up a pair of favors arranging the buy. People know I set it up—people who aren't such good people. The kind of people you like to think I know so well. My guess is these people, or some of their friends, or somebody they work for, will be coming down here when they find out about that plane blowing up. They'll be coming down to pay me a visit and find out what this little airborne conflagration was all about."

Cooper rolled a shoulder, easing a crimped nerve with a little stretch.

"What I'm saying is, if you did this, Cap'n, it's you who brought that on me."

Cap'n Roy stared at him, Cooper surveying the look but unable to read it. Back held ramrod straight, face all but blank, Cap'n Roy's eyes were saying something, but it wasn't anything Cooper could read. He knew enough about the man to know Roy would work hard to avoid giving him any response or reaction—Cap'n Roy's way of telling him to fuck off.

Go fuck yourself, Cooper. Figure it out for yourself, mon.

Cooper tried to get his mind to do some more quick work on the matter at hand—to think about who might be behind all this crap if Cap'n Roy wasn't the man. He didn't like the place his mind went: while there were people like Susannah Grant who knew something or other about the shipment, the fact of the matter was, the Keeler murder, and now the detonation of the plane, had come, first and foremost, following a bust by the U.S. Coast Guard . . .

He came out of this brief mind-drift to realize that Cap'n Roy appeared to be waiting for something. It looked almost as though the chief minister of the British Virgin Islands, in fact, was seeking Cooper's permission to depart. Then Cooper realized Cap'n Roy wasn't looking for that at all.

He isn't waiting for permission to leave—he's waiting for reassurance that he won't be the next to go.

"Watch your back, Cap'n," Cooper said.

Cap'n Roy turned and walked away. As he watched the man turn the corner around the terminal, it appeared to Cooper that Cap'n Roy had been swallowed by the night precisely the same way the plane had a few minutes before.

15

Laramie loaded up on coffee with Sadie, Bill, and Sid in a place called the Circle Diner, to which Bill had driven them in one of the black-on-black Suburbans. The diner was four miles up the two-lane highway from headquarters, and Laramie took note of the fact there was actually some activity here—customers, waitstaff, people eating and serving dinner to the clink of dishes and silverware.

While Sid and his senior staff were perfectly polite and informative, Laramie learned little at the caffeine-intake session outside of the fact that the task force meeting in the ballroom of the Motor 8 Luxury Motel had more or less been staged for her benefit, at the order of some senior administration official or other. Admitting as much, Sid told her the bottom line on the progress made by the task force since their last fully attended session was close to zilch: they were pretty much where they had been a week ago, when they'd stood pretty much where they had one week before that.

Enter me, Laramie thought—emissary from God knows where, here to show these twenty-year veterans of counterterrorism how it's *really* done.

Following a lift back to the Motor 8 in Bill's urban assault

vehicle, Laramie retreated to her room, where, just after
dark, a series of files was delivered to her. She answered a
knock at the door and a young male agent, clean-cut and
suited up like everyone else, wordlessly handed over a tall
stack of three-ring binders. He withdrew something resembling a UPS man's delivery pistol and, with it, swiped the
bar-code sticker affixed to the spine of each binder. Laramie
waited calmly; the little gun beeped each time it got a reading, and then the agent departed without so much as a nod.
Laramie was quite familiar with the classified-intel-logging
device; it was used in Langley too.

Since she didn't plan to study the files on caffeine alone,
Laramie had taken some advice proffered by Sid during
their meeting at the diner and called room service to get a
meal sent up. She found the room's ice bucket on the bathroom counter, headed down the hall to fill it, and came back
to her room and kicked off her shoes. It was only another
couple of minutes before a second suited-up young fellow
arrived to deposit a Cobb salad, bereft, by Laramie's request, of eggs and cheese, dressing on the side, packaged in
a clear plastic enclosure with accompanying Saran-wrapped
plastic utensils. She jammed into her ice bucket three of the
six-pack of Diet Cokes she'd added to the tab, and popped a
fourth.

Then she came over and sat at the room's lone, circular
table to confront the binders.

As Laramie understood it, investigations of international
terrorist acts played out pretty much the same as ordinary
homicide cases, only with more people, more organizations,
and—ostensibly—greater secrecy. The investigators assigned to either sort of case did mostly the same things,
primarily because they were *looking* for the same things—
evidence, suspects, motive—and, by definition, acts of terror typically involved homicide anyway. This meant, among
other things, that a terrorism-incident version of the homicide detective's "murder book" was usually created by antiterror investigators.

From what Laramie had heard, even following the intelligence reform enacted by Congress in 2004, rarely was the "terror book" held in its entirety in one place, and whichever agency housed it rarely shared its contents with other agencies. This, however, did not appear to be true for the Emerald Lakes incident. By Laramie's count, there were 3,697 pages in the three binders combined, and if there were pages missing, or kept somewhere else, she had some difficulty determining what the content of those pages might have involved.

The task force, she found, had been thorough. Every cubic inch of the Emerald Lakes blast site had been scoured, accounted for, studied. The entire curriculum of any number of graduate forensics programs could have been taught from the work performed on the casualties; the page count on the binder packed with interview transcripts—emergency room doctors, friends of the Achar family, Achar's widow, in-laws, eyewitnesses to the explosion, local law enforcement and civic officials—tripped the meter at just over one thousand sheets of single-spaced printouts, give or take a few interrogations.

Laramie read all of them. In the area where it seemed the task force had focused their investigation—the forensics piece—Laramie concluded these guys had watched too many reruns of *CSI.* She skimmed her way through these voluminous sections. The last 124 victims of the outbreak died the same way the first had, so how many different photographs of orifice-hemorrhaged corpses did she need to see? The pages provided by Sadie, the Centers for Disease Control's designate, made it pretty clear that all 125 had died from the same pathogen—the "filo," as task force investigators seemed to relish calling it.

It took her a few hours, but Laramie got through all three binders before dawn, spending at least some time on every page. Salad long gone, Diet Coke supply dwindling, she took a restroom break—splashed some water on her face, mashed her cheeks into one of the barely absorbent towels on the rack—then came back to the table for a second read.

This time she took aim on two specific parts of the terror book. She plucked pages from the binders and set them out on the bed, the floor, the laminated cabinetry holding the television. She set them out in order of what she cared about, what occurred to her, what she couldn't figure out. Most of her selections focused on Benny Achar—everything she could find that the task force had gotten on him, from interview transcripts to cell phone and credit card statements, all the way through to his career-long UPS delivery schedule, tracking number by tracking number. She also pulled the pages on the conspiracy theory stuff: the doomsday scenarios, the extrapolations and forecasts on what *could* have happened had Achar's complete stash been disseminated—what *could still* happen if there were other Benny Achars, living in other suburban housing developments around the country under false identities stolen from Mobile, Alabama's town hall, or wherever else one stole identities.

Sometime around five-thirty, she found herself nodding off. She closed the binder she'd been looking through, pushed a few of the checkerboard of papers aside, reached for the phone, requested a wakeup call for eight-fifteen, dropped the phone on its cradle, and let herself fall back onto the bed.

Eyes drooping, Laramie fell asleep under the spell of a familiar sensation. A puzzle unsolved, an itch unscratched— the sense of incompletion, of un-wholeness, that, when exposed, drove her nuts . . . and, when solved, made her tick.

She flipped on the coffeemaker that came with the room, took an extremely hot shower, and worked through two cups of coffee—half a packet of Equal, a thimble-size container of half-and-half in each—while she suited up like the rest of her newfound colleagues. She decided to go with the black pantsuit one of Ebbers's people had packed for her, picking a gray tee to wear underneath.

She found Bill on the cell number he'd given her and logged her interview requests for the day. Today, she'd decided, would be agent-debriefing day: she'd meet with individual members of the task force to start with. Mainly those she thought could clarify certain questions she'd generated upon consuming the terror book.

Once he'd taken down the names, Bill asked whether she wanted them in any particular order.

"Nope," she said. "Whatever works."

Bill suggested a room at the Motor 8 they had used for most of their interrogations.

"Actually," Laramie said, "I'd rather hold the interviews in my room."

He said he'd have the first agent there in thirty minutes.

Laramie returned the papers to the binders in the order they'd arrived, stacked the binders on the table, called the number Sid had told her to use for library purposes, and handed off the documents to the agent with the tracking gun when he came to retrieve them. She switched the A/C console to MAX/COOL, put away the blow-dryer and the selection of clothes she'd decided not to wear, then headed into the parking lot with a third cup of the room's very bad coffee. She sat on the cinder-block wall on the far side of the parking lot, leaned her head back with her eyes closed, and let her pores soak up the sun.

It must have been fifteen or twenty minutes she'd been sitting like that when she opened her eyes to observe, strolling across the hot parking slab, the first subject in the long list of interviews she'd set for the day: Mary, the profiler.

Coming across the parking lot, Mary looked to be about a head shorter than Laramie, four-eleven tops—Laramie sympathizing with the woman, considering Laramie didn't consider herself much more than a runt to begin with. Mary shook when Laramie offered a hand and Laramie led her into the room, closing the door but leaving the curtains open. When Laramie motioned for her to do so, Mary took one of the two seats at the little round table.

"Diet Coke?"

"Why not," Mary said.

Laramie pulled a can from the ice bucket, popped it for her, and slipped it across the table. Laramie sat on the edge of the bed near her side of the table. Mary took a delicate sort of three-gulp swig of the soda, Laramie thinking the profiler looked a little overheated, maybe from walking over from her room—where she'd probably sat in a prep meeting with Bill, Sid, or some designated interview coach.

Laramie decided to start with some small talk—see if she could loosen Mary up before getting into it.

"Where you based?" she said, thinking, *Nice opener, Laramie.*

Mary set the can on the table.

"Quantico."

"You live nearby, or you commute an hour like the rest of us?"

The profiler nodded. "Manassas—around forty minutes."

"It's a little longer for me." *At least it was,* Laramie thought.

"I'm hooked on it. Can't stand being on these road trips."

Laramie turned a little sideways, waiting for Mary to clarify.

"Audio books," the profiler said, grinning a calm, pleasant, clean smile. "I'm a junkie. Mostly nonfiction."

In the brief flash of smile, Laramie saw that Mary had maybe the whitest rack of teeth on the planet, a walking toothpaste commercial. It made her slightly self-conscious, Laramie fighting the urge to reach for her teeth and see if she'd missed anything with her toothbrush.

"Haven't tried them," Laramie said. "I pretty much just do the NPR thing."

"Probably have a hundred CDs of books in my trunk— find me after and I'll send you some when we're out of this and back in the groove."

Laramie stretched her arms then pushed her hands under her thighs.

"Do you find it odd he didn't own a truck?" she said.

"Pickup truck, you mean?"

"Yes."

Mary thought for a moment.

"I see what you're saying," she said.

"You live in suburban Virginia like I do," Laramie said, "you see SUVs everywhere. But a low-income Central Florida housing development?"

"Normal guy living there, you're right—he'd be more likely to own a truck."

"You said yesterday his disguise was too pat," Laramie said, "and in reading your report, I agree. It just occurred to me as I was reading your profile that you could add 'no pickup truck' to the list."

Mary nodded and took a swig of Diet Coke.

Laramie said, "You think there's any chance Achar was an American?"

Mary said, "Pulled a Timothy McVeigh under a fabricated identity?"

"Yes."

"It's possible. The profile I put together has mostly to do with his not being real. His disguise was a good one but, as we agree, too good in some ways, maybe missing a piece or two. But as to where he's from—if you read my full report, you've seen I took a couple guesses, with my favorite being the one I mentioned yesterday—frankly, out of sheer racial profiling, or at least profiling based on his likely ancestry. Central or South American heritage, at least partially. Of course he certainly *could* have been from here, but he'd have been putting on a disguise that hid his background either way."

Mary paused, thinking for a moment, during which time she tilted her head to the side a notch. "And I'm not sure somebody living here would skip the pickup truck part of the disguise," she said.

Laramie nodded. "Tell me about the woman at UPS," she said.

"The dispatcher, yes," Mary said. "We've been over this, but it isn't taking us anywhere. As you know, I only included in my report the one statement from one of Achar's fellow drivers. I interviewed them all, and this was the only mention of her, the only comment on the two of them seen together. Based on the driver's remark, I think it's safe to say Achar and the dispatcher, whose name is Lori Hopkins, were friendly. I remember exactly what he told me: 'The way they joked, you could tell they had a little something going.' He didn't elaborate, said it more or less the same way in a second interview, but he seemed to have, well, written off his own suspicion by then. This is pretty normal—you look back on a victim or suspect's life after he's dead, you check all the phone records and the e-mail accounts the way we did here, and you'll usually know beyond a reasonable doubt he was sleeping with somebody, presuming he was. In fact, you'll usually find a lot more evidence of flirting between coworkers, affair or no, than we found between Hopkins and Achar. Amazing what people say and do when they think nobody sees what they're doing. But we found absolutely nothing between them. No e-mails, no corroborating suspicions, no flirtatious conversations on the tapes of the dispatch communications, which UPS holds for a few weeks at a time. Nothing—zilch."

"A deep-cover sleeper would probably be good at hiding an affair," Laramie said.

"True. One of our agents checked her out, grilled her pretty hard, as you probably read in the transcripts. I'm assuming you have most or all of the interviews. But more important, affair or no, there doesn't appear to be any evidence of foreign contact—between her and some outside foreign national, or possible representative of such. Still, it's interesting you asked me about this. The comment from the driver bothered me, and still does."

"In what way?"

"It could be they spent some time on the radio, or in the dispatch center, joking around, tossing out the occasional innuendo, and none of it got recorded. Only this one driver noticed anything at all. But the way the guy put it . . . it just sounded as though Achar and Hopkins knew each other better than the rest of the evidence suggests. A familiarity that went beyond the water cooler. I don't feel we should clear her just yet."

"All right, then," Laramie said. "I'm public enemy number one. I've got ten sleepers planted around the U.S., ready to disperse filo serum on my command. I teach them the ways of all things American—except we follow the SUV sales statistics instead of heeding the blue-collar credo of owning your own pickup truck." Laramie scratched a shoulder and went on. "Doing my planning from my cave in Pakistan or wherever it is I'm from, I see at least two moments of vulnerability in each of my sleepers' useful life spans. The first is the moment he or she takes delivery of the 'pathogen,' or the 'filo.' The longer they own it, the more vulnerable they'll be, so I'll probably get it to them late in the game. Second is the *Manchurian Candidate* moment. You see the movie?"

"The original," Mary said, "not the remake."

"What I mean is the playing cards—the signal. Getting the message through: *Time to blow yourself up.*"

"Understood."

"Here's my question," Laramie said, "and I ask you because you've studied Achar the person, rather than the 'perp,' or the fragments of his body, more and better than anyone on the task force. At least by my read. As public enemy number one I'm trying to get this delivery to Benjamin Achar. Once I succeed, I'm then trying to send him the signal. How do you think I should do it?"

Mary looked at her for a second then shrugged.

"We've talked about that," she said. "At the request of—well, I took a pretty hard look at his routine and marked some places where he could take delivery of goods, or messages, without detection." Laramie hadn't seen this breakdown in any of the binders, but let this go, thinking it would have been naive to expect that everything had been included in the version of the terror book they'd provided her. "Suffice to say," Mary said, "there are few professions better suited to receive such packages or messages than a UPS driver. Achar could have received thousands of deliveries and hundreds of activation messages every week, more or less undetected. But you asked the question in a slightly different way, I think."

"Yes."

Laramie was getting to like Mary the profiler.

"I'd have somebody tell him something in person, with nothing in print, no e-mail, no record. Or maybe even set the date a few years in advance. Tell him to move forward on September 12 of such and such year unless he gets a signal to the contrary. In any case, I *don't* think I would use a person the sleeper is known to spend any time with."

"What do you mean?"

"Be better," Mary said, "to send somebody he's never seen before, has never been seen talking to at the water cooler, who might deliver a simple verbal code, or a business card of a certain color—whatever. Anyway, there's less chance for detection if it's a randomly appearing person."

Laramie thought about Mary's answer. She kept thinking she was going about this the wrong way—that they all were. That she was asking stupid, standard questions, looking at all the same, wrong things. The only problem being, she didn't know what sort of different approach she should be taking, or which questions were the stupid ones.

Neither, it seemed, did the esteemed members of the multijurisdictional task force.

Laramie stood.

"Thanks for stopping by, Mary," she said.

"Thanks for the Diet Coke."

Mary offered Laramie a flash of her bright white smile on the way out.

"Among humans, the infection rate of Marburg-2 is approximately the same as we find for the H5N1 virus in animals," the biologist said from his seat at the little table in Laramie's room. "M-2's symptoms are far more severe and progress more savagely—although the forecasted avian flu mutation could do similar damage."

The task force called the local filo Marburg-2—M-2 for short—due to its similarity to and evolved improvements over the Marburg filovirus. The biologist seated before Laramie was an infectious diseases specialist who did free-lance work for the Centers for Disease Control.

Laramie thought of something.

"Marburg-2 hit animals," she said, "just as hard as people?"

"Yep—I'd say this is your basic avian flu doomsday scenario, but with more deadly results once the symptoms kick in."

"So how wide did it spread in the animal kingdom—birds, rabbits, deer? Frogs? Crickets? Cicadas?"

"It killed just about everything it came into contact with."

"What about ants?"

"Ants?" The biologist shifted in his chair. He was a little

heavy, a tight squeeze at the little table. "We haven't really had the time to fully analyze the impact on the insect population, but my guess would be no."

"Why not?"

"Ants, scorpions, and cockroaches aren't typically susceptible to viral infection. In fact, they aren't susceptible to much of anything. Cockroaches and scorpions, for example, would be the primary surviving species following a global thermonuclear war. Ants aren't that hardy, but they're pretty tough."

"But whatever *consumes* ants," Laramie said, "would have died."

"Pretty much across the board within the infection zone," the biologist said.

Those ants, Laramie thought, *took over the Emerald Lakes housing development, and took a few chomps out of my ankle while they were at it, because no predator survived to eat them.*

Their population was probably multiplying geometrically.

"According to your report," Laramie said, "M-2 infected animals, and spread across species, following the gathering places of those animals—swamps, streams, pine barrens. Geographically speaking, how far did it reach? In the animal world, I mean."

"It spread across a slightly wider range—about double the human infection zone. The quarantine we set up was engineered to stump the spread of the filo on animals too; it took a little longer than the human quarantining, but it worked—mostly due to the preponderance of housing developments and golf courses."

"What do you mean?"

"The wetlands over here are mostly landlocked, so an infected fish couldn't, for instance, swim more than a couple miles south before bumping into a berm designed to keep the swamp water off the fairway of the eighteenth hole, or somebody's backyard."

" 'Over here'?"

"Sorry?"

"You said something about the 'wetlands over here,'" Laramie said.

"Oh," he said, "I'm not sure exactly what I meant. I suppose it's my fear of what *could* have happened if we didn't contain it, or if the perp disseminated M-2 twenty miles east or south of here."

"What are you afraid of?"

"Well, 'over here,' so to speak, we're cut off from large portions of the Everglades. But if you were to disperse more of the perp's stash of Marburg-2 a half hour to the south or east—no quarantine's going to shut down *that* epidemic anytime soon."

Laramie thought about this.

"I get the remaining portions of the Everglades being south of here," she said. "But why would the same thing happen if you blasted the filo into the wind an hour to the east?"

The biologist nodded—a scientist in his element, laying out the facts. "Lake Okeechobee's one of the main faucets keeping the Everglades wet. The water supply runs south into the 'Glades from the lake. A little over twenty miles away—to the east. And it isn't so much the water, but the creatures that inhabit, or frequent it—kind of works like an infection-spreading pipeline."

"So if Benjamin Achar's garage were on the banks of Lake Okeechobee, the filo would still be spreading."

"Among animals? No doubt."

"What about people?" Laramie said.

"Them too."

17

Maybe even two or three weeks ago, Janine Achar had been very attractive. Now her hair was a flattened grease stain, and her formerly bright blue eyes had darkened to a dreary kelp, lost in a sea of blackish skin sacs beneath. Laramie thinking it was less the look of a woman who hadn't slept in sixteen days, and more what you'd see from someone who'd just learned that God didn't exist. *Takes some serious shit to get you this far over the cliff*—such as your husband blowing himself up and revealing his fake identity, plus the fact that he was a terrorist, in so doing.

Janine smoked a cigarette from her seat in the Hendry County sheriff's interrogation room, the coagulating smoke lending greater pallor to the already pallid chamber. The woman's son, Carter, held court in a shorter chair some deputy had scrounged up, eating chicken nuggets and French fries out of the cardboard nuggets container. An unopened burger, chicken sandwich, and soft drink sat beneath the haze of cigarette smoke on the table before Mrs. Achar.

Worked on me when Ebbers tried it—doesn't seem to be doing the trick here.

"My deepest condolences," Laramie said.

Janine kept hold of the perch she'd made at the edge of the table, smoke curling to the ceiling from her Pall Mall, eyes unfocused. According to one of the memos in the terror book, one week ago, Mrs. Achar, in a screaming fit of rage, had demanded that her son be kept with her at all times; the task force had obliged, isolating a wing of holding cells where she and Carter could reside together under physical conditions suitable for an eight-year-old, while still remaining under lock and key.

May as well get started.

"If you could, Mrs. Achar, please take me through the days leading up to and following your husband's—" —glancing first in Carter's direction, she quickly decided Janine had been the one to insist on her son's presence, and that demand shouldn't dictate direction in the interview— "his suicide bombing," she said. "I'm aware you've been through it dozens of times with multiple interrogators. But I don't care. I'd like to hear it again. I came because I wanted to hear what you have to say. I wanted to hear it directly from you."

Laramie didn't add the words she was hoping Janine would infer: *woman to woman.*

I want you to tell me what happened, woman to woman.

Janine took a drag on the cigarette and exhaled slowly, allowing some of the smoke to journey through her nostrils. She punched out the butt in the ashtray Laramie had provided, opened the pack she'd kept beside the burger and chicken sandwich, fired up a fresh one with the matchbook stored at her elbow, took another long drag, completed exhale number two, and then—engaging in her first actual expression of any kind—she shrugged.

"That'd make a hundred and forty-two, then," she said, and flipped her hair back, doing it in a way that made Laramie remember the pictures taken of her a couple months ago—a woman who'd been poster-sexy, a displaced auto show model holding down the domestic fort for Benny and Carter Achar there in the Emerald Lakes housing development. Maybe the kind who knew how to use that hair flip, and a couple other tried and true methods, to get what she wanted.

Janine told her story again, Laramie staring into the woman's glazed, angry eyes while she told it.

Benny Achar had purchased airline tickets for his family—via CheapTickets.com—for a round trip to Seattle from Miami. They'd planned to spend six days with Janine's mother at her home in Kent, the Seattle suburb Bill had mentioned in the task force session. Two days before they were scheduled to leave, Benny told Janine he wouldn't be able to make the outbound flight—that an illness in the UPS driver rotation required him to work two out of the five vacation days he'd put in for. At a cost of $290, Janine had changed Benny's reservation so he could fly out and meet up with them two days after they'd headed west on the original itinerary. They kept the back end the same—they planned to return home together.

One day before Janine and Carter's flight, Achar made multiple trips to The Home Depot and an additional stop at a liquor store. Janine noted, as she had in prior interviews, that her husband acted strangely most of the evening, speaking little, head drooping, mood uncharacteristically sullen. After dinner, Benny offered to put Carter to sleep, something he rarely did. Once the boy had gone down, Benny cracked the bottle of Stolichnaya he'd picked up at the liquor store, poured them each a shot, and sat down with Janine at the dining room table to share a toast—this, between a man and wife who did not normally drink—and to tell Janine he would miss her and Carter for the two days they'd be in Seattle without him.

According to Janine Achar in both her prior interviews and here in the interrogation room now, that was all Benny had said to her. Janine repeated her prior recollection that this, along with his odd mood and The Home Depot runs, were the only indications that anything had been amiss.

This testimony, Laramie knew, among other factors, had

led the task force theorists to conclude—logically—that Benny Achar the deep cover "sleeper" had received his sign, the trigger telling him it was time to act. Probably, the theory went, he'd caught the sign on the day he'd told Janine about the shift change. Laramie knew from the terror book that nobody had taken ill at UPS, as Achar had told his wife—that he had never been asked to work the vacation days he'd put in for. Somebody had informed Janine of this along the way, one of many tidbits she maintained she had not known.

Laramie listened as Janine told her the rest: Benny kissed her and Carter goodbye the morning of their flight, she drove with Carter to the airport in their Altima—agreeing that Benny would hitch a ride to the airport from one of his fellow UPS drivers and they'd take the Altima home together. She said she'd called Benny as the plane was boarding to say goodbye.

Janine had maintained in each of her interviews that she hadn't found it odd that Benny had refused to take her to the airport. He needed to get to work early, and Janine didn't want to wait around the airport with Carter for three-plus hours.

Word of her husband's act of destruction had come just after six o'clock that night, Pacific time, in the form of a cryptic call placed by an FBI agent to Janine's mother's home. The agent had asked Janine a number of pointed questions, but hadn't given her much in return. Janine had not been able to determine what was going on. Two hours later, she received another, less cryptic call from the FBI man, in which he asked another set of questions, then informed her the FBI required she return immediately to Florida. She learned later that the bomb had been detonated while she and Carter were in the air on the way to Seattle.

When Janine declined to return to Florida of her own volition, a pair of federal agents had been dispatched to her mother's home, only to learn that Janine and Carter Achar had fled. Laramie knew that this had initially cast a cloud of suspicion on Mrs. Achar, but the task force later learned that

Janine had surfed the Internet immediately following her second call from the FBI agent, learned in a news story that her husband had been one of the victims in a "gas main explosion," and supposedly panicked. She used cash, Janine told Laramie, to get a room in a motel in Tukwila, near Kent but closer to the airport. They stayed there for ten days—until the cash she'd traveled with ran out—and then Janine had used her ATM card at a nearby Key Bank. Not the most savvy move by somebody on the lam, and certainly, the task force judged, not the move of a deep cover sleeper: following her use of the ATM, an FBI canvas of the neighborhood where she'd made the withdrawal netted Carter and Janine that morning, during their daily breakfast stop at the McDonald's across from the motel.

They were taken into federal custody and held in Seattle for seven days, primarily because issues with the filo outbreak didn't warrant a return to LaBelle. Once the quarantine contained the spread of the M-2, the feds had flown Janine to Fort Myers and taken her and Carter here—to the holding-cell facility in the Hendry County sheriff's offices.

Mother's tale complete yet again, Carter poked his head up from his meal and asked if he could go to the bathroom. Laramie used the phone on the wall to summon a deputy and told Janine they'd resume as soon as Laramie could get her hands on a cup of coffee.

"I think you're lying."

"Excuse me?"

"After reading up on you, and now, hearing you out in person, I'm prepared to recommend that the task force reconsider their assessment," Laramie said. "To tell them they got you wrong. Completely. I don't know if they've told you this, but they were ready to clear you. Did you know that? But I'm going to recommend they hold you indefinitely."

Janine glared silently at Laramie over the cigarette in her hand. Laramie didn't wait for further reaction or response.

"It's the motel room, Mrs. Achar. You took enough cash with you to pay for ten nights—at least fifteen hundred bucks based on the rate of the hotel you chose—and you had that much on you *before* you received the call from the FBI. Ten nights—long enough for the small amount of pathogen dispersed by your husband to run its course and be all but contained. You've been lying. He told you something, warned you, gave you instructions, who knows, and you knew enough to travel with sufficient cash in your purse to spend a week or two in a motel—anonymously."

Janine violently snuffed out her cigarette.

"Are you fucking kidding me?" she said. "You think I *knew*? Who the hell are you, coming in here offering me your condolences—the first interrogator to do that, so I thought you might be somebody decent. Then trying to tell me I *knew* something more about my husband? Something that isn't true anyway? Goddamn you—goddamn *all* you people. *Fuck you.* You can't imagine what I'm going through—what *we're* going through. Or maybe you do, since it's all lies anyway, and *you're* the people making up the lies. First the papers call it a gas main explosion. Then your people tell me that wasn't it at all—that he blew himself up! And now he's a *terrorist*—a terrorist? Benny? A *suicide* bomber? Do you know how ridiculous that is? And then you tell me he wasn't Benny at all and that I'm not even Mrs. Benjamin Achar—that Benny wasn't even *real*? Let me ask you something. Do you know why I have my son with me?"

As she said this, Janine reached over and touched her son's shoulder in a way that made Laramie think suddenly that she was a very good mother.

"You know why? I knew you'd ask the same horrible questions that everybody else asked me, and that I'd be making him hear it by bringing him with me, but you know what? *I don't believe you people, and I don't trust you either.* You lie about one thing, then another, you lie to the media, to the public, you lie to me, I don't even know who you're lying to on any given day, who can keep track? Maybe you're lying to everybody. It can't be a gas main explosion *and* a suicide bombing, can it? It can't be the flu and a terrible disease bomb, can it? I don't believe you that Benny isn't Benny, and I don't believe you that he did this. You know what I think? I think *you* did it. I think somebody ran a test. They made a bomb. The CIA. FBI. Whoever. They wanted to try out their bomb, and they decided to blame Benny. Did he say something you didn't like, something about the *government*? Or was he just *convenient*, you sons of bitches—oh my God, he's gone . . . *I don't trust you people!* You get it now? For all I know, you're planning to take my son next. You'll tell me he isn't Carter after all, I bet. *But you'll fucking take him over my dead body.*"

She suddenly reached over with her other arm and grabbed her son in a bear-hug embrace.

"Fuck you people, *it's not true!* None of it! *Get out!*"

Laramie sat still while this played out, Janine sobbing into Carter's shoulder for a few minutes running. She felt the urge to join in on the hug, to comfort them in some way, but there wasn't exactly anything for her to do, particularly anything like joining the hug, so she thought things through instead.

The motel thing had bothered her from the minute she'd read about it. It had bothered the other investigators too, to the point where they'd suspected her of being in on it, until her background check came out clear, and then interrogator after interrogator sat and listened to Janine say the same things she'd just told Laramie, in almost exactly the same way. This bolstered the case for her innocence—had she been lying, it seemed impossible she wouldn't have got caught up in even the smallest inconsistency given the multiple repeats of her tale.

But the motel bothered Laramie in a different way: it made something register in her analyst's mind, something that didn't quite fit the rest of the puzzle. It was the timing. She couldn't pin down exactly why or where the timing was off initially, but she knew it was.

When the sobs died down, Laramie decided to come at it a little differently.

"Listen," she said, "if it were true that all this—"

"*ARE YOU STILL HERE?*"

Laramie let Janine's shrill bellow hang out there for a moment.

When the noise of the outburst felt to her as though it had faded, Laramie said, "Janine, listen to me. I don't trust our government any more than you do. In fact I know *not* to trust it—*them*—by experience. But just in case it were true—in case it isn't all one gigantic lie—there's something I'd like to hear from you."

"Why should I tell you *anything*? I told everybody everything already anyway."

Laramie heard it in the speed of the woman's second sentence and knew immediately she'd been right about what she was about to ask.

"Mrs. Achar," she said. "You're lying."

"Go to hell. I'm sure that fits your conspiracy just like everything else—"

"You're lying because you're trying to protect him."

This seemed to quiet her down, if only temporarily.

"I think that despite all the evidence—the identity theft, the timing of your trip, all of it—I think that you know, deep inside, that he wasn't honest with you. And that he did something terrible here."

"Don't you tell me what I know or don't know."

"*Let me finish.* You had your say, now I'll have mine." Laramie felt like a bully, running an interrogation with a distraught widow and her eight-year-old son by yelling in their faces. Too bad. "In reading everything you said in all the interviews, and in hearing you now, I think you will never believe he did what the government says he did. That your husband would not have tried to kill thousands of people, or a million people, or whatever it was the government is saying he was trying to do. It bothers you, because you think he was lying to you, but you know he wouldn't have been trying to do what they've accused him of. So you're protecting him."

Janine just stared at the floor, holding her son.

"What did he tell you before you left?"

Janine didn't change expression or the direction in which she was looking, but Laramie felt something shift in the room.

"You knew to be ready to disappear. I know that part. You had the kind of cash on you that nobody carries around anymore. Not unless they're looking to book ten days at a local Holiday Inn under a false name. What I want to know is, What did he say? Was it during dinner? After he put Carter to bed? Over the drinks? Help me out here. Nobody else—"

"Help *you?*—my God, you *are* just like the rest—"

Preparing to repeat the question, Laramie suddenly realized what it was that connected the motel and the M-2, and answered her question as to the timing. The feeling was as familiar to her as the sense of un-wholeness that had greeted her that first night in the Motor 8, only this time it was a sense of completion. Of the tumblers in the keyhole racking into place.

When she asked the question, repeating it to compel Janine to focus, Laramie felt some saliva escape from her mouth and spray halfway across the interrogation table.

"What did he tell you!"

Janine said nothing at first, but in a moment, something did come.

Tears.

There were only the tears—Janine didn't outwardly cry, and there came no sobs, only the dual streams of the silent tears coursing down her cheeks.

"He saved my life," she said, almost inaudibly. "He saved Carter's life."

Laramie nodded slowly.

"I just don't understand," Janine said. She was talking to herself, quietly enough that Laramie caught most of it by watching the widow's lips move as she spoke. "He would never do what they say he did. What *you* say he did. It just isn't . . . *possible*. You can tell me whatever you want to tell me. *Us*—you can tell us anything. Show us any evidence. But it won't matter. It won't make any difference. I know my husband. *We* know him. Even if we didn't know his real name. We know him—*him*—and he would never have done it. He would never have tried to kill thousands of people. Never. *Ever.*"

The tears continued in their twin streams down the sides of her haggard face. She was leaning back in her chair now. Her left arm remained draped around Carter's shoulders. Carter's chin was pressed against his chest and Laramie couldn't see his face. With her right hand, Janine wiped away a tear, but it was like trying to divert a river with an oar.

Thinking she might have to assist Janine in connecting the tears and the widow's thoughts to words, Laramie said, "But you said he saved your lives. How did—I know you don't just mean Seattle, the trip to Seattle. How is it he saved your lives?"

In due course, Janine looked up at Laramie through her tears.

"He told me—" she said, then stopped, and now the sobs came, the woman taking in a big, heaving, choppy breath of air that sounded almost like a rattle—"he told me that if something happened—"—a kind of wail escaped her throat and merged with the sobbing and crying, Laramie nearly cringing at the raw outburst from this desperate, grieving widow with no source of hope or comfort—"he told me that if something happened while I was gone, I would need to hide. To go away. For as long as I could. But for no less than seven days . . . oh, Christ . . . *for no less than seven days!*"

The piercing wails that followed prompted Carter to burst into tears, the boy calling for her as he grabbed her around the neck and waist.

They cried into each other's bodies for many minutes. After almost ten minutes had passed without the sobs lessening, Laramie decided she couldn't take it any longer. She rose, came around the table, reached down, and placed a hand on the widow's shoulder. Nothing changed—the wails continued, the sobbing cries, Carter burrowing into his mom's bosom, his cries of "Mommy, mommy," muted by her storm of wails—but at least, Laramie thought, she isn't pushing my arm away.

Laramie stayed there, touching Janine Achar's shoulder, for a while. When the pitch of the wails seemed destined never to shift or end, Laramie decided there was nothing more to be asked or done. She had learned what she needed to learn. She could do nothing more for this person—not that she had done anything for her anyway. Not that anybody could—probably ever.

Laramie opened the door and left the interview room.

18

He waited until they came all the way in—until the very instant before they grabbed him. While the cell door was open and he was still free to move. He felt their presence, he heard that the door had not yet closed, and he took his shot.

Sidestepping, he spun, seized the pistol from its nook in the ammo belt of the guard closest to him, and fired blindly. He fired blindly because of the obvious—he wore a blindfold and his hands were cuffed behind his back—but he managed to empty the revolver's chambers in what he estimated to be the vicinity of the three men. Then he dove into the hall, smashing his chin and ear as he bounced on the hard stone of the passageway.

He had grown so emaciated and his musculature was so weak following his imprisonment and starvation that he was able, and quickly, to pull his cuffed wrists down past his ass and under his squatting legs. He felt his hands partially dislocate from the wrists as he did it, but this weird bending of his frayed bones allowed his wrists to slip from the cuffs like twigs from a bucket. The dislocation should have hurt, but he never remembered any pain from that moment.

He remembered only that he had discovered his hands to be free.

He still dreamed, often, of the house of horrors that followed. As much as he had been trained to kill, as any soldier was, he later admitted the actions he undertook on that day were the actions of a killer—not those of a soldier trained to kill, but those of a murderer. One who kills pathologically, for sexual pleasure—the more brutal the act, the better. He viewed himself differently from that point forward, and this altered view of himself hadn't changed over time. He knew it never would. That it never could.

Once he got the blindfold off and had slipped out of the cuffs, he looked up and found he'd downed two of them. The felled men were making noises—grunts and curses, each man far from dead. Cooper saw the third man, coward that he was, turning the corner ahead of them in the passageway. Going to get help—going, Cooper knew, to the chamber of horrors. What came next, he knew God would never forgive him for. That He couldn't, and shouldn't. Presuming there was even somebody upstairs, which he often found hard to believe—Cooper considering it would be better if the attic were empty, given the toll the big man would undoubtedly collect once Cooper's time came around.

He found another gun on one of the men he'd shot, snatching it as the bloodied guard realized what was happening and, too late, made a grab for it. Cooper held the pistol to the man's chin, leaned in close, eye to eye, screamed some obscenity he'd never been able to remember, and pulled the trigger. He watched from two inches away as the man's face erupted, chin to hairline, blasting across the floor in wet fragments of bone, tooth, flesh, and gristle, a triangular spray that deflected off the floor and rained out and up, catching his own chin and cheeks with wet warmth as it shot forth. Ears ringing—for the moment, deaf besides the ringing—face burned from the muzzle blast, one eye partially blinded by the bright burst of the shot—Cooper pocketed the pistol. He knew he would need it for what he would do when he caught up to the third man. The coward—running for the chamber of horrors.

First, though, the second of the three.

Cooper found the man gurgling in pain on the floor of the passageway, rocking slightly, busy trying to get oxygen into his flooded lungs. Pulling the machete the man kept on his belt, memories registering of the slices this one had made on his arms, legs, even once across his cock, Cooper grinned a diseased, insane, murderous grin—and swung. He sliced clear through one of the man's arms and Cooper heard the machete clang on the rock floor of the passageway. It felt so good to him that the tremors of an orgasm came searching for his loins, but his testicles had endured so much pain by then the tremors were met by a brick wall and retreated. Cooper sought more of the pleasure, savagely—an addict going for the ultimate hit, slicing, whacking, chopping, exhausting himself as he diced his former captor into what he remembered counting as nine pieces. He went back, then, to the man with no face—the one he had shot. The man was already dead, but the addict craving another hit could not shake his need, and so he lifted the man by his remaining hair, held his body in a seated position, and beheaded what was left of the guard's skull with the machete.

Thrusting the machete under the arm that held the faceless head, he drew the stolen pistol again with the other hand and began to run. Not away—not yet. Head in hand, holding it out ahead of him, he ran, screaming at the edge of his deteriorated larynx, sprinting headlong down the dark tunnel . . . to the room.

He came at them with the pistol blazing. They were ready for him, warned by the fleeing coward, and they shot at him and hit him more than once from their hiding places. He saw where they were hiding—one crouched astride the open doorway, one prone beside the chair, the third standing behind the wooden post that kept the ceiling of the ancient room from caving in. Without adequate training and the requisite balls, however, felling a target shooting back from close range was one of the most challenging tasks in combat, and these men were no match for the addict seeking his next hit.

Bullets whinging and pocking on the wall and floor around him, Cooper found his opponents to be pathetic, the cowards generating miss after miss. He was struck in the left forearm and outer thigh, but with the pain tolerance he'd developed—that they'd fostered in him—he didn't even notice. With the five shots he had remaining in the revolver, the addict went five-for-five against the three opponents. He knew exactly who each man was: the guard who had fled in the passageway had been the one feeding him the crusty tortillas; the one beside the chair was the one who had whipped and strafed him; the one behind the post, the man with the mustache, was the one who'd always done the talking as the other whipped him with the serrated paddle from hell.

Two bullets made it into each of Whip-man and Tortilla, one into Mustache. The direct hits disabled them, and they fell, and whether two of them had survived the initial bullet strikes, Cooper had never known. He knew that Mustache had not been killed, because he gutted him with the machete while the man screamed and flailed on the floor. He laid waste to the other two in like fashion, Cooper screaming, a constant yell, as though he held no need for breath in the process of emitting the steady, curdling wail that escaped his throat. When he was through with the men, he took to the chair—the chair—and killed it with the machete like he had the men. When he had chopped it to pieces, he took all of the guns in the room and emptied them at the remaining pieces of the chair, blasting away until each revolver clicked on an empty chamber. Until there were no more bullets to shoot with.

In the process of his committing these inhuman murders, the door of the chamber had somehow eased shut. He remembered seeing this, feeling the deep cringe of ungodly fear, as though the devil himself had closed the door and would shortly be setting the oven to broil. He'd made an im-

possible escape, accomplished vengeful, disturbingly satis-
fying retaliation—and yet it seemed he would remain
trapped for eternity in the chamber of horrors.

He dropped the first man's severed head, which he realized
only then he had held on to throughout; he dropped the pistol
he'd just exhausted. Then he scrambled for the door, slipped,
and fell. On his face. And hands—he remembered his hands
from that moment, the sight of them in the torch-lit room, because he found them coated in blood when he looked at them.
Dipped and soaked to well above the wrists. He felt the same
blood dripping from his face, and chin, and neck, and as he
stood, he saw that he had become coated with it, with the
blood of his enemies, that he was standing in a puddle of it, of
the blood he had shed, a puddle the edge of which he could not
see. His shoeless feet were immersed in it, toes nearly covered.

He slipped and skidded through the blood, all but wading,
as though he were dreaming of trying to run through quick-
sand. He grasped the handle of the door, the handle he had
wanted so badly to grasp all those times, and his hands
slipped on it, and he thought for a terrifying moment that it
was locked, that he had somehow locked himself in, but then
he tried it again and it opened.

He didn't know which way to go, but he knew that if he
followed the lost light he could find his way, that hint of daylight reaching through the darkness and the torches lighting
the tunnels, the drab gray mist of daylight brighter around
each succeeding corner and stairwell, and then there was a
massive wooden door with a round, windowless opening in
the center, and he grasped its handle with his bloodied hand,
pulled it inward, and felt the blinding assault of equatorial
sunshine on eyes that hadn't seen daylight in months. He collapsed from the blinding daylight—the pain striking him in
his eyes, a place he was not accustomed to feeling pain.

He rose slowly, recovering—squinting, so that he saw the
world only through the miniscule slivers between his inter-
laced eyelashes.

Then he ran.

Somebody saw him, shot at him from above, and hit him in the back. The shot knocked him down, but he got up again, and found he could still breathe, and still run. So he did. He ran until he could only walk, walked until he could only crawl, crawled until he collapsed, then awoke to the sounds of a river, the river he had known from the operations maps would be to the east, assuming they had kept him anywhere near where he'd been caught. That was the direction he had tried to run. Twenty miles, thirty, fifty—he had no idea, but he heard it, then found it—the Rio Sulaco. As he fell into it, the thousands of mosquitoes that had been feasting on him separated and floated away in a grimy cloud on the surface of the wide, gentle tributary.

A mile downstream he whacked his head on a boulder, passed out, and didn't remember a goddamn thing from the next three years of his life.

Journey complete, Cooper sat on the last plank of the dock. He took his pole, disengaged the hook from the guide nearest the reel, then set the pole down until he'd dug out one of the worms from the bucket and slid it, wriggling, full bore onto the hook. Then he took the pole, pointed it out over the water, flipped the catch on the reel, and slowed the pace of the hook-and-weight's drop into the water with his thumb pressed against the spool of filament. When he felt the weight hit bottom, he flipped the catch back into place, reeled in about a foot and a half of line, and set the pole across his lap. He draped his arm across the pole and clasped it in his hand midway up the pole.

Cooper was doing the food-chain thing, a sort of timed experiment he liked to do from this decrepit dock, situated around the corner from Conch Bay. The old man with the goats had built the dock maybe twenty-five years ago, then let it fall into utter disrepair. Cooper would walk over the hill behind the club, stop and dig for worms or sand shrimp, and head down to the dock. He could usually wrangle about a dozen baitfish in under an hour; once he caught the smaller fish, he got serious, switching out the original hook and weight for some heavier drag, a bigger, barbed hook, and a steel leader.

Then he'd find a couple footholds on the rotting dock and have a few casts under the light of the moon—and just about every time he came out, he'd catch a couple monsters before running low on the baitfish. It was always a hell of a fight, trying to keep himself out of the water on the rotting old pier while he reeled in the fish.

Cooper knew the Cap'n Roy theory was the easy way out, the simplest possible explanation behind Keeler's death and the subsequent vaporization of the plane. And he couldn't deny the scheme might have made sense for the top cop: take a payoff from Keeler in exchange for refusing Homeland Security's request for his extradition, spring him, then cap him on the yacht transporter's way out through the prison gates; complete the cash sale of the tomb-raided treasure trove, then blow the evidence clean out of the sky, those gold artifacts mangled and sunk to the bottom of the Sir Francis Drake Channel. This plan left nobody alive—at least nobody besides himself and Cap'n Roy's merry gang of day players, each having pocketed his own share of the bounty—who knew anything about the money Cap'n Roy had secured.

But Cooper had to face facts: Cap'n Roy Gillespie, dirty though he was, didn't work that way. Cap'n Roy took every handout available and leaped at the chance to avail himself of such sticky situations—or, Cooper thought, such ordinary police duties—as murder investigations. But he didn't have killing in him—seeing this kind of thing in people being easy for Cooper. It was easy because he knew exactly what it was to be the opposite.

And Cap'n Roy was not the same as him.

If Roy wasn't good for it, things became much more complicated. One big question, for instance, was why he and

Cap'n Roy were still around at all. If somebody had wanted to shut this thing down at the source—hiding what, Cooper couldn't figure, unless somebody had an oddly extreme case of the racial-profiling rage Cooper had felt for the statues— then Keeler, the boys on the plane, and the goods themselves were the least of anyone's troubles. He, Cap'n Roy, and a small army of semidirty RVIPF cops probably knew more than Keeler did, and damn well knew a lot more than anyone on that detonated plane had known.

There was the possibility that whoever it was who'd done the deeds hadn't known Cooper had interviewed Keeler, and therefore didn't realize that Cooper knew the shipment had come originally from a man called Ernesto Borrego—El Oso Polar. But any conspirators worth their weight in palm fronds would, Cooper knew, assume that Cap'n Roy had interrogated the man, and that some minimal degree of information on the chain of ownership would therefore have come to light.

Meaning that somebody, by this theory, must have proactively decided *not* to kill him and Cap'n Roy. There was also the issue of Susannah Grant—though nobody would have been able to track his trip to Austin. He'd done it with fake ID having nothing to do with his current identity.

No, he mused—Susannah aside, there was, in all this, a nifty fit with a highly uncomfortable notion.

It was this: whoever was doing the killing seemed to possess no particular desire to fuck with government employees. If the conspirators knew who he and Cap'n Roy worked for—or at least, in his case, who he *technically* worked for— it followed that the conspirators might have intentionally refrained from crossing the "government line." The concluding wrinkle in this theory was that it offered a pretty good chance that the conspirators got their own bread and butter from a government payroll too—American, British, or otherwise— thereby explaining their heightened sensitivity to, and proactive decision against, the murdering of fellow U.S. or British G-men. They were trying to keep quiet whatever they wanted kept quiet, but were only willing to go so far in doing so. As though by scaring other government people off, only without crossing the cop-killer line, these people were looking to put the hush on things without having the hushing come back to bite them in the ass.

Or it could just be a crooked thief with brains enough to know he ought to avoid the cop-killing stigma.

The first monster catch of the night came around eleven; after hauling in what he guessed would be a twenty-pounder, he almost laughed when the slippery little shape of a baby albacore, no more than a foot long, broke from the water and flickered against the moon, wriggling on his hook. Looked as though he'd eaten the entire six-inch baitfish Cooper had used to catch him too.

Keeping the pole in his right hand, Cooper reached out with his left hand and got hold of the hook. It took a balancing act, but he managed, as usual, to set the pole down, pull the hook from the hungry tuna's mouth, pull the kill stick from his swimming trunks, whack the fish between the eyes, underhand it back to the beach, set the hook into another baitfish, and cast the food out at the pool where he knew that bigger fish than the hungry tuna gathered at night.

Around twelve-thirty, with nothing more than a couple further nibbles that had gone nowhere, Cooper gathered his gear—along with tomorrow's lunch—and headed back over the hill. An unlucky night—rare were the pickings so slim from the old dock, though he'd had more unlucky nights than usual in recent months.

He saw the lights as he crested the hill. You could always see the lights of Road Town once you stepped over the lip of the trail, at least whenever a fog hadn't rolled in for the night and obscured the five-mile view.

But tonight it was a different sort of light.

It looked, to Cooper, to be happening somewhere along Blackburn Road, a mile or so east of the harbor. The lights swirled red and blue, piercingly bright even all the way across the channel. He could see there was more than one set of them too; maybe the whole set of them, as close to the entire motor pool of the Royal Virgin Islands Police Force as you'd encounter in any single incident.

Cooper knew upon seeing this that it had been one hell of an unlucky night for someone else too. He felt a sort of white heat rise in his chest as he swung through the half-empty restaurant.

"Son of a bitch," he said, and decided to make a stop by bungalow nine. He'd get out of his clothes and change into something that didn't exude the scents of worm and fish.

Probably best to look a little more presentable for what he figured he was about to see in Road Town anyway.

19

Cooper crested another hill, this time from the interior of a minivan taxi, and when the cabbie said, "Can't go no farther, mon," Cooper paid him, let himself out, and talked his way past the patrol cop manning the road block. Cooper hadn't seen the patrol cop more than once or twice before—kid might have been nineteen, and looked more like an eighth-grader in a policeman costume than a law enforcement official. Even the trademark RVIPF cap was too big for his head. Still, without knowing the kid worth a damn, he could read his expression like an open book.

The RVIPF cruisers were parked in an array of angles across and along the side of the road, and what Cooper had suspected from his view across the channel was confirmed now: the carnival of police and other authority types was gathered, more or less, at the front door of the chief minister's house—the residence of none other than Cap'n Roy Gillespie.

Visible from the road as Cooper marched the fifty yards downhill to Cap'n Roy's house was a stripe of yellow crime scene tape, draped across the twin rails that flanked the home's main stairwell. Set directly back and up from the stairwell, in the area of the property Cooper knew to house the pool, a number of lights had been set up. A camera flash popped a couple times while Cooper stared. Over to the right of the pool, a light pole was up, and he could see a couple RVIPF caps moving to and fro behind a hedge near the top of the slope.

The cop at the base of the stairwell normally functioned as a kind of desk sergeant in the department's main offices. As he stood aside to let him pass, Cooper realized there was, among other emotions, something like fear in the cop's eyes.

Either the desk sergeant or the kid out front must have radioed ahead, since, as Cooper elbowed open the gate to the pool deck, he found Riley there waiting for him. The lieutenant didn't say anything, didn't really offer up any particular expression on his wide-boned, normally cheery face—he just nodded solemnly and stepped back to fall in behind him as Cooper came out onto the deck. It was on the deck that he saw, sprawled halfway between the French doors at the back of the house and the lip of the pool, the splayed, bug-eyed, and clearly dead body of Cap'n Roy.

Cooper stood over the body. It took a few minutes, but in time, the investigative function of Cooper's mind began to engage itself, and Cooper found comfort in it: *two visible bullet holes placed three or four inches apart near the geographical center of his chest; a bloodied, formerly white robe still wrapped partially around him, the robe's terrycloth belt partially untied, maybe from the gunshot impacts and subsequent fall, but still curled around itself enough to hold the robe in place; dark blue swim trunks, but otherwise unclothed beneath the robe; one flip-flop fallen off his foot, the left, on the wood planking of the deck, the other still adorning his right, its rubber thong wedged between his toes; a hand, his right, placed against his rib cage, slightly beneath the wounds.*

Cap'n Roy had been shot as he exited his house, intending to come out for a swim in his infinity pool. The pool's underwater lights were on, as though Roy had flipped them on before strolling out for a few laps—a little relaxation, here in the man's chlorinated oasis, a pool that featured a view of the Caribbean to match the most luxurious of resorts.

After a while, Cooper unsure of how long it had been, Riley came up beside him. The other cops, formerly busy taking photos and performing related investigative activities, resumed their work; Cooper realized they'd stopped to let him have a look at Roy.

"Cap'n had a two-man security detail watchin' him," Riley said, "morning, noon, and night. Told me it was your words made him do it—'Spy-a-de-island tell me I better watch my back,' he said to me, 'so watch my back I will.'"

Riley shook his head in utter disgust.

"We were it, mon—Tim and me. Arranged it to go 'round the clock—one man on, one man off, goin' 24/7." He brushed gently against Cooper's shoulder and Cooper looked up, realizing as he did it that this was why Riley had brushed him—so he would look up and see the places Riley was about to describe.

"Tim was hidin' out over there," he said, pointing to a defunct stairwell from the home that had been here before Roy had built his shadow-funded luxury residence in its place. "Standin' where he could watch the street and the house at once. Thing is, I was comin' up the stairs down low, readyin' for the shift change, when Cap'n Roy come walkin' out and get hit. Two shots, mon, and he down and dyin' right away."

Riley had been motioning in the direction of the hill just beyond the deck, and the second pool of light and activity there—Cooper realizing what he meant from the way he was telling it.

"The shots came from up there," Cooper said, the sandy mumble of his voice rough and thick.

"Yeah. Shit, mon, two-man security detail failed at protectin' its one and only charge. Maybe the killer, he too good for us island cops. But I'll tell you this—that two-man security detail be too good for the killer when he lookin' to get away."

Cooper sharpened his focus on what Riley was saying.

"Without a way out o' here by way o' the deck or them old stairs," the cop said, "there only one steep slope to the street, or a cliff down to the rocks. He tried for the slope but I knew he'd be tryin' it. Didn't waste any time. Or energy, mon. Not going to let our assassin head on down that hill and away."

"You shot him," Cooper said.

"Many times."

Cooper nodded. They stood that way for another moment, beside each other, beside Cap'n Roy's body on the deck, both looking off toward the pool of light and activity they knew to contain the dead target of Riley's vengeful wrath.

"Let's have a look," Cooper said after a while.

On the slope, the carnage wrought by Riley's bullets on the killer's body was disguised by scrub and wildflowers. Even under the lights, it was hard to make out the corpse in the knee-deep bed of weeds; once Cooper waded uphill to the spot, though, he felt even worse about the killing of Cap'n Roy, and who it was that might have been responsible.

It fit his developing theory all too well.

"Crap," he said.

"Yeah, mon," Riley said beside him, "once I started I kept on—emptied two clips. Twenty bullets. Don't think a single one of 'em missed."

"No," Cooper said. He could see now, taking a look at the body, that Riley had literally destroyed the physical frame of the man who'd shot Cap'n Roy from his sniper's post on top of the hill. But he hadn't looked at the body until now, and Riley's carnage hadn't been what he was complaining about. "More bullets the merrier. What I'm talking about is who you shot."

"What—you know him?"

"Not him. Not this one man. But I don't need to. I know what he is. I know what he does. Christ. Look at him—I could probably take a good guess at some of the places he trained. Maybe tell you right now his top two or three rifles of choice."

"You see all that," Riley said, "lookin' at his bloody remains in the weeds?"

"I see it from his face. From his fucking haircut. His race. It's like a serial killer—there's a standard profile. And this motherfucker is it. Crap," he said again.

"So? Who he be, then? A spook? Like you?"

Cooper shook his head. "Not quite. Probably hired by spooks, though."

"This mean you no longer thinkin' Cap'n Roy take down the smuggler and the plane?"

Cooper turned to look at Riley when he said this. He saw, looking at the man, more than a little rage coming back at him, Riley defending the honor of his fallen chief with a measure of bravado. Cooper understood. He held the challenge of Riley's gaze.

"I'll have to think about it," he said.

Riley eased a little closer to him. Close enough so that his chin, which was kind of jutting toward Cooper, nearly touched his own.

"You let me know when you finish up with thinkin' it through," he said.

Cooper kept his thousand-yard stare on the lieutenant who would probably soon be chief of police. Then he said, "Why don't you show me the rifle he used," and dropped his eyes to let Riley feel like the winner in the contest determining who was defending Cap'n Roy's honor best. Cooper wasn't sure whether Cap'n Roy had any honor to defend in the first place, but he was thinking he already missed the son of a bitch as much as anybody else would—including Lieutenant Riley.

Cooper followed Riley over to the rifle, which was still in its place in the weeds where the assassin had dropped it before tumbling a few yards downhill under the onslaught of Riley's twenty-bullet barrage. Without touching it, Cooper examined the rifle, bending down to get a closer look. When he'd finished, he stood and shook his head again.

"That one of those 'top two or three rifles of choice'?"

"Yep."

They had a view of the water from where they stood,

Cooper taking a look out across the channel. He was just able to make out the pale yellow safety lights of the Conch Bay Beach Club on its squat little island across the way. Cooper stood there, looking, hands in the pockets of his Tommy Bahama swim trunks. Riley looked too, hands on his hips, one of the hands a little lower than the other because of the holster that rode on his hip.

"Unlikely," Cooper said, "this'll be the end of it."

Riley thought about that.

"Yeah, mon," he said.

Cooper kept staring out at the black water and sky.

"Goddamn that Cap'n Roy," he said.

After a long silence, Cooper heard Riley's barely audible reply.

"Yeah," he said, all but whispering. "Yeah, mon."

20

Her seventy-two hours were just about up—a point which Laramie already understood, but which her guide emphasized further with his knock at her door. It was six A.M. when she heard his shave-and-a-haircut sound out; Laramie was already showered, dressed, and blown dry, sitting there at the little round table sipping her second cup of bad coffee while she thought through the things she would lay out for Ebbers. They hadn't given any number for her to call, or any other means by which to report in, so she'd assumed they'd be reaching out to her, and now they had.

Her guide drove her to an abandoned two-story stucco complex near the municipal building. The name of the strip mall behind which this building found itself was the Brick Walk—named, by Laramie's guess, after the brick sidewalk that wound its way past the 7-Eleven, nail salon, and computer store to the stucco office building with its chunky sign: SPACE AVAILABLE FOR LEASE.

Inside, her guide pass-keyed their way to a conference room bereft of decoration—unless, Laramie thought, you counted the collection of broken phones and ancient computer monitors stacked against the back wall as interior decor. Her guide unlocked a drawer in a small file cabinet, withdrew an insect-looking device about eight inches in diameter, and plugged it into a jack at the base of the rear wall. He punched the small red button on the lower-right corner of the device and a dial tone blared, the noise sounding like a Who concert in the silent, empty room.

Her guide leaned over the phone and dialed a number he blocked Laramie from seeing by the way he stood. It took two rings for Lou Ebbers's Carolina lilt to hit them from the speaker.

"I'm assumin' you've got her with you," he said.

Laramie's guide nodded as though Ebbers could see him. "Yep."

"All right, then, Miss Laramie," came Ebbers's normally friendly tone, sounding garbled and sinister on the speaker. "You're on."

Laramie found herself wishing she'd forced her guide to make a pit stop at the 7-Eleven so she'd have the additional java boost of a third cup—might have helped keep her on her game, and she figured she was going to need all the help she could muster. Without the aid of a bonus cup, she felt an all too familiar sinking sensation—it always seemed to happen this way, and no matter how much time she'd spent arranging her thoughts in the room, it was happening again. She was bold and brave in private, devising her grandiose theories on the evil that lurked in the world—usually while studying satellite images in the lab—but emerge from your motel-room library and the bottom falls out. Her faith in her theories evaporating before she'd even started in on them— Laramie feeling that twinge of fear that her boss would see right through her rookie interpretations and grasp how big a mistake he'd made in hiring her.

Shut up and get going, Laramie. She decided she'd get right to the point, rather than working her way to the punch line.

"As you promised," she said, "the task force was pretty accommodating. I'm not convinced they showed me everything, but I had access to enough. Enough to tell you I believe the investigation is proceeding under at least two fundamentally flawed assumptions."

A crackle of static popped from the speakerphone.

Then Ebbers said, "All right."

The sounds that came from the speakerphone had an odd digital quality to them, Laramie thinking of whatever Cher song it had been that took the singer's voice and ran it through a synthesizer. Maybe it had been all of them.

"One assumption *I've* made," Laramie said, "is that you're not interested in seeing a 'terror book' from me—that you want nothing from me in writing. I'm prepared, of course, to put everything I will tell you today, and more, into a report if you so choose. I'm also assuming you know more about this case than I do, or at least just as much. So I'll keep the background short—even skip it altogether."

No answer came from the static-ridden phone line, which Laramie took to mean, *Then why are you giving me so much background, Miss Laramie.*

"The first flawed assumption," she said, "is that the greater Miami metropolitan area was Benny Achar's intended target. I agree it seems the obvious choice due to its population density and basic proximity to the blast site—the filo spreads beyond the hundred-plus victims it killed and infects any part of greater Miami-Dade County and you've got a few hundred thousand casualties, maybe more. Achar didn't get his whole stash airborne, of course—if he had, or so the theory goes, he'd have delivered his evolved viral hemorrhagic fever serum to the entire population of Miami. Therefore it must have been his target."

"Go on," Ebbers said.

"Like the much-discussed potential seen in the avian flu, however, the Marburg-2 filo infects both humans and a number of animal species. All humans it comes into contact with die; for many animal species the same is true. The virus spreads from one infected species to the next with no apparent resistance. My point is that when you examine the geographical choice of Achar's blast site, there is a strategic positioning to it that is worse, from a casualties perspective, than Miami. Lake Okeechobee."

Laramie paused, half expecting a sarcastic comment along the lines of, *His target was a lake?* Getting none, she launched into an abbreviated version of what the freelance biologist had explained about Lake Okeechobee providing the Everglades with its water supply.

"Even if it isn't the case, we need to consider this scenario as a possibility," Laramie said, "because if an unobstructed waterway feeding the Everglades had been breached by the M-2 virus, that's pretty much all Achar would have needed to take out the whole state. Virtually every animal touched by the ecosystem that is the Everglades would act as a carrier of the filo, and that means just about every animal and human in Florida. It's possible that if this scenario were executed properly and quarantines were put into place a few days too late, a death rate among the human population here could run in the high ninetieth percentile."

Noisy digital silence came from the speakerphone. Laramie decided not to wait to find out whether Ebbers had any comments in response to her theory.

"I'm not saying that looking at Everglades wildlife as the target is going to get us anywhere special right away—but what it gives us, if in fact he wasn't acting alone, is a number of other regions in which to look for other sleepers. Say there are ten others. One may be assigned the Colorado River; another goes after the Mississippi; another the Hudson. I was never much for geography, but give me ten minutes and even I can come up with a scenario by which ten or eleven sleepers, placed correctly and armed with the equivalent stash of M-2 Achar kept in his basement, could bring down seventy-five to ninety percent of the population of the entire country by infecting areas of high animal population that overlap with the human population of nearby cities."

Ebbers spoke up again.

"Not sure," he said, "I want to hear about the second mistake."

Laramie felt a sudden tingle of fear. It hit her veins like a shot of espresso and moonshine: *Christ, he might just think I'm right . . . and what if I am?*

"The second, well, not mistake, but my opinion on the second flawed—"

"*Fuckup,* then," Ebbers said, almost yelling to make sure she heard him over her own voice. "Tell me where they're wrong, Miss Laramie."

Laramie blinked. "Well, if you're a cop, you're supposed to bust somebody based on evidence. Not just a hunch. But my hunch is that Benny Achar did not make a mistake at all. He is not a 'perp.' This is what the task force believes, and it is the way they refer to him: as a perp. Instead, I believe him to be a deep cover agent gone native."

A silence ensued, the digitized snap, crackle, and pop of the encrypted line the only audible emission from the phone. Laramie tried to picture Ebbers sitting there doing the math on what she'd just told him.

His voice came level and flat from the phone.

"I'm familiar with the term," he said, "but considering he killed over a hundred American citizens by suicide bomb and pathogen dispersal, I'm having trouble grasping how the idea of his 'going native' applies."

Time to get in as much as you can.

"I think it's not only possible," Laramie said, speaking quickly, "but likely that he turned on his employers. Or his country—or whoever it is he was 'sleeping' for. I think that instead of the perp he's been characterized as, Achar was a turncoat—for our side. I think he did exactly what he planned to do. I think he carefully and deliberately calculated exactly how much filo to disperse, and when to do it—in particular, right after his wife and son took off from Miami—in order to achieve three objectives."

She kept on, barely taking in air as she went.

"First: cause the least number of casualties while still displaying the pathogen's effects. Second objective: reveal to such people as you and me his role as a deep-cover sleeper agent. And third: make it likely the M-2 epidemic that results remains, in size and scope, an outbreak that would be contained within the length of time he told his wife to hide. Seven-plus days, or thereabouts. So she could survive, and his son could too, while he nonetheless accomplished his other objectives."

Laramie left it at that.

It took a while, but at length the tinny, double-encrypted voice of Lou Ebbers said, "He told his wife to hide for a week? I didn't see that in the book."

Laramie didn't waste any time—since he'd bitten, it was time to set the hook.

"He told her to hide for 'no less than seven days.' She told me in my interview with her in the Hendry County sheriff's interrogation room. She admitted that he warned her—I'm fairly certain he didn't tell her what he was up to, but he warned her before she left town that 'if something should happen,' she would need to hide out for that period of time. Which she did—armed with enough cash to stay at a motel anonymously for that length of time."

"So he knew what he was about to do? That proves nothing."

"I think what he told her proves he knew approximately how far the virus would reach. How long it would continue spreading before it might run out of gas, particularly assuming the kind of response the CDC would enact in our terror-prone time. He spreads the whole batch with nobody positioned to quarantine its effects, the epidemic would still be active to this day. He knew it wouldn't happen like that— because the amount he chose to disperse could be contained in a week to ten days. Bottom line: if you assume Achar warned his wife in order to save her life, then you must conclude he intended to disperse only the amount of M-2 filo that he actually did disperse."

"*If.*"

"If I'm right, then he didn't intend to kill the people of

Miami at all. He didn't even plan to infect the entire Everglades, though I do believe this was his original mission. What he *did* plan to do was to send a signal. To us."

"If that was his intention," Ebbers said, "wouldn't it have been easier to walk into his friendly neighborhood FBI office and confess?"

"There's at least one explanation why he wouldn't have done that," Laramie said.

"Which is what?"

"He'd have gotten his wife and son killed. Let alone the skepticism he'd be met with."

"Got them killed how?"

"If his employer knew he'd sold out—gone native—it could be there was a threat on his family or the likelihood of retaliation. But if he succeeds in pulling it off the way he did, it might just seem to his employer that he made a mistake. This is exactly what we thought, at least to start with. It's still what the task force thinks. But if you see it my way, Achar has succeeded in sparing his wife and son the wrath of the 'bio-dirty bomb' he was sent here to detonate, while still revealing to Lou Ebbers & Company that the enemy's troops are out there."

After a few clicks of static, Ebbers's voice came again.

"Others," he said, "who haven't gone native."

Laramie nodded as though he were standing there.

"Theory being," Ebbers said, "his love for his wife and son drove him to do this?"

"Maybe, sure—he became his cover and didn't want them to die."

"Assuming you're right," Ebbers said, "it follows that he'd have left us more clues."

Laramie thought about that. She noticed the sound of the traffic on the highway outside—the rumble of a passing semi, the wash of a few sedans, the whoosh of an SUV floating into the conference room from somewhere past the end of the red brick road. She didn't say anything, and Ebbers didn't say anything either, not for quite a while—

long enough for Laramie to wonder whether they'd lost the connection.

Then Ebbers's smudged voice came from the speakerphone again.

"All right, then," Ebbers said. "Find them."

"Find . . . his other clues, you mean?" Laramie said.

"The other clues—and the other sleepers."

The job she'd been interviewing for, it seemed, had just become a little more permanent.

"I'm a little unclear on how to do that, though, sir—will I be able to utilize certain members of the task force? Some of the men and women I interviewed were pretty forthcoming, and I'll need the help if I'm going to—"

"The task force is being disbanded. You'll be taking over."

"Pardon me?"

The hiss and crackle of the line reigned for a few seconds. Then Ebbers's voice, in its digital monotone, said, "What part didn't you understand?"

Laramie thought for a moment about what she'd found so far, and the kinds of places she'd have to look to find more. The people she'd need to talk to, the resources she'd need to deploy. None of this was her specialty. How would she . . .

"Look, Lou, um—I'm capable of being pretty industrious, but as you certainly understand, I'm no operative. And my analytical experience, as you also know, doesn't have much to do with terrorism. Actually, it doesn't have *anything* to do with terrorism. I'm probably the last person you should—"

"No kidding, Columbo."

"What?"

"Isn't that what your father used to tell you?"

Laramie felt some heat pop up into her neck and snake toward her cheeks.

"Listen," she said, "I already know you know everything there is to know about me. Congratulations. In fact, can you tell me when I'm menstruating next? I'm occasionally a little inconsistent, mostly based on my diet, or how far I run in the mornings. So maybe you could tell me when I'm due again—

that'd plug in nicely with the Columbo thing, the coffee, the sandwich, and the things your people packed in my Tumi bag. But in the meantime, I am flattered by the job offer, if that's what this is—but I'm not your man, Lou. You don't need me. You need paramilitary people. Spies. And counterterrorism experts to run them. I don't mean to sound ungratef—"

"As in, a 'compartmentalized counterterrorism unit'?" Ebbers said.

His tone of voice was business as usual, as though Laramie's menstruation-themed outbursts were to be expected.

"Better yet," Ebbers said, "maybe we should use the term 'counter-cell cell' to describe the team you're talking about. Or 'C-cubed' for short."

Laramie more or less forgot to breathe for a moment. She would need no further clarification from Ebbers as to what he was talking about, and what he meant by saying the things he'd just said. The terms "counter-cell cell" and "C-cubed" were quite familiar to her: this was what she had called the structure she'd recommended the government use to confront today's terror threat—in her independent study paper. The one Ebbers had revealed to require the highest security clearance in the federal government to read.

"We recruited you," Ebbers's digitized voice said, "to function as the leader of just such a 'cube.' I used the term, 'No kidding, Columbo,' because you were right: yes, you will need to select a team. The paramilitary operatives; other analytical minds; any counterterrorism specialists you feel become necessary. To be clear, your team's sole responsibility—the assignment of your 'cube'—is to identify, isolate, and, as directed, take steps to eradicate the person, people, or organization for whom Benjamin Achar was working. Along with the suicide-sleeper colleagues of his who remain at large."

Laramie closed her eyes and counted silently in her father's recommended fashion. She spoke only once she'd counted her way through the cycle.

"In selecting the team," she said, "will I be able to work from both a pool of recruits, or volunteers, as well as from my own, independently generated choices? Of personnel, I mean."

"Yes. We are not organized precisely as your paper proposed, but in this respect the setup is similar. The pool of recruits includes a roster of ordinary citizens, government officials, and military personnel, each of whom has been identified, approached, then solicited to volunteer, or vice versa. Most offered themselves in some capacity during the immediate aftermath of 9/11. Each has been background-checked to their birth, often further back than that. With regards to the independently generated choices you may pick, we would of course need to conduct similar background checks on each of your choices before such personnel are approved. I have the feeling, however, that you know the answer to your next question already."

"Did—did I have a next question?" Laramie said.

After a while, confronted by the volume of the silence, Laramie decided she might as well give up on her short-lived facade.

"Christ," she said. "If you're saying you believe there's somebody I would call first, then you're correct. My next question was going to be whether you know him, and whether you think he'd check out. But of course you know him."

"He's already on the approved list."

"Of course."

They know pretty much everything, don't they, she thought, and if they knew pretty much everything, they certainly knew about *him.* They knew he'd be the first one she'd think about reaching out to, at least if this was the kind of job they were giving her. She wondered whether the reason Ebbers picked her in the first place for the assignment had more to do with *him* than anything she'd written in school, or analyzed afterward.

One of the only things they don't *know is that he might well be on* their *approved list, but he certainly isn't on* mine.

Actually, he was on her least-approved, most-annoying list—a list that spanned one person.

Still, his expertise could prove highly valuable, and she had a pretty good idea she could trust the son of a bitch.

"You can go ahead and place the call," Ebbers said.

Laramie didn't say anything.

Ebbers too was silent again for a minute, or maybe ten, Laramie couldn't tell, until his voice crackled through the speakerphone one last time.

"Nice talkin' to you, Miss Laramie," he said. "Break a leg."

Then he hung up.

21

Planted on oil reserves more bountiful than those beneath most OPEC states, Venezuela had, by the early twenty-first century, failed to lift more than a token percentage of its people from abject poverty. The oil revenues were routed through the government-owned Petróleos de Venezuela S.A., with profits promised to the poor but usually distributed only according to the whim of the nation's chief politician. So despite the black gold mined from beneath it, for each of its six decades of independence from Spanish territorial status, the Bolívarian Republic of Venezuela remained a nation of high-profile leaders, sleek, modern city centers, and—mostly—shantytown *barrios*.

The latest chief politician was Hugo Chávez, a man imprisoned for leading a failed military coup before he went on to win a pair of presidential elections. Along the way, he managed to snuff out the standard South American sort of political challenges—a referendum seeking his ouster, a successful but short-lived coup, a few assassination attempts. Chávez routinely conducted a number of foreign-affairs initiatives geared solely, it seemed, toward alienating U.S. officials, with considerable success. Americans consumed the majority of Venezuela's oil, and probably always would—but the discord resulting from Chávez's anti-American bravado was enough to make a visit to Venezuela by any American citizen a tremendous pain in the ass.

Cooper circumvented the would-be four-hour customs detainment of American tourists by buying his ticket at the Copa Airlines counter in San Juan with a MasterCard under the name of Armando Guttierez—which name the ticket agent also found printed alongside Cooper's picture on the Colombian passport he was breaking in today.

He rented a car, and after a stroll through the soupy heat to the vehicle, found his way to the *autopista* and headed south for Caracas. It took him about an hour in the gridlocked traffic to reach the exit he'd pinned down as the correct choice in an online atlas search from the porch of his bungalow.

He'd pinned down some other things too with a phone call or three, namely that Ernesto Borrego, aka El Oso Blanco, was, in fact, as Po Keeler had claimed, into a lot of shit. Borrego's businesses, operating under the Borrego Industries banner, included trucking, intermodal shipping, home electronics and personal computer importing and exporting, wholesale distribution, and order fulfillment. This according to the backgrounder Cooper had ordered up from Langley, which he presumed to be far from comprehensive.

He'd called some other people and learned that Borrego liked to hunker down in his rat-trap of an office within the confines of the Borrego Industries distribution center south of the city. Apparently Borrego rarely left the place, and instead preferred to all but live out of the facility. It was from the Caracas distribution center that he took his meetings—of which there were few—while logging fourteen or fifteen hours of phone calls a day. He was said to hold frequent video teleconferences, the man's preferred meeting format.

It was also well known locally that Borrego consumed massive quantities of takeout. Rarely leaving the windowless office space in his massive warehouse building, he cycled through a set delivery rotation of offerings from local eateries, his favorite being the two-foot hoagies stacked high with meat that a nearby deli ordinarily made for birthday parties and corporate events.

Once he found the distribution center, Cooper drove around the perimeter of the place for a look around. It was a massive facility that made Cooper think suddenly of New Jersey—a vast, sprawling campus of one-story buildings equipped with loading docks, surrounded by what had to be ten square miles of parking lot. The place appeared to be accessible, from the road anyway, via two secure entrances, each equipped with a guard booth and gate. One was much bigger than the other, the larger serving as the egress point for tractor-trailers, Cooper losing count at 237 rigs being loaded or unloaded behind the sea of buildings. He saw a couple of the semis leave, and a couple others come in. The guards granting this access didn't seem too diligent, but Cooper didn't have an eighteen-wheeler on hand.

The second gate was your standard corporate-campus security booth, same in any country—swipe your pass card across the black panel on the post astride the guard booth and the gate would open to let you in. While Cooper watched, he saw the guard manning the booth wave to or otherwise greet every driver coming in. That was the nature of the second entrance—it was the administrative parking lot, all cars and no rigs, the autos lined up outside the only building on the lot that lacked loading docks.

This would be where Borrego kept his office.

Cooper had some trouble devising a painless way in, but on his ninth loop around the complex, he noticed the trains. There was a switching engine pulling container cars in and out of the facility, five or six at a time. Even Cooper, beach denizen though he was, could admire the intermodal transportation system Borrego had going: rail cars held the shipping containers today, but a truck or ship might hold them tomorrow. The switching locomotive was busy plucking select cars from a pair of mile-long trains parked on a set of spurs, set off to the side of the main rail thoroughfare. The tracks may well have served other facilities in the area, but the main stop appeared to be Borrego Industries.

Cooper ditched his rental car on a dusty shoulder between a roadside junkyard and a service station. Locking it with the remote, he strolled around the back of the service station as though headed for the restroom, but kept going until he hit the switching track behind. He doubled back a couple hundred yards so that he could hide behind the junkyard, then waited there until the switching engine came rumbling along, the rhythmic *bong bong* of its klaxon announcing its passage. The engineer had four of the container cars hooked up this time around.

He stayed hidden behind a stack of punctured tires until the locomotive passed—Cooper making sure the engineer couldn't clock him—then stepped out and jogged alongside the slow-moving train until he found a good handle and pulled himself aboard. He clung to a ladder beneath two towering twin-stack shipping containers while the train pulled onto the property, waited for the hydraulic *hiss* of the train's brakes, jumped off, walked around the side of the building, found his way to the sidewalk lining the administrative building, and strolled through the glass doors and into the main lobby.

Coming in, he saw it did not appear there was much pomp or circumstance here. Judging from the number of cars in the lot, there couldn't have been more than twenty-five people working in the business wing to begin with—none of them, apparently, working in particularly luxurious digs.

He approached a stern-cheeked receptionist. She sat behind a fold-out desk that might have been a card table in another life.

"Afternoon," he said, going with English for no particular reason.

There was little life in the look she shot back at him.

Cooper added, "I'm here to see the Polar Bear."

"Pardona me?" she said, struggling even with the two-word foray into English.

"El Oso Blanco," Cooper said, grinning as though he were a salesman here to hawk business-to-business long-distance telephone service. "Good old Ernie."

Appearing mildly relieved by his use of Spanish, she returned to the comfort zone of her native tongue. "Security hadn't told us—"

"Sí," Cooper answered, "they were pretty busy up front."

"I don't have you on Mr. Borrego's calendar."

They were sticking with Spanish now. Cooper noted where her eyes went as she dropped Borrego's name: the double doors at the end of the hallway to Cooper's right. Not that he couldn't have guessed which office belonged to the main man upon entering the otherwise Spartan complex.

Cooper said, "You mind if I just . . ." and, keeping the salesman's smile plastered on his face, headed past the card table and on down the hall.

Standing, the receptionist pronounced her objections at great volume, then punched a button on her telephone console and began yelling something about *"Seguridad!"* into the phone. Cooper opened one of the double doors at the back of the short hallway, entered, then closed and locked the door behind him. He turned and encountered exactly what—or at least who—he had expected to find, only on a much larger scale than anticipated.

Seated before a tropical fish tank that looked about twenty feet long by eight tall—Cooper putting it at fifteen, twenty thousand gallons—was a man with one of the largest heads ever seen on a human being. Adorned with a wireless telephone headset, outfitted in an off-white three-piece suit that made Cooper think of Tom Wolfe, the man Cooper presumed to be Ernesto Borrego was digging in—big-time.

Cooper watched as the man called the Polar Bear, unfazed by his entrance, continued working from a tub the size of a deep sea charter's bait bucket. He used a serving fork to stab a mound of the pasta within, wound it in a tight spiral with the aid of a ladle-size spoon, then lifted the fork-bound coil of semolina and sauce into his monstrous facial cavity.

Skin the color of the moon on the clearest of Caribbean nights, suit protected from the elements by a gigantic red-checked napkin, Borrego was working on a bottle of red too, a decanter's worth resting on his big desk alongside the tub.

Eating the food the way he was, the man not the slightest bit disturbed by his entrance, it struck Cooper that Borrego looked about like . . . a polar bear.

Borrego shoveled another mouthful of noodles into his maw. When he'd chewed and swallowed, washing it down with a sip taken directly from the carafe, he wiped his mouth with the bib and said, "Who the fuck are you?"

As far as Cooper could tell, Borrego hadn't yet looked up to examine him.

"May not resemble one," Cooper said, "but I'm a canary."

Borrego chewed a new spool of noodles. He looked to Cooper to be conducting two operations: the sensory function of enjoying the flavors of the pasta, and the intellectual act of solving the half-ass riddle. When he'd finished masticating, Borrego made a clicking sound somewhere in his huge mouth before returning for another backhoe-dig with the serving fork.

"Canary in a mine shaft, you mean," he said. His English was clean—middle-America news-anchor clean.

Muted voices came from beyond the door Cooper had his back against. Somebody tried the knob; Cooper wrapped his hand around it just in case the lock hadn't done the trick. There came more muted chitchat from the hall.

"More or less," Cooper said. "I'm not expecting to pass into bird heaven anytime soon, but the fact remains that the people who're currently considering offing me will probably come after you next. Or even first."

Borrego looked at him while continuing to eat, seemingly observing him for the first time.

"So am I the canary," he said, "or you?"

Cooper shrugged.

"How'd you get in here?" Borrego said.

"The guards in your booths don't concern themselves with the trains."

Borrego stopped chewing for a moment then started up again.

"Have to fix that," he said.

The knob spun in Cooper's hand and he was yanked backward by the opening door as he tried to keep it in his grasp. He'd expected the intrusion but still had to switch his weight from one foot to the other to avoid falling. He soon found his fancy footwork didn't matter, since as he regained his balance, the well-muscled shoulder of an exceedingly large individual plowed into his spine, a pair of muscle-bound arms wrapped around him, and what Cooper pegged for a three-man private security detail gang-tackled him. As he hit the floor chin first it felt to him as though he were being pig-piled, and once they had him pinned they jammed both his wrists against his respective shoulder blades and crammed his face into the wall-to-wall carpeting Borrego kept in his office. Somebody found and took from him the Agency-issue FN Browning tucked against his back, and it began to occur to Cooper he'd been a little too thrilled with his infiltration game. It became equally apparent these boys didn't appear to possess handcuffs, since by now they'd have slapped him with a pair.

A powerful hand was keeping Cooper's face against the rug, so he couldn't see Borrego as the Polar Bear said, "Careful there—canaries are known for their delicate constitutions."

Cooper felt a little easing of the pressure of the tough spirals of rug against his lips.

Probably deserve that.

None of the people who had entered the room said anything. He heard the *bong bong* of the switching engine, the distant sound of a ringing phone, but that was about it—until there came a low rumble, which Cooper first thought to be coming from the floor. It began as the sort of trembling bass you got from a subwoofer, then clarified and sharpened to a more familiar noise—at which point Cooper realized Borrego had just performed a polar bear's equivalent of a chuckle. The chuckle soon accelerated into a great, braying belly laugh.

"Ah, shit," El Oso Blanco said, the laughs crashing from his larynx like southern California surf. "Ah, *puta mierda* . . . !"

Finally the laughing surf retreated. As it did, so too did the pressure from the hand on Cooper's head. The hands that had been holding his arms against his back released too, and soon he was lying unrestrained on the carpet. Realizing that Borrego must have given his security team some kind of gesture ordering his release, Cooper turned on his side to get a look at the security men and saw, to his consternation and embarrassment, the nature of the army that had just subdued him: there stood looking down at him only one man, a behemoth with a wafer-thin waist who looked more velociraptor than human despite his half-decent suit and not-inexpensive wingtips.

Cued by another unseen gesture, the velociraptor stepped away from Cooper and retreated to a place against the wall beside the double doors. He clasped his hands in front of his groin.

"That was funny," Borrego said. "Funny." As Cooper worked his legs around and sat upright on the floor, he could see Borrego smiling over the tub at him. "So again," he said, "who the hell are you, what the fuck do you want, and what or who is it that's poisoning the mine?"

Cooper checked his lips for blood but they were dry— rug-burn dry. He started slowly, mainly because his numb lips had some trouble mouthing the words.

"A trail of bodies has begun to turn up in the wake of a shipment of gold artifacts," he said. "The artifact shipment would be the same load of boxes you checked aboard the good ship *Seahawk* in La Guaira. One note you may find equally discouraging is that the artifacts themselves were destroyed too. Or at least sunk to the bottom of the Caribbean."

Borrego, who had begun eating again, shrugged.

"That'd be one of the reasons they call it the black market," he said. "Involves some risk."

"I'm assuming you'd be one of the bodies now too—especially considering how easy it is to get past your security detail—"—Cooper flipped a look in the direction of the velociraptor-bodyguard as he said this, hoping for a reaction but earning none—"except, by my best guess, whoever's leaving the trail of bodies doesn't know you're the one holding the luggage tags."

The Polar Bear made a *humph* sound. "They'd be right," he said. "I'm not. At least not anymore."

Cooper stood, sort of bending at the hip in hopes of readjusting his spine as he did it. No such luck—there remained a sharp pain in one of the meaty muscles in his lower back. He pulled himself into one of the chairs that faced Borrego's big desk while he thought aloud through what Borrego had meant.

"You're not holding . . . you didn't check the bags, you mean."

"Right. I sold 'em."

"Funny," Cooper said, "so did I."

"No surprise there—so did somebody else before me. That's how it works," Borrego said. "I don't even get the prime cut. And while antiquities *are* a passion of mine, I'm into them as a margin guy. You know—buy very low, sell not quite so low. Little or no risk—get in, get out."

Borrego stopped eating just long enough to grin, and Cooper saw that the Polar Bear had sharp teeth that looked almost brown against his white skin and whiter suit.

"Except for the fact that I usually pluck a few of 'em for myself before getting all the way out," he said.

"Well, that's something else we've got in common. What about the two idiot gunslingers you required the shipper to take along for the ride to Naples? If you didn't check the bags for a colleague of yours to retrieve on the other side, what do you care about protecting the merchandise?"

"Idiots is right. But while our conversation thus far is chippy and neat, I'd like you to answer my other questions now," Borrego said.

Cooper considered this.

"You mean, 'Who the fuck am I,' and, 'What the hell do I want?'"

Borrego thrust him a thumbs-up over the top of the bucket.

"I've got a few made-up names I can pick from," Cooper said, "but the one most people use is Cooper. And I'm not one hundred percent positive what the hell I want, but if you are the middleman you claim to be, there are two questions I've got for you. I'd like to know the names of the people you sold the shipment to, and the names of the people you bought it from."

"You know what I'd like to know?" Borrego said. "I'd like to know why you didn't just give me a call. Slip past my secretary that way. I usually even call back."

"I'm old-fashioned."

"Meaning you like to discuss such things in person."

"Sometimes."

"Or you just prefer to be a pain in the ass, in hopes it'll get you somewhere the phone call wouldn't."

"Come on," Cooper said, "why the gunslingers?"

El Oso Blanco shook his massive head.

"You tell me, 'Cooper,'" he said. "The guns came at the behest of the buyer. Stupid and unnecessary, no matter what you're shipping. Unless you're running dope, the U.S. task forces don't give a shit what you're shipping. Might get a little sticky from all the red tape if you're caught, but those boys think they're fighting a war, and they don't have time for anything but the front lines. I advised the buyers as much, but I was paid what I asked to get, and the goodies were out of my hands the instant the wire transfer landed. I knew they wanted the gunslingers, so I worked that into the

PUBLIC ENEMY • 181

shipping terms in advance. That's what they wanted, so that's what they got."

"As it turns out," Cooper said, "that shipment was worth quite a lot of money."

"Oh, I know what it was worth. It was obviously worth quite a lot of trouble too."

"You know what happened with the Coast Guard?"

"Sure." Borrego pointed with his fork at the computer screen on the desk. " 'Coast Guard Guns Down Smugglers at Sea,' or something to that effect."

"You get a call from the buyers once the story broke?"

"I wouldn't get that call directly anyway, but no."

"You find that surprising?"

"That I didn't get a call?" Borrego shrugged. "Mildly."

"Who'd you sell to?"

Borrego began packing up the remains of his meal. "Considering that you've come and alerted me to the 'string of bodies,' as you put it, I'd be happy to break protocol and give you a name. He isn't the buyer, of course. Only another middleman. A fence. But unless he's relocated already, which is something he frequently does, you can find him in Naples."

Food and silverware pushed aside, Borrego removed the napkin from around his neck, pulled a pen from a drawer, wrote something on a Post-it, and held the Post-it across the desk for Cooper to take.

"Should be able to reach him here."

Cooper leaned in and took the Post-it.

"Appreciate the help."

"Appreciate the warning."

"What about the source?" Cooper said.

"You know, *Señor* Cooper, you are one greedy bastard."

"Selfish too," Cooper said. "Also angry."

There came that brownish-yellow grin again. It faded, though, and the Polar Bear said, "No cigar there, *campañero*."

"Why not?"

"Only way this artifact-acquisition system works is to retain the anonymity of the seller. I've got people out there—South and Central America, Africa, China—do my buying for me. And when they buy, they do it on a no-questions-asked basis. We pay close to the lowest price, but you always know you'll never be ratted out by the Polar Bear."

He grinned again, pleased at this declaration of his reputation.

Cooper thought for a moment. "You know where your people bought it, though," he said. "Geographically speaking. And I imagine telling me *that* wouldn't be 'ratting out' on your suppliers."

"Interested in a tour through rebel-infested Central American jungle?"

Even hearing the term *Central American jungle* made Cooper's stomach roil. He tensed up, Cooper starting to get pissed off at the indecipherable presence of butterflies that kept lightening his midsection whenever he put too much thought into the source of Po Keeler and Cap'n Roy's goddamn gold artifacts. He thought for a moment of the statue of the priestess, camped out on the shelf in his bungalow: *Yeah, Cooper,* he heard her decayed, gritty voice croak, *we up here in the afterlife waitin' for your help. Up here lookin' down at a slice o' Central American jungle, about where you lost track of a few things yourself.*

"I'm not following you," Cooper said.

"No joke, *amigo,*" Borrego said. "I like to get out there once in a while—two, three times a year, minimum. Head out with my boys and do the buy myself—maybe even coax some tomb raider or other to take us along for the spelunk."

"Spelunk," Cooper said.

"The journey belowground—into the caves. The tombs, if you can find them. Still plenty of 'em out there—Inca gold, Mayan antiquities, art and treasure been hidden for a thousand-plus years. Technology and civilization just now getting us in on some of it."

Cooper didn't say anything about the relative youth Susannah Grant had pinpointed as to the origins of the Keeler artifacts—a hundred and fifty years at most.

"Appreciate the offer but I'll take a pass," Cooper said. "You go along for the ride on the shipment in question? If not, why don't you just tell me where you got them."

"Well, that's the point. We purchased them in a remote, mountainous region along the border between Guatemala and Belize—but we'd have to get out and track down the sellers, among other things, to pin it down any better than that. I could track them down if I nosed around those parts for a bit, but there isn't exactly a phone number."

Borrego waved the receptionist in from the perch she'd clung to in the doorway, and she came in and cleared the remains of his lunch, shooting Cooper a series of dirty looks along the way. *Or maybe she's taking the time to admire the sharp crease of my cheekbones.*

Then the Polar Bear stood and extended a hand.

"Offer stands," he said.

Cooper, who tended to tower over the average guy, had to look way up as he took hold of El Oso Blanco's paw and shook. Man had to be six-nine, maybe taller. An effective guess on his weight seemed impossible.

"While I enjoy a nice eco-tour as much as the next soul," Cooper said, "that part of the world isn't exactly my favorite. I'll be getting hold of your Florida buyer, though."

"Fence. You going to call him?"

Cooper cocked his head a notch, unclear as to what Borrego was asking.

"Just curious," the Polar Bear said, "if you were planning to call the man on the phone, or whether you'd ride in on a train to get past his security guards."

Cooper released Borrego's paw from the handshake.

"What *I'm* curious about," he said, "is when I can expect to get my gun back from your army of one."

Borrego motioned to his bodyguard and Cooper turned and caught the Browning as the velociraptor threw it.

"Hasta luego," Cooper said, and took his best shot at stepping on the bodyguard's toe on his way out of the office. The security man pulled his wingtip back as Cooper passed—and Cooper might have caught the velociraptor smirking at his lame attempt.

Despite the relative humiliation, Cooper exited the administrative building and headed for the train tracks.

22

It was six o'clock in the morning when Cooper heard the phone ring forty or fifty times. Somebody finally silenced it—meaning it wasn't too much of a stretch to peg the three hard whacks at his door for Ronnie, coming to say the call was for him.

"Rise and shine," Ronnie said, "you sorry rummy fuck!"

Cooper's first thought was, *Who's dead now?* But doing his best to ignore this thought, he reached under his bed, picked up, then heaved his Ken Griffey Jr. Autograph-Special Louisville Slugger in the direction of the front door of his bungalow.

It wouldn't do anything to Ronnie but scare the daylights out of him—Cooper was too tired to get up and take the swing that would have done the trick—so he made sure of his aim, watching with satisfaction as the heavy bat careened off the concrete floor of the bungalow in a single hop then rocketed into the jalousie panes on the door. The bat shattered all twelve louvered panes to splinters, gouging a hole in the screen beyond—Cooper hopeful, though unable to see whether the hardwood handle of the bat had reached far enough through the screen to strike Ronnie in the shin.

"Keep out!" he bellowed.

Through the window near the foot of his bed, Cooper saw Ronnie stroll down the stairs and pass out of view—middle finger extended all the while, dropping a foot with each step taken down and away from the bungalow.

A fuck-you puppet show, Cooper thought—what a fine way to start the day.

He found a saggy set of black shorts with an *AND1* logo on the thigh and slipped on his Reefs. He ignored, even enjoyed the eighty-five-degree rain as it dumped its thick drops on his mussed hair and naked, weathered shoulders. He came through the dark, empty kitchen with its huge stainless steel appliances—detecting, as with every early morning, the faint scents of hops, barley, rum, and conch fritters emanating from the floor, probably inherited as much from the old mop used to scrub it clean as from the food and drink spilled on it the night before.

In a cubbyhole behind the kitchen sat a hulking phone. It seemed Ronnie had left the receiver off the hook.

"Yep," he said upon snatching the receiver.

"Good morning, Professor."

Upon hearing the sound of Julie Laramie's voice, Cooper instantaneously jerked the phone from his ear and dropped it from great elevation onto its cradle.

He made his way leisurely back through the garden to his room, where he removed the *AND1* shorts and slid beneath the sheets again. He could feel some sand in the covers, the way he always felt some, even if he'd had the sheets washed thirty minutes prior.

The ringing started up again, and after twenty-one of the phone's shrill, bleating rings, the clamor ceased. To Cooper's great relief, the sounds of the diminishing rain on the metal rooftops and wind-rustled palms washed over the club.

Then he heard those goddamn footsteps coming up the porch again.

"Fuck's sake, Guv," Ronnie said. "I hung up on her, but she's waking up all the guests."

"The hell you expect me to do about it?"

"Don't know how many times I need to tell you, old man. Give these fucks your sat phone number and maybe the rest of us can sleep till six-thirty—maybe seven."

"You sleep till seven, Woolsey'll have your ass, 'Guv.'"

"Be my pleasure," Ronnie said. "Bleedin' 'ell, I been trying to get 'im to fire me since my first day here." He went silent for a minute, but Cooper didn't hear any footsteps, so he knew the errand boy was still standing there.

"Was nice havin' her around, you know," Ronnie said. "Why don't you take her call, you effin' stump?"

Cooper, his voice almost delicate, said, "Ought to mind your own business."

He heard the pooled raindrops dripping from the gutters, from the railings, from an occasional wide, waxy leaf. The rainfall itself began to abate, and the wind, too, slowed. After a while, Ronnie's departing footsteps mingled briefly with the regular mix of sounds.

After another while, Cooper lying in his sheets listening, the last of the sounds of draining water ended too, and the silent heat began to beat down on the places the rain had moistened, and warm the roof of his bungalow, and infiltrate the depths of his room.

Another day has begun, he thought, here in Conch Bay.

Cooper sat in the blistering inferno that was his porch, the old stoop made that way by the direct sunshine that struck and cooked it every afternoon between the hours of two and five. It hadn't been designed quite right to handle the direct, oppressive afternoon sun. He'd once planted a thermometer out here to measure how hot it got, and the thing had actually sprung a mercury leak. It had registered higher than 140 degrees on the day it broke, but Cooper had decided this wasn't quite possible—that he'd simply bought a faulty unit that wasn't made for direct sunlight.

Around noon, the kitchen phone had started up with another ring cycle, and somebody had taken down the number of the woman everybody had already been told not to bother to come get him for. Now, baking in the afternoon heat, Cooper, bored with too many options on how to spend the remaining hours of the day, begrudgingly punched in Laramie's number on his sat phone. He was informed by the man who answered that he'd reached the LaBelle Motor 8 Luxury Motel. As instructed by the information scribbled on the slip of paper, he requested room number eighteen.

She answered on the second ring.

"All right, what is it," he said.

Laramie's interpretive delay lasted only a couple seconds.

"Why did I call, you mean?" she said. "Maybe I was calling just to catch up."

"Maybe not."

Cooper leaned slightly forward in his deck chair and planted his elbows on his knees, the sweat pouring out of him in the heat of his outdoor oven. He'd never tried it, but frequently wondered whether eggs would fry out here if he cracked open a pair on the reading table between the chairs. He reflected that for a few months, on and off—between trips aboard the Apache to a string of resorts—Julie Laramie's rear end had logged its share of oven-hot hours in the other chair on this deck, but not many; not enough. Laramie hadn't liked the afternoon heat—she preferred the porch at night, under the stars.

Though as it turned out, she hadn't preferred much of that, either.

"I'm—" Laramie said, then stopped. "This is mildly awkward." She hesitated again, Cooper suspecting she was hoping for an encouraging word or two—*Go ahead, Laramie*—but he didn't bite. Effectively maintaining his reputation as a grouch.

Laramie went on anyway.

"I'm in a complex and difficult situation," she said. "I've been given permission, and instructions, to speak to you— officially, I mean. To recruit you. As a member of my team."

Cooper sat silently for a while, elbows pressing reddish indentations into his thighs.

"That is awkward," he said.

"I'm in Florida. Obviously I'm unable to discuss why, or what we need you to help us with, on the phone. We'll pay for you to come meet with us."

Cooper began a kind of repeating, monotone chuckle.

"I know I've offered to pay you before and you laughed at me then too. I know you don't need—"

"No problem," Cooper said. "If I were interested in coming, I'd happily pay my own way. Actually, I'd charge it to my expense account, so it's just a matter of which department pays." He realized something, thinking of Laramie's call in a slightly different way, then said, "Or which agency."

"It's important for you to come up here and meet with us. With me. There isn't really a choice."

Cooper said, "No choice, eh?"

"We'll discuss it when you arrive. I can't until then. You'll need to trust me. But we'll get you up here the fastest way we can do it."

"Not interested," he said.

"No, it's not—look, you have to come. You're necessary."

"Not sure," Cooper said, "how I was unclear."

The occasional, distant ping of interference over the satellite connection did its audio dance while neither of them said anything for a while.

Then Laramie said, "If you don't come, the people I work for have told me they will consider freezing your assets. They have the capability, and you've told me where you put enough of it for us to get hold of a significant portion of your money."

Cooper's monotone Morse chuckle resumed then quickly overtook him, verging on an all-out belly laugh of the sort the Polar Bear of Caracas had levied on him two days before. After about a minute of this, Cooper finished up his laughter as though it were a delicious drink and sighed.

"I'm sorry," Laramie said, "but the people I work for instructed me to tell you that this would be our only recourse were you to decline my initial recruitment effort. It's that important. And I don't have time to ask more than once. If I need to force you to come, I'll do it."

" 'Initial recruitment effort,' " Cooper said. "That's nice. You know, I find it amusing the way the American government believes itself all-powerful in places it has less pull than a gecko. Good luck to you."

He took a great deal of time removing the phone from his ear, holding it beneath his chin so he could find the button, and plowing his thumb into the word End printed in red letters on the upper-right corner of the keypad. He set the phone on his reading table, leaned back against the rear spine of the deck chair, and closed his eyes to soak in the convection waves of mercury-busting heat.

He considered, with enormous satisfaction, that he still had at least another hour and a half before the temperature would sink below three digits again.

23

Throughout Collier and Lee counties and all
the way back to Miami, Ricardo Medvez was regarded by
all—rich, poor, chic, nearly everyone in between—as the
news anchor of choice. Their trusted man, host of the six and
eleven o'clock news, telling it like it was from his seat in the
studio of the Fort Myers NBC affiliate.

In certain, less public circles, Medvez was also known for
some other things: a gambling addiction, frequent trips
down the crystal meth, coke, and freebase superhighways,
and a generous propensity for lump-sum payoffs engineered
to discourage numerous paternity suits from making the run-
down of his own news broadcast.

Having largely succeeded in keeping his evening and
weekend activities under wraps, however, Medvez—who
otherwise considered himself starkly heterosexual—had,
one night, made a tape. Perhaps it'd been the freebase talking, or maybe he'd just unlatched a long-locked closet door,
but one night Medvez, jumping on the phone, ordered up
half a dozen male prostitutes, punched the record button on a
couple of camcorders, and made a private porno flick that
made *Deep Throat* look like a Pixar movie. He got plenty of

mileage out of the tape, taking it with him wherever he knew he'd possess sufficient private time with a VCR.

The odometer wore out, though, when one of the people he owed a hundred grand in gambling debts to got hold of the tape. From that point on, the interest rate on his gradually accumulating vig jumped a few dozen percentage points and Medvez assumed he was fucked for life.

This remained the case until a year and a half later, when the olive-skinned news anchor stumbled across a high-stakes card game in Key West. A few of the guys in the game kept referring to the weathered, baritone-voiced card shark taking all of their money that night as the "spy on the island," and Medvez wondered what this meant. Afterward, putting his finely honed interviewing skills to work—dulled somewhat by the lines of coke he'd done in the bathroom between hands—he ascertained that his fellow gambler was in fact a spy of sorts, and resided on an island in the British Virgins.

Medvez propositioned him on the spot.

"What would it cost if I wanted a favor done?" he asked.

Cooper sized up Medvez, the two of them out on the sidewalk in front of the restaurant they'd used for the game.

"What kind of favor," he said.

When Medvez explained, Cooper pondered the request for a few minutes—standing there in his Tommy Bahama short-sleeved shirt at four in the morning—then said, "I won't kill anybody for you, but this shouldn't be too hard to handle. I'll need whatever information you have on them, everywhere you've seen or associated with them, who you think they might work for, and so on."

Then he asked what Medvez had to offer in return.

"You like boats?" Medvez asked.

"Sure."

"Wanna take a walk?"

"How far?"

"Old Key West Marina. Five minutes, tops."

Parked as it was, roped beside the fuel depot in the island's marina of choice, Cooper would always remember his first encounter with the squat-hulled, off-white-and-burnt-orange Apache 41 custom racing vessel. For him it had been like meeting that woman you were meant to be with—he felt he'd known her all along. Upon further inspection, the forty-one-foot boat revealed its brawny twin engines, luxury quarters belowdecks, and nearly untouched, mint-condition state. He knew the boat to be worth somewhere close to four hundred thousand dollars.

"I'll take it in advance," he'd told Medvez back then, "but if I can't solve your problem, you can have it back."

Medvez agreed, and in an odd way—because of his own love for the racing boat he'd had built to his exact specs—he found himself, over time, to be mildly disappointed by the lack of contact from the people Cooper had somehow silenced. Medvez never asked Cooper whether he'd actually retrieved the tape, and ultimately didn't really want to know.

Cooper took the name and number El Oso Polar had passed him on the Post-it and ran them through three separate wash cycles—the reverse-directory services of CIA, FBI, and one private think tank. The machines returned three neatly pressed but slightly different packages. Between them came one post office box, three residential addresses—two in South Florida, one in Louisiana—one business address, two different versions of the man's name, his social, printouts of four different credit bureau reports—the kind the manager at a car dealership pulled when you went in to buy a car—plus a basic breakdown of the person's various bank and credit card accounts and loans and various supposedly current addresses.

Cooper didn't have much interest in placing phone calls to people he didn't know, who didn't expect his call, and who wouldn't have any interest in answering the kind of questions he intended to ask. He did, however, have an interest in finding out who had sent the contract killer to take out Cap'n Roy. And his only current lead—at least outside of the entire federal government of the United States of America or anyone else who had access to reports or radio communications from U.S. Coast Guard antidrug task force fleets—was the name of the fence the Polar Bear had provided him. Cooper figured an in-person conversation with the man might yield some answers on who else had been aware of the intended transaction.

He took his boat up to Naples—it was a long haul, but he was in the mood for a challenge. Including a couple of half-hour breaks, he made it in a shade under nineteen hours, bay to bay: five A.M. departure from his Conch Bay mooring and an arrival one hour shy of midnight at the fueling pier near downtown Naples. He'd made an average speed of forty-eight knots.

Double-parking against a lengthy yacht that looked something like Po Keeler's *Seahawk,* he kicked the bumpers off the edge, tied the two boats front to rear, then strolled through the rear cabin of the other boat on his way to the dock. He knew it was unlikely anybody would be using the big yacht anytime soon—with these kinds of boats, people liked having them more than using them. He took a cab to the single-building television station on the outskirts of Fort Myers.

In the lobby of the television studio, Cooper told the receptionist he had a story their evening news anchor would want to hear about. He told her it was about a film that had been made of a famous celebrity without the celebrity's permission, and that competing media outlets would leap into a frenzy to cover the story if Ricardo Medvez didn't come out and capture the scoop while he had the chance.

At 11:23—Cooper watching the weather segment begin on the eleven o'clock news on the monitor in the lobby—Medvez barged into the lobby in the suit Cooper had just seen him wearing on television. The contrast between the dark fabric of the suit and the white shirt he wore made the anchor's Latino skin tone appear even darker than Cooper's island tan—though Cooper could see pale orange smudges of pancake makeup on the edge of the man's shirt collar.

Medvez saw it was Cooper who'd made the thinly veiled

threat and grinned. He nodded to the receptionist that all was cool, saw Cooper had been watching the monitor, and opened the door to the newsroom.

"Wanna watch the rest from back here?" he said. "We're just wrapping up."

"Why not," Cooper said, and followed Medvez into the newsroom.

Medvez was good—very good. Cooper watched the last segment of the news from a folding chair four feet behind the assistant director. The AD gave Medvez his cues; besides the weather girl and sports guy, Medvez anchored alone. Seated in there watching the studio lights banging off of Medvez's glistening hair, it wasn't much of a stretch for Cooper to grasp the man's appeal—old ladies and blue-collar men's men would relate to the guy equally. Red state, blue state, displaced Cubans, blue hairs fresh off the links—no matter who you were, there was something in Medvez for you.

Including the denizens of the narcotics, gay porn, and gambling industries.

When they wrapped, Medvez offered Cooper a seat in the cubicle he inhabited in the center of the newsroom. Even after the last newscast of the day, there was a restrained but constant swirl of activity buzzing around them in a way that made Cooper think of a police precinct house. Medvez kept his jacket and makeup on but loosened his tie.

"So to what," he said, "do I owe the honor?"

"I actually have a story for you," Cooper said. "One with considerable sex appeal, in fact. Though not as much sex appeal as that tape of yours."

Medvez's eyes went hard and shifty and Cooper could see most of the on-air aura drain from the newsman's olive-orange skin.

Cooper got on with it.

"There's an antiquities smuggling ring," he said, "part of which is operating out of Naples. May even be a good old-fashioned curse involved, since a string of somewhat up-standing citizens have recently met their demise in connection with the smuggling operation."

Medvez leaned back in his chair.

"Florida's got plenty of murders to go around," he said.

"Well, you can scoop the competition on this one," Cooper said, "help yourself hold on to that anchor seat and keep getting babes—or whatever. Either way, I've got something you're going to do for me, so you may as well mix in a story along the way."

Medvez glared at him, his crumpled-up chin looking as though he'd just bitten into a lemon. Cooper pushed across the desk the complete stack of data related to the Polar Bear's Naples-based fence.

"The man described in these credit reports," he said, "is the broker for the U.S.-based buyers of the pillaged artifacts. The reason I'm giving you his papers is I want you to find him. What's in there should be enough for an ace reporter like you to track the guy down."

Cooper checked his watch.

"I'll give you until tomorrow afternoon. By then I'll need to know exactly where I can find him. I'll come by after the six o'clock news, and once you wipe that fucking makeup off, you'll take me there and we'll have a talk with the man. I'll get you back by eleven and you can stay famous for another night."

Medvez lifted the stack of papers, Cooper thinking maybe to clock the guy's name, then dropped the stack back on the desk.

"What the hell you need me for?" he said. "I'm no reporter. I sit behind the desk wearing my 'fucking makeup' and say what other people tell me to say. I even wear shorts most of the time I'm on the air—the cameras can't see below your waist."

Cooper stretched and yawned.

"I've been looking forward to a nice, long run on the beach," he said. "The kind you don't get living on an island with only a quarter-mile stretch of sand. I'm sleeping in, tracking down some huevos rancheros, then scooting out for as long a run as I can handle. Presuming my mostly broken-down legs can take it, I'm taking a shot at seven miles out, seven back. When I'm done, I'll shower off at my hotel, load up on seafood fettuccini at Vergina on Fifth, then stroll over to the Tommy Bahama store and re-stock my wardrobe with the latest in tropical silk fashions." Cooper stood. "With all that on my plate, it just seems counterproductive, spending my brief stateside time doing something like scrounging up a current address on some black market art smuggler."

Medvez shook his head, expression still puckered and nasty. The anchor was well aware of the fact he didn't have any choice in the matter.

Cooper smiled, then mimicked the words Medvez had used to sign off from the news.

"You take care, now," he said. "See ya tomorrow at six."

24

Sore from the run, and full after a Polar Bear–size helping of seafood pasta, Cooper rode in the passenger seat of
the news anchor's S500 AMG sedan. Medvez, unmasked,
had the wheel. With his deep bronze skin he didn't look
much different without the makeup—Cooper thinking
maybe a decade older, provided you were examining him
from as close a place as the passenger seat.

"You can see his place from here," the anchor said.

He pulled into a parking lot serving a set of shops and
restaurants called Tin City and parked in a slot that faced the
main drag, so that when he tugged the emergency brake they
were staring out the front windshield at the condominium
tower across the street. The Tin City parking lot was nearly
empty; Cooper could see the roof of a tour boat parked in the
channel beside the parking lot. He knew the inland-most
edge of Naples Bay to reach past Tin City and under Highway 41, where it squeezed down to the size of a creek and
dissolved into salty marsh. It was long since dark, and rush
hour, what little downtown Naples had of it, had just about
wound down for the night.

Medvez handed him a pair of binoculars.

"Second story, corner unit, right side of the building," he said. "Pretty easy to see most of his place with those curtains pulled."

Cooper adjusted the lenses and had a look.

"Left his lights on," he said.

"Place looked that way at six A.M. and again at noon when I came back," Medvez said. "Unless he gets up real early, I don't think anybody's been home since last night."

"What about the other addresses?"

Medvez shrugged. "Couldn't reach him at any of his numbers; no answer on his e-mail. Answering machine at the condo you're looking at gives you one of those computer voices telling you the machine is full. I checked all four of the addresses your documents listed as his places of residence during the last ten years—turns out two were business addresses, two residential. One of the businesses is now one of these banks that pop up every couple of weeks around here, Sun Coast or whatever. Bank just moved in two months ago. One of the residentials is an apartment four miles east on Highway 41, where a single mother and her two loud teenage sons live. The other business address looked pretty much vacant to me, and this was the other address on the list."

Cooper dropped the binoculars and eyed Medvez.

"Back in the reporting groove, eh?" he said.

Medvez offered another shrug.

"Broke a couple investigative stories to earn the anchor's seat," he said, "but that was a long time ago."

"What do you mean by 'pretty much vacant'?"

He nodded. "Warehouse. Seafoods, it says, but it doesn't look or smell dirty enough for that. Might be a cold-storage place—definitely not retail, not where it's located, over on the bay in about as bad an area as you'll find around here. Couple of fish-packing firms and tour boat offices next door. There were a few things going on even as late as five in the other buildings, but nothing in your guy's warehouse. Lights out all day. Nobody working there, no cars in the lot, no boats on the pier. Actually the pier's busted and rotting, hasn't seen a boat in a couple hurricanes. Parking lot ain't much better—quarter-mile dirt road gets you there and you find nothing but the warehouse at the end. The neighboring operations have separate entrance roads and their own asphalt parking lots."

"You go in yet," Cooper said, motioning with the binocs, "take a look around the condo or the warehouse?"

Medvez's face pinched in on itself, that lemon-chewing look again. "Reporting compelled by extortion, yes. Unprompted breaking and entering? No."

Cooper set the binoculars in the well behind the emergency brake.

"I'll educate you on the latest techniques," he said. He motioned in the direction of the building. "What's a place like that go for? Looks like a two-bedroom, maybe three at most."

"Right in town here? Seven-fifty, eight."

"For a territorial view of Tin City and the marsh?"

"Relative paradise, my dear extorter."

Cooper nodded. He liked the term—*relative paradise*—if not the concept.

"Let's have a look," he said.

The middleman's Uniden answering machine contained twenty-seven messages. Cooper listened to all of them, determining that twenty of the messages had been left during the prior five days. There did not sound to be anything of substance as to his whereabouts for the evening, at least not that Cooper or Medvez could understand. Cooper took notes on a pad the middleman kept beside the answering machine.

The guy's car and condo keys, residing on the same ring, sat on the counter in the foyer. Most of the lights in the place were on, including those in both bathrooms. The condo turned out to be a two-bed, two-bath, the second bedroom set up as a home office—Dell desktop, HP printer, Ikea file cabinets, boom box, telephone handset nestled in its charging base. The office had a view to the marsh.

With Medvez leaning, half hidden against a hallway doorjamb, Cooper rummaged through the office. He dug up little more on the man than the credit reports and related documentation provided by his sources had already told him—couple of contacts he hadn't known about before, written here and there, but that was it. He took a few dozen shots at the password that would unlock the computer, but couldn't hack his way in. He knew a few people who could, but that wouldn't do him much good at the moment.

In the master bedroom, Cooper flicked on the light and discovered a very neat room, decorated about the way you'd expect a bachelor to decorate a bedroom. The drawers contained clothes that looked as though somebody else did the folding; the closet displayed two dark suits and a reasonable selection of tropical leisure wear.

There was some milk getting close to the spoil date and a pair of Bud Lights in the fridge, but nothing else worth noting anywhere in the condo.

Medvez, who had not moved from his place against the doorjamb, said, "You know what you're doing, don't you?"

Ignoring the comment, Cooper made one last swing through, his tour concluding in the foyer, where the answering machine lay. He had the sense, from no specific evidence, that the man who'd been living here was no longer around—at all.

He jerked his chin at Medvez.

"Why don't we go see how vacant that warehouse is," he said.

Medvez shrugged and followed him out the way they'd entered.

Looking at the old building from the interior of the Mercedes, Cooper experienced a vision of being eaten by an alligator the minute he stepped from the car. There was just something about any partially developed area of Florida swampland—the look of the pines, the shrubs, the fat tropical leaves—that always gave him the sneaking suspicion there were some nasty critters laying low, looking for an easy meal.

Shrugging off his Yankee's sense of dread, he exited the car and crunched across the gravel parking lot—thinking, as he went, he'd have called it that, *gravel,* rather than dirt. Monitoring the edges of his peripheral sight with an eye wary for gators, he strolled the perimeter of the warehouse.

He found pretty much what the anchor had described: the aging wooden structure was built on undisguised landfill, and reached partway out into a narrow, swampy portion of the bay as a kind of wharf, the wharf's single, dilapidated dock offering little in the way of support. There was only enough latent light from the neighboring buildings for Cooper to see the exterior features of the place, but when he tried to examine the interior through the caked-over windows he found it a useless effort.

Cooper found a window with its lock hinge out of whack, fought the friction brought on by the couple dozen layers of peeling paint, and swung himself inside the rickety warehouse. He quickly found a light switch, and with the sound of a dying mosquito, a pair of tin-coned lights flickered on from the ceiling. He turned to observe Medvez climbing in behind him—the man unable to resist.

Between its rows of boxes and bookshelves—racked to the gills with yellowing paperbacks—the place looked to Cooper like a distribution center for the crap they put outside head shops. He saw painted wooden statues depicting various native peoples, totem poles, dark hardwood furniture, tables full of brass and cast-iron figurines, and stacks of large picture frames wrapped in protective material.

Cooper thought he detected something—it was very faint, but it was there, kind of lingering in the humid interior of the warehouse. Probably not the best environment for paintings and first-edition book collections. Also probably not so good for what he was afraid he smelled.

He came into a smaller back room, the part of the building that overhung the water, where he picked up on the heavy buzz of big freezers. In here Cooper saw the first evidence of a legitimate business operation run by El Oso Blanco's fence: a series of signs, labels, Ziploc bags, and low-slung freezers were all marked with a logo featuring a crab's claw and a slogan printed in red: Snow Country King Crab Legs, Frozen North of the Border and Brought Fresh to You.

From one corner to the other, Cooper thought—a nation of consumers on whom the concept of *fresh* had been lost a long, long time ago.

He was thinking it could have been the crabs he'd smelled, but knew it wasn't. He found a switch on the wall and got some more lights on. He opened, then rooted through the first of three big waist-high freezers, cutting his fingers a half dozen times on the frozen crab legs within as he moved them around for a better look.

It was in the second unit that he found, jammed in beside an otherwise fully stocked selection of plastic-wrapped imported king crab legs, the uncovered but completely frozen body of the man Cooper judged to be the stateside fence used by Ernesto Borrego.

He couldn't be sure, given the frosted-over nature of the clothes adorning the body, but it looked to Cooper as though there were at least a double-tap's worth of bullet holes grouped precisely in the vicinity of the late fence's ventricles. He brushed off some of the frost from the guy's face and confirmed his identity based on the couple of pictures he'd seen in the condo.

Cooper dropped the freezer lid. Medvez was hovering behind him.

"In case you were wondering," Cooper said, "I'm not particularly surprised."

"No? Well thanks for bringing me along for the ride," Medvez said. "Something I've always wanted to see—fresh-frozen art smugglers. Eleven ninety-nine a pound."

Cooper nodded dully.

Government affiliation or no, Cooper had a pretty good idea whose turn would come next. He flipped off the light.

"Come on, Mr. Nightly News," he said in the dark. "We get out of here quick enough, nobody'll know you did my detective work, and we might just be able to keep you off the list."

25

Laramie answered groggily.

"Yeah?"

"Rise and shine," came the familiar baritone. In her sleep-deprived state she almost slipped right into the routine, that voice feeling like a comfortable old shoe. She could sense his presence beside her, and thought of the sand they'd always felt in the sheets, no matter which resort they'd picked. Laramie stretched lazily in the sheets—

And snapped out of it.

"Christ," she said. "What time is it?"

She pulled herself up against the headboard.

"Early," Cooper said, "or late. Depending."

She confirmed this with a glance at the dim green numbers on the alarm clock in her room: 4:42 A.M.

"Up and at 'em," Cooper said. "If you don't get your tail out of bed pronto you'll be late for your seven A.M. breakfast meeting in Naples."

"I've got a seven A.M. breakfast meeting in Naples?"

"The Sunrise Café. Known for its eggs Benedict, though they serve a mean doughnut too."

Laramie got her head wrapped around things. She knew better than to say what she wanted to say—*So this means you've reconsidered our offer?*—or, better yet—*What are you doing in Naples?* Be wiser, she thought, to wait until they were face-to-face to pop her questions.

Still, she couldn't resist the temptation of at least one toe-dipping probe.

"And you think I'd be interested in driving, I don't know, an hour or so, at this time of the morning, why?"

"I happen to be in the area. I figured I'd do you and 'the people you work for' a favor. Save them some time—you know, in case they've started spinning their wheels in a vain hunt for the numbered account my initial extortion dough got siphoned into, or any of the many hundreds of investments my attorneys subsequently made with it, scattered around the globe like little financial Easter eggs. And don't get your hopes up on your own personal knowledge contributing to the hapless mission of the federal government finding any of my assets—just because we hung out some doesn't mean you have any more concept than the sea turtles south of Conch Bay as to where that money lives."

"Ah," Laramie said. *I knew I shouldn't have said anything . . .*

"Anyway," Cooper said, "since they're not ever going to find any of it, not in a couple generations' worth of IRS investigators, I'll save them the trouble and have a cup of coffee with you—as per your 'initial recruitment effort.' As to the driving part—among the reasons you'll need to be the one logging the miles is the fact that I'm not meeting you anywhere near the people you work for."

"Fine."

The phone line kind of sat there between them, part noise and part silence.

"You said you'll have a cup of coffee," Laramie said. "You drink coffee now?"

"Helps with the headaches."

"What are the other reasons?" Laramie said.

"For drinking coffee?"

"You said 'among the reasons'—that avoiding coming anywhere near 'the people I work' for was 'among the reasons' I'm the one who has to do the driving. Why else?"

She heard some kind of muffled sigh rumble from the receiver.

"Laramie, after our breakfast rendezvous, I'll be hopping back aboard my refueled speed machine and heading south. Conditions are expected to worsen as the tropical storm currently dumping six inches of rain on Cancún moves into the Gulf, so if I don't clear Key West by ten, said speed machine will wind up as fiberglass kindling somewhere near the halfway point of my intended voyage."

"What if the storm moves faster than that?"

"Then you'll be eating your granola alone."

Fair enough, Laramie thought.

"All right," she said. "Storm allowing, I'll see you at seven and brief you there."

"You can brief me all you want," Cooper said, "and I'll give you my thoughts on whatever it is you've got going. But if you were asking me then, and you're asking me now, and you ask me over coffee, to come work for whichever people it is you're working for now, I'm not interested."

A bonking rattle sounded out, and Laramie knew he'd dropped the phone on its cradle.

She leaned back against the headboard, allowing some of the fog to clear from her sleep-deprived brain. She sat there with her eyes closed for a minute, or maybe five, then flipped off the covers and rolled her feet off the side of the bed.

She wondered, as she stood, what the simplest way might be of procuring one of the task force fleet's black-on-black Suburbans at five in the morning.

"It's only a matter of time."

After swallowing the sip of black coffee he'd just taken, Cooper attempted and failed to determine what it was Laramie was talking about. He was certain she wasn't talking about what had slipped into his mind once she'd uttered the words.

"You want to run that by me again?"

"The caffeine addiction," she said. "You didn't used to drink any coffee. Now you look suspiciously like a two-cups-a-morning guy to me. Addiction can't be far behind."

"Maybe," he said. "But last I checked, there were a few other addictions chewing up most of my real estate. Not sure there's room for any others."

Cooper was feeling irritable—or highly uncomfortable, at any rate. Upon Laramie's arrival at the table, it seemed there had been a slight quickening of his pulse. It was a familiar sensation—familiarly annoying. He'd thought himself impervious to it, which was what made it so annoying: he had assumed his year-plus of rage at Laramie's decision to abandon him and his island way of life, coupled with the so-preposterous-as-to-be-humorous threat Laramie had made in her "initial recruitment effort," would function as a kind of force field. A moat.

Here he was, though, a mere three minutes into his breakfast meeting, and the force field had already disintegrated in favor of the same old quickened pulse. He thought of an imaginary wall suddenly detonating into a million digital pixels and the pixels fading to reveal an image behind.

"You're an asshole," Laramie said.

Cooper blinked.

"You're an infantile, inconsiderate, uncontrolled, obnoxious child," she went on, "in an aging, sunbaked, time-and-fisticuff-abused adult male shell."

She did not appear particularly incensed, or even emotional, Laramie just leaning forward with her forearms crossed on the table, telling him off over coffee. Cooper took a few slow sips, letting time pass, swirling the bitter, chocolately fluid around his mouth with each taste, depositing the cup on its saucer between sips to draw out the time between each sip-to-taste-to-swallow. Knowing there was more on the way from the analyst across the table.

"An adult human being," Laramie said, "would respect another adult human being's decisions and, despite such decisions being difficult and painful, or even hurtful, retain some sense of interpersonal decorum. Even a bratty child, taking a friend's tormented, thoughtful, deliberate decision to return to work *personally,* would *eventually* come to grips with his boorish overreaction and call, maybe apologize, or even, for Christ's sake—you horse's ass—*take* my goddamn call when I show the maturity and patience to dial up that goddamn beach club in search of you, knowing Ronnie's already been told to screen my fucking call."

Her words were delivered in so matter-of-fact a fashion that Cooper felt as though he'd tuned into one of the lower-rated local newscasts that competed with Ricardo Medvez's nightly displays of knowledgeable warmth.

Despite being in no mood to explain himself—despite never being in the mood to explain himself—Cooper said, "Hell, I called. Twice now."

"Popping your rude head above the surface after ducking me for a year is not the kind of 'eventually' I was talking about."

" 'Eventually' is a relative term," he said. "Subjective, even."

She looked at him for a while, still leaning on her forearms, but losing some of the detachment factor. A little color worked its way up the sides of her neck in pinkish splotches against her pale skin. He could feel the crackle in the air as she fought to keep the color beneath the collar of her blouse.

"Here's what's going on," she said.

Then Laramie started in on the sordid suicidal exploits of Benny Achar and the ramifications of his act as incurred by a hundred and twenty-five late and former citizens of Hendry County. She covered Achar's false identity, the reality and likelihood of what could come to pass if Achar were one of many, and the engineered version of the facts as presented in the news media. Then she told him she had been asked to head a counterterrorist unit whose purpose was to identify and possibly destroy Achar's comrades, if any, and those responsible for compelling Achar to action in the first place.

"So that's all," Cooper said.

Laramie ignored him and concluded with a brief explanation of her theory that Achar had meant to use his bomb-launched spread of the filovirus as a message—as bread crumbs for them to follow. She didn't mention the similarity between the counterterror strategy she'd outlined in her independent study paper and the organization she now appeared to be working for. Including Cooper's interruption, it took Laramie thirty-four minutes to lay out her briefing.

Since Cooper's fourth cup of coffee was giving him a headache, he ordered eggs Benedict from the menu. When Laramie attempted to wave off the waitress, Cooper asked the woman to bring Laramie an order of granola served with seasonal fruit.

"Skim milk, please," Laramie said before the waitress padded away.

When they were alone again, Cooper said, "That was interesting how you told the whole story of Benny Achar and your role in matters," Cooper said, "without mentioning who it was who put you on the case, or whose jurisdiction this 'counterterrorist unit' happens to fall under."

Laramie didn't say anything.

"Also," Cooper said, "I find it just as interesting when a five-foot-four female satellite intelligence analyst with smooth skin and tremendous legs tells me it has become her job to 'identify and possibly destroy' international terrorists. Perhaps," he said, "instead of offering you advice, I should loan you the gun I'm packing just east of my right hip."

Laramie leaned back slightly from the table and folded her arms across her chest.

"Wow," she said. "Was that your only-partially-infantile way of offering me an apology? The smooth skin and tremendous legs part?"

"I'm not sure I'd go that far."

"Knowing you as I do, which, I believe, is marginally better than you know yourself, I'll take it as your apology. I know it's all I'm going to get."

They were silent until the food came. Cooper was halfway through his breakfast, and Laramie one bite in on her first wedge of cantaloupe, when Laramie said, "So what do you think?"

"Of the Achar predicament, you mean?"

"Yes."

Cooper considered the query.

"Who do you have on your team," he said. "Your 'counterterrorist unit.'"

"I've been interviewing from a pool of candidates. Volunteers from various walks of life who've been background-checked to the hilt. Plus," she said, talking faster, "I've contacted a former professor of mine, who we'll probably bring on board."

Cooper looked up from his eggs Benedict with a look of moderate disgust. "You've got to be kidding me." He thought of something else to say, then decided his growing irritation with matters wouldn't be helped much by the nasty comment he had in mind, shelved it, and said, "And how is Professor Eddie doing?"

"He's doing fine."

Laramie left it at that.

"To give you answers," Cooper said, "or advice, I'd need to know more than what you included in your half-hour speech. Probably need to dig into whatever documents you've got—I don't know, transcripts of interviews, maybe whatever paper trail you've got on the guy back to whenever it was he first turned up under his false identity. I do have some experience in crafting a new identity, of course. But other than my own background, I'm not sure—"

"Wait a minute—unless you're skipping the boat trip, there's no way—"

"I thought you wanted my advice?"

"But I can't just send you off on your boat with a copy of classified files—"

"Sure you can."

"Look. You know I want—*we* want—*need*—your help, but it won't work if you're providing it from Conch Bay, or San Juan, or wherever it is you're heading on your boat."

"No? Well thanks for the breakfast, anyway. Always prefer to set sail on a full belly."

He waved for the waitress to bring the check.

"You can't just say no, or dictate how this is going to work," Laramie said, and Cooper could see the pink coming up her neck again. "You do understand that if Achar was one of a dozen sleepers, each targeting a vast water table or some other vital area, that thousands—even hundreds of thousands, or more—could die." She leaned in again, full of emotion for a change. "And you're just going to go back and lie out on the beach?"

"Actually," Cooper said, "yes."

She stared at him.

"Perhaps," Cooper said, "you and Professor Eddie can continue to work with your team of Salvation Army volunteers and solve your little riddle on your own."

The check came and Cooper deposited a couple of twenties on the tray without checking the total. He thought of a story he'd once heard about Frank Sinatra and Sammy Davis Jr.—outside a Vegas casino, Sinatra asks Sammy if he's got change for a twenty, and Sammy says, "Twenties *are* change, baby." Cooper couldn't remember who'd told him the story, or whether Sammy had been the one asking for the change, but he'd heard it a long time ago and it had stuck with him since.

"Listen—wait, you goddamn pain in the ass," Laramie said. She had reached her hand across the table but didn't quite touch his arm with her fingers. He felt their warmth, though, resting an inch from his wrist on the cool glass surface of the tabletop. "I can get you some of the documents in a diplomatic pouch. They'll be encrypted and I'll work out a way for you to get the code. But it won't be everything, and you'll need to weigh in quickly—if Achar's suicide bombing wasn't ordered by his employers, they may have discovered what he's done by now. Rung the alarm, I mean—and that could mean the other sleepers may be activated. We might have a month, a week—a day."

Cooper smiled without putting any heart in it and got to the business of setting the hook.

"I'll take a look at whatever you send me," he said, "and whatever you call to brief me on later. But I'll only do it if the people you work for are willing to make it worth my while."

"What?"

"I've got a deal structure in mind."

"Wait a minute, you did hear the part about the others *volunteering* to work on the team—are you actually saying you're looking to profit from a terrorist—"

"Yes."

She stared at him, silent, Cooper seeing in her look a hostile kind of pity, Laramie clearly upset with him for displaying such a lowlife's priority scheme. He found himself to be both thrilled and disappointed by the reaction. It was the way she'd made him feel from the beginning—like he was constantly getting in trouble for his rambunctious behavior.

"Here's what I suggest," Cooper said. "I suggest you take this back to the people you work for. Inform them that one of the members of your team would, upon further consideration, have ultimately decided to sign on for the sake of national security *pro bono*—except for the threat they suggested you make in hopes of coaxing me to join up. Since you, and they, went ahead and made that threat, I'm therefore going to charge whatever organization is involved for my services. Homeland Security? NSA? Somebody new? I don't give a shit who it is. You want my expertise— what little I have—it'll cost you. It'll cost you exactly what it cost our late, mutual former boss Peter M. Gates eighteen years ago, plus interest. Though because we know each other so well, I'll play nice and keep the interest to a nominal, even token rate of, say, four-point-five percent per annum."

"Christ," Laramie said, her look of pity now deteriorating to one of disgust. "What kind of money are we talking here?"

"Not much. What Pete paid was twenty years of salary beginning at the GS-14 level, including annual merit raises, periodic promotions, and the usual annual hazard bonus. Plus the interest, of course."

"You're kidding. I can't—"

"Did they know you knew me before they hired you?"

"What?" Laramie blinked, then glared. "Why are you assuming somebody else hired me?"

"You mean, somebody besides CIA?"

"Yes."

"They don't work this way—they don't give anybody the kind of authority it sounds as though you've been granted. Not anymore. Not unless you extort them into it, anyway."

He grinned.

Laramie sighed. "What does it come to?"

"Rounding off, we can just call it twenty million."

"Come on."

"I thought I was necessary?"

"Maybe I shouldn't have put it that way."

"Maybe you shouldn't have. I'll need it as a single lump-sum disbursement. I'll provide you the relevant numbered account into which they'll need to do the disbursing. And the account will vanish a few seconds after the money is posted to it, so don't get any ideas."

He thought for a moment, then reached over and retrieved the pen from Laramie's side of the table and wrote four phone numbers, all with the same area code and prefix, on a napkin stained with a splash of Tabasco sauce.

"You can find me at one of these numbers for the next eight days. Forty-eight hours per number; they expire and switch on a more or less annual cycle."

He handed her the napkin, stood, then promptly spun and walked off.

26

Cooper spent most of the ride home from Naples thinking through recent history as crafted by, or against, Po Keeler, Cap'n Roy, El Oso Blanco's stateside fence caught sleeping with the frozen crabs—and the anonymous killers who'd snuffed them out. Cooper thinking of them as *snuffer-outers*—the *snuffer-outers* who'd hired the killer Lieutenant Riley had shot on the hill beside Cap'n Roy's infinity pool.

He decided he would call Lieutenant Riley to see whether they'd found a ballistics match between the bullets that killed Keeler and the gun the assassin had used on Roy. He'd guess it'd turn out that way—as the body count added up, the game of connect-the-dots was getting easier. This much he knew: everybody who'd been offed to date had been immersed in the shipment, seizure, or resale of the gold artifacts stash. The list of duly immersed parties still among the living wasn't long—himself, El Oso Blanco, Lieutenant Riley and his staff, and Susannah Grant, whose involvement he estimated couldn't be traced. Either way, though, unless he found some way of identifying and taking down the snuffer-outers, chances were he and his surviving associates would soon show up in the dead pool.

He continued to find it odd there hadn't been an attempt on his life already, and if he could presume El Oso Blanco was continuing to chow down on a daily rotation of bucket-served take-out luncheons—which he should probably no longer assume—it was just as odd that Borrego too had not had the pleasure of an assassination attempt. He wondered whether it had been assumed by the killers that Lieutenant Riley would be scared into silence by his chief minister's murder, or whether Riley was being crafty about keeping an eye out—or possibly that the snuffer-outers just hadn't yet dispatched a second contract killer to take aim at the lieutenant. Still, if the snuff-out mandate remained in effect, Cooper figured Riley for third in line.

He and the Polar Bear would be vying for top honors.

It didn't compute, though, that the snuffer-outers, in wanting the trail of the gold artifacts stamped out, wouldn't have thought to kill the Polar Bear first. Maybe they hadn't known of the big man's involvement to start with, though Cooper found this unlikely—Borrego had been the one to kick-start the whole goddamn thing. Maybe Borrego was just a tough guy to kill—but that theory didn't hold water, particularly given the Swiss cheese security configuration at his Venezuela headquarters.

Could be, he mused, that the Polar Bear *is* the snuffer-outer—but however snugly the pieces might have fit for this answer, Cooper decided it was hogwash. There was nothing in it for Borrego, same as there'd been nothing in it for Cap'n Roy.

Despite multiple hours of theorizing, he kept coming back to the same conclusion. The snuffer-outers hadn't killed him yet because of who he worked for. Now that Cap'n Roy had been taken down, it was clear it wasn't just a government thing—the snuffer-outers obviously didn't mind taking down the chief minister of a small, though NATO-allied, island nation. They did, however—at least by his working theory—hesitate before snuffing out an employee of a federal agency of the good ole U.S. of A.

Meaning the snuffer-outers were probably U.S. of A. types themselves—specifically, U.S. of A. *government* types. Other hues fit the color scheme of this picture too: the contract killer, for instance, was the kind of man certain federal agencies of the Evil Empire would hire. Cooper thinking that if you threw in a botched assassination coup, the impossible survival of imprisonment and torture, a reverse-extortion scheme, and maybe a couple decades of sun and alcohol, then that contract killer would probably look reasonably similar to someone else.

Plowing through the crest of a fifteen-foot swell fifty miles east of Cuba, he found himself—following a few hours of brooding—in exactly the same place he'd started.

Cap'n Roy was dead. Somebody, probably somebody on Uncle Sam's payroll, didn't want anybody finding out about the antiquities stash El Oso Blanco had bought, sold, and shipped. Among a set of stupid, greedy people, Cap'n Roy had simply been unlucky enough to emerge as either the stupidest, greediest, or both—and got himself killed for it.

It struck Cooper that in case he were to find himself in a vengeful mood—*And when do I not?*—he'd need to find out who the snuffer-outers were. And unless he felt like yanking the stateside fence's hard drive from the marshfront condominium and spending a few weeks tracking down every single name on the man's electronic Rolodex, which he already knew wouldn't tell him a goddamn thing about the snuffer-outers anyway—

Hell, I'm going to need to go in the other direction.

The only problem with looking in the other direction was that everyone on that side of the equation was dead—except one: the six-foot-nine behemoth of a pale-skinned intermodal transportation kingpin called the Polar Bear.

Maybe if he gave El Oso Blanco a ring—test the man's claim that he actually returns his calls—the big guy could shed a little more light on the source of the artifacts. Something more than the way he'd put it in his office, slobbering across that bucket of pasta: *somewhere along the border be-*

tween Guatemala and Belize. Not a place Cooper preferred to spend his leisure time; not a place Cooper preferred to spend any time.

It didn't really seem to Cooper there was any other way of going about it—even if what Borrego had said was true, and they'd need to travel to the source to find the kind of specifics Cooper was looking for. He didn't have any fucking choice—not now, not after the ghost of the twelve-inch priestess statue had been joined in his skull by the wraith that was once Cap'n Roy Gillespie. Cooper hearing the greedy, stupid son of a bitch coming at him in two-part harmony with the equally annoying priestess—*'Ey, Cooper, we up here waitin', wrongly departed, and now you all we got. Oh, yeah, the truth shall set us free, mon, and then maybe we start to thinkin' 'bout settin' you free too!*

Looping past Anegeda into the Sir Francis Drake Channel, Cooper concluded there was a pretty good chance Cap'n Roy wouldn't be resting in peace anytime soon. That the chances were, following one last phone call that wouldn't yield a goddamn thing, "the spy-a-de-island," as the late chief minister preferred to call him, would just have to plan on watching his back a little more closely than usual—at least until the curse befalling all who came in contact with the shipment of gold artifacts and their annoying twelve-inch priestess had blown over and gone the hell away.

27

Laramie's diplomatic pouch beat Cooper home. As was generally the case when these things came, somebody—presumably Ronnie—had already brought it up and left it on his porch. Cooper presumed further that a courier had brought it to Conch Bay in the first place and been instructed to deliver the pouch only to him, but that Ronnie, or somebody on the staff, had convinced the courier to chill out at the bar, got him hammered, and sent him packing on whatever boat or pontoon plane he'd come in on.

Initially, Cooper ignored the pouch's presence on his darkened porch, ambling into his bungalow after seventeen hours on the high seas and plunging directly into his pillow for however long a snooze the goat-of-the-day would let him enjoy.

He awoke to the sounds of people and music, shocked by the midday illumination creeping through the jalousie panes, his first thought that the snuffer-outers might have succeeded in taking out the goddamn goat.

He checked his watch to find it was lunch, not breakfast, underway down at the Bar & Grill.

The restaurant's music selection always included the

same rotation of Caribbean-themed songs, but he never failed to find them pleasing to the ear anyway. The lifestyle many planned for a whole year or more just to ingest for seven nights—the sounds, the rum, the sun, the sand, the lapping waves, the fish, the reefs, the SCUBA and snorkel gear—Cooper took in every day of the year, and never grew tired of it. Never. It got a little more crowded every year—there seemed one less layer to the sheen every time you took a close enough look—but in his view, the British Virgin Islands could have trademarked the elixir bubbling up from every lagoon in the chain. It was the essence of the Caribbean—at least the essence of the part you could enjoy if you had enough money, or had decided along the way that money didn't matter all that much.

Maybe he'd call Lieutenant Riley and recommend the RVIPF apply for a patent—with Cap'n Roy gone they'd be needing a new revenue source.

Unaccustomed to his good mood but writing it off as the fruit of his long sleep, Cooper moseyed onto his porch, cooler today than usual, and eyed the diplomatic pouch. *Can't hurt to be prepared—just in case my preposterous $20 million request gets the thumbs-up from "the people she works for."*

"Ronnie!"

Cooper screamed this at considerable volume. It didn't take long for the ponytailed errand boy to wander over through the garden and approach the base of his stairs.

"Ham sandwich, conch fritters, bottle of Cabernet."

Appearing no more annoyed by the embarrassing form of summons as usual, Ronnie started off wordlessly, taking a couple steps down the garden path, then stopped, turned, and laid a quizzical, narrow-eyed look on the grizzled permanent resident of bungalow nine.

"Cabernet?" he said.

"Just get it."

Cooper took a seat, unzipped the bag, and withdrew the short stack of files from within. He set them on the floor, plucked the first manila folder from the stack, and started in on the recent and tumultuous history of Hendry County, Florida, and the opinions of the small army of people who'd examined that history since. Laramie had left a message on his sat phone with the decryption code.

When Ronnie came with his food and the open bottle of wine, Cooper poured himself a glass, took the first sip, remembered as he always did how much he didn't like the taste of wine as it first hit the tongue, then got himself through the predicament with a second sip and a few more in succession.

He ate, read, and drank. When he'd finished the last of Laramie's files, Cooper set it on the stack he'd already read and settled a creak deeper in the chair.

"Well, Benny Achar," he said aloud. "How do we find the old you?"

He thought a little of his own disappearance—an unwilling, unwitting one—and his subsequent reappearance as a man of his own crafting. A man with a made-up name, one with a new home, new habits, new neighbors—everything different. With no contact from the people or world of his past. Not that he'd had much of anybody around from before anyway, not by the time the ties with that old life had been severed, against his will or no.

Maybe that's what Benny Achar had faced. Back home, wherever home had been—maybe he didn't have anybody there. Maybe whoever he'd had in his life was gone. Dead, or killed. He must have had something, though—if only hatred, or anger, or misery—considering what he signed up to do. If Laramie was right about Achar's intentions—and Cooper knew Laramie usually turned out to be right—then Achar, as his new self, had possibly discovered the opposite: satisfaction, happiness, or better. And because of these new companions—maybe found by way of his wife and son— Benny decided to abort the mission. To send the warning; to lay the bread crumbs.

Cooper could relate to the satisfaction Achar may have

found in his new life—there was a measure of that for him here in Conch Bay, at least during the hours following a good night's rest. And he'd had another measure of satisfaction too—at least until the woman serving up the dose of contentedness of a sort he'd rarely known decided to cut off his supply and head back to the civilized world.

Ah, the civilized world, he thought, his musings made palpably clear by the effects of the Cabernet, *home to such nifty things as "counterterror units."*

He considered for a moment how somebody might go about unearthing *his* former identity. It wouldn't be too much of a challenge—the information wasn't exactly buried, covered up, or otherwise classified. He knew himself to be listed as buried—dead—killed, supposedly, in a plane crash that'd had nothing to do with the way he'd actually vanished. He supposed that somewhere, buried in some compartmentalized file cabinet, there would be documentation on the mission that actually got his fellow special-ops goons killed. The trip that had erased the old version of himself.

Maybe there was something to that—the part about his being officially dead. Maybe the real version of Benjamin Achar was dead too. In the same way he'd assumed the identity of someone who'd died, maybe he'd abandoned a similarly, if only officially dead identity he'd once worn around.

Or maybe there wasn't anything to it at all, and it wouldn't matter anyway.

Cooper observed that he'd polished off the sandwich, fritters, and all but a quarter inch of the last glass of Cabernet. He also observed that with the whole bottle of *vino* inside him, he was feeling pretty good.

Not quite all the way to satisfied, but still pretty good.

He swallowed the last swish of wine, found the fax Susannah Grant had sent him, and punched in her number on his sat phone.

She answered on the third ring, prompting Cooper to decide this was all the confirmation he needed. He clicked off—no need to heat up any of the bad blood from their aborted rapture session in Austin. She was doing fine, and even if her phone had its caller ID feature intact, she wouldn't know anybody besides RESTRICTED NUMBER had just called. The snuffer-outers would have got her by now if they knew about her.

Cooper punched in a second set of digits—the Caracas number for Borrego Industries. When he asked the receptionist to connect him to the Polar Bear, the woman shot back a terse reply, struggling as she had in person with her English.

"Who is this?"

Cooper felt a pit form in his stomach on hearing her tone.

"Tell him it's Cooper," he said.

"What does this regarding?"

"Just tell him it's Cooper."

She put the call on hold and Cooper waited. After about a minute, the call was answered by a man whose voice Cooper didn't immediately recognize, except that he recognized it wasn't Ernesto Borrego.

"Why are you calling here," the man said. He had a deep voice, almost as deep as Cooper's, with English as heavily accented as the receptionist's—along with a kind of masterfully projected audio scowl discernible to Cooper even across many thousands of miles of sky.

"Well, I called to speak with Borrego," Cooper said. "That would be why I asked for him."

"He is not available."

"I thought he was proficient at returning calls?"

"Proficient?"

"Expert. Good. Skilled—"

"I'm aware of the meaning of the word. Proficiency is difficult to achieve, however, when you are dead."

Crap.

"When?" Cooper said.

"Please. We have already notified the *policia* you have called."

"Well give them my regards—"

"You are the chief suspect in his killing. I suggest you turn yourself in to the authorities in Tortola, where you live."

Not quite, Cooper thought, but close.

"Yeah," Cooper said, "I'll do that first thing. Who is this?"

"Who do you think?"

"I bet you're the friendly neighborhood bodyguard who took my gun," Cooper said.

The velociraptor paused at the other end of the line.

"Sí," he said. "And I will take it again if you show yourself here. Only I will use it on you—not give it back."

"Good luck. I'm a suspect because I came by for my visit last week?"

"You're a suspect because you shot him."

Cooper said, "I need the names of the tomb raiders Borrego bought the gold artifacts from. The Caracas shipment that was headed for Naples. Borrego told me you would give them to me."

"Bullshit. And I wouldn't tell you even if he told me to. You know what? I will kill you myself," the velociraptor said. There came a muted *pfft* sound, which Cooper assumed to be the sound of the man spitting. "I'll kill you with my own hands. I know where you live."

Cooper wondered whether Borrego's thug had spit on the floor, or a desk. He also wondered whether this guy had been reading too many comic books.

"Been tried before," he said flatly, and hung up.

Between the long run on the beach in Naples and the longer boat ride home, Cooper was experiencing a kind of dull ache in what felt to him like every joint in his body. He wondered whether it was really the run and the ride. Maybe it was something else, like the wine. Maybe, he thought, I need to live on a longer beach, where I can take a long run every day, without needing to turn around for another lap every five hundred steps like I do here. Or maybe what I really need is to find another beach, long or short, where the paradise isn't relative. At least not yet.

Where I don't wake up after a rare morning of sleeping in—only to learn I'm next up in the dead pool.

Maybe there's a beach like the one I'm thinking of in

Tahiti, or Fiji, or Malaysia. Maybe there's a spot where I can find a different bungalow, make up a new name, and finally accomplish the fucking escape from insanity I tried to pull off nineteen years ago. Maybe I'll even be able to find, in that place, a total absence of the memory, phone calls, and predicaments of Cap'n Roy, Po Keeler, the Coast Guard, this fucking twelve-inch golden idol on my shelf, that goddamn Polar Bear, the Polar Bear's stateside fence and his king crabs—even an absence of the other guy with a made-up name, good old Benny Achar, who'd blown himself up, killed a hundred-plus Floridians, and annoyed a government agency or two in the process.

"Or maybe I wouldn't find anything different at all," he said, and shouted out for Ronnie to bring him another bottle of wine.

28

When he sold his third paperback, Wally Knowles bought the place in New Hampshire. A rambler with two bedrooms and one small bath, the size of the place topped out around six hundred square feet. Nineteen acres of forest had come with the house, though, and almost four hundred linear feet of the property nosedived straight into Sunapee Lake. Cost him $62,900, which price he paid some eight years prior to the time people started realizing the ski-resort town of Sunapee was as good a place to hang out in the summer as in winter—and began paying ten times what Knowles had paid for his whole property just to snatch up an empty half-acre building site.

His wife left him two weeks before he bought the lake house. Having come to agree with her view of his unimpressiveness, Knowles, who for his third novel got a $75,000 advance—his first of any kind—decided he'd better figure out how to live as cheaply as possible. He'd have to, if for no other reason than the measure he'd just undertaken to address his escalating midlife crisis: upon signing his divorce papers, Knowles promptly resigned from his $38,400-a-year job as public defender in the Bronx and went ahead with his plan of writing for a living. He put a chunk of his advance down on the house, wrangled a thirty-year fixed rate mortgage to cover the rest, and on the day of his closing found himself observing the view from a lakefront home, in which it would cost him $208.71 per month, escrow included, to write for just about as long as he damn well pleased.

Had she not been killed before a dose of positive karma struck her ex-husband, Mrs. Knowles might have come to regret saying, in the divorce, that "she didn't want a red cent" and relinquishing the fifty percent interest she could have taken in her husband's "pesky little books." Book number five, it turned out, seized the second slot on the *New York Times* best-seller list its first week in print, and did not relinquish a place in the top five for nearly three years. Thirteen million copies sold. This led, among other things, to sales of just over six million copies of his first four titles.

Knowles did not regret for one instant having retreated from life as he'd known it. As the only African-American for miles, a man with a penchant for black suits, black Ray-Bans, black shirts and ties, a black ten-gallon hat, and no interest whatsoever in conversation, Knowles was known, simply, as "the black guy on the lake." Although he'd heard the descriptions of him change, over time, to something like "the author," the fact remained that despite his success, people still considered him an odd duck and a half.

And that suited Knowles just fine.

As "the black guy on the lake," Knowles, by choice, had a lot of time to himself. He spoke to no one but his editor, but nonetheless spent most of his time assembling computer systems, database subscriptions, satellite and high-speed cable connections, and virtually any other gadget which, for most, normally assisted the process of communication. For Knowles this collection of toys and access served a different purpose: it allowed him to keep clear of everybody and anybody while still remaining abreast of everything. Knowles, for example, was the first individual not affiliated with a university to possess an Internet-2 connection, initially an exclusive, multiple-university-controlled next-generation high-speed Internet. Armed with the roster of research services and corporate intranets to which he belonged or had access, the novelist liked to think he could find out anything, or locate anybody, faster than any other civilian.

When his wife was killed, Knowles engaged in two main actions. First, suffering from a four-month case of writer's block, he utilized his equipment to bury himself in research and news. He learned everything there was to learn about those who had wrought their fury on his ex-wife, those who had failed to protect her, and the government's plans for retaliation. His blood pressure skyrocketing, fury his constant companion, Knowles sequestered himself in a single room in his lake house. Movies ran repeatedly in his mind's eye—films depicting his ex-wife arriving in her office at eight-thirty as usual, going about her usual morning, maybe having a look out the window of her office with the kind of view of the city you only found from the 103rd floor of One World Trade Center. The films always ended in the same way, of course—white paper, floating everywhere. Gray clouds billowing to earth, roiling outward, then up again. Toward the end of the four months in that one room, Knowles devised the plot of the novel that would become his breakthrough hit, but above all, he realized he still did carry a torch for the woman who'd been his wife.

The other action Knowles took, he shared with a man named Dennis Cole.

Cole was a homicide detective for the NYPD, 23rd Precinct. Cole had once liked to keep his day to a little under eight hours, maximum, so he could spend as much time as possible with his new wife. Cole's junior partner was hungry enough to pick up the slack without saying anything. It wasn't long, though, before his partner didn't have to pick up any slack at all—Cole started staying late, coming in nights when there wasn't any work to do, finding just about any reason to avoid the fact that Cynthia Cole was staying out one hell of a lot later than her duties as a bond trader required. After two long years of made-up expensive dinners, gala events, and—though Cole chose not to face this—a great deal of fucking that did not include her husband, Mrs. Cole demanded a "trial separation."

Unlike Knowles, who initially hadn't minded particularly when his wife left him, Cole pined away for Cynthia like nobody's business. It was after her separation from him that he started in on the bottle—though this was just the beginning. The fact that Cole was pining away for his wife meant, among other things, that when she failed to call in or make it home from work on that second Tuesday in September— that when she failed to show despite Cole's descent into the hell that was downtown on that day, and when she failed to emerge, in full or part, following Cole's statuesque, indefatigable presence irrepressibly visible over the course of three full weeks in the triage unit a block from ground zero—it meant that Cole had been able to convince himself that it might still have worked out.

If, that was, the 767 with its topped-off fuel tanks hadn't pulled the plug on her supposed desire to reclaim his embrace.

Literally right after the funeral in Stamford, Cole got back to work—a morose ride on Metro North into Grand Central and he was back at it. Picking up the pieces from the three unsolved murder cases he and his partner had been served before twenty-eight hundred murders happened all at once a few blocks down the street. He broke all three cases with a vengeance, becoming one of the most deadly effective homicide investigators on the force. In the year that followed, he cracked his cases at the rate of one hundred percent— sixteen for sixteen.

After hours was another story.

When he wasn't on the job, Cole, a five-foot-eleven-inch, two-hundred-and-ten-pound former athlete of a man, behaved more or less like a bulimic teenager. Starting sometime approximating 5:01 P.M. each day, Cole drank, ate, and

then—between the hours of three-thirty and five A.M.—
purged. He drank so much at night, so consistently, that his
aching liver demanded a postmidnight caloric intake sufficient to nourish an elephant. This, in turn, led to an early
morning ritual, of which he partook with savage consistency: just prior to four, he would stumble down the hall in
his one-bedroom shithole walkup in Queens, usually rising
from odd, ever-new places in the apartment where he'd
passed out the night before. Sometimes falling and denting
various bones on the hard surfaces in the bathroom that was
his destination—sometimes smacking a knee on the floor or
a shin on the edge of the tub—every morning, he roamed in
there and loudly vomited his guts out.

It always seemed his traumatized body had failed to digest
even an ounce of the food and beverages he'd consumed
hours before, all that food and drink just hanging around his
belly waiting to be ejected. And eject it he did. Painfully.

His stomach expanded over time, becoming first soft, then
thick, then monstrous, until the weakened muscles around
his ribs became little more than a source of stabbing pain as
he repeatedly blotched his guts into the 1930s-era American
Standard nobody had seen fit to replace because the fucking
thing kept working just fine.

It was in approximately the same manner, at approximately
the same time, that Cole and Knowles expressed their common rage in an uncommon way. During the same week in
early January—four months to the day on which they'd lost
their ex-wives—each man composed his own letter to the
Central Intelligence Agency.

Knowles's note was more eloquent, but the point in each
was the same: Knowles and Cole each expressed, in approximately one and one-half pages of handwritten text, a desire
to serve his country. Each told the story of his murdered
wife, of his desire to retaliate. Each confessed a suspicion he
was too old, that it was too late for him to volunteer as a sol-

dier, at least in the strictest sense. Thus, each man said, the logical choice of service was either the intelligence or, more specifically, antiterror ranks of the federal government.

In the years that followed 9/11, Cole and Knowles were not alone, and CIA was not the only recipient of such offers. Both CIA and FBI recruiting personnel, obsessed as they were on developing HUMINT assets fluent in Arab languages and cultures, tended to simply keep such letters on file, occasionally offering the names of the volunteers to other inquiring agencies.

Following repeated interviews, deep background checks, and some in-person monitoring of day-to-day routines, it was precisely because of each man's rage, and the letters that rage spawned, that Dennis Cole and Wally Knowles came to be included in the pool of names from which Julie Laramie had been instructed to assemble her "counter-cell cell."

A former TraveLodge gone private, the single-story
motel had been given a fresh coat of paint, a sickly beige
that drew a strange contrast with the trademark blue-and-
white "sleepy bear" still standing vigil above the lobby entrance. The billboard beside the bear proclaimed the place
the Flamingo Inn, though the old TraveLodge insignia could
be seen peeking out from beneath the new name, which
somebody had painted in pink with a sweeping cursive flour-
ish. The bear, chipped and fading, still wore his blue paja-
mas and nightcap out front.

With the help of her guide, Laramie had procured two adjoining rooms as an office, opening the door between to
connect them. In one of the rooms they moved all the furniture except one table against a wall, then added some folding seats and the armchair they'd discovered in a closet.
Toss in a dry-erase board retrieved from LaBelle's only
office-supplies store, and they had themselves a poor man's
war room.

Wally Knowles wore a black linen suit, black loafers, and
Ray-Bans. He sat on the bed with his legs crossed, his trademark black hat on the bed beside him. Dennis Cole, who'd

chosen one of the folding chairs, came in jeans, a green polo shirt, and a seersucker blazer. Laramie's guide sat just out of sight in the adjoining room doing something on a laptop. She knew he would soon be leaving to retrieve their third recruit of four from the airport—a tenured professor of political science at Northwestern University named Eddie Rothgeb.

Rothgeb was the professor with whom Laramie had worked on her two independent study projects—as well as a few other things maybe she shouldn't have. Bringing him to the table wasn't exactly a move that put her squarely in the comfort zone, but he was the best at what he did and his was an expertise she could use right now.

Laramie had also been given the green light to pay Cooper—recruit number four, as her guide had called him upon relaying the message from Ebbers, or whoever it was who made such decisions. There had been no questions asked and no negotiating: twenty million bucks, approved with little or no red tape, for a single man. She decided she'd have to ponder the meaning of that later, but one thing it meant was that somebody—CIA, NSA, DIA, FBI, DEA—*whoever*— was taking the antics of Benjamin Achar very seriously.

Meaning that the guests of my little convention here at the Flamingo Inn aren't exactly gathered to suck down piña coladas by the pool.

Overnight, each had been given an abridged version of the terror book, inclusive of some of Laramie's conclusions, which Knowles and Cole had read in the privacy of their respective rooms at the inn. Rothgeb, she mused, should be listening to his version right now.

Laramie stopped fiddling with the dry-erase marker she'd been holding.

"So," she said.

Cole raised his eyebrows and dropped them. Laramie thought of the way she remembered Tom Selleck doing this on reruns of *Magnum, P.I.,* except that she remembered Magnum being a lot better-looking than Cole.

"You might have wondered initially why you were summoned here," Laramie said. "Or why you were asked to read the package of documents with no explanation or preamble. That was intentional. The document you read last night is this incident's version of a 'terror book,' aka murder book, as it is usually known in domestic homicide cases. We didn't explain it in advance because we wanted you to form your own impressions. To give weight where you chose to give weight, to consider circumstances the way you naturally would upon reading the document."

She grabbed hold of the dry-erase marker again, popped off the top and tacked it back on again with her forefinger and thumb. She'd rehearsed parts of this speech but had ultimately decided to more or less go with the flow.

"You've each volunteered your services in defense of the country. You've been screened for suitability and liability and, for now at least, you've passed. Congratulations. You now work for me. I work for someone else. The man in the other room keeps an eye on all of us; he also gets us what we need. There will be another member of the team arriving here shortly."

To the extent the $20 million fee would buy his time, Laramie had decided to use Cooper in the way you were supposed to use field operatives—secretly. She wasn't yet sure how they'd be putting him to use, and until she'd figured that part out, she wasn't planning on telling the other members of the team about his involvement.

"Operating alone, in whatever degree of secrecy one finds at the Flamingo Inn, here is what you will now be asked to do," she said. "Despite the indirect references to the contrary in the terror book, we are operating under the assumption Benjamin Achar was not acting alone. We are assuming that five, or ten, or twenty or more fellow deep cover operatives are living within our borders under assumed identities, armed with an equivalent stash of Marburg-2 filovirus and the wherewithal to disperse it over a much wider zone than Achar succeeded in reaching."

There came no expression from Knowles, whose sunglasses remained planted on the bridge of his nose, the man a poker player.

"I'll anticipate some of your questions because we don't have time for process particulars. We'll work out of this motel for now. Food and laundry services will be provided. There are rules, but we'll get into that later. You are now, but only temporarily, members of a miniscule, clandestine counterterror unit. That oversimplifies it, but it's the closest and best explanation. We have support personnel who will perform back-room investigative work—research, fingerprint matching, forensics and other technical analysis, if needed. There is an operative available to us for investigative work, surveillance, or certain preemptive acts as needed. You could also look at it this way: you have just joined a counterterrorism video game already in progress—or board game, if that helps the translation for any of you as old-fashioned as me—except that it is real. Our combined role in the 'game' is simple: we use the clues, tools, and ingenuity available to us to identify and stop Benjamin Achar's fellow sleepers and the individual or organization who sent them."

Knowles cleared his throat and Laramie inclined her chin in his direction.

"The difference between the definition of 'counterterror,'" he said, "and 'antiterror' centers around proactive measures designed to preemptively combat the terrorist threat—you're proactive in 'counterterror,' reactive in 'antiterror.' I assume your choice of words reflects and considers this fact. Do we have a commando team in this tool kit of ours?"

Cole frowned and made a sighing sound.

Laramie said, "If you're asking me whether part of our assignment is to kill the enemy, I'm not entirely clear on that. Our actions may lead to that, however, so if you have any problem—"

"No problem here," Knowles interrupted.

Laramie nodded. When Knowles passed on following up

with more questions, Laramie gestured with the dry-erase marker, first toward Knowles, then Cole.

"It is anticipated that you, Mr. Knowles, may function as the chief scenario builder, and that you, Detective Cole, would contribute primarily as an investigator. The third member of the team is a reasonably well-known diplomacy and foreign affairs professor who has consulted with the federal government from time to time. He will assist us in narrowing the list of likely nations, or people, who might have sent the sleepers here. Despite this general orientation, there are no titles, there exists no hierarchy besides my leadership, and there are no lines dividing your roles."

She set the marker lengthwise on the table like a tower and took a sip from the latest in a long line of bad cups of coffee. For once, she didn't feel much need for the caffeine. She swallowed the sip and replaced the coffee on the table beside the marker.

"Unless you convince me otherwise," she said, "we will be operating under the theory that Benjamin Achar did not make a mistake in blowing himself up or dispersing the amount of pathogen he did. According to what his wife revealed to me—which you would not have seen in the terror book—Achar told her to be prepared to hide for 'no less than seven days' if anything happened while she was out of town with their son. He knew he was going to do what he did when he did it, and I believe he also knew how much filo serum it would take to do some damage but not cause a plague."

"Used his flare gun," Cole said gruffly.

Laramie couldn't quite hear.

"Sorry?"

"He used his flare gun. Fired one into the sky for us to see. Saying, 'Look what's about to happen if you don't do anything about it.' So we can do something about the others. That's the way I read it too."

"Really," Knowles said. His tone was laced with sarcasm—indicating very clearly he believed Cole was playing the role of teacher's pet, adjusting his theory to get some extra credit. Laramie saw Cole steer a challenging look at the author. Thinking she was already being made to feel like a day care supervisor, Laramie addressed Cole.

"Then I suppose you'd also agree," she said, "that if the whole explosion was a flare gun, he probably left some firecrackers lying around too. Or bread crumbs. Depending on the analogy."

"Yes," Cole said, holding his evil eye with Knowles.

"Second question," Knowles said. Loudly.

"Second answer," Laramie said. "Maybe."

Knowles almost appeared to Laramie to have smirked, but if he had, the movement of the straight line that was his mouth vanished as quickly as it had come.

"How much do you know about the lies in the media?" he said.

Laramie waited, considering her answer.

"Not much," she said. "Why do you ask?"

"I don't have a lot of faith in your average reporter," the author said, "but maybe you can help me here. I study the news like religion, and I can tell you with assurance that there has not been one single leak of the facts as they've been shown to us in the 'terror book.' I find this an unlikely if not impossible set of circumstances. Except, that is, if the so-called crisis you've dropped us into is nothing more than an exercise."

Laramie almost smiled at the very serious Wally Knowles.

"I'll agree, it does seem unlikely," she said. "My introduction to this incident came six days ago in almost exactly the same way you're getting this intro now. Is it an exercise? Same question I asked. Answer: it could be. I don't know. I no longer think so, but you'll have to judge for yourself."

"I always do," he said.

Cole pulled his glare away from Knowles.

"How about you?" Laramie said to Cole. "Any questions? Doubts? Challenges?"

"None," the cop said.

"If he has none," Knowles said, "I'm happy to move things along. There is no evidence—paper, photo, or image—of Achar's existence before January 1995?"

She gave his question, and her answer, some thought.

"No," she said, "none we've got."

"Idea, then," he said. "We'll need five or ten photographs of Achar to do what I'm thinking—ideally, spaced out over the past ten years, so we get shots taken of him at various ages. We'd also need a computer with high-speed access, and permission from whoever has kept the lies intact to hook into my home system."

Laramie waited to see whether her guide would appear in the doorway between rooms and acknowledge Knowles's requests. He didn't.

"An image search?" she said.

"Correct. Two companies and a series of universities have been compiling a national image database along with an accompanying search technology. The database includes video. I'm in possession of the beta version of the search engine, but searches can only be conducted by computers with Internet-2 access, which I have, but only at home. The only images that will show up are those that have been archived into the national database, of course. But ours is the age of the camera, and that was true eleven years ago too."

"Meaning he could have been photographed, or videotaped, by somebody, somewhere, in his prior identity," Laramie said.

"Yes. The search engine is rudimentary and it's been claimed that three percent of the world's images have been digitally archived to date. My guess? It's actually far under one percent. But worth a search anyway."

"Assuming," Laramie said, "all this is true—not an exercise."

"Yes. Assuming that. But either way, it's a good idea."

One the task force hadn't thought of, Laramie thought. *At least not that they revealed to me.*

"One thing people do to you when you're a cop," Cole said from his chair, "especially when you're working a homicide, is lie."

Laramie, day care instructor that she was, rotated her attention to the cop.

"Mostly people do it at first," he went on, "then give in after a while. Eventually, they all want to confess—in one way or another."

He seemed to leave it at that, Laramie getting the idea he didn't intend to go on.

Knowles spoke, brimming with sarcasm again.

"And?"

Cole shrugged.

"I think it happens because everybody's carrying secrets around," he said, "and in their everyday lives they've grown used to keeping them stashed, like cash under the mattress. In a murder investigation, we're basically turning lives upside down and shaking, so we can see what falls out. At first, people try to hold on to their secrets at all costs. I'm talking the stupid ones—totally unrelated to the murder most of the time. Like how many times a guy who's married says he's talked to a girl he likes. But once you call their bluff and break through the first layer, they tend to get suddenly comfortable, and start confessing everything they've ever lied about. Like they'd paid for the interview by the hour. Like all along they had to get it out."

Laramie waited for more, but Cole appeared to have completed his train of thought. Knowles—strangely, Laramie thought—began nodding with some enthusiasm.

"You're saying Achar didn't appear to reveal who he was, but that maybe he did," he said. "To somebody."

Cole nodded without looking over at Knowles.

"Guy's whole life was a lie. He had to want to tell at least some of it to somebody. Even if he didn't plan to leave any bread crumbs besides the so-called suicide mistake, chances are he left some anyway. And if we're right about the flaregun theory, he probably tried more than one way to tell us about what he was up to. I'd like to get my eyes on all the videotape you have on him too, get a look at the man in life—but where I'll be able to do my best work is to conduct, or re-conduct, all relevant interviews myself."

Laramie said, "You mean anybody interviewed by the task force?"

"Yes. Everybody. Nothing against the FBI, CIA, the rest of the task force, or you, but when I can, I prefer to do my own work. I might be able to learn what he was trying to tell us if *I* talk to the people he told—I'll have a better chance at it anyway as compared to reading transcripts."

"I'll see if we can get you started today."

Laramie stood, and on the dry-erase board wrote two lines in its upper-left corner: *Internet-2 image search* and *Re-interview all*.

"I've got a few other thoughts," Cole said, "in case you want to hear them."

"You've got a lot of thoughts," Knowles said.

Cole didn't acknowledge the author's comment. Laramie had a fleeting thought that the day care dynamic was only going to get worse once Rothgeb showed up. Considering the much sharper turn for the worse things would undoubtedly take were she to plug Cooper into the equation, she quietly thanked herself for keeping their "operative" compartmentalized.

"Have at it," she said to Cole.

"Birth certificate thefts," he said. "I'd start in Mobile, where Achar got his, then maybe expand outward. Didn't see anything about the task force looking into it, though I can't believe they wouldn't have."

"Not sure," Laramie said, then, climbing the learning curve on Detective Cole, figured she ought to finish the thought Cole was likely to leave hanging. "So you're saying we check and see whether more than one birth certificate was stolen from the place where he grabbed his?"

"Yeah. And other places. Problem is, when the kind of

birth record he used is taken, sometimes there isn't any record of it being there in the first place."

"We should go the other way and look at the deaths," Knowles said.

Cole rotated his head to take in Knowles, considered what he'd said, then nodded.

Laramie wasn't grasping it yet.

"Little help?" she said.

"What—"

"It—"

They'd both started speaking at the same time, then stopped. Laramie almost flinched in anticipation of the argument she figured would ensue.

"Go ahead," Cole said.

Knowles nodded. Laramie raised her eyebrows.

"It doesn't do any good for our kind of guy, a sleeper," Knowles said, "if he's stolen the identity of somebody who's alive. The way it's done—at least the way I understand it— is you swipe the birth certificate, or just use the Social Security number, of a dead person."

Catching up, Laramie said, "Nobody's around to argue that you don't exist."

"Yeah." Cole took the baton. "The most effective way to do it is by stealing the Social of somebody who died young. Would just make the most sense either way for it to be somebody born twenty-five or thirty years ago."

"So there isn't anybody still, what, actively grieving for him?"

"Well, yeah, that too, but what I'm talking about is the records. Last couple of decades, most jurisdictions have been keeping an electronic copy of birth certificates and death records in the same system. Before that, you could be born and die in the same town and the only record of either event was buried in separate files in different buildings. Plus you're getting the age right on the Social Security number. But maybe the most important thing is, if we're talking an early death—such as the real Benjamin Achar's death from SIDS—there isn't any significant record of life that'll register with the federal government based on the Social. In many cases, Socials weren't issued to children until they were six, eight, ten years old. Not until recently."

Laramie considered this.

"So if you're Achar, or his employers," she said, "you steal a birth certificate from some town hall, making sure the person whose certificate you're stealing died young. Preferably before the electronic-records era. And then, what, you apply for a new Social Security card using the birth certificate?"

"That's right," Knowles said. "Or get a new one. Say you lost yours—or they never gave you a number to begin with. And what *we're* saying is we could find some Socials to check up on, doing it the same way Achar might have chosen *his*—by digging out names of people who died young in the same time period as the real Benjamin Achar, and checking to see whether their Socials have, after a long gap, eventually popped up on recent credit reports or tax returns."

Laramie reached back and wrote *Birth certificate thefts—dead—Mobile/other* as their third note on the board, but was already thinking through some of the problems presented by this investigative strategy before she finished writing the words.

"Lot of dead people to check on," she said, "in a lot of places. Plus we'll need to find the deaths how? From town halls?"

"Libraries would be better," Cole said. "In old newspaper files stored on microfiche."

"Whole thing adds up to one hell of a thought, Detective," Knowles said.

Laramie almost laughed out loud at these guys. She said, "Might test the resources of the support personnel we've got at our disposal, but it certainly is an interesting idea."

Laramie noticed the salmon-colored hat first. She then realized what it was—her guide was standing in the doorway between the rooms.

"Headed for the airport," he said, then thrust a thumb over his shoulder. "I set up some coffee and bagels in twelve. Door's open."

"What," Laramie said, "no doughnuts? We've got an officer of the law here this morning."

Cole swiveled his head to observe her guide—interested, Laramie thought, in the answer, and thereby confirming the truest of all stereotypes.

"No worries," her guide said with a half-assed grin. "They're even Krispy Kremes."

Cole turned back around.

"I assume you heard the last part of our conversation," Laramie said. "Can you accommodate that too?"

"We'll get some investigators on it starting now," he said.

Knowles stood and put his hat on.

"As chief scenario builder," he said, "I'd say it's a good time to get some chow."

"Hear, hear," Cole said.

The homicide cop rose and followed the author out of the room.

Laramie succeeded in waiting for both of them to leave the room before snorting out a laugh that wouldn't stop for a while.

30

One of the more influential people Laramie encountered at Northwestern University—in ways both good and bad— was the sandy-haired, ageless professor of political science with the round, wire-rimmed glasses and piercing blue eyes whose name was Eddie Rothgeb. Before you got to know him, he was Professor Rothgeb, or maybe, if you were feeling loose, Ed. Only a few people came to call him Eddie— among them Laramie, Rothgeb's wife, Heather, and the professor's two sons. Laramie often excused certain things that had happened between her and Professor Eddie by labeling herself as too young and too stupid to know better.

Once Laramie and her guide retrieved Rothgeb from the airport, her guide—at Laramie's request—deposited her and Rothgeb at the Krispy Kreme. She asked her guide to wait outside while she spoke with Rothgeb alone.

He looked the same. He always did. He even dressed the same—exactly the same, as though the jeans, V-neck sweater, blazer, and Converse All-Stars were a uniform the university required him to wear. Even his neatly trimmed beard, she decided, was exactly the same length as it had been the last time she'd seen him.

Rothgeb selected an original glazed, which he began consuming in small pieces, breaking them off while he sipped from a decaf mocha. Laramie thinking, *Me and the rotating band of coffee-shop sissies, sampling oversweetened coffee concoctions from north to south.* He sat before her at one of the restaurant's Formica tables while Laramie worked through another cup of full test, having decided, on hearing Rothgeb's order, to forgo the milk and sweetener.

Somebody's gotta be a man about this coffee thing.

"So," she said, laying out her usual opening. "I'll begin this with a question."

Rothgeb broke a piece from his doughnut and chewed it with some moistening help from his mocha.

"All right," he said.

"How do you catch a sleeper?" Laramie said. "And I mean a real one—not some recent Arab immigrant with a heavy accent and a card-carrying membership in a radical mosque, but one who's long since embedded himself. A deep-cover operative, awaiting orders, displaying no apparent affiliation with the people from whom he awaits orders, having long ago established a fully legitimate fake identity. How do you catch him—how do you even find him?"

Laramie's guide had arranged—she didn't ask how—for Rothgeb to listen to a one-play-only MP3 file on a portable device during his flight from Chicago. The content of Rothgeb's file included Laramie's findings and theories at the tail end of the recording.

The professor tilted his neatly trimmed head to the side, pondering the question.

"You know," he said, "twenty years ago, this was considered a rampant problem." He drew out the word *rampant* as though it were a curse that he relished using. "I've heard it speculated that hundreds, if not thousands, of Soviet sleepers are still here, having stayed on, as Americans, after the collapse of the USSR. Stayed asleep—or awakened, I don't know how you'd put it."

He broke off another piece of doughnut but did not lift the

piece to his mouth nor say anything else—an academic, lost in a sea of his own complex thoughts. Laramie, growing weary of the verbal fencing it took to get these guys to share what they were thinking, said, "And?"

"Well, we've never been good at stopping this. I'd love to recommend some sleeper-busting specialist I've met along the way, but either such experts retired along with the sleepers or I just don't know the right people. Maybe whoever it is you're working for now could track somebody down."

Laramie spun the Styrofoam cup of coffee slowly between her hands, wondering idly how it was everybody seemed to know she wasn't doing this for CIA.

"Well," she said, "instead of tracking down any such specialist, the people you're referring to decided to recruit . . . *me*. Though maybe they called me additionally, and they're working with some other specialists separately. You never know."

"No," he said, "you don't, do you?" He ate the broken-off piece of doughnut, which wasn't much of a mouthful. "But your Benjamin Achar was similar to the Soviet sleepers, at least in the way they were rumored to have been positioned. Assuming he wasn't some American ex-con running from a shadowy past and looking to emulate Timothy McVeigh, you'll need to consider that he was *trained* in all things American. Mannerisms, accent, job skills, and so forth."

"But not the inclination to buy a pickup truck," Laramie said.

Rothgeb blinked but otherwise ignored her comment. "Point being, there would have to be a facility, or facilities, where Achar was trained. And unless they only had this one agent, it'd be logical for the trainers to need to cycle instructors through, and to put more than one student together for the training sessions."

"An Americanization campus," she said, and took a swallow of the bitter, undiluted coffee. "There was a novel written about that, wasn't there?"

Rothgeb nodded. "Nelson DeMille. Maybe a check of

satellite intel on terrorist encampments could yield a clue as to its whereabouts, presuming it exists in some visible place."

"I think I've examined enough SATINT for ten lifetimes, but that isn't a bad idea," she said. "Wherever it is they trained is likely to have been abandoned long ago, though, isn't it?"

"Because he's been here for ten years? Still," he said.

"Yeah. Still."

She took another sip.

"How have you been," she said, and thought, *Now is when he clams up*.

Rothgeb shrugged. It was an uncomfortable gesture for him to make, in that it was imprecise. Everything else, the man did with precision. The shrug came, she suspected, because he needed something to do while avoiding the question, without being too obvious about it.

"Just fine, I suppose," he said. Coming dangerously close to the last of his diversions, he broke off another piece of doughnut, ate it, took a leisurely sip from his coffee, then said, "It's our weak spot, you know."

Laramie looked at him. "Sleepers, you mean."

"Yes."

"I would tend to agree we're vulnerable," she said, "but what do you mean?"

He ate his next-to-last bite.

"We still haven't learned to adapt. The big bureaucratic machine engineered to battle the Soviets needed to redirect itself and focus on someone else, somebody specific. So once some new group hit the radar, the machinery targeted it: al-Qaeda. Palestinians. Internally, certain Arab-Americans or Arab immigrants, as you say. We mobilize the big, slow machinery, get set up to fight people who look like that, or come from there, and hope the power steering works."

Laramie nodded absently.

"You think about the business of spying, though," he said, "and it's all about immersion. So here we are mobilizing to attack, while the smarter enemy is busy immersing themselves in our culture. Assimilating."

Laramie watched his eyes and his mouth as he spoke. She remembered soaking up his words, and watching him say them, while she was immersed in her new life in Evansville. Now, listening to him rant on like the self-absorbed academic he was, Laramie wondered whether she'd made the right move in bringing him here. Maybe that was the real reason she'd stopped by the Krispy Kreme before bringing Rothgeb to the Flamingo Inn: maybe she wanted to make sure it wasn't too stupid an idea. Adding a pompous blowhard to the mix might spur stimulating debate in their "war room," but she had her doubts he would help them pinpoint strategies and action plans. Which is precisely what it was going to take—if there were anything at all to be done.

Too late now, Laramie. You brought him here, your guide retrieved him from the airport—you going to send him home already?

Besides—he's already hit on something.

"You still read spy novels as much as you used to?" she said.

Rothgeb smiled neatly, the motion more compact and precise than the unwieldy shrug in which he'd earlier engaged.

"Aren't as many good ones as there used to be," he said. "But I still partake of the occasional best-seller."

Laramie slipped the plastic lid back on her half-drunk cup of coffee.

"Then let's head over to the Flamingo Inn," she said. "You're in for a treat."

31

The velociraptor's name was Jesus Madrid.

Madrid was currently functioning as interim business manager of Borrego Industries. As with his late boss, he worked with no pretense, but lived lavishly—there was, it seemed, a great deal of money to be made in the shipping and fulfillment industries.

At the end of each of the six days since Borrego's disappearance, Madrid followed approximately the same luxurious routine—one he would follow on this day too. At the conclusion of the workday, Borrego's driver chauffeured Madrid to the spa he and Borrego frequented, and Madrid did as he always did there: shower, hit the sauna, subject himself to a full-body deep-tissue massage, subject himself to twenty minutes of rapture with the masseuse who'd deeply massaged his tissue, shower again, and return to the car. He listened to a jazz playlist on an iPod nano in the back of the car, waited while the driver pulled into one of Borrego's take-out joints to retrieve an order of spicy tuna sushi rolls for him before ferrying him home.

It was closing in on ten-fifteen when the driver, armed with the remote, opened the gate to Madrid's estate and navigated the quarter-mile driveway that took them up the hill to the mansion. Madrid's home was a misplaced English Tudor of just over eight thousand square feet featuring numerous amenities—seventeen plasma screens, for instance. As he had the night before, and the night before that, Madrid retreated to the master bedroom to change into his workout gear—black spandex pants; Asics running shoes; a tank top with *BI SECURITY* stenciled across the chest—then retrieved a bottle of Gatorade from the Sub-Zero fridge in the kitchen and came downstairs to his workout room.

In size and feel, the room resembled your average suburban health club, outfitted with a circuit of weight machines, barbells, dumbbells, the latest in cardio equipment, and one glaring exception from the norm: a floor and wall design aimed at re-creating, in miniature, the soccer pitch used by Madrid's favorite team. The field was Old Trafford Stadium, the team Manchester United. The surface of the floor, painted with penalty and goal boxes and a midfield stripe, was covered wall to wall with the latest in artificial turf technology—FieldTurf—its green plastic reeds of imitation grass longer and softer than prior generations. As was well known among football and soccer pros who played on it, though, if you were tackled into FieldTurf, it would still give you nearly as wicked a burn as AstroTurf had.

This turned out to be unfortunate for Jesus Madrid, since Cooper—having observed the velociraptor's routine for a couple days running, and stolen in here to nab him—decided from his place behind the water cooler that his best means of subduing the Polar Bear's bodyguard was to offer up a reciprocal tackle-and-pin maneuver.

Cooper got his full body weight planted into the small of Madrid's back, pulled the velociraptor's arms around behind him, and pile-drove the man chin-first into the turf.

"*¡Hijo de la gran puta!*" Madrid spat.

Cooper pretzeled both of the man's wrists against opposing shoulder blades and stabbed a knee into the lowest vertebra in Madrid's spine. With the hand that wasn't occupied,

Cooper snatched his Browning from his waistband and secured the velociraptor's chin to its spot near the top of Trafford's penalty box, barrel of gun to rear of neck.

"Ain't payback a bitch," he said.

Cooper wore a blue-and-green Tommy Bahama short-sleeved shirt featuring a recurring pattern of parrots and palm fronds, khaki shorts with deep pockets, and his travel sandals. He allowed himself a look around the massive workout room.

"You built a weight room on a soccer field?" he said.

"*Sí*," the velociraptor said. "Old Trafford Stadium. Man United."

"Man United, eh," Cooper said. It occurred to him that Conch Bay's staff of soccer-loving Brits, most of all Ronnie, would appreciate this odd expression of untold wealth better than he. "You know, you're doing pretty well for a bodyguard. Especially for an incompetent one."

A kind of grunt came from the tall FieldTurf beneath Cooper's hand.

"Pretty safe guess," Cooper said, "Borrego was having you handle a few more things than physical-protection services, he paid you like this. But I don't care what else you are. It occurred to me that your mildly late, but highly effective appearance in Borrego's office during my visit was a couple notches too casual. Born, the way I saw it, of endless and constant routine."

"So what?"

"Just saying I'm guessing you were always around the man. Everywhere he went. All the time. Including the trip to Central America the two of you took to buy the artifacts Borrego was shipping to Naples."

Even though he hadn't really asked a question, Cooper, upon gaining no response, angrily mashed the barrel of his pistol into the musculature of the velociraptor's neck and sharpened the prod of his kneecap on his spine.

"Who'd you buy them from, where'd they get them, and how do I find these people?" Cooper said. "Start answering."

He thought he heard Madrid say something, pushed the Browning a little deeper into his captive's neck, heard another mumble that lost itself in the turf, then, ticked off, Cooper stood all his weight on his knee and said, "Say again, motherfucker!"

Madrid turned his face from the blades of the turf with a grimace.

"I said it's not that simple!"

"Go on."

"*Maldita puta,* this fucking turf hurts," Madrid said. Then, turning his head another quarter inch toward Cooper, the velociraptor appeared to Cooper to smirk—or at least a corner of his mouth performed an upward curl, whatever expression was intended. "We had a pretty good idea you'd be paying us another visit. So we're ready to answer your fucking question. Just not like this."

"No? Why not? I kind of like the way this conversation's arranged."

Despite enjoying his reply, Cooper found himself mildly disturbed by the velociraptor's use of the word *we.*

"Because, *gringo,* there's somebody else you'd rather talk to about it than me."

"Yeah?" Cooper felt a slow sinking sensation in his stomach—he'd been had.

"*Sí,*" the velociraptor said. "What's the expression you Americans use? Better you hear it 'from the mouth of the horse,' I think?"

"Close enough," Cooper said, already knowing what was coming before the bodyguard said the rest.

"Then you and your expressions probably agree it'd work out better," Madrid said, "if you get your answers *de la boca del Oso Blanco.*"

Cooper sat there for a minute, planted as he was on the velociraptor's back. Thinking he was getting pretty good at being taken to the cleaners.

From the mouth of the Polar Bear.

Doing it quickly so as not to lose the edge, Cooper stood

and stepped back, keeping the Browning pointed at the velociraptor.

"On your feet, then," he said, "Mr. Man United."

Madrid drove about the way Cooper figured Dale Earnhardt Jr. did, wending around so many bends at speeds registering near 140 kph on the speedometer of his BMW M5 that Cooper began to think he'd need to break down and take a dose of Dramamine for the first time in his life. Despite the speed, the velociraptor wasn't frantic in the way he drove—listless, Cooper thought, was a good way to put it, Madrid about as enthusiastic about the many gear changes, braking, and acceleration leaps as the driver of an airport rental-car shuttle might have been about his wheel-bound duties.

It took about twenty-five minutes for the M5 to deliver them to a lower-middle-class neighborhood at the base of a long hill, the place maybe four hundred times wealthier than ninety-eight percent of Venezuela but with tiny homes, built too closely together on narrow, unkempt lots, Cooper tagging it immediately as a place where the police didn't get much cooperation from the residents.

A dozen long blocks from the thoroughfare they'd come in on, the velociraptor zipped the M5 around a final series of turns, slowed, then pulled almost daintily into a short driveway beside a slovenly, two-story house with a dilapidated Spanish-tile roof.

Madrid triple-flashed his high beams as he parked.

The place, Cooper observed, had "safe house" written all over it. Good pick of locations for it too—nobody in this kind of neighborhood bothered you much, asked you anything, or otherwise got in the way of whatever you felt like doing. Cooper thinking maybe *he* should consider a spot like this—it's missing a beach and a few snorkeling holes, and there's no hammock, porch, or dock, but what the hell: Lieutenant Riley and friends wouldn't bother him here, would they?

The velociraptor took them to the side door, which was

answered by a pair of men who looked vaguely like Madrid—at least the way Madrid looked while on duty, each of these guys sporting a suit and tie and exuding a quiet sort of menace. They did look a bit stupider than the Polar Bear's A-number-one man, which quality they quickly exposed when both men failed to mask their surprise at the somewhat effeminate workout gear their boss had shown up in.

The twin looks of mild shock were quickly concealed and the men parted. The velociraptor came into the house between them; he didn't give his men any evident signal to take down Cooper, so Cooper followed him in. In the kitchen, the lights were bright and the shades drawn. In here, another four armed bodyguards were playing a card game at a folding table that looked as though they'd brought it solely for the purpose of the game. The four guys watched Madrid, Cooper, and one of the doormen swing through the kitchen and down into the basement through a door beside the fridge.

While oddly misplaced, the bottom floor of the dilapidated row house was supremely outfitted. A widescreen plasma set looking somewhere north of a hundred inches wide played, in silence, an action movie featuring a submarine and a series of torpedoes chasing it. Within and beside the TV cabinet were multiple decks—DVD, stereo, and otherwise—along with a tower full of CDs and a case of face-out DVD boxes. Cooper recognized most of the titles.

The television was playing silently, since the sounds of the film were being monitored by Ernesto Borrego by way of a fat set of earphones. The headset's coiling connecting wire stretched, limply and partially airborne, to a plug on the face of one of the many decks in the TV cabinet.

The Polar Bear ignored the presence of Cooper and his security men until the climactic moment of the scene he'd been watching played to fruition. When the submarine had avoided the torpedoes, Borrego depressed a button on the remote control he'd been holding, removed the headphones, and turned to Cooper.

"Wondered how long it would take," he said with a flash of those sharp yellow-brown teeth. "Not long, turns out."

Since none of the Polar Bear's crack security staff had seen fit to take away his gun, Cooper racked a bullet into its chamber and pointed it at the couch-bound Borrego.

"I've got a few questions," he said.

"Ask away." As usual, there wasn't any discernible tension in the Polar Bear's tone.

"I was thinking of taking you up on your spelunking offer," Cooper said, "when it turned out you were dead. So I thought I'd come see your guy here, and see if I might compel him to tell me the things you wouldn't before."

"You mean the answer," Borrego said, "to your question of who I bought the artifacts from."

"And the additional question," Cooper said, "of exactly where the sellers found these things. Plus how any of this might explain why somebody's killing everybody who had anything to do with the loot."

"I think we've got the same questions," Borrego said. Cooper was enjoying the Polar Bear's no-nonsense manner. "And I do know a little more than I told you—but not a lot. We'll still need to go find them—the sellers, I mean—in order to find out the rest."

Cooper surveyed the behavior of the velociraptor and the doorman. They hadn't noticeably moved and didn't seem particularly on edge.

"What made you think I'd show up?" Cooper said.

Borrego shrugged.

"You struck me as a sharp cookie."

"No doubt," Cooper said. "Why else?"

"I believe I told you I found it odd I hadn't received a call when the shipment didn't show in Naples. After you left, I tried to reach my fence. Couldn't. I had a vague idea as to his preferred list of buyers—always a good thing not to rely too heavily on a middleman—so I called three or four of them. Also not reachable. Missing—dead, I expect. Like my fence. Caught the story online in the Fort Myers papers."

"A story broken first on the nightly news," Cooper said, "by one Ricardo Medvez."

Borrego thought for a moment, digesting this.

"You went there, then," he said.

Cooper nodded. "Found his body. Frozen in an icebox beneath a couple hundred pounds of Alaskan king crabs."

"In Florida?"

"Fresh frozen," Cooper said.

"This Medvez a friend of yours?"

"Wouldn't really call him that."

"You gave him the story, though."

"Maybe you're doing the killing," Cooper said.

The Polar Bear didn't shift, fidget, or change expression. He didn't say anything either.

After a while, gun still drawn, Cooper said, "If it isn't you, I don't really see any other way of finding out who the snuffer-outers are, and why they're taking people out, besides paying a visit on whoever it is who found the artifacts and having a look at whence they came."

" 'Snuffer-outers'?" Borrego said.

"That's what I've come to call them."

Borrego considered this.

"Snuffer-outers it is, then. Incidentally, you should know," he said, "that we may not find a thing."

"Maybe so," Cooper said.

He backed up, shuffled one step to his left, and kicked the place on the doorman's hip where the man had been keeping his gun. As Cooper had suspected from the drape of his jacket, the gun, a fat, black automatic pistol, hadn't been housed in a holster, so it dislodged from its spot in the waistband, sort of leaped up into the air, and clattered to the floor. Cooper retrieved it and placed both it and his Browning beneath his own waistband.

In no rush, the Polar Bear disentangled himself from the leather sofa and rose.

"Jesus and his boys will pack a few things for us," he said. "We can leave in the morning. You want us to find you a place to sleep, or do you still suspect me of doing the snuffing?"

Cooper said, "I'll take that M5 Jesus just parked in the driveway and bring it back in the morning. You an early riser?"

"See you at six," Borrego said.

He inclined his chin in the velociraptor's direction and Madrid tossed Cooper the keys.

"Hasta mañana," Cooper said on his way up the stairs.

32

Cooper took the call when he saw the area code on the caller ID readout display the same number he'd used to invite Laramie to breakfast. Ordinarily, there was nothing remarkable about his taking such a call, but since Cooper did so while seated aboard the Borrego Industries Gulfstream G450, winging it over the Caribbean to Belize, he found the clarity of Laramie's voice mildly surprising.

"Your proposal has been accepted," she said, "and the payment wired. You can call whoever it is you need to call to confirm the wire."

The pilot hadn't warned him not to use the phone in the air, and neither Borrego nor Madrid made any motion to stop him now. Cooper knew that the prohibition on the use of standard mobile phones on commercial airliners was horseshit—the weak wireless signal had no effect on an aircraft's instruments—but he wondered about the signals sent by a portable satellite unit.

Cooper thought he'd choose his words carefully—no need for the Polar Bear and his lieutenant to learn anything they shouldn't on the topic of the Emerald Lakes affair.

"Enjoyed the book you sent," he said. "A real thriller."

It only took a short pause for Laramie to say, "You're not alone?"

"Nope. But it doesn't really matter. Seems to me your boy Benny did one hell of a job leaving his real self in the dust."

"That's your analysis? That our sleeper hid his true identity well? You aren't exactly giving the federal government its money's worth."

"You getting your money's worth from Professor Eddie?"

Another pause, slightly longer this time, then, "He's working at a slightly lower pay grade. But we do have some ideas, so I'll be in touch. I was going to recommend you get going on the reading, but it seems you anticipated the government's response."

Cooper said, "I know that you can be very persuasive," then wondered immediately why he'd have said something like that.

"Sometime in the next two or three days, I'll be calling you back with the rest of the team on the line. It may be sooner rather than later if an assignment crops up."

Cooper eyed the landscape passing a few miles beneath the Gulfstream jet.

"I may be a little busy," he said. Thinking of something, he pulled the phone from his ear and regarded the caller ID numerals. "I can reach you at this number?"

"Room eighteen."

"I'll be in touch," he said, and broke the connection.

The pilot came on over the intercom and informed his trio of passengers they should buckle up for the descent into Belize City.

Belize, a tall, skinny nation occupying the western edge of the Caribbean Sea, rests just south of the technical demarcation between the Caribbean and the Gulf of Mexico. Cooper had been here a few times, mainly by boat and mainly to dive along the country's celebrated barrier reef. What he'd seen gave him the impression of a landlocked Caribbean island: dark-skinned locals, colorful paint jobs on weather-ravaged buildings, fishing boats everywhere you turned.

After a brief taxi through Philip S. W. Goldson International Airport, the G450 cooled its jets before a private hangar, where Cooper observed a waiting two-vehicle convoy consisting of a black Cadillac sedan and a dull yellow jeep. Upon closer inspection, Cooper observed the jeep to be a Land Rover Defender, probably worth a hundred and fifty grand outfitted the way it was. If nothing else, Cooper thought, considering the M5, the Land Rover, and the Gulfstream, the top brass of Borrego Industries certainly did travel in style.

It turned out the Caddy was merely there for the driver of the Defender to hitch a ride home; upon handing the key to the velociraptor, the guy—looking to Cooper like Derek Jeter's long-lost brother—hopped into the sedan via the passenger-side door and it sped off across the tarmac. Madrid opened the luggage hatch on the side of the plane and set to transferring their bags to the back compartment of the Defender. The man, Cooper thought, seemed endlessly willing and able to accomplish any task, of any type, that Borrego didn't want to tackle himself. Hell, Cooper thought—pay me as much as Borrego probably pays good old Jesus, and maybe I too would be happy to sign on as a multihyphenate comrade.

When Cooper came down the stairs and hit the tarmac beside Borrego, the Polar Bear smiled.

"This is us," he said, and motioned for Cooper to join him in the Land Rover. As Borrego offered him the passenger seat, Cooper was thinking of shooting for a bout of politeness when he noticed the setup in the rear of the Defender. Beneath the vinyl top, just aft of the jeep's roll bar, sat a custom-built throne resembling something between a Recaro racing seat and a La-Z-Boy. The seat's color scheme matched the exterior of the jeep, black and muted yellow, and there were sealed baggage compartments on both sides of the seat, into which Madrid placed the last pieces of luggage. Once the velociraptor locked them, it was hard to tell the compartments were there—they simply appeared to be part of the jeep's floor, raised as it was to accommodate the special design of the throne. Cooper assumed there were some monster fuel tanks built into the vehicle too.

The three-hundred-plus-pound Borrego hopped over the side of the jeep without opening the driver's-side door and climbed nimbly into the back, Cooper thinking of *The Dukes of Hazzard.* He located a cooler, dug out a bottle of Gatorade, and plunked it into the movie-theater-style cup holder built into an armrest in the throne. The Polar Bear seized and buckled his seat belt, took a long pull on the Gatorade, and—once Cooper had clambered into the passenger seat—popped open the cooler and offered him a beverage.

"Why not," Cooper said, and palmed the cold plastic bottle.

Madrid slid behind the wheel and bounced them out of the airport.

After a pit stop by the Polar Bear at a quasi-governmental building near Belize City's sprawling container docks, Madrid piloted the Defender through a series of narrow streets and the kind of colorful, worn-out overcrowdedness Cooper had grown accustomed to seeing in the Caribbean and points south. They made their way out of the waterfront district, Cooper turning for one last look out the rear of the Defender at the cool blue Caribbean, obscured somewhat by a forest of industrial piers but still there, making him feel good. The velociraptor sloped them up a highway ramp and Cooper watched the tall cranes of the container terminal fade into the distance.

He asked the enthroned Borrego where they were headed.

"Kind of a laundromat for cars," Borrego said. This, between chugs of Gatorade. He bent down between bumps in the road, returned his empty bottle to the cooler, brought a new flavor out, twisted off the top with two fingers, and put away half of it. "Belize City's maybe the third or fourth most corrupt port in the Americas. Maybe every two months or so, a regular shipment of—how does Lexus put it?—'pre-owned' cars comes into the docks, probably a couple hundred vehicles in the hold. Comes in at night. The customs agents policing the docks don't seem to mind as the shipment is divided and loaded aboard six or seven smaller ships. The smaller boats hit a few ports around the region to unload their abbreviated load of Honda Accords, where people like the people we'll soon be visiting clean off the VINs and send them on their way."

"And this," Cooper said, "has what exactly to do with the artifact shipment?"

"The tomb diggers I bought from are all working at the laundromat."

Cooper considered this.

"Day jobs," he said.

"Right. I stopped by the port authority first because we need to find out where the laundromat is operating today before we can get there. Normally," he said, "the port authority personnel taking the payola to keep that sort of information quiet don't exactly part freely with it."

Cooper eyed the outskirts of the city as it passed by along the side of the highway.

"But some of those containers back at the shipping terminal," he said, "are yours?"

"Most."

Cooper nodded. He didn't exactly need to whip out a calculator to assess how easily Borrego, as the local shipping kingpin, could glean the whereabouts of the "laundromat" from the "port authority personnel"—each of whom, he supposed, Borrego was probably paying two or three times their salary in cash just to keep them friendly.

After an hour on an increasingly winding, thinly paved, oft-cracked highway, Borrego dug into his cooler and began distributing triple-decker club sandwiches. He explained that the facility they were visiting lay just outside a seaside village called Dangriga, known for its enormous lobster haul.

"Be good to stick around for dinner," he said, wolfing the sandwich as he spoke. "Nothing like a four-pound Belize lobster."

Cooper didn't argue.

A couple miles past the Dangriga town line, Madrid hauled ass onto an unpaved side road that climbed into the hills. Cooper was about to toss his half-digested turkey club on the velociraptor's lap when a towering, razor-wire-tipped cyclone fence appeared on the right-hand side of the road—along with some buildings, mounds of squashed cars, and a series of other, less identifiable structures, all lurking behind the coiled edge of protective fence.

Not your usual used-car lot, Cooper thought, but maybe a hell of a place to blank-slate some late-model American sedans for redistribution around the globe.

Madrid found the entrance, a gated break in the fence, and pulled the Defender alongside a pole-mounted mesh speaker with a white button on its face. Madrid punched the button with his left hand; Cooper noted the proximity of the velociraptor's right hand to the holster on his hip.

"Yeah," came the static-ridden sound of a man's voice from the speaker.

"We're here to visit some friends," the velociraptor said in crisp English.

After a brief silence, the voice said, "Who that?"

Madrid rattled off four names Cooper hadn't heard before.

A longer silence ensued. When Madrid appeared ready to speak up again, the voice from the box said, "Only one of them here today."

"Well," Madrid said, "we'd like to see him."

"He agree you friends, I ask him?" came the voice.

"Sure," the velociraptor said. "Just tell him it's the Polar Bear."

Another pause. "The Polar Bear."

"That's it," Madrid said.

Cooper had long since caught the security camera peering down at them from the top of the gate. He expected the voice wouldn't need to ask whether they were cops, since the Land Rover couldn't really be mistaken for a Belize City PD cruiser.

A click and whine sounded out as the gate swung inward, opening with a jerky but consistent pace, as though it ran on rusty chains. Madrid brought them inside as though he knew where to go, though Cooper suspected he didn't. A thick-jowled man with deeply brown skin, wearing a pitted-out T-shirt and grubby jeans, emerged from a kind of lean-to not far from the gate. Cooper found it interesting that the man did nothing but stand and observe the Defender's progress.

Madrid parked in an open patch of dirt beside the junk-yard's main building, a huge prefab corrugated-aluminum structure Cooper figured a strong wind would knock down. He also figured the building could easily be relocated in half a day if you knew how to take it down and had a flatbed truck handy to do it with. A partially shredded blue tarp dangled like a curtain over its main opening, so you couldn't see inside but could push your way in with a brush of the hand. Madrid led the way in, having a look around before holding the tarp aside to allow Borrego to pass.

Cooper ducked in behind the Polar Bear and found his senses immediately assaulted by the sights, smells, and sounds of an auto-body shop. Maybe fifteen men of varying ages worked on different parts of different cars in different stages of repair, the activity taking place in clumps, almost like a virtual cubicle environment—workstations divided by function but not walls. And while the work continued without pause, every man in the place, in his own way, took careful stock of their arrival. Cooper took stock in return—black, white, and brown faces alike, some of them adorned with welding helmets, some in baseball caps, others in overalls, or plastic ponchos splattered with different colors of paint—all of them wore the hangdog slouch, that edgy angle of repose common to guys on probation or parole.

Giving the impression of lazy indifference but ready to bolt on a dime.

One of the laborers stood off to the side, welding torch idle in his hand, helmet tilted back. To Cooper the guy looked Guatemalan, but he wasn't sure whether his idea of Guatemalan was accurate.

Borrego waved to the man with a kind of cocksure effusiveness that immediately dispelled the air of skeptic tension from the army of ex-cons. By the time he shook hands with the Guatemalan, everybody seemed comfortable in his own skin again, and the pace and noise had kicked up a notch. Cooper and Madrid followed Borrego over but held back, close enough to listen but not to participate.

As Borrego shook with him, the Guatemalan covered his face with his off hand and sneezed. He wiped his nose with the back of his wrist, which caused Cooper to notice the red chafing around his nostrils.

"Mierda," the Guatemalan said. The conversation, which Cooper understood perfectly well, continued in Spanish. "Sorry—been sick as a dog."

"Yeah? We'll get you some vitamins, you want," Borrego said. "I've got a guy in the city'll take care of you, vitamin pouches that'll turn you around in a day."

"No gracias," the Guatemalan said. He held up his hand. "I'm getting better. Can't say the same for the others."

"No?" Cooper appreciated the way Borrego held a conversation, speaking as though he got what the man was saying when he clearly had no idea what the guy was talking about.

The Guatemalan lowered his voice and Cooper pretty much had to read his lips to understand his next words.

"It's the curse," he said. "The goddamn curse."

Borrego laughed. "Come on," he said.

The Guatemalan wasn't quite shaking, but he definitely had the look of a cornered mouse. Seemed to Cooper Borrego wasn't the cat he was scared of—Borrego was everybody's buddy, including the Guatemalan's.

"That where your pals are—out sick?" Borrego said.

"Sick?" The Guatemalan chirped out a nervous laugh. "Shit, Oso—they're dead."

Cooper felt a gut-twinge as his concentration locked in. He assumed Borrego was experiencing a similar pinch.

"How?"

"I'm telling you, Oso, it's the curse. You know—the kind they tell you about in museums? Strange shit taking out anybody fool enough to raid an ancient king's tomb. That's what we got, getting those artifacts we sold to you. Fuck! I've been in bed for a week. And I'm the lucky one."

Cooper heard Borrego say, "So they were sick, like you."

"They were sick all right. And they caught it from that fucking town. The caves. That isn't how they died, though. Not all three."

"No?"

"It was bad luck. Kind of bad luck you get from a tomb-robber's curse. Radame was shot, got killed by a stray bullet in Dangriga. Eduardo too. They were together. Caught in the middle of some gang shit—"

"I get it," Borrego said, and turned his body slightly to look over at Cooper. Cooper raised his eyebrows and shook his head half a shake.

"All right," the Guatemalan said, "but you wanna know how Chávez bit it? Got hit by a fucking bus, that's how. Fucking school bus, and there weren't even any kids in the thing. Dumb luck. Bad luck. The fucking curse. I'm lucky I survived so far."

"Could be just that," Borrego said. "Dumb luck."

"Could be, but lemme tell you—I don't care. I'm out. Retired." He motioned with his left hand to the welding torch in his right. "You see this? This is what I do, and this is what I'm going to keep on doing. This or something like it. Nothing like the other shit. Not anymore."

Borrego clamped a paw on the Guatemalan's shoulder. The guy flinched but didn't bolt, Cooper thinking maybe because he couldn't with Borrego's grip planting him in place.

"I can understand how you'd feel that way," Borrego said. "And since you're now out of the business, I'd like to ask you something I don't normally ask."

"Hey," the guy said, "whatever you want."

"I want you to tell me where you got it," Borrego said.

"You mean the shit that came with the curse?"

"Yeah," Borrego said. "The shit that came with the curse."

"Hell, I'll tell you exactly where it is. I kept the map in my bag 'cause I figured there'd be more. You know, that we didn't get it all, 'cause nobody's been up there. Not before we went and probably not after. So I was thinking, before the curse got us, I'd be going back. Not now, though. Fuck!"

His last F-bomb came out a little loud—a few of the ex-cons flicked their eyes in Borrego's direction to check whether anything was developing.

The Guatemalan lowered his head.

"I should have known," he said, more quietly.

"Should have known what?" Borrego said.

"Should have known we'd all get the curse."

Cooper could see Borrego's face since he'd turned his body earlier in the conversation. He watched as the Polar Bear narrowed his eyes.

"Why," he said.

"Because everybody else had the fucking curse," the Guatemalan said, "that's why."

"Everybody else where?"

"In the place where we found it."

"Who?" Borrego asked.

"All of them," the Guatemalan said. "Could have been a thousand years ago—I don't know. I just know they were dead. Every one of them."

Borrego said nothing. Madrid said nothing. Cooper continued to say nothing. From behind one of the mostly painted cars Cooper saw the figure of the heavy-jowled guy with the pitted-out T-shirt appear. It was unclear how he'd come into the building, but Cooper supposed it didn't particularly matter. He wasn't there to ambush them—he was there to pressure the Guatemalan to get his ass back to work. The Guatemalan felt the man's presence and swiveled his head to take in the sight of his super.

"You want me to get you the map, then?" he said to Borrego.

"Be great," the Polar Bear said, and lifted his paw from the Guatemalan's shoulder.

When the Guatemalan returned from his locker with the rumpled piece of paper, Borrego took it, but not before handing the cornered mouse a chunk of bills, the denominations of which Cooper couldn't quite read. Then the man moved off and blended back into the shop.

Without any visible prompt from Borrego, Madrid strode purposefully to the heavy-jowled super, handed the man another chunky wad of bills, then came back and led them out through the blue curtain.

When they were situated in the Land Rover, Borrego leaned forward in his throne and clamped down on Cooper's shoulder with that big fat paw of his.

"Don't know about you, *amigo*," he said, "but with all this talk of curses, I've got myself worked up into a four-pound-lobster kind of mood."

33

The Guatemalan's map suggested a route that, on paper and highway alike, may well have been the most convoluted possible means of approach on their destination. Nonetheless this was the route they took—nearly six hundred winding miles, some of the way paved but most not, the first four hours spent worming their way out of Belize, the remaining twelve dedicated to working their way around, then up, what Cooper decided had to be one of the more treacherous mountain ranges north of the Andes.

"They're good," was all Borrego had told him in answer to Cooper's objection to the length—and path—of the line drawn on the map. "They know what they're doing."

"The dead tomb diggers, you mean?" Cooper said.

"Yes," Borrego said.

"You say so," Cooper said.

Around sunset, they hit a rebel checkpoint.

It had been eight hours since they cleared the Guatemala border crossing. That had been fluid—show your passports, hand over some cash, and away you go, Borrego explaining nobody was looking to keep people out of Guatemala, since anybody who came in was usually a tourist ready to spend some money. Check out the Mayan ruins, drop some coin on a guide or two—there existed no reason for the authorities to concern themselves with the pesky issue of border control, at least on the immigration front.

The challenge, Borrego explained, came at the rebel checkpoints.

The leftist rebel groups in Guatemala had been soundly defeated by American-backed government forces in the mid-1980s, but had more or less never given up. As a sort of consolation prize they had claimed certain remote regions of the country as their own, and been allowed to do so—mainly because almost nobody lived in the areas they'd been sequestered to, and even fewer people wanted to go there. Accordingly, there was little harm in allowing the armed factions who'd once waged war on the streets of the nation's capital to reside and rule in relative peace in the remote countryside.

Try to do some business out here, though, Borrego telling Cooper, and you were in for some serious taxation. That, he said, was one of the main reasons he had such a skinny margin on his antiquities-wholesale business: most of the places you found original, as-yet-undiscovered artifacts—in Guatemala, Egypt, northern Africa, or anywhere else for that matter—you had enough local strife, usually inclusive of civil war, to require payoffs rivaling the profits you stood to make in the first place.

The other part of it, Borrego said, was no matter how much you paid these guys, they still tended to want to seize whatever you had on board, and sometimes, just for the hell of it, they'd toss you in whatever sort of jail they'd been able to assemble.

"Kind of a raw deal for anybody doing the bribing," Cooper said.

"Raw—or stupid," Borrego told him between gulps of Gatorade. "Plus, the boundaries are always changing, so you never quite know who's controlling what."

"So once in a while," Cooper said, "you've paid the wrong guy."

"Most of the while," Borrego said. "Meaning you wind up paying two, three guys before you're through. Of course, that's about how we do it in Caracas too."

For an insane moment, as they approached the two guys in fatigues, Cooper thought he recognized one of the rebel soldiers—and that the soldier recognized him. Madrid eased to a stop, and for a very real instant, Cooper caught eyes with the soldier on his side of the Defender. He suddenly knew he'd been caught—*caught*—the man seeing his picture on a "Most Wanted" flyer posted following his escape, the guard knowing immediately he'd found an enemy of the state—

We know you, the soldier's eyes telling him, *and now we have you.*

Panic welled in his chest like bubbling bile, and he almost made a knifing move for his gun, thinking he could take both of them with two quick shots—

When he remembered where he was. They were in a *different* Central American country—goddammit. Cooper also recognized how young the kid with the rifle was. Seventeen at best, but probably fourteen or fifteen with the tough country life he must be living out here.

These guys weren't even born when you were last in the neighborhood.

The velociraptor had some words with the soldier on his side, among the words Cooper overheard being *Oso Blanco* and *dinero*—and for another instant, Cooper's eyes locked with the kid on his side of the road.

Then the teenage rebel dropped his look and waved them past with a relaxed, menacing swish of his rifle, and they were through.

They camped beneath some willow trees, then set out before dawn. Two hours into a climb in the Defender up a muddy road, Cooper said, "Assuming your tomb raiders were as good as you say, and this is the easiest way to the site, then I've got a question."

"Shoot," Borrego said, lolling back and forth, belted into his throne as the Land Rover tossed them around.

"How the hell did they get eight crates of gold artifacts out of here—at maybe half a ton each?"

Borrego smiled and those yellow teeth gleamed.

"That's the trick, isn't it?" he said.

Cooper waited. Madrid steered around a rut but hit another one and Cooper had to struggle to avoid taking a dashboard to the chin.

"To be honest," Borrego said, "I'm not entirely sure. I've done my share of digs in the area—at least the general vicinity—and the places you usually find something, it tends to be the case that nobody else has been where you're going. Lot of the undiscovered ruins are in the middle of an active volcanic range, spots that were once populated by Mayans, or whichever native set you're pillaging—but these places have seen a few thousand landslides, earthquakes, even volcanic eruptions since. People move away, nobody goes back in but some recreational hikers, the rain forest overtakes the village, and anything of value the former inhabitants kept takes some hard labor to pull out."

Even with the four-wheel drive, Madrid was losing traction on the muddy slope. The road had become so steep that Cooper felt as though he were reclined in a business class airline seat.

"You still haven't answered my question."

"Getting there," Borrego said. "Point I'm making is, nobody's going up sheer cliffs or scaling the edge of a volcanic crater with the two or three trucks of equipment it takes to excavate the goodies, so, like us, the tomb raiders take their equipment in on the low road. But once you get your hands on the statues, or the mummies, or the bags of gold—whatever—you're usually not too far from some pretty steep slopes. Hell—in these parts, it can sometimes be—literally—a thousand-foot sheer cliff."

Cooper held on for his life as Madrid rolled them around a bend at the peak of a particularly steep incline.

"Anyway, when you're talking slopes like that," Borrego said, "it winds up being a lot easier going down than up."

When they came around the turn, Cooper observed they were now faced with a hill that looked to him the way it might if he'd been looking up an Olympic ski jump. At the two or three miles an hour Madrid was doing, there was no way they could generate enough speed to climb the hill.

"Hang on," Madrid said, then jerked the wheel hard left and, flooring it, sped madly for all of ten or fifteen yards before wedging the Defender into a thicket of ferns and short, stubby trees. Then he flicked off the ignition and locked the parking brake.

"End of the line," he said.

The Polar Bear unlatched himself from the throne and leaped deftly, even lightly, out onto the muddy ground. Once he got his feet under him, he looked at Cooper. Even with Borrego standing on the ground and Cooper high up in his seat, Cooper had to glance up to look the Polar Bear in the eye.

"If I read that map right," Borrego said, "we've got this tall hill, some mountain climbing up above it, and maybe six or seven miles of jungle to go before X marks the spot." He grinned. "Feel like a hike?"

Cooper took another look up the slope. It looked to be one hell of a long way before the incline eased—and that was all in advance of the "mountain climbing," which he didn't really want to think about.

"Piece of cake," he said.

Cooper's feet were blistered silly by noon, and it wasn't until two-fifteen that they crested the lip of the crater to observe, beyond its edge, a short downward slope and what looked to Cooper like an endless ocean of jungle.

Borrego scrambled nimbly up behind him and stood beside Cooper to take in the view.

"An unnamed rain forest plateau," he said. "One of a few thousand such gardens of Eden found here."

There were mountain peaks on every side of the forest, and Cooper realized the plateau was part of a volcanic crater, or possibly a few of them decayed and overgrown together. There seemed to be two main patches of green—the first being a larger circle of forest closer to them, the second another, higher plateau. The two regions, taken together, formed a sort of figure eight. He wondered how many archaeologically important ruins, Mayan or otherwise, were buried in vines and rot in this plateau alone—then thought again, considering it would be strange for anyone to live up here, now or ever.

Madrid arrived, hauling a little more than the others in his backpack, and stood up straight to take in the view.

"For you history buffs," Borrego said, "this is the kind of place Mayan Indian culture thrived for as long as a thousand years beyond the period in which they have traditionally been declared extinct. Up here, you didn't get any visitors until recently—not for six or seven hundred years at a time. And if you know how to do it, you don't need more than what you've got in that jungle out there to live as long as you want. Forever, even—except for the continued encroachment of the rest of us human beings into all corners of the planet, and the diseases we bring with us."

Borrego pulled the map the chop-shop laborer had given them and examined it for a while. Then he looked out at the jungle plateau, scratched his head, and pointed to what Cooper believed to be the northwest corner of the woods.

"If his sketch is legit," Borrego said, "that's where we're going."

Cooper shuffled his aching feet on the rocky earth of the crater's edge.

"So that'd be the six or seven miles you were talking about," he said, shaking his head.

"Yeah," Borrego said. "Only it looks more like ten to me."

"Christ."

"Hard to believe, isn't it?" Borrego said.

"What's that?"

The big man pointed again toward their destination.

"That the answer to who the hell your 'snuffer-outers' are, and why the hell they're doing their dirty work, might actually lie out there. In the goddamn jungle."

Cooper let his tired mind roam to thoughts of Cap'n Roy, and Po Keeler, and the frozen corpse buried beneath the Alaskan king crabs—seemingly so vastly distant from the time and place they'd flown, driven, and climbed to. A world away from this—how had Borrego put it?—garden of Eden. Planted square in the middle of a mostly irrelevant third world country—geopolitically speaking.

Even the original Eden wasn't rumored to have been all peanuts and popcorn, and he expected no different here. In fact, there was something out in that rain forest crater the chop-shop laborer and part-time tomb raider had seen that convinced him this place, and anyone who visited it, was cursed.

Cooper didn't really want to think much more about what they were about to find. At least not yet. He reached up— way up—and offered Borrego a friendly whack on the shoulder.

"Let's see what there is to see," he said.

34

They found the village just before dusk.

Cooper encountered the first of the structures, an over-grown rectangle made of clay and dark hardwood timbers that had barely rotted at all. He almost missed it, mainly since it wasn't the kind of ruin he was expecting to find. Not that he should have expected one type of ruin or another—but where were the Mayan stones, crumbling into dirt as the jungle overtook them?

Soon he saw another such structure. Then another. The three of them had been working about fifty yards apart, covering as broad a swath as possible while still remaining within earshot, if not within eyesight. Cooper whistled.

"Got something," he called out. "Not sure what, but it's something."

"Same here," Borrego said, his voice arriving from somewhere off to Cooper's left. Cooper heard Madrid, or some large animal in any case, approaching from the right.

It was getting hard to see, but not that much harder than it had been to see the whole time. The canopy of wide-leafed trees kept out most of the light. Everything was wet, and it was hot, maybe eighty-five or ninety degrees. Four or five times during their march through the woods, Cooper had heard, more than felt, rain showers, pelting the trees at the top of the canopy, the frequent rains seeping their way through over time, basically creating one giant soupy mud puddle underneath.

Madrid arrived and, along with Cooper, examined the small buildings.

"Not too old," he said.

In the one Cooper was currently examining, there were cooking utensils, a wooden table and bench, two pots—worn out and dirty, but made, it seemed, of gold—and, up against one wall and aside the bench, two sets of human bones. Cooper poked his way over to the structure Madrid was looking through and found it nearly identical to the one he'd been examining, only it was slightly bigger, and featured three sets of bones rather than two.

When Borrego didn't swing by, Cooper made his way over to the place from which he'd heard the Polar Bear answer his whistle. Madrid followed. It took them a few minutes—darkness was upon them now—but after shouting his name a couple times they found the big man crouched down on one knee. He appeared to be examining some bushes.

"You find your share of skeletons over here?" Cooper said.

Borrego rotated his flashlight from the bush he was looking at. Even pointed at the ground, it was nearly blinding because of the way their eyes had adjusted to the rain forest twilight.

"I did," Borrego said, "but I found this too."

He shone the flashlight out ahead of where he was crouched, where Cooper saw there appeared to be some kind of road. It was partially overgrown, but as Borrego worked the flashlight beam along the ground, Cooper could easily see tire tracks through the thin cover of brush.

"My guess," Borrego said, "is this is where they dragged the artifacts out. Those are mechanized wagon tracks, kind of a specialized minitank today's tomb raiders utilize as their excavation vehicle of choice. I'd bet we've circled back a ways—the edge of the crater closest to Belize isn't far from here. There's probably a steep mountain face a few miles from here at most, where they could have passed the artifacts down the cliff with ropes and pulleys."

Cooper flicked on his own flashlight and walked around for a while, taking a look at whatever he could see that wasn't a tree, bush, insect, or snake. He heard Borrego and Madrid fall in behind him, and they marched around that way in the dark, examining some additional structures, including one made of more traditional-looking stones. He found a few fire pits too. Everywhere they wandered, the sounds of the jungle were overwhelming—screaming insects, frogs, or some other creature, Cooper had no idea. There was the rustle of snakes, rodents, and maybe birds, plus the occasional, more intimidating growl. Cooper didn't know what the sounds were, but he did know he hated them. He hated almost everything about this place—the look of each leaf, the width of the vines that wound up the tree trunks, the scents of rotting things and new, green growth. He found he had to clamp his jaw to keep the insanity and fear—an instinctive desire to run—from overtaking him.

He knew the reason: it seemed there existed no difference between this jungle and the one through which he'd fled—the one in which he'd been held, and into which he'd stupidly, arrogantly jumped.

His jumpy need to bolt came in waves, between which he paid close attention to what he saw—and what he saw, besides a reasonably primitive Central American Indian village, were more bones. Skeletons—lots of them.

Or, as the tomb raider in the chop shop had put it, *all of them.*

It was becoming rapidly clear—particularly given the positioning of the skeletal remains in their many different, seemingly casual angles of repose—that every single inhabitant of this village had died, or been killed, at almost the same time. Some had been attended, some not, but it seemed pretty obvious everyone had died fairly quickly.

Curse, indeed. Christ.

A wave of fear and nausea overtook him briefly and he set his hand against a tree to steady himself. As he did, he heard her. It was faint at first, just another part of the jungle sounds, but then her screeching, singsong tone ramped up in volume and he knew who it was. It was that goddamn golden idol of a priestess, calling out to him across the Caribbean. Her voice was deeper now, distorted, throat dry and scratchy—

Oh, yeah, Cooper, you come to find us, and now we been found.

You come to free us at last. So take us away, you dumb old paramilitary goon. Let us escape our damnation. An escape arranged by a soul as damned as we . . .

Cooper bent down and squatted beside one of the skeletons and had a closer look. This one was reclined partially against the wall of the structure it occupied and partially on the floor, as though the person, in life, had been sitting against the wall when he or she died, the bones collapsing somewhat over the course of the body's decay.

"Why don't we set up camp," Borrego said. "There's a clearing back a hundred yards or so, seems like a decent place to do it. We can use a fire as a home base and take a look around in spokes—out and back, out and back, so we know where we've been and where we haven't, with the fire as our compass."

Madrid cleared his throat.

"Might just be better," he said, "to wait for morning. *Then* have a look around."

Borrego chuckled.

"What," he said, "and wait around all night? If you can stand to wait another ten hours to peer around every nook and cranny of this little city—hell, if you can get any sleep in this racket—you're a better man than I."

"All right," the velociraptor said, lacking Borrego's enthusiasm for matters. "I'll get going on setting things up."

Borrego tossed Madrid an enthusiastic thumbs-up and turned to lead the way.

Working in tag teams, with one of them manning the camp—usually Madrid—they had a look at the entire village, or at least what appeared to be the entire village, examining everything within range of the flashlight beams while they headed six or seven hundred yards out and back on each "spoke." It was about three-quarters of the way around the wheel where Cooper and Borrego, about a hundred yards east of the fire, found the stairs going down.

There were two stone columns that had recently been knocked to pieces, but had obviously once marked the entrance to wherever the stairs went. Stone slabs composed the stairwell, which, upon illumination, revealed itself to lead down beneath the rain forest floor. Cooper counted thirty stairs and estimated the level of the passageway visible at the base to be twenty feet below ground level. Dirt, leaves, sticks, fallen stones, and broken slabs of rock were strewn across the stairwell and the passageway beneath. There were also footprints, straight-line depressions, and, on the surface, near where they stood, the tire tracks again.

"I'm guessing this'd be where they found the goodies," Borrego said.

"And maybe the curse." Cooper felt queasy at the prospect of heading underground.

"Oh, hell, no," Borrego said with a chuckle. "You get the curse over where we set up camp."

"Very funny."

"After you."

"Even funnier."

"I could get Madrid," Borrego said. "Send him in ahead of us. Maybe he can set off the booby traps."

"Thought you were an experienced spelunker?" Cooper said.

Their dual flashlight beams remained trained on the base of the stairwell.

"I am."

"So?"

"You're the canary," Borrego said, "aren't you?"

Aw, what the hell, Cooper thought, and started down. He turned so he could keep an eye on Borrego as he went. He didn't do it for any reason other than instinct—you just never knew. Borrego started down behind him cautiously, some of that spring he'd shown along the way missing from his step.

In the passageway, some of the stones and beams that held the walls together had broken apart and fallen. There were mounds of dirt where the earth had caved in, but most of the cave-ins appeared to have happened prior to the raid—tire tracks, footprints, and scrape marks evident on the mounds of dirt too.

Protrusions from the wall were visible at shoulder height every ten steps or so, on alternating sides; looking more closely at them, Cooper realized they were there to hold torches or lanterns. As with the rest of the architecture, they didn't seem particularly old.

The hall turned to the right, and Cooper first saw darkness, and then, as he rotated the flashlight beam into the blackness—vastness. Borrego came up alongside him, and between their two flashlights they were able to partially illuminate the room.

It was a massive, stone-walled chamber, with a number of benches built in rows along the floor. The benches were made of the same dark hardwood as the structures on the rain forest floor. Along the two longest walls, rectangular cavities had been carved out at regular intervals, the flashlight beams revealing the cavities to be empty. Because of the way the spiderwebs, dust, and dirt were patterned within the cavities, Cooper caught the distinct impression of something recently taken.

A similar emptiness of grime and dust showed itself under their beams in a rectangular shape along the shorter back wall of the room; Cooper thought immediately of the gold tapestry he'd seen on display in Cap'n Roy's Marine Base Barn.

"Looks to me," Borrego rumbled from Cooper's left, "like a church."

There were a pair of doorways, one on each side of the place where the tapestry had hung. Cooper took one of the openings at the back of the room and Borrego the other. They wound up in the same room—this one much wider, with a shallower ceiling. As he watched his flashlight beam illuminate the features of this particular chamber, Cooper felt an icy tingle inch up his spine.

"Or a funeral home," he said.

Stretching away from them, in multiple rows, stood a sea of caskets. These too were made of the same hardwood. They looked more weathered than the timbers used to build the shacks—older, Cooper thought.

"This is their cemetery," he thought out loud.

"So it seems," Borrego said.

Most of the caskets appeared to have been opened and re-closed; their lids were mostly a little bit askew but remained on the coffins despite the disturbance they'd endured. There were cavities built into the walls of this room just as in the other, and these—along with the boxes beside the coffins, Cooper and Borrego examining a few of them—were also empty.

"Your boys did a pretty thorough job of cleaning house," Cooper said.

"Told you they were good."

"Not that this comes as any great surprise," Cooper said, "but I'm not exactly feeling like Sherlock Holmes here. Everybody's dead—okay—that makes the place no different from every other Mayan ruin, except it's pretty obvious whatever killed these people killed them quickly. Then we've got the thorough cleaning job by your tomb raiders—other than these evident facts, we ain't exactly stumbling across an explanation behind the multicontinental snuff-out currently being conducted by persons unknown."

Borrego's flashlight beam moved bumpily around the walls of the room; Cooper took a look at him and saw that the Polar Bear had entered into a massive, slow, ecstatic kind of stretch. As though to emphasize the satisfaction the full-body stretch gave him, he opened his mouth and undertook a wide, trembling yawn.

When he'd finished, Borrego said, "Guess you could see it this way: either it's got something to do with the whole village being dead, or this trip was one big waste of time. Other than good exercise and great lobster, of course. Let's head up top—see if Jesus has the tents up."

Cooper shrugged, said he didn't see why not, and followed the Polar Bear up and out.

35

They had a fire going, not to keep warm—no need in the tropical heat—but to brew some coffee. The changing sounds of the forest had awakened Cooper just before dawn.

On one of the "spokes" they'd traversed the night before, he'd encountered a narrow river. It was on the outskirts of the village, to the north. This morning, once he'd arisen, he found the aluminum pot Madrid had used to cook some condensed hiker's food, and made his way to the river to fill it. He got the fire going by kicking its embers around, boiled the water in the pot, took a coffee filter and pouch of grounds from his backpack and custom-filtered some brew into the cups Madrid had packed into each of their backpacks.

Borrego and Madrid came awake the minute the smell of coffee hit the jungle air.

Food, Cooper thought—*it's all about food with these guys*.

Once they'd found three suitably distant bushes in which to relieve themselves, the trio of explorers sat around the fire and worked on putting away the coffee.

"You notice the shreds of fabric on some of the bones?" Cooper said.

"Yep," Borrego grumbled.

"Your tomb raider was right. Everybody here died. But he said it could have been a thousand years ago when they caught the curse, if that's what it was. I'm fairly certain that's not possible."

"The artifacts certainly aren't that old."

Cooper nodded, electing to ignore the fact that Borrego already knew this and hadn't said anything about it along the way.

"Correct," he said, "a hundred and fifty years old at most, according to an archaeologist I asked. But the presence of the fabric in the homes would indicate the citizens here died a lot more recently than that."

"You're saying the clothes on the skeletons," Borrego said, sipping from his cup, "would have rotted faster than that."

"I'm not exactly up to speed on the latest forensics theories, but no way do fabrics like those stick around a rain forest more than twenty-five years."

Borrego nodded.

"Definitely not a hundred," he said, "or even fifty."

"So everybody died here. They died quickly, and more or less all at once—less than fifty years ago."

Borrego nodded again and took another sip of coffee. Madrid too sipped.

"Maybe that's what the snuffer-outers don't want anybody finding out," Cooper said.

"Could have been something else," Borrego said. "Like tribal warfare, say."

"Could have."

"Or civil war within the tribe—two factions battling to the death. Hell," Borrego said, "could be they all listened to their crazy leader and downed some arsenic-laced indigenous version of Kool-Aid. But given the other factors that brought you into my office on that switching train, I'd say your theory is in the lead."

Cooper dumped the gritty remainder of his coffee on the fire and stood.

"Gonna look around some more," he said.

Borrego looked up at him from his seat beside the fire. He didn't have to look very high despite Cooper's relatively tall frame—six-nine goes a long way, Cooper thought, even when you're sitting down.

"Longer spokes?" Borrego said.

"Longer spokes."

"Let me lace up my boots," Borrego said. "I'll join you."

Madrid looked over at Cooper, and then at his boss, who was already busy securing the double knot on the first of his hiking boots.

"How about I stick around and make some more coffee," the weary velociraptor said.

Neither Borrego nor Cooper said a word while they worked around the hundred-plus square miles of the crater in silent synch. They encountered other signs of the civilization that had been—pots, tools, the occasional small, rotting structure—but little else. Around three-thirty Cooper encountered the creek again. It ran a little faster here, kind of a scale model of rapids, maybe four feet across at most. Following the creek's upstream course, he saw that the creek was rushing along at this pace because it had just completed its tumble down the edge of the crater. He hadn't realized he was so close to the edge of the forest.

Cooper caught Borrego's eye with a wave and the Polar Bear started over. Cooper headed uphill, enjoying, even in his first few steps, a fresh supply of newly forming blisters. He thought of the figure-eight shape they'd observed upon cresting the crater's edge the day before—that was where he was headed now, the higher, smaller plateau in the figure-eight. He followed the creek as it leveled out and slowed and the stroll became less arduous. He could hear Borrego behind him from time to time, the occasional broken twig, the brush of the big man's bulk against a tropical leaf.

The light had begun to fade when he found it.

There wasn't much to find. The toe of his hiking boot

bumped against it, and he felt whatever he'd bumped shift. A quick look down revealed a distinctly unindigenous scrap of particle board. Charred, wet, and mostly rotted through, the flat chunk of wood still managed to look as out of place as a man like he did in the West Indies: yellowish-white and soft in a forest of hard, dark trees. Cooper picked it up and discovered nothing else out of the ordinary about it: unpainted, it held no bolts, displayed no telltale shape, and otherwise simply seemed to be what it was—a scrap of compressed sawdust being slowly uncompressed by the wet woods around it.

It was about a hundred yards onward when the smell got to him.

It wasn't exactly an unnatural fragrance, but neither was it familiar to him in the three days he'd spent here. He placed it as the smell of an old, doused fire—of burned, water-soaked wood.

Borrego caught up to him. Cooper showed him the particle board.

"Smell that?" he said once Borrego handed him back the wood.

Borrego said that he did.

Working wordlessly again, they started covering this section of the woods in opposing crescents, Cooper examining the foliage and earth beneath it as he went. Besides the chunk of particle board, all that remained of whatever had burned was charcoal, long since blended into the soil.

It occurred to Cooper that whatever had burned to the ground here had been exceedingly large—the charred footprint, while mostly hidden beneath the foliage now grown over in its place, stretched at least sixty yards in one direction and a hundred in the other. There were fewer trees growing in the footprint than elsewhere, and those that were growing here had a long way to go to catch the other, taller trees in the crater.

He looked up from his reverie and saw that Borrego, up ahead, was staring off into the woods. When he saw that

Cooper was clocking him, the Polar Bear said, "You see those?"

Cooper looked where he was pointing and saw stones in the river.

Stones, but not stones. Broken concrete—the water eddying lazily around chunks of it, some with straight or sharp edges but most busted into rounded, rocklike pieces. They converged on the rubble and saw depressions in the soil, presumably indicating some of the places from which the concrete had been excavated. The exposed portions of the foundation had been broken off, knocked to pieces, and tossed into the water.

"Looks to me," Borrego's deep voice said from behind him, "like somebody worked very hard at hiding whatever this place was."

"Didn't do too good a job of it, either," Cooper said.

"At least not if you're standing in the woods under the rim of a volcanic crater that sees city slickers like us maybe once a century."

"Yeah," Cooper said. "Fly by or something, you've got no idea."

"Bad winds in here too. There's something about the humidity and the winds together that makes it impossible to fly through most of this mountain range. Even with a helicopter."

"Suppose a smart person would have asked you the question back in the Land Rover," Cooper said, "as to why we weren't flying in aboard a helicopter to start with. There's my answer."

Borrego shook his head.

"Tough to get hold of one without arousing too much rebel attention anyway," he said.

Cooper said, "Crap."

Borrego nodded, then shook his head. Cooper understood the combination of gestures with a kind of precision: *What a shame—lot of people killed here.*

"Somebody spilled something," Cooper said. "Killed off

a whole village full of people in the process, then headed for the hills."

"Looks that way to me."

"Then whoever it was decides—"

Cooper stopped.

"Fuck me," he said.

It was getting dark. He flipped on his flashlight. It created a million sparkles of light on the surface of the river as it swirled through the chunks of concrete.

"What is it," Borrego said. "You hear something?"

"No," Cooper said. He hadn't shared with Borrego the part of his theory he'd started out with—the theory on who the snuffer-outers worked for, or were associated with, the very association that caused them to decide not to snuff him out too. Wouldn't be too much of a stretch that somebody in the federal government of the good old U.S. of A.—his chief snuffer-outer suspects—might have had something to do with this fucking chemical spill, or whatever the hell it was about this place that had killed an entire Indian village. The treatment of the locals here being fairly consistent, he thought, with the treatment of other localities around the globe by the Evil Empire.

He still didn't see much reason to share his theory with Borrego. What would he do with it anyway? Get mad at Uncle Sam? Or, more likely—get killed by someone *sent* by Uncle Sam.

Cooper started out along the river, heading upstream again. Borrego clicked on his own flashlight and fell in behind, following the rhythm they'd maintained throughout the day. Cooper liked that Borrego didn't press him further. Working with the flashlights in the increasing darkness, they made their way out from the rectangular burn site in the same spoked paths they'd used back in the village. Cooper found himself growing angrier with every spoke. With every passing minute, in fact.

Almost a dozen spokes had come and gone when Borrego finally said, "You want to tell me what it is we're looking for?"

"Any goddamn thing at all," Cooper said, "that'll show me who was here."

Or confirm it—since I already know who it was.

Cooper crossed the stream and found the woods didn't last long in this direction—the rocky crest of the crater stood like a steeply angled wall a hundred yards from the creek. They approached the crater wall and Cooper saw it almost immediately.

A cave.

"Should have looked here first," Borrego said—almost, but not quite, causing Cooper to break the scowl distorting his face.

Ignoring his knee-jerk fear of lurking predators, Cooper barreled into the cave, descending into a cavity the size of a squash court. It occurred to Cooper that the Indians from the village must have known or found these underground caverns to exist in the crater, and used them to their advantage. The way Indians and other smart people did, he thought—use what nature gave you to its fullest—unlike the way whoever ran *this* facility worked. Theirs being—literally—the scorched-earth philosophy.

All the more corroborating evidence on the identity of the snuffer-outers.

As with the aboveground portion of the former riverfront factory—or prison camp, or movie theater, or whatever the fuck it had been, he thought—there wasn't much to see in the cave. They'd burned whatever had been left in here too, the blackened, moist, smelly soil that coated the floor of the chamber consistent with the ash and coals he'd been kicking around up top. Neither Cooper nor Borrego could stand up straight except near the middle of the cavity; they shone their flashlights around the room in search of anything besides the evident rock, moss, dirt, and puddles.

"Maybe they stole from the Indians too," the Polar Bear

said from somewhere behind Cooper. "Kept the loot in here."

"Maybe," Cooper said idly.

"Whatever it was, though, seems to me it wouldn't keep."

"What do you mean," Cooper said, peering around.

"Right now's dry season. My guess'd be half the year, maybe more, this room's a pond. Underwater."

Cooper, brain dulled from too many days with too little food and too much humidity and exercise, took upward of thirty seconds to hear the coupler engage within the confines of his head. Trying to fend off some of the fatigue and flex his brain, he made the connection his mind was trying to tell him it had already made:

Underwater.

Along the back wall of the cavern, the floor was two or three feet deeper than the spot where he stood now. It was there, at the back of the cave, where the puddles stood. He walked to the back wall, moving slowly so as not to stir up too much mud, and shone his flashlight into the water as he worked his way along the wall.

The puddles reminded him of blackened tide pools. He poked around with his foot, feeling from behind the protective sheath of his steel-toed boot. Some of the puddles were deeper than others—two inches here, six there.

You're burning something, and part of that something happens to be underwater, it could be you didn't burn all of—

He heard the muted scraping noise first. Cooper and Borrego met each other's gaze for an instant, and then Cooper pulled his boot out of the puddle, crouched down, and slipped his hand into the muck to find what it was he'd nudged. He came out with a short length of rotting wood.

Holding it up in the light, he could see it was close to eight or nine inches long, two or three inches wide in one direction, and thinner than his pinkie in the other. Its edges were jagged, blackened, rotten—a piece of it fell off and slopped into the puddle as Cooper rotated it in the beam of his flashlight—but when he got it turned around, Cooper, and Borrego beside him, saw that there was actually something to see.

The wood on the back side of the board, which had been submerged in the mud—or algae, or whatever else it is you find in a mud puddle in a rain forest cave—was pale. The color on the back side of the board was probably close to the original, natural color of the wood before the fire and rot had got to its other side.

Along this pale side of the board, stenciled in black, were two complete and legible letters, and half of a third. The three letters, at least by Cooper's guess, were ICR. Below the letters were the rounded tops of an incomplete sequence of numbers, Cooper thinking it might be a serial number or ID labeling of some kind, but this portion of the markings on the wood seemed impossible to read.

Cooper looked at Borrego and pointed the wood in his direction.

"Mean anything to you?" he said. "Appears to be part of a crate, and you're the biggest shipping magnate in the cave."

" 'ICR,' you mean? Not offhand."

Cooper put the rotting piece of wood in his pocket, kicked and felt his way through the remainder of the puddles, found some other boards, splinters, and chunks of wood—all similar to the one in his pocket, but none with any markings.

Then he stood and took in the sight of the massive, hunched form of Ernesto Borrego.

"Might mean something to somebody somewhere, though," he said.

Borrego nodded. "Otherwise we came all this way for a stick."

Cooper almost smiled again.

Borrego's bass rumble of a voice came next.

"Had enough?" he said.

"Of this place? For a lifetime."

Borrego turned, pointed his flashlight beam toward the exit of the cave, and led the way out.

"Good," the Polar Bear said. "'Cause I may be dead, but I've still got a business to run."

36

Laramie was in her second hour of sleep following forty-eight without when an obnoxiously loud and persistent knocking dredged her from her pool of slumber.

"I *hear* you."

She got her legs around and found the floor, retrieved a pair of jeans, and pulled them on beneath the oversize Lakers T-shirt she always wore to bed—another detail it seemed Ebbers had instructed his minions to heed. A look through her peephole revealed Wally Knowles, looking as chipper as she'd seen him, the man even showing the presence of mind to put on his hat before coming down to see her. She checked her watch—3:43 A.M.—then unlatched the chain and opened the door.

"I think we may have found our boy," Knowles said.

Laramie perked up. He must have meant they'd got a hit on their custom computer setup—that it had yielded a photograph of Benny Achar taken before he'd adopted his new identity.

When Laramie asked Knowles if that was what he meant, the author jerked his head sideways and disappeared from the door frame, headed back in the direction of his room.

"Better to show," he said, "than tell."

They'd imported some serious computer equipment during the past few days, which Knowles had set up on his own in his room. Even to Laramie—who preferred to leave anything with computers to the tech guy who serviced their workstations in Langley—the setup was impressive. A pair of gunmetal gray Power Macintosh towers anchored a system featuring two huge flat-panel monitors, a laser printer, and a box with a strip of green and yellow lights down its front that Laramie figured for the cable modem. As she came in behind Knowles, Laramie saw that Cole was on the phone, using—as instructed—the room's land line instead of his cell phone. On one of the monitors she could see a grainy, smudged image of a life raft overflowing with people. The boat looked to be out on the ocean, but was about to make landfall—some of the people on the boat were reaching for a dock Laramie could just barely make out on the right-hand side of the picture.

Cole continued with his phone call, offering Laramie a lazy salute with his off hand as Knowles took the seat in front of the monitor and motioned for Laramie to join him for a look. He worked the mouse and the image rewound. Laramie noticed it happened digitally, in that way where pixels and squares could be seen as the image shifted backward in time.

"We got lucky," Knowles explained, "considering such a measly portion of the actual available pool of images from the past twenty years has been digitized and stored in the consortium's archives. Most of what *has* been digitized comes from broadcast and print media, however, which turned out to be useful."

The image started playing, the raft—almost a small barge, she thought—rolling in the waves. There wasn't any audio, but Laramie could see a buffeting of the surface of the water, as though from a helicopter—the source of the camera shooting the video, she assumed. The men crammed aboard the boat appeared very animated, most of them gesturing toward the right side of the image, where Laramie knew the dock would soon appear on-screen.

"This is a boat full of Cuban refugees," Knowles said as the video played, "shot by a local news chopper as the vessel docked somewhere south of Miami."

The call letters of the local station appeared above the word *NewsFile* in the lower-left corner of the screen.

"It's file footage from the local station, dated December 1994. We'll play the whole clip for you, but this is the part that matters, when the videographer zooms in. I believe U.S. policy was the same then as now—'wet feet, dry feet.' If a Cuban refugee makes land here, he's eligible for asylum. If he's picked up en route before he makes it in, the Coast Guard has to send him back. These guys made it—by the end of the clip they all climb onto the dock and out of frame. There."

Knowles pointed to the monitor as the image zoomed in, and six or seven of the men's faces could be seen more distinctly. In another second or two, a brightened circle of the kind Laramie had seen on police-chase reality shows spotlighted one of the men, and the video image froze.

Even with the granularity of the station's old footage, Laramie had no problem recognizing the face.

"That's him," she said.

Knowles nodded. "Search engine scored the hit about two hours ago. I had an alarm rigged for when the system found a match. Woke up, checked it out, and got Cole in here the minute I saw what you just watched."

Laramie heard Cole wrapping up his phone call— something about "Thanks, I owe you one"—then he hung up and came over.

"If it's December of ninety-four," she said, "that's only a month or two before Achar showed up in the first Florida docs."

"Yep." Knowles eased back in his seat, looking somewhat overwhelmed with self-satisfaction.

"He was Cuban, then," she said. Then she thought about this some more. "Or at least he came here from there."

"Yep," Knowles said again.

Cole had come over to stand silently above them.

"Castro's last-ditch effort to take down the capitalist pigs up north," Laramie said, "seems an unlikely version of this conspiracy at best. No way he cares enough anymore. Or has the resources."

"We're in agreement on that," Knowles said. "But the guy may still have been Cuban."

Laramie said, "Maybe. But somebody could have dumped the raft in the water, or put the people on it, to make it seem that way."

Knowles nodded. "Could have," he said. "Of course that's not the only clue this image gives us."

Laramie had the idea they'd been through all of this before he'd come to get her, and decided she was irritated they hadn't called her over immediately. Though maybe they'd wanted to do some follow-up first—have some "show rather than tell" ready for her by the time she came down the hall.

"The other people on the boat," she said, her brain starting to click.

"Right."

"If we search in the other direction," she said, "working from the faces on the boat, then maybe we find some other sleepers."

Cole nodded.

"Already under way," he said. "Been dipping into some of the data banks your friend the guide knows how to get into. Once we got some hits on the faces—meaning matches with photos in the federal or local databases Wally and I plugged into the search engine—we were able to determine that two of Achar's pals aboard the boat were busted for armed robbery—manslaughter charges were part of it too—and sent to prison in Dade County in 1997. Two others have been in and out of jail for smaller crimes, possession and so on, for most of the eleven years since they came over. We're shooting for some other angles, but so far it looks like nobody else on the boat can be shown to have stolen the identity of somebody who died. At least not yet. It's a maze—we need to find each man's Social Security number from a starting point of his image on that tape, then check whether the Social registers as one belonging to somebody who's already dead. Like we talked about, almost none of this kind of thing is kept electronically, but we're starting that way just in case—it's faster than our other search method if it works."

Laramie looked at the image on the monitor and counted—twenty-two men on the boat.

"We're checking for other boats from the same time period too?"

"Yep," Knowles said. "And the search engine's still working on the other faces from this boat. Assuming the search comes up dry, all this really means is that our pal, public enemy number one, doesn't appear to have shipped all of his sleepers over on one boat, all at once. Assuming there's more than one."

Laramie nodded. "Suppose it was too much to expect for ten of them to be caught on tape, all on the same boat."

Knowles looked at Cole, who nodded his affirmation of something.

"It's late," Knowles said, "but we're up. We were thinking we'd give you the other updates now, get back to sleep, then get back on it around nine or ten A.M."

Laramie had planned to do a roundtable at eight, to include Rothgeb, and maybe even Cooper by phone. Now she might just have something for Cooper to do. There might be some investigative work to be done in Cuba—work up a notion with Eddie Rothgeb on what sort of "Americanization facility" he should be looking for, then send Cooper on his way.

Maybe I could even go with him.

She immediately became infuriated with herself for thinking this final thought, and nodded quickly at Knowles in a vain attempt to expel it from her brain.

"Go ahead with your update," she said.

Cole retreated to his seat by the phone and started in.

"Been interviewing, interrogating, and otherwise hassling every name that popped up in the terror book," he said. "Plus a few more that didn't. If you care, I think my tally is up to fifty-two interviews so far, and I've set another fourteen for today. Besides the fact that most of these conversations are basically putting me to sleep, I'm on to something—some kind of pattern, I think—I'm just not sure what. There are some consistent, and unique, pieces of his weekly routine— two events per week, I believe—which may have served as the 'bread crumbs' we've been speculating he may have left. I'm just not positive my theory makes sense yet."

Laramie considered this for a moment but couldn't grasp how it would work.

"You're saying he might have left messages in those places?" she said. "In the bar where he hung out with his buddies on Thursday nights, or—"

"Yes and no," Cole said. "Probably not literally. And not that obviously. But what I was thinking is, it might be in the numbers of the get-togethers."

Knowles said, "Fourth day of the week at seven, for instance."

"Right. I'll have more today after I wrap up the circuit of interviews, but if I'm right—if he's trying to give us a couple sets of numbers as the clue—then this guy was very, very good. For example, I've found no evident 'confessions' like we talked about before, and that's pretty rare. Almost contrary to human nature if you're talking ten years of under-cover work. Even cops love to give themselves away to anybody who's smart enough to figure it out. I'll give you an example: I met a guy once who'd done some undercover work, and the name they gave him in his cover job on the docks was 'Bobby Covert.'"

"As in covert operations?" Laramie said.

"One and the same."

"You're telling me nobody figured it out?"

"Nope—the guy busted a whole tier of New Jersey organized crime chiefs while working undercover at a trucking company under that name the whole time."

"You said there were two pieces of his routine," Laramie said, her mind a few lines back.

"Yeah," Cole said. "That's what I'm thinking. But I'm not positive."

"Involving numbers?"

"I think it's twice per week that he set regular appointments he never broke, but I haven't boiled down the consistent, well—I guess you'd say least common denominators of the get-togethers. You know, which pieces, such as time of day, that might give us a code from the weekly arrangements he made."

Laramie said, "But maybe the meeting times, if that's what you're talking about, are giving us numbers?"

"Not sure. There's a hundred possibilities, from address to time to day and date, and so on. But he had two weekly things going—outside of obligatory work stuff, ordinary kid stuff, and dates with his wife. If you look only at the day of the week and the time, there's a few ways to get either two or three numbers for each get-together. What are you getting at?"

"Two numbers, each in two or three sets," Laramie said, "could mean he's giving us GPS coordinates. Latitude and longitude in, what—'degrees, minutes, seconds,' right? Three sets. The third set, the seconds, sometimes being left out."

Cole sat up a little straighter in his chair. For a moment, Laramie thought she was able to catch a glimpse of the lean, athletic cop Cole might once have been.

"Christ," he said. "Here's the thing—I wanted to flesh this out before going over it with you. Reason being, it's insane at best to consider two weekly outings with friends a pattern, and a pattern expressing a code on top of it—"

"Go on," Laramie said.

"Well, outside of work, his wife, and any practice, games, or class appointments with his kid, it's looking like Achar kept two, and only two, regular appointments each week. One on Monday, when he would take his break at quarter after four and get two coffees from the Circle Diner. He'd bring the coffees back to the UPS facility and hand one off to the dispatcher, the girl named Lois—"

"When did you find that out?" Laramie said, amazed he'd found this when even Mary the profiler had not.

"Spent quite a while with her." Cole offered a smirk and left it at that. "I don't think they had anything going either, by the way, and I'd also discount the theory of her being some sort of control. But she confirmed to me that on Mondays, and Mondays only, he would radio in his break, and when he did, meaning each Monday, he'd always come back from the break with a coffee for her on his way back out to the job. Extra cream, one sugar."

"Okay," Laramie said.

"Second consistency was Tuesday night, for pool and darts at a tavern called Latona with seven of his buddies from work."

"Seven, specifically?" Laramie said.

"Yep, interviewed them all, talked to Janine Achar for confirmation. Dispatcher not among the 'buddies from work,' in case you wondered. Anyway, he and the fellas met at five-thirty at the Latona every Tuesday after work."

Laramie remembered seeing something about this in the terror book.

"Anyway, the reason I wanted to flesh this out on my own," Cole said, "besides it maybe being nothing, is the huge list of numbers or factors that could plug into a code. There's day of the week, the date, the time, the address of each of the events—coffee shop, pub, *et cetera*—plus, it could be the names of the places or the streets are figured into the code, if there is one. Maybe even the number of people involved at each event. But it's interesting when you raise the GPS issue. If GPS coordinates have three sets of—"

"Either two or three sets of one- or two-digit numbers," Laramie said, "more or less. Depending on how specific the reading is. If it's just the latitude and longitude in 'degrees' and 'minutes,' for instance, and not down to street specificity, then it's two sets for lat, two sets for long. If it's more pinpointed, 'seconds' are provided too."

"We work from there then," Knowles said.

Cole had begun nodding.

"Two or three numbers would make sense as the simplest pattern you can generate from his appointments," he said, "because you can come up with numbers solely from the days and times—or maybe the days and times and number of people involved. So, for instance: Monday—first day of the week; four-fifteen P.M. is the time; two people in the get-together, including him. Pick the numbers as you see fit. Tuesday's day two, at five-thirty—and either seven or eight participants—depending on whether you count Achar in the number again."

Knowles moved the mouse and the dual monitors came back to life, long since having gone to sleep. Laramie watched as he Googled a GPS translation site, asked for a repeat on the first shot at numbers Cole had just taken, then entered one combination of degrees, minutes, and seconds for both latitude and longitude based on what Cole had stated. Laramie noticed Knowles mouthed the numbers to help himself remember them.

"Here's what we might get," Knowles said, "using the factors you suggest and in the order you mentioned them."

He hit the Enter key. A fairly slow-loading map came up in a box, a red crosshair graphic centered on the map—over the middle of the Indian Ocean.

"Store that just in case," Laramie said, "but I don't see any relevance in an Indian Ocean location. Try again."

Knowles found a pad and began taking notes while he entered numbers on the computer. "I'll keep track of all the combinations," he said.

Another location popped up on the map, this time off the coast of Greenland. Knowles kept at it with various combinations, eliminating one after another, as a variety of unlikely locations for anything related to Americanization training or sleeper agents popped up in the crosshairs on the map.

"Doesn't matter," Knowles said. "Trial and error. Let's reverse it."

Cole said, "You mean, people first, then day of week, then time?"

"Right."

Cole laid that version out for him: *two, one, four-one-five; eight, two, five-three*.

Laramie thought of something as another few open-ocean locations resulted from what Knowles entered.

"Simplify it," she said. "Eliminate the seconds. If we're going with this order, the seconds would be the minutes past the hour of the meeting time."

Knowles punched in 21-4 for latitude, 82-5 for longitude.

Cole mumbled something about trying the addresses, and was in the process of rising to retrieve his notes, when the crosshairs centered on a section of the Caribbean just south of the western portion of Cuba.

None of them said anything for a moment.

Cole said, "That where they dumped him on the boat, maybe?"

"Sunday," Laramie said. "Not Monday."

Cole looked at her.

"Sunday's the first day of the week," she said. "First day of the work week is Monday, but—I took French in my training program, that's what made me think of it—you're learning French, you know what they teach you early on? That the French count Monday as the first day of the week. *Lundi, mardi, mercredi* . . . But *we* count Sunday as the first day of the week on our calendars. And if he was being formally Americanized, that's what they would teach him early on. That's the way he would assume *we* would think of the days of the week, because that's what he'd have been taught."

Knowles already had the boxes filled in: 22-4, 83-5. He hit Enter again.

Resolving itself in the same, slow fashion, the red crosshairs centered over the Cuban landmass this time—a hundred miles from the southwestern tip of the island.

"I'll be damned," Cole said.

"Map kind of speaks for itself," Knowles said.

Laramie looked at the map, and its red crosshair graphic.

"San Cristóbal," she said, naming the city adjoining the red crosshair graphic. She offered Cole a whack on the shoulder. "Nice work, Detective."

"You ain't kidding," Knowles said. "Also, we might want to go back in and add the 'seconds' based on the number of minutes past four and five P.M. that he held his meetings. Could be he narrowed it down even better than this."

Something occurred to Laramie about the location of the crosshair, but she decided she could confirm her suspicion later. She'd take a look at what she figured to lie in the crosshairs—just as soon as she got a hold of the operative they'd paid twenty million bucks to place in their tool kit.

She thought of something else that had been working its way around her head during their discussion.

"Now we know the role Lois the dispatcher played," she said.

Knowles and Cole looked at her, not grasping it yet.

"By my guess," she said, "he made friends with her because she was the one who could ensure he keep his schedule—week in, week out."

Knowles considered the notion, then nodded.

"You may be right," he said.

Laramie stood.

"I think it's about time I gave our operative a call," she said.

37

Cooper had a feeling it wouldn't be easy digging up the dirt on "ICR," whatever the letters stood for. For starters, the third letter on the board was partially cut off by the frayed edge of the wood, so that the company name, if that's what it was, might have been "IC Rentals" or "ICRT" as easily as it could have been just the simpler acronym "ICR."

More out of laziness than anything else, Cooper decided to place his bet on the easy version, which meant searching for a three-word company name, or individual's name, with current or former holdings in Guatemala or Central America. Though he knew just from the scent of the soil it was unlikely that ICR, the person or company, would be claiming any involvement with the facility built, operated, and burned in the upper portion of that figure-eight of volcanic crater where they'd taken their little hike. Whoever or whatever it was, ICR probably wouldn't even admit to being in Guatemala at all, meaning searching based on a geographical presence would probably turn out to be a waste of time.

There were six relevant, classified databases he could search, and more than a few techniques he knew to employ with ordinary search engines, to hunt around for the dirt.

This morning he'd picked the veranda as the operations center. It was almost dawn, Cooper lucky it wasn't pouring rain the way it almost always did before the sun came up. Ronnie, he knew, would soon emerge to slice his melons, and probably want to talk—ask him where he'd been, tell him about some crap one guest or another had pulled, a crazy request he'd been asked to provide.

Cooper usually answering, *That's what you get for being an errand boy. You get to run errands,* or something to that effect.

While he still had the peace and quiet, Cooper did his work—and found nothing. He started with Google and some other less reliable ordinary search engines, working through Spanish-language variations first, separating the letters, trying one Spanish word beginning with I, then two words beginning with I and C, and so on. He tried the other techniques he'd honed during his many hours with nothing to do, but other than a few individuals' names—Inez Charon Rodriguez, for instance, who, he learned, lived in Argentina and enjoyed water sports and horseback riding—there was no name, company or otherwise, that popped up showing any apparent relevance. He tried more and more variations, using some standard Spanish words, working through the logical ways a Spanish-language company name would be structured, but again found zilch.

He switched to English variations and after another forty minutes of looking, found only a number of obscure entities that seemed to have nothing to do with corporate or government business.

He tried some of the slower, though occasionally more thorough federal databases he liked to use, but soon concluded he was wasting his time. There wasn't any publicly named organization with known ties to Central America that used the initials ICR, at least not that related to a chemical spill or the manufacturing of materials that might have caused one.

Not that he'd expected to find anything to go on anyway.

He closed his PowerBook, putting it to sleep automatically, then tossed his left ankle over his right knee, crossed his fingers behind his head, and leaned back in the plastic deck chair that he knew would break if he put too much weight into his lean.

Earlier he'd placed the strip of wood on the white plastic table beside his PowerBook, the wood's letters beginning to fade. Cooper lifted his bare foot to shove one end of it and spin it in place on the tabletop.

He had plenty of people he could call—among others, any of a number of the individuals Cooper kept on his long list of corrupt souls he'd caught in action and was always pleased to blackmail or extort when opportunity beckoned. He'd try a few such souls later today, see whether they could give him some goods on the letters printed on the scrap of wood—but he knew it'd only be due diligence, and nothing more. He had that sense he sometimes got—that he'd already found all he'd be finding. The rest was nothing more than a waste of energy and time.

Particularly if the snuffer-outers, and by extension the chemical plant torchers, were, as he suspected, "of government" and "of Washington," or at least somewhere in the States.

"Crap," he said.

Maybe I'll just sit out on the beach and wait around until the snuffer-outers work their way around to me—

He heard a noise and realized that somebody had begun slicing melons behind him. Without turning to look, he already knew it wasn't Ronnie—the errand boy, he knew, wouldn't have got to work without offering up at least a snide remark, or hangover-heavy greeting. Cooper listened, still facing the beach and not the melon slicer, and detected the bubbling gurgle of a pot of coffee brewing somewhere behind him too. Finally, it seemed a form of calm—or maybe he'd have to call it a fluid sort of transition—had come over the veranda and its surrounding garden.

Because of this, he knew who it was who was doing the slicing.

The man with the knife cut a tall, lanky shadow against the nearest bungalow wall. He cut the fruit with an expert, if rusty hand, doing it a little more slowly than when he used to do it every day. Meaning that when Cooper turned, he found the proprietor of the Conch Bay Beach Club looking back at him, an almost imperceptible nod offered while the man continued with the slicing and dicing. His name was Chris Woolsey—a tan, fit, cheery-looking fellow maybe half a decade younger than Cooper but much healthier—and much healthier looking—than the permanent resident of bungalow nine.

Woolsey didn't spend as much time in Conch Bay these days—there were a few other properties to manage—but when he did, it was evident to gecko, plant, and person alike that this was a man who'd found his place in life.

As with Cooper, that place was here.

"The hell'd you do with Ronnie," Cooper said.

"Even the putz gets a vacation now and then, Guv."

"Where've you been?"

"Mostly the Caymans," Woolsey said. "Little while in Aruba."

Cooper nodded. He knew what Woolsey meant, and specifically where the proprietor had been on the islands he mentioned.

Cooper sometimes admitted to himself he envied Woolsey for his generally friendly manner—it was utterly genuine, and in fact he'd grown more effusive in the two decades Cooper had known him. Cooper envied Woolsey for it but couldn't quite grasp how it might be possible to always be in a fine mood. Though on the other hand he could see how a person might be capable of acting that way, had that person not been subjected to near-fatal torture, nor dug himself a spiritual hole and taken a nosedive into the abyss in the years that followed.

"You know, the lagoon's beginning to look like shit," Cooper said. "Saw a fucking beer can down there the other day."

Woolsey nodded.

"Got a notion to cut back on the rezzes," he said. "Put a limit on it. Maybe raise the prices. Cut 'em back either way."

"In the meantime let's get Ronnie down there with the net to clean it out. When he's back from his little sojourn, that is."

"Not entirely clear he's comin' back, mate."

Cooper turned to look at his friend.

"Feeling guilty?" Woolsey said after a little while.

"Why would I feel guilty?"

"Seeing that you've been even more than your usual horse's ass recently."

"Christ," Cooper said. "You too?"

"It's usually funny as effin' hell, mate," Woolsey said. "Almost a tourist attraction in and of itself, having a bitter, angry old fuck such as yourself in the last bungalow in the row. Angry and sad—make that depressed—are bloody different, though."

Cooper turned back around to face the water.

"See," Woolsey said, "somebody's pissed, you argue with him, even laugh at the bloke, right? Take some barbs but who gives. Somebody's in a funk, it's different—kind of rubs off on you. Rubs off on the whole effin' place. Rubbed off on Ronnie anyway."

Cooper lowered his eyelids. "He quit?"

"He will," Woolsey said, "you don't quit driving him into his own depression. Hell, Guv—lucky anybody's even coming by any longer. Place has the atmosphere of a funeral parlor. Maybe one with a sad old dog sleepin' in the corner."

Cooper didn't say anything. Woolsey, who had finished slicing the fruit, stacked a few cubes of each kind on a series of plates. When he had the servings assembled, he wiped his hands on a towel he'd been keeping in the waistband of his board shorts, turned his back, reached for the pot of coffee, and poured two white mugs full enough to prohibit the addition of any milk. He grabbed both mugs and came over and handed one to Cooper.

He took a nearby seat and the two of them sat there, facing the very short crescent of sun as it began to show itself, fatten, then rise above the horizon. Cooper sipped, Woolsey sipped, and they said nothing. Cooper didn't disturb his PowerBook, or the piece of wood. He just kept sipping, and looking out at the water and the sun.

When they were finished with the first round, Woolsey brought the pot over and poured them each a new cup and they drank that too in silence.

When they began to hear some footsteps on the garden path—the telltale sound of flip-flop on gravel—Woolsey stood.

"Time for the world-famous continental breakfast," he said.

Woolsey stood there, sort of glaring down at Cooper, until the guests behind him were only a few steps away. When they were nearly within earshot but not quite, he said, "I trust we understand one another."

Cooper didn't look up at him, or do anything else to acknowledge the comment, but Cooper knew better than to think he could get away with the silent treatment on a friend as old and good as Woolsey. He understood Woolsey perfectly well—this didn't mean he was ready to admit anything—far from it—but Woolsey knew as well as he did that their little get-together had gotten under his skin. They certainly did understand one another—for nearly twenty years now, they almost always had.

When the bubbly conversation arrived along with the married couple on the veranda to spoil the solitude of his morning paradise, Cooper stood, folded his PowerBook beneath an elbow and the strip of wood in the pocket of his swim trunks, and headed out onto the beach—opting, as he usually did, to take the scenic route on his walk back to bungalow nine.

38

"Time to earn your money."

Upon hearing Laramie's voice over the earpiece of his sat phone, Cooper checked his watch—ten of twelve. He decided he had no idea when he'd fallen asleep—ten minutes ago? Twenty? However long it had been, it hadn't been enough. If nothing else, at least the beers he'd put in the icebox would be cold now, so he'd be able to drink something chillier than piss-warm brew.

He thought immediately of asking Laramie to look into the letters "ICR" for him—admit he was a failure as an investigator, that he'd be better off swimming laps, consuming lukewarm beer, and taking his cherished late-morning naps, and leave it at that. Rub her nose in the scent, he knew, and Laramie could find just about anything—including how to get her goat like nobody's business. Julie Laramie, he thought—the woman he'd once referred to as the human lie detector machine. Maybe I'll just put her on the case.

Since Cooper wasn't thinking any of these thoughts out loud, Laramie went on.

"You'll need to get us into Cuba," she said. "The sooner the better."

"Us?"

"You and me. Or, if you prefer to think of it this way, the operative and his commanding officer in the 'counter-cell cell.' "

Cooper thought for a moment, reclined as he was in the hammock that stretched between a pair of palms at the far end of the beach. He couldn't see the restaurant from where he lay, which meant that nobody in the restaurant could see him either. Either way, it was the ideal time of day—the sun was high and hot, the sky clear, and most of the guests had headed into the restaurant or their bungalows from the beach, either eating lunch or readying to do it. A pair of kids played in the water all the way down the other end of the beach, but no one else was around.

"Whatever it is you want done on Fidel's home turf," he said, "if you're calling me to do it, it can't be good, and if it's nasty business, you've got no business going along for the ride. Even as commander-in-chief of your empire of dirt."

He had a feeling the skin on Laramie's neck was turning a splotchy, pinkish red right about now.

"I'll be the judge of that," was all she said.

Cooper said nothing, unimpressed with the reaction he'd failed to earn.

"How do you go about getting there?" Laramie said. "I know you've been plenty of times."

"Cuba?" Cooper said. "Pretty much the way you'd go about getting anywhere."

He heard something that sounded like a sigh over the phone.

"I understand Cuba is happy to take tourism dollars despite the U.S. trade and travel embargo," Laramie said. "I'm not talking about a pleasure cruise. We'll need to go there in secret. Probably under false names. And preferably—"

"Going that way's simple for somebody with your connections. And mine. Book a seat aboard a military transport into Guantanamo Bay and sneak in from there. That's the preferred means of entry for CIA. Everybody, including Fidel, knows it, and no one really cares anymore. Once in a while the Cuban government'll toss an American in prison, hold him for a day or two—"

"I don't want to use my 'connections,'" Laramie said, "and I don't want you using yours, either. Technically, the investigation we're conducting is nonexistent. I think the people I work for would be more concerned about my operating through CIA or military channels than if we were to get in there in some way that alerts the Cuban government to our presence. Anyway, it seems to me this is one of the main reasons we have you on the team—to generate HUMINT. Unconventionally, if need be."

"*One* of the reasons," Cooper said, not quite making it a question.

After enough silence had passed for Cooper to be forced to admit Laramie had refused to bite, Cooper said, "By boat, then. I'd do it by boat."

"Yours?"

"Hell, no. Always a chance Fidel's Revolutionary Navy'll take your boat if they find out what you're doing and don't like it. It's a small chance, but still a chance."

"How do you do it then?"

"If you want to do it undetected, or relatively so, you just sail on in. Literally. Preferably on a pretty quick boat, but one you can afford to lose. When you say 'sooner the better,' how soon are we talking about?"

"However soon you can get us there."

"Also, where we going? Pretty big island, Cuba."

It took a moment for Laramie to answer. "Near the western tip, on the south coast. San Cristóbal," she said.

Cooper flipped over his wrist and checked the time on his Tag. He'd need to make a couple of calls, and they'd need to get themselves on a couple of flights—neither of which tasks would put them past midafternoon.

"Unless things have changed in the last five years, there's a three o'clock nonstop to Cancún out of Fort Myers," he said. "American. Get yourself on the flight and I'll pick you up outside the baggage claim. I were you," he added, "I'd pick up some Dramamine in the airport gift shop. Don't take it until after you land—it'll be another hour from there before we're out on the water."

Cooper knew it would take at least six hours by sea, maybe more, before whatever shitbucket his friend Abe Worel procured would deliver them to the land of Fidel, Che, and good baseball—and that Laramie would probably be heaving her guts over the side maybe fifteen minutes into the trip, regardless of how many Dramamine tablets she took. But the drug usually mitigated the effect, if nothing else.

After a moment Laramie said, "You're saying we're going in tonight?"

"That soon enough?" he said. "Call if you miss the flight. Otherwise I'll see you at the baggage claim."

Cooper ended the call.

With nothing much else to do during the usual delays on the pair of flights he was taking to get from Tortola to Cancún, Cooper brought Laramie's terror book along for the trip and reread most of the material. He couldn't concentrate particularly well—whenever he hit a boring passage, which was always, he'd begin experiencing visions of the various dead ends in his triple-murder, seek-to-save-your-own-ass case— the golden-idol priestess screeching for help, Cap'n Roy dead by his pool, Po Keeler's tarp-covered body down in the Dump, these images all sloshing around his sodden mind's eye between thoughts of Belize City, the contract killer, U.S. Coast Guard cutters, the Polar Bear, and that strip of wood from the bottom of the fucking cave in—

Guatemala.

He read the word on the page just as he thought it. He focused on what he'd been reading, realizing he hadn't comprehended a word in the past ten, maybe fifteen pages. He was camped in the section covering the "filo," authored by somebody from the Centers for Disease Control; it seemed there was a mention of a case of hemorrhagic fever in Guatemala in the early 1980s that the CDC indicated was a fairly close match, symptoms wise, with the "Marburg-2" bug Benjamin Achar has loosed upon the Central Florida population.

Having just returned from a trip in which he'd witnessed the skeletal remains of a village worth of Indians all dying quickly and at about the same time—in the same neck of the woods as the case of hemorrhagic fever outbreak mentioned in the report—Cooper decided he'd have to consider the unlikely possibility of a connection. He found this hard to believe, but as he pondered it, the scenario actually sounded more plausible every minute.

If the "isolated remnant civilization" he and Borrego had discovered to have been killed sometime less than fifty years ago *hadn't* been dispatched by a Marburg filovirus, the village had certainly been exposed to something *like* it—which, in turn, he had to assume had been released, whether intentionally or no, by the torched-to-the-earth facility formerly occupying the upper portion of the crater. Maybe it wasn't a chemical plant after all—but a *biological* weapons plant.

Any further connection became rapidly more disturbing.

It seemed obvious that his own discovery might be of great value to the commander-in-chief of the "counter-cell cell" by which he was now employed—but he also wondered whether there might be something from Laramie's case, or the connections possessed by "the people she worked for," that could aid him in solving his own, seemingly endless sequence of dead ends.

Cooper flipped back to the last paragraph he remembered paying attention to and reread from there. The "filo" dispersed by Achar was an airborne filovirus, or hemorrhagic fever pathogen, easily caught by and transmitted to both animal and person. According to the report, there were synthetic components of the "filo's" makeup, meaning it had been bioengineered. The CDC author mentioned numerous laboratories, hostile regimes, even one clandestine American facility in Utah as possible institutions where filovirus engineering had taken place within the "preceding decades," but stated that no evidence existed indicating such a revolutionary technological breakthrough as found in the "Marburg-2" had been achieved at any of these labs.

"In our effort to find the origin of the organic portion of the pathogen," the report went on to say, "the CDC followed two investigative paths. First, we accessed CIA's most current intel on the inventory and status of all facilities known to have done illegal biological weapons research. We isolated three active facilities that have, at one time or another, been known to focus on filo-related R & D: one in Malaysia, operated and funded by the Jemaah Islamiya terrorist organization; a second, possibly run by al-Qaeda, in Algeria; and a third housed on the grounds of a privately held pharmaceuticals company in the Ukraine. At the urging of the task force, the Pentagon sent [REDACTED] . . ."

By necessity, Cooper skipped the blacked-out portions of the report and kept on. He wondered whether Laramie had blacked out sections she didn't want him to see, or if she'd received the report this way.

"The second angle we're taking in our search for the origin of the strain assumes the organic portion of the filo serum is a naturally occurring bug," the report said, and here, Cooper saw, was where the report referenced Guatemala, and the outbreak the CDC had focused its investigation on.

He read that in 1983, a caregiver's journal documented the outbreak at a health care clinic in "rural Guatemala"— the report, Cooper found, offering no greater precision than that. Before the caregiver ran out of gas herself, she described the symptoms of the outbreak, as incurred by the entire clinic's staff. The CDC had recovered the journal from some vaguely explained source. The symptoms of hemorrhagic fever, Cooper read—uncontrollably high fever, total breakdown of all organ functions, bleeding out through every orifice, rapid death—were similar wherever the pathogen struck. But the specific characteristics of the La-Belle outbreak matched the symptoms suffered by the victims in the Guatemala clinic very closely, at least per the caregiver: the incubation and infection periods, aggressive symptom development, and other disease "mile markers" tracked in the missionary's journal matched the LaBelle fever death pattern nearly to the minute.

The journal described a local teenage girl "of Indian dialect" who had been treated in the clinic for flu-like symptoms and subsequently released before the onset of the symptoms among the staff.

Cooper leafed back to check the date again: 1983.

Poor man's forensics team though he and the Polar Bear made, he and Borrego had put the deaths of the members of the Indian village somewhere in that basic time frame. Yet another disturbing match—it wasn't too far-fetched a scenario to presume that the filo-infected girl "of Indian dialect" had strolled into the health clinic the same week, or month, or year that the Indian village was taken down by some similar outbreak.

Cooper checked for and found no further reference to the fate of the girl in the passages from the journal as photocopied into the binder.

Christ—a survivor?

He closed the binder and stuffed it in the bag he'd brought along for the flights, Cooper thinking the CDC report had decided it for him: he *would* be asking Laramie the lie detector about "ICR," in addition to recommending that she, as the "counter-cell cell" commander-in-chief, plug into her suicide-sleeper equation the connection he'd just unearthed.

The only problem being what and who it all seemed to connect *to*—unfortunately, by way of that fucking burned-down lab, he thought, the bioengineered filovirus and the murdered village seemed connected to none other than the fucking snuffer-outers. The snuffer-outers he now felt safe assuming to be camped out in Washington, or Langley—or wherever the hell it is that powerful government assholes camp out these days.

Meaning that the minute he brought Laramie into the loop, he may as well be signing her death warrant—as surely as Po Keeler and Cap'n Roy, in their innocent greed, had signed their own.

"Crap," he said, realizing, without caring, that he'd said it aloud on the small plane he shared with fifteen other passengers.

He closed the terror book and fixed his eyes out the window. The plane ducked below the clouds and the Yucatan Peninsula revealed itself a few thousand feet below.

39

They were able to get ninety minutes of the voyage out of the way before the sun ducked behind the ocean. Cooper was powering them along at twelve knots with the catamaran's eighty-horse motor, and the surface of the Caribbean was about as flat as it got—slow, rolling swells of the sort that never went completely dormant, but utterly lacking in wind and chop. This meant, among other things, that Laramie hadn't yet begun to purge the contents of her stomach, slim as Cooper assumed the contents to be given Laramie's usual intake of such things as small-size salads with nonfat dressing on the side.

The boat was a 30' Endeavorcat. Cooper had got Abe Worel, a longtime charter captain based out of Virgin Gorda, to reserve the boat for him through a Cancún outfit Worel had a stake in—Cooper suggesting to Worel that he secure comprehensive insurance as part of the rental arrangement and leaving it at that. Worel told him where to go to find the boat and that it would be ready for him anytime after four. By six, Cooper and Laramie were pushing off from the rental company's dock.

As the sun began its hastened retreat below the horizon,

Laramie explained her team's theory that an "Americanization campus" of some sort would be what Achar had directed them to with his GPS-coordinates code. She also told Cooper her secondary suspicion about the site, generated when she'd seen the coordinates represented on the map of Cuba: she believed that whatever they'd find, they'd find underground.

Cooper said, "So we're heading to this place, presuming we've got the location correct, to do what? Ask who's in charge?"

"Maybe," Laramie said.

"Why don't you just snap off some satellite shots and whip out your magnifying glass? After you isolate what it is you're looking for, the people you work for can send in somebody properly equipped to crash the party. Such as, I don't know, possibly the U.S. Marines."

"I already have snapped off some satellite shots, and you're slowing down as you age," Laramie said. "This isn't the party we need to crash. If it's an Americanization campus, then it follows it's run by whoever sent the sleepers, but it doesn't change the fact that he, or she, or they, have already planted the sleepers. It's the sleepers we need to 'crash,' not the training grounds. And who knows—maybe we'll find something altogether different. It could be— however unlikely it is at face value—that Castro's the one behind this, and the GPS location represents the place where he actually keeps the list of sleepers."

"Or maybe we find nothing."

"True."

"Then why are you going?" Cooper said. He checked the glow-in-the-dark compass and flicked the wheel slightly to starboard, adjusting the catamaran's course by a few degrees.

Laramie didn't say anything for a while. She didn't do much either—just kept her head set back against the cushion in her seat. Maybe she's keeping quiet, he thought, because the reason she came was to seize the chance, international terror crisis or no, to wing it southward with the ex.

Ex? Cooper made an attempt to withdraw the thought,

something he always found himself trying yet failing to do in the presence of Laramie—and only Laramie. Otherwise, he was usually quite pleased by his own thoughts. At the moment, though, he found some fury swell up within, along with a question to himself: *How could four months in the islands qualify as a relationship?*

Well, that's what you called it: you just referred to yourself as the "ex." One in a long string of thoughts, words, and other annoying acts I'd usually prefer I never thought, or said, or did. Laramie—still the lie detector she always was, a goddamn truth serum you didn't even have to drink to begin suffering its effects.

"I'm coming along because I need to see it for myself," Laramie said, interrupting his thoughts.

Cooper wasn't buying.

"Even though you don't know what it is?" he said.

"What we're finding?"

"Right—if it's anything at all. You're going just because you need to see for yourself?"

"I'm going," she said, "because I have no idea what I'm doing."

Cooper tried but failed to make the connection, but he didn't need to prompt her, Laramie forging on with no delay.

"Somebody I used to work for," she said, "who's currently working somewhere else, recruited me to do what I'm now doing. Meanwhile, I think it's still not quite four and a half years since I was pulling a string of all-nighters cramming for my undergraduate poli sci exams—"

"Working with one hell of a professor, the way I understand it," Cooper said.

"—so here I am, not even five years later, and I'm overseeing a 'counter-cell cell,' which—unless my new boss, or somebody else in addition to him, has also recruited other unqualified persons such as myself to do the same thing . . . look, if you believe the theory that there's ten, or twelve, or twenty other sleepers out there, this 'cell' they've got me in charge of currently holds the fate of thousands, even tens or hundreds of thousands of American lives in the balance. Solely. I'm having some trouble with this. It doesn't make any sense. Or, it does in a strange way—I wrote a thesis for an independent study project in school, and the people I work for are employing a strategy that is pretty much a carbon copy of what I recommended in the paper. It's the way I thought to be the proper means by which to fight today's terrorist threats. But who cares? Somebody else certainly thought of the same thing—they probably just stumbled across my paper and tossed it in the vault once they realized the similarities. And, well, I mean, I'm pretty good at solving puzzles, I guess you could say. But this is one hell of a serious puzzle. I'm not remotely qualified for this."

"Just don't shrug," Cooper said, "Ms. Atlas."

Laramie turned, aiming, he surmised, to eye him sharply, but even in the encroaching darkness he saw a softness hit her eyes when she caught his. She turned away, looking out at the vanishing horizon again, the direction she'd been facing for the majority of their conversation. Fending off the seasickness, he thought. She'd soon lose that battle. Once the horizon disappeared, so too would her equilibrium.

Laramie kept at it.

"I thought if I got my nose out of the terror book," she said, "and saw something live and in person, then maybe something, *anything,* would occur to me. Maybe nothing that would explain why I was chosen for the job, and why there isn't somebody else, or thousands of somebody elses, possibly including the U.S. Marines, more qualified than I to be out there searching for Benjamin Achar's true identity—and the identity and whereabouts of his fellow sleepers. But I thought I might see something that'd make the four or five puzzle pieces out of a thousand we've found thus far orient themselves on the jigsaw board. Christ," she said, waving her hand, "whatever. We've found virtually nothing besides these GPS numbers, so maybe I just want to see what we've found."

Cooper looked at her, and couldn't see it in the dark, but thought suddenly of the tiny mole he knew existed just above her right ear, which he remembered having noticed the second time they made love. It had been an awkward session—each of them recovering from fairly morbid gunshot wounds but still finding the places each needed to find.

Another thought I need to purge.

"Of course, even if you found nothing," he said, "you figured you might just be able to use this Havana vacation of ours to talk things through with your operative. Maybe catch a little R & R, even, before returning to strategy central and good old Professor Eddie."

"Stop it," she said. "This may surprise you, but I'm not necessarily interested in taking any R & R. Don't you realize the stakes here? What's wrong with you?"

Cooper almost grinned, thinking he'd finally struck paydirt.

"I'm trying to figure out who these assholes are, and you're goofing off?" she said. "No, I take that back: you're flirting."

"Me?"

"Stop it."

She was staring at him again, maybe shooting him an evil eye, but Cooper couldn't really see her in the failing light. He locked the steering wheel, stood, balanced his way forward, found the onboard fridge he'd loaded up before they left, withdrew a Budweiser longneck for himself and the bottle of Chardonnay he'd brought for her. Might not last long in that landlubber's stomach of hers on the ocean in the dark—but Laramie, he thought, needs a goddamn drink.

He came back to their spot near the helm, opened the bottle, poured and handed her a paper cupful of the wine, popped his Bud, then did his best to clink his beer against the paper cup for a toast.

"Relax, lie detector," he said.

After a while, Laramie said, "Yeah?"

"Yeah," he said. He slid back into his place behind the wheel, discovering, as he settled in, that he was feeling something close to what he'd felt during those times when he'd been away from Conch Bay for a week, or month, and took his swimming goggles and headed out to poke around the reef. Familiar territory, warming his cold soul like ninety-proof bourbon going down the hatch.

"You know what we're going to find?" he said.

"No," she said.

"We're going to find what we're going to find," he said.

Laramie didn't say anything for a while. He assumed she was drinking some of the wine.

"That's very Zen of you," she finally said from the darkness.

"Live slow, mon," Cooper said, and put away some of his beer.

Two hours later, nursing his fourth Budweiser, Cooper found to his amazement that Laramie had not yet fallen victim to a bout of seasickness. During those two hours, while they rode in relative silence, Cooper considered, then made his decision, reflecting, as he went in circles, that he didn't have a choice. Any way he looked at it, he was going to have to tell her what he'd found. As she'd put it herself, too much was at stake.

He was just going to have to do a better job of keeping the snuffer-outers away from Laramie than he'd done for Cap'n Roy.

Plus, there was the selfish angle. He wasn't quite willing to accept himself as a good soldier, obligated to perform good deeds in service of the safety of American citizens. These citizens were part of a nation that had fucked him over, up, and down—with little remorse—more than once. And according to the theory he was following as to the identity of the snuffer-outers, somebody with considerable power, working for the government of that nation, had arranged the killing not only of Cap'n Roy and a few other relatively innocent souls—but, by intention or utter, careless negligence, of an entire Indian civilization.

And by invoking Laramie, the human lie detector machine, he might just be able to turn her against the people she worked for in service of his own case—and the vengeance those voices in his head were asking him to seek.

The people Laramie works for, he thought, are bound to know something—or maybe everything—about that fucking factory, the people who burned it to the ground, and the chief snuffer-outer I'm looking to put at the top of *my* dead pool.

And considering they've made the mistake of hiring the human lie detector machine, maybe I can put this to my advantage and squeeze some info out of the equation.

Cooper peered into the shadows where Laramie was seated and tried to determine whether she was awake. He couldn't, so he said, "You actually took the Dramamine?"

She had never abided by his suggestion before.

"I did," she said from the darkness.

"We've got a few hours to kill," Cooper said.

When Laramie didn't say anything, Cooper realized what it sounded as though he was implying—or proposing. He enjoyed the moment of crackling tension, imagined or real, before explaining himself after a while.

"Reason I mention that," he said, "is there's a story you should probably hear."

"A story," Laramie said after her own measured delay. "What about?"

Cooper grunted. "Among other things," he said, "a twelve-inch priestess, a murdered chief minister, and a guy who calls himself the Polar Bear."

The sound of waves, and a mild rush of breeze, came at them for a moment.

"Sounds like one hell of a story," Laramie said.

"You've got no idea," Cooper said, and commenced to killing time with his tale, careful to clarify how he thought it may well connect to the intended wrath of the suicide sleepers she hoped to thwart.

40

Cuba's Revolutionary Navy, Cooper knew, wasn't particularly adept at protecting its own coast, with the notable exception of a few ruthless attacks on Cuban citizens, conducted during the citizens' attempts to flee the regime. Castro's army, the Revolutionary Armed Forces, was nearly as ill-equipped, essentially operating on a zero-budget basis since the COMECON money train—the Soviet Union's foreign-aid package for communist partners—derailed in the early nineties. The FAR, as it was known, had succeeded in shooting down the occasional Cessna, and its army managed to keep Fidel alive—but such expensive tools of modern warfare as effective coastal radar installations were, for the Republic of Cuba, the stuff of nostalgia.

San Cristóbal was part of the Pinar del Rio province, on the southern side of the island, just over a hundred and twenty miles from the western tip. They made good time on the flat seas, coming in around two-thirty A.M. to a beach Cooper had used before. He'd navigated tonight strictly by compass, thinking, as he flicked on his flashlight and aimed it toward the beach, that the old Cuban fisherman in Hemingway's famous book couldn't have worked his way to San Cristóbal any better. He killed the engine as they hit shallow water and drifted in; after a few seconds the twin hulls made a dull scraping noise. Cooper secured the outboard and slipped over the side into the shallow water. He'd left his Reefs in the boat and felt the grainy sand noodle up between his toes as he touched bottom. He pulled the boat onto the beach and told Laramie she could jump out.

They unloaded their gear—two Mongoose touring bikes and a pair of tall backpacks, the backpacks outfitted with a variety of equipment, food, and drink. Then Cooper pushed the boat back into the water and guided the catamaran to the eastern end of the beach where he dragged it behind a mound of driftwood. Laramie watched as Cooper vanished into a thicket of bushes, broke off some branches, and came out again to lay them across the boat. He came over and pulled the bikes and backpacks up the beach, tucked them too behind some driftwood then came back down to Laramie, who'd stayed firmly planted in the sand in order to shake off the last of the effects of the sea.

"Made good time," he said, peeking at his watch. "Sun'll be up in three hours. May as well catch some zzzs while we're here at the Mambo Beach Resort. Road's right past those trees, but it won't do us any good heading out on our little *Tour de Cuba* before we get some light."

Cooper got busy doing some things behind the driftwood. When he was done, he poked his head over one of the up-ended stumps and saw that Laramie was seated in exactly the same place as before. Wordlessly, he came out from behind the logs, strolled down the beach, extended a hand and, when Laramie took it, pulled her to her feet.

He turned and let go of her hand once she was up, but Cooper thought he caught a glimpse of a hard-edged kind of stare as the pale moonlight glinted off the whites of her eyes. He wondered whether it might only have been the angle of the light. But if it hadn't, and the glare had been real, it struck Cooper that he had seen that look before.

Laramie crawled out of her sleeping bag and found the backpack he said was hers. She dug through two compartments before finding the place he'd stored her toiletries. She withdrew a tube of toothpaste and her toothbrush and took them east along the beach with her, over where Cooper had hidden the boat. Still wearing the khaki shorts and sweatshirt she'd used for the voyage over, she stuffed the toothpaste and toothbrush in her pockets, made her way carefully into the brush, and pulled down her khakis to take a leak.

Then she came back down the beach and brushed her teeth. She brushed for a while. She thought about the things Cooper had told her he'd found, but she'd been thinking about those things, and what they might have meant, for most of the trip. Scraping the brush against her teeth, looking out at the Caribbean—or listening, at least, in the darkness—she thought about some other things. They were there during the darkest moment you found in the West Indies, the sky in that predawn, moonless state of blackness beneath the blanket of the morning cloud cover, and Laramie couldn't see too far beyond her wrist. But she could hear the waves lapping and breaking in their relentless approach and retreat, and there was another sound out there too, a distant sound that resembled a gently clanging bell. Might, she thought, be nothing more than a piece of metal banging somewhere in the wind—maybe on a dock fallen into disrepair a mile or two down the coast.

As far as Laramie was able to tell, Cooper remained asleep in his sleeping bag.

When it became apparent her eyes would never quite adjust to the darkness, she closed them and let the sounds of the water, and the tradewinds, and the tapping piece of broken metal sing to her. It wasn't, she decided, much different from the sounds of the trains she used to watch in San Fernando, back home, where she'd sneak up to a bluff and close her eyes while the freight trains rumbled by in a wash of hot wind.

Laramie supposed she should have expected what was occurring to her, sitting on this beach. She even supposed she'd brought it on herself by coming on this trip at all. She thought through some more things, then got sick of thinking through all the possible scenarios.

"Goddammit," she said, and opened her eyes.

She stood and kicked off her khaki shorts. She was already in bare feet, and kicked off her panties next. Pulled her T-shirt over her head and flipped it onto the sand behind her. Standing there in the darkness and breeze, she first walked, then jogged into the water, feeling the sand squish beneath her feet with every step, and then, when the water had reached her waist, she pushed off and dove into the warm blanket of the Caribbean.

She swam around in the shallow water, mostly balancing on her knees or floating around on her back, the water feeling like a hot bath in the cool night. She might have swum for fifteen minutes, or half an hour, Laramie losing track by intention as, after a while, she stood erect, leaned forward against the drag of the water, and walked out of the sea and up the gentle slope of the beach. She flicked her fingers through her hair to shed most of the water from her head, but otherwise didn't bother to dry off. The warm wind was already doing it for her anyway.

She passed by her rumpled mound of clothes, turned the corner past the driftwood, and, mostly without grace, located her empty sleeping bag by dropping down and feeling around on all fours. Once she found the soft mat of her own sleeping bag, she aimed left and kept crawling along until she encountered the bulky form of Cooper, hidden beneath the folds of his own bag. She found his zipper, opened the bag until she had enough room, then slipped in beside him and zipped the bag back closed behind her.

She knew from the way their skin touched that he had never actually fallen asleep.

In the tight quarters of the bag, she managed to get her arms around his chest. She rolled him over on his back, lay her body on his, and found his lips with a long, heavy, salty kiss.

41

It took them two and a half hours to reach San Cristóbal on the mountain bikes, the sun rising, then beating down and heating up the roadway beneath their wheels. Cooper thinking as he pedaled that if you wanted to see Cuba—the real Cuba—the trip was best made by bike. Spend your time in what was left of the old tourist havens, or the bustle of Havana, and you saw the propaganda, the illusion that the communist nation's economy and overall health of its citizens were on the up-and-up. Put your ass on a bicycle seat, though, and head out on a country road, and you'd catch the real deal. The jovial but understated people who lived here, desperate for a few bucks from any and every wayward tourist, long since accustomed to the disaster that was the Cuban economy but still doing fine.

Keeping the Caribbean attitude alive, he thought: governments, conquerors, hurricanes, wealth, and poverty came and went, but the sun was always hot and the sand and sea and earth were always there. *Live slow, mon*—though they didn't say it quite that way in Fidel's homeland.

He pointed to the sign as they rode past—part makeshift billboard, part poster, the wooden placard set back from the road announcing to them in a cursive scrawl that they'd arrived in San Cristóbal. Palm fronds and a batch of weeds had grown to partially obscure the sign. Cooper had been here before; he had expected then, and found himself expecting now, to see some symbol of the past—a communist propaganda billboard, perhaps—advertising what the town had become world famous for: in aerial photographs taken in 1962 and 1963, an American spy plane had identified it as one of the main construction sites which Cuba and the USSR had been gearing up for the installation of Soviet ICBMs. Ground zero, as it were, of the Cuban missile crisis.

But this morning, same as during his first visit, Cooper found there existed no local clue that any such thing had taken place. The town seemed as ordinary as you got— another busy village at the junction of a few country roads, home to the usual farm-oriented bustle found in just about every such town south of Texas.

They steered off the road into a gravel flat, flipped down the kickstands, and looked directly at each other for the first time since they'd got themselves untangled from Cooper's sleeping bag. Laramie handed Cooper her portable GPS unit.

"Here are Achar's numbers," she said, and pointed to the color screen. "And here's where we are now."

Cooper saw from the graphics on the screen that they were approximately four miles from the place Benjamin Achar had supposedly told them to go. Their destination was on this side of town, but judging from the GPS unit's directional arrow, it would take finding a side road or two to get them there.

Cooper handed the device back.

"You want to review our story, or are you all right with it," he said.

They were bohemian newlyweds out seeing the world on an extended honeymoon. Cooper had their fake passports— they'd used these identities before, during their aborted resort-hopping trip.

Laramie shook her head. "I'm good."

Cooper secured his backpack and swung himself onto the Mongoose.

"I'm assuming if there's anything worth seeing," he said, "somebody's going to be there keeping undesirables out."

"Like us," Laramie said.

"Correct. What I'm getting at," he said, "is if the shit hits the fan, I shoot, and you run."

Something twitched slightly at the corner of Laramie's mouth, but Cooper didn't exactly feel comfortable calling the expression a smirk.

"You're the operative," she said.

Cooper disturbed some gravel as he led the way back out onto the road.

Following the GPS unit's directions, they turned onto a narrow, paved ribbon of road that cut through a dense stand of trees. After a short ride, Cooper encountered a metal gate set back off the right side of the road. The gate blocked entry to what might once have been a dirt or gravel road but had long since been retaken by nature. He'd expected something like this, and he supposed Laramie had too: grown over and hiding the remnants of John F. Kennedy's beef with Nikita Khrushchev stood the usual Caribbean blend of indigenous and imported foliage—part pine forest, part palm fronds, but mostly weeds.

Stenciled in faded, red letters on a yellowing sign secured to the gate by two pieces of wire, there hung a warning against aspiring visitors.

PROHIBIDO EL PASO—PROPIEDAD DE LA F.A.R.

Cooper pulled his Mongoose into a shallow ditch at the side of the road, propped it on its kickstand, and was approaching the gate for a look around when he saw the slight shimmer of movement between the trees.

He ducked low beside the gate and Laramie followed his

lead. From his hiding place, Cooper was just able to make out the unmistakable figure of an armed, though distant human being. The guard stood on a hill about half a mile back from the gate, barely visible over the peaks of pine and palm. Perched on the near side of the summit was a dilapidated hut—looking no different, Cooper thought, than the endless stream of fruit stands they'd encountered on the way here, but with the alternate purpose of housing the guard currently strolling about it.

The sentry walked out of view behind the shack, then reappeared on the other side. He wore fatigues and had a rifle slung over a shoulder. He was doing something with his hand, Cooper having trouble making out the miniscule activity from this distance until he realized the guard was having a smoke. Cooper watched him for a couple of minutes, rapidly becoming satisfied that the guard looked the way a guard looks when he isn't too concerned about the threat of encroaching trespassers.

"So we've got company," Laramie said. "As expected."

He felt her right breast kind of pillowing against the back of his left shoulder. It bothered him that he noticed which body part had touched him as she leaned in for a look, but he dismissed the increasingly, irritatingly common sensation of helplessness and did his best to train his brain on the situation at hand.

"We do."

"Could mean nothing," she said. "Could be Castro has kept somebody posted here for forty-four years for no significant reason. At least nothing outside of sentry duty over an abandoned military base."

He didn't say anything.

"Or it could mean they've got something worth protecting," Laramie said.

Cooper backed away from the gate, falling in behind the stand of pines that blocked the sentry's view of their spot on the road.

"In the mood for a hike?" he said.

"Lead the way."

They found the perimeter fence about two hundred yards into the woods. It was chain-link fencing with rusting barbed wire trellised along the top. PROHIBIDO EL PASO and PROPIEDAD DE LA F.A.R. signs of the same style as they'd seen on the gate were wired to the fence, alternating at fifty-yard intervals. Cooper tried lifting the fence in a place midway between poles and succeeded: there was plenty of space for them to crawl underneath.

"Congratulations," he said as he came through behind her and got to his feet. "You're now trespassing."

"I've never been good with boundaries."

They'd been prowling for close to three and a half hours when Cooper fell into a hole.

He felt his ankle roll, attempting and failing to transfer his weight to the other foot before the sprain engaged and a stab of agony rocketed up his leg. He swore at the pain, planted a knee, then had a look around: it seemed he'd fallen into a six-foot-deep depression, which he now observed had been masked by a sea of dead leaves.

"You all right down there, operative?"

Laramie was smiling at him, and Cooper was about to devise some wiseass reply when he realized she was pointing at something behind him.

"I think you may just have found the way in," she said.

Cooper turned to see that he hadn't fallen into a hole at all—more of a dry canal bed. Infested with weeds and stunted pine trees, the depression was shallowest on the end Cooper had fallen into, and graduated to ten or more feet below the surface over the course of the length of a school bus. At the canal's deepest point, Cooper saw what Laramie meant: a set of 4' x 8' plywood sheets, one nailed to the next, covered some sort of door. Cooper counted four sheets of the wood, not a single one of which was holding up worth a damn, all four boards stained a moldy brown-green and covered in moss and mushroom bursts.

Laramie was already in the canal and pulling at the plywood wall as Cooper grunted his way up and limped over. He joined in, reaching under one of the sheets of decrepit wood and pulling. A chunk of the board broke off from its host and crumbled from his hands. He did it again, pulling off a larger chunk this time. In a matter of minutes, they had enough room to walk through the opening.

Cooper deployed the Maglite he'd brought along in the backpack to reveal that beyond the plywood barrier, a short length of tunnel ran away from them, partially interrupted along the way by something resembling chicken wire. Behind the chicken wire there stood the wide, inert blades of a massive fan. The housing for the fan appeared more solid-state than the exterior section of the tunnel. It had wide spaces between the blades—wide enough for them to crawl through.

The chicken wire moved aside with little resistance, its footings long since rusted out. When Cooper got to the fan, he unstrapped his backpack, got down on all fours, and crawled under one of the blades, pushing the backpack ahead of him on the floor of the tunnel as he went. He had the sensation of crawling into the belly of a submarine, passing the vessel's propeller as he snuck into the engine room.

Aided by the beam of the Maglite, Laramie followed him in.

They could walk upright in the tunnel. They hit a fork and Cooper chose a direction at random. He attempted to keep track of the fastest way out; he heard Laramie's footsteps shuffling behind him. There was grit, mud, and the occasional puddle at their feet, and a kind of consistent, moldy stench. The walls were made of thin concrete, Cooper aiming the flashlight at the wall while he poked around a few places to find that the substance crumbled apart as easily as the plywood had. He wondered how grave was the risk of a cave-in.

Then they turned a corner, and Cooper caught a glimpse of blue.

It hadn't exactly been a light at the end of the tunnel—when he dropped the beam of his flashlight and waited for his eyes to adjust, there was nothing to be seen. But when he raised the flashlight again, he saw it again—a shimmer of blue, almost the color of the sky on a clear day.

"You're seeing it too, then," Laramie said.

"I am."

In twenty steps, the sky blue glow became more pronounced, and when Cooper raised the beam of the Maglite they could see a louvered panel up ahead—the end of the line, and the source of that sky blue glow.

He moved the flashlight around some more, trying different angles, but it was always the same: it seemed no light was coming from beyond the louvers, but when he pointed the light in the direction of the panel, a blue glow would hit them. Soft—muted—but definitively sky blue. There were no sounds coming at them through the louvers.

Cooper brought the light around so they could see each other's faces.

"May as well have a look," Laramie said.

They hunched down at the base of the panel, listening. But there was nothing to hear.

Cooper reached up and tilted one of the louvers. He held the flashlight up and pointed the beam through a space between slats, and the two of them raised themselves to their elbows, more or less in unison, and had a look.

That was when they found themselves staring at the oddly displaced sight of an American strip mall.

42

Facing them was a full-size, brightly painted
7-Eleven sign, below which stood the store, beside which
store stood a crop of surrounding businesses built on opposing sides of a main drag. The street came complete with left-
turn lanes and accompanying traffic signals.

The source of the blue glow, she saw, was the color the
walls had been painted above the buildings and street—sky
blue, to duplicate the sky. Every store along the boulevard
appeared to be fully stocked with merchandise; in fact,
everything appeared to be picture perfect, at least outside of
the fact that it seemed utterly lifeless. The power had been
shut down, and not a single person was in sight.

After what might have been five minutes of silent observation, Laramie got a hold of herself. She turned and looked
at Cooper.

"It's Disneyland," she said, "inside out."

Cooper considered what she meant. "A theme park," he
said, "featuring the parts of Anaheim you find outside the
park."

"Or Orlando," she said.

"Or anywhere."

They stared through the panel at the odd view for a while longer.

"I'll be goddamned," Cooper said.

"So will I."

Laramie considered the meaning behind what they'd just found. Despite the facility's being abandoned, the apparent lengths to which the builders had gone in their attention to detail was staggering—or, she thought, *disturbing*. You're the leader of a cell, or nation, or faction intending to lay your wrath upon the Great Satan, and you certainly don't erect an underground suburban-America adventure ride to train *one* deep-cover sleeper agent.

"More like an army of them," she said.

As Cooper turned and eyed her, she realized she'd spoken her thought.

"Come again?"

"Just trying to comprehend this," she said.

"Far as I can tell, it means your 'counter-cell cell,' " Cooper said, "has got its work cut out for it."

"It's your cell too, Mr. Operative."

"Suppose you're right."

Laramie watched as Cooper worked his flashlight around the rim of the panel, her operative and onetime island-hopping companion examining the anchors that held the panel in place. He turned to dig through a pocket of his backpack, came out with an ordinary Swiss Army knife, and used the screwdriver tool to unscrew the panel's fasteners. He managed to detach the panel without dropping it the twenty feet or so down to the street, and with Laramie's help got it turned sideways so they could pull it inward. Laramie cringed as it scraped loudly, then made a noisy metallic *bang* on the concrete floor of the tunnel as they brought it in and released the grip they had on the thing a little early.

No follow-up sounds came.

Laramie poked her head over the ledge and discovered that a ladder was built into the concrete wall of the interior, rungs painted blue like the wall. She climbed out and started down the ladder.

After ten minutes of strolling wordlessly around the shops along the street, they came to stand in the middle of the 7-Eleven parking lot.

"It wouldn't be too expensive to pull this off," Laramie said. "I just can't believe nobody stumbled across it in the ten or fifteen years it's probably been here. Maybe it's Fidel who's behind this after all."

"Maybe," Cooper said.

He suddenly wondered whether his cash-paying participation in Castro's invitational Texas Hold 'Em poker challenge hadn't been the best of ideas. Then his thoughts of regret made him consider why Castro operated the poker tournament—and why Castro did just about everything he did, outside of rant and rave about the capitalist pigs ninety miles to the north:

For sheer profit.

"He rented it out," Cooper said.

Laramie, who'd been stealing a look at the "sky," looked down from the ceiling at Cooper.

"You mean Fidel?"

"It's his MO," Cooper said. "He'll take cash for anything he's got access to. Including, for instance, the San Cristóbal underground missile transport caverns. He'll take other things—oil, for instance—but basically the man will sell or rent anything he's got if you've got U.S. dollars to fork over. You name it—soldiers, prisoners, boats, property, whatever. Gotta keep the war chest funded so he can keep the revolution alive."

Laramie considered this.

"So if you're right," she said, "the trick becomes identifying the tenant. Most likely a revolutionary crony of Castro's—or at least somebody with access to the cronies."

"Ten or fifteen years ago, anyway," Cooper said.

Neither of them said anything for a while, Laramie considering some names, recalling photographs she'd seen in the international press of Castro's many labor-movement, socialist, or anticapitalist-themed diplomatic summits—and the guests he'd hosted at those events, or who'd invited him to theirs. Thinking that she'd brought Eddie Rothgeb aboard for a reason, and this was it: he'd be able to pin the list of America bashers down to the top ten, or top five suspects most likely to emerge as public enemy number one—and chief tenant of Fidel's rental park.

Cooper rotated the flashlight beam, pointing it down the road that led past the strip mall and turned a corner in the cavern at another traffic light maybe a hundred yards distant.

"Let's take a walk," he said.

Laramie came out of her Castro-comrade daydream. She knew they shouldn't spend any more time down here than necessary, but she would need to see everything while they had the chance.

She dug into her backpack and came out with the digital camera her guide had procured for her before she'd boarded the plane in Florida.

"I'll do the tourist thing," she said. "Lead the way."

They started down the street.

Cooper was riding too fast to turn them into the woods in time.

They came around a bend in the road, about half a mile toward the highway from the gate, and had to control their skids to avoid crashing into the side of the FAR jeep that had parked sideways across the road.

Blocking the way out.

Cooper had his hand on his Browning before the bike had completed its skidding halt, but the young man in fatigues seated behind the wheel of the jeep had his AK-47 trained on Cooper's chest.

"No, no, no, no, no," the man said.

Laramie swore as she skidded along the dusty road behind him, turned sharply and crashed, mostly to avoid plowing into Cooper's rear tire. She stood slowly, uninjured, and the

Cuban's gun rotated to point somewhere between the two of them. The man was smoking a cigarette, the white stick dangling, ash-heavy, from his lips. The setting sun hung over the trees behind the guy, so it was hard to see through the glare and get any definition on his face.

Either way, the guy looked to Cooper as though he'd seen a couple too many James Dean or John Wayne films.

Cooper suspected this was the guard they'd seen manning the shack at the top of the hill. The cigarette, the way he held the gun—it had been a long-range view, but if he was right, and this was the only MP around, Cooper figured they had a pretty good chance of shooting their way out of here.

Making it all the way back to the boat was another matter.

"American, eh? Both of you," the soldier said. His accent was there, but his English was strong—practiced, Cooper thought. Almost formal.

"Yes!" He regretted reaching for his gun so early—*Rust comes in many forms, and this form might just get me killed.* "This is our honeymoon. Backpacking trip."

"Yes, yes," the soldier said. "But this is military base. *Prohibido el paso.*"

They were almost a mile from the highway, which wasn't visible ahead on the winding road. Unless they bolted for the woods, there wasn't much to do but try to talk their way out of this.

"Is that right? We didn't realize. Did we, honey?"

"No," Laramie said. "Sorry, sir."

"You like what you find? Strange, no?"

Cooper and Laramie avoided looking at each other.

"I will need your passports. You are under arrest."

Cooper observed that despite the caustic tone of the soldier's statement, the guy didn't make move one to reach for their passports.

"No problem," Cooper said, but remained still.

"How did you travel here?"

Cooper couldn't find a good reason to make something up.

"Sailboat," he said.

"Which is where," the soldier asked.

Cooper motioned in the direction of the beach where they'd made landfall, trying out a measure of honesty to see whether it would get him anywhere. "A couple hours that way by bike. Not sure what the town is called."

Laramie said, "Can we pay you for your trouble?"

Cooper raised his eyebrows—brash, but maybe it'd work. The soldier swiveled his head to her, then back over to train his eyes on Cooper again.

"It is almost dark," he said. "When were you planning to leave?"

Cooper narrowed his eyelids at the direction the line of questioning seemed to be taking.

"Tonight," he said.

"Are you CIA?"

"No, we were just married," Laramie said, "and—"

"Yes," Cooper interrupted. "Both of us."

She turned to look at him as though he'd lost it. The soldier nodded.

"Where are you going on your boat?" he said.

"Southwest," Cooper said. "Mexico."

The soldier nodded again, and that was when the sun lost some of its power, a cloud, or the tip of a tree, obscuring enough of its declining rays so that Cooper could read the soldier's face a little better.

Well enough, in fact, for him to see a couple things. First, how young this guy was—maybe twenty-five at most. He could also see the soldier's scheming eyes—not much different from the look Cooper had seen from Po Keeler during their conversation across the half-ass Plexiglas shield.

Cooper grinned and threw it out there.

"We can take you as far as Cancún," he said. "My friend here can arrange the rest. Assuming, that is, the final destination you've got in mind is north of the Florida Keys."

Laramie turned to look at him—wondering exactly how that would work, he assumed. But he knew "the people she worked for" could find a way to pull it off.

The guy turned to look at Laramie again.

"Including paying me for my trouble," he said.

Laramie glanced back at Cooper again with a look he decided he'd have to call priceless.

"Sure," she said. "Including that."

The soldier set his rifle on the passenger seat, took one last drag, then tossed the cigarette into the road.

"Climb in, Yankees," he said.

43

It was ten after midnight in Knowles's room at the Flamingo Inn. Rothgeb opened the door to let Laramie and her guide inside, at which point Laramie observed that Wally Knowles's computer system had expanded to seize every available surface in the room. Newspapers and stacks of printed sheets of white paper stood in neatly organized partitions in the few portions of the space the computer system had failed to overtake.

All business, Laramie shut the door, said her hellos, and got right to briefing them on their discovery of the San Cristóbal theme park. She fed them the working theory—that Castro had rented the place out—then asked them to generate a list. The list, she said, should include whichever of Castro's allies they believed to be the most likely theme park tenant. She and Cooper had gained little additional info on the theme park—outside of the patrol schedules and the long-term inactivity of the place—from the FAR refugee her guide had arranged to be flown from Cancún to Washington aboard a military transport, where he would be granted asylum after they held on to him for a bit.

Laramie then spent almost an hour walking her cell

through their operative's discovery of a possible connection between the genetically engineered M-2 filo, some sort of industrial facility in Guatemala that had been burned to the ground, and the lost Indian village that coincided, in place and time period, with the hemorrhagic fever outbreak the CDC had identified at the clinic in "rural Guatemala." She told them about the letters "ICR" that Cooper had found on the piece of wood near the facility.

"If the connection is real," she said, "let's find it."

Once she'd wrapped up, Laramie watched as Knowles, Cole, and Rothgeb looked at each other and came to some unspoken agreement.

Rothgeb then piped up as the cell's newly appointed spokesperson.

"Why don't you give us till nine A.M.," he said.

Laramie did the math. "Eight and a half hours? That's not much—"

"We've become something of a well-oiled machine," Professor Eddie said. "And while you've been out on your Caribbean vacation, we haven't exactly been sitting around with our proverbial thumbs up our rear ends. We've got some progress to report, but it's probably better if we brief you all at once. Eight hours should be plenty of time to isolate the top theme park tenant suspects."

Knowles nodded; Cole did too.

Laramie thought that she should have expected it— Rothgeb, assuming the spokesperson duties for her ragtag clan. She wondered idly whether he'd barged in as the pompous professor of diplomacy and foreign affairs he was—spokesperson, self-appointed—but couldn't detect any animosity from Knowles, or tension from Cole. Strangely enough, she thought, it seems this dysfunctional bunch *has* in fact become a well-oiled machine.

She told them nine A.M. would be fine and left the machine to do its work.

They gathered in Laramie's room—Laramie watching as her team arrived and its members chose their seats in approximately the same arrangement as the morning Laramie had given her introductory speech. Knowles perched on the edge of the bed; Cole, wearing shades today, took the chair near the door to the adjoining suite, where her guide was sequestered as usual. Laramie had the same chair at the room's lone table, only this time around, Professor Rothgeb sat beside her at the table. Cooper was listening in on the device Laramie had decided to call the "spiderphone"—the odd-looking contraption her guide had employed for her first report to Lou Ebbers.

She introduced Cooper as, "Our operative, whose identity will remain classified."

Rothgeb got right to it. For Laramie, it was a repeat of Foreign Policy 101—only with a sinister edge.

"In seeking to isolate who is most likely to have entered into a lease with Castro for the San Cristóbal theme park," he said, "we took into account the following prerequisites, evidence, and variables. First: relationship. Whether head of state or rogue terror financier, he or she needs to have had some relationship with Castro ten to fifteen years ago. And while we all know Castro would probably take money from anybody interested in paying, he was clearly involved in some way here, and that means ideology's gonna be key. That's second on our list—ideology—since Castro wouldn't have cooperated to such lengths without this guy being left of left. Third, and quite obvious: this person has a beef with America. Fourth: resources. It doesn't take billions to build a stadium-size theme park, but it does take a few mill. Plus, our guy would need to be capable of recruiting, training, possibly maintaining, and absolutely paying his sleepers. In almost all cases, the families of suicide bombers are handsomely rewarded by the faction for which they make the supreme sacrifice."

Rothgeb gestured toward the phone.

"Fifth is access to the filo. And while we can't yet point to a specific connection between the facility our operative discovered in Guatemala and the R & D it took to develop this bug, the confluence of factors is too significant to ignore. Bottom line here: any current or former Castro crony who's got a beef with America, sufficient resources to assemble these sleepers, and who either hails from or maintains ties with Central America generally, or Guatemala specifically, is moving very high on our list. There are a few other factors we've plugged in, but we need to work with what we know, and the elements I just described are pretty much what we're aware of."

Despite the serious issues at hand, Laramie was having difficulty suppressing a smile at how familiar Rothgeb's overly formal semantics sounded to her. She'd sat in too many lectures, among other things, to take him nearly as seriously as he took himself.

"There's a list maintained by the federal government, which used to be called the 'Strongman Ranking'—back in the days when Manuel Noriega and Moammar Khaddafi were our chief enemies of state—and now seems to be referred to more pedantically. I think it's called 'Terrorist Most Wanted' now. Point being, it's unofficial, so it isn't shown around, but it exists, and is regularly updated as a joint effort of numerous agencies, based on a number of anti-American activities and other factors conducted by the people on the list. We have a copy of it, and while our guy doesn't *need* to be one of the names on the list, if our suspect is one of those guys it's another notch against reasonable doubt."

Knowles passed around copies of the list, which had various headers and passages blacked out. The list was heavy on Middle Eastern names, and Laramie saw at least a few that shouldn't have been there but for their public opposition to certain American policies.

"Coming back to Fidel," Rothgeb said, "the man has held summits with virtually every enemy of the state, of our state at any rate, on a semiregular basis, in some cases annually, in some cases monthly, some for as long a period as the past thirty years. Anyway, in searching out staunch, fellow anti-U.S., anti-imperialist Castro allies, we're talking about a long list. With our other factors plugged in, the list narrows, of course—and look, there may well be an unknown, undocumented multimillionaire behind this sleeper operation, and if so, then we're making a mistake. But we're prepared to stand by our pick, primarily due to the geographical proximity of the 'filo lab' *vis à vis* his background—and largely because of his background itself. We believe public enemy number one is Raul Márquez, or somebody associated with his regime."

Laramie's eyes dropped to Márquez's name on the most wanted list. She knew who he was, and knew of his loud "beef"—many beefs—with America. On the resources front, she had her doubts, but he was certainly a Castro crony—

"He was the longtime head of organized labor in El Salvador," Rothgeb said. "He's held a position of influence and maintained a friendship with Castro for over fifteen years. His first candidacy for the presidency was a rout, and he hasn't looked back; plus, he's played a major role in helping organize labor and socialism-related movements with considerable political clout throughout Central and South America, to the point where you could say he is, in effect, a coalition leader of a number of socialist states, all of whom have a major beef with the U.S. and its 'imperialism.' You know his rhetoric—he and Hugo Chávez are the current heads of state who've essentially taken the anti-America torch from Fidel. The part of it bin-Laden isn't already holding."

Knowles adjusted his own sunglasses from his seat on the bed and jumped in, apparently on cue, since Rothgeb leaned back just as Knowles got started.

"We could make the case against Chávez, and a number of other figures, pretty effectively," he said. "But for a variety of reasons, we've eliminated each of the others. Chávez, for instance, remains in dire need of the economic health of the United States—we buy most of his oil, among other reasons, and it's his oil money that keeps him in power. His beef isn't with U.S. citizens, but U.S. regimes. Finally, though, there's one specific reason we believe we're right to pin it on Márquez. He's of native Central American descent—of Mayan ancestry. It's said that if you'll listen, he will tell—though only privately—where it is his hatred of all things American originated, and the accounts we've found of this tale are pretty consistent."

Knowles the storyteller grew a little more animated.

"During the Reagan era," he said, "the U.S. funneled big sums of foreign aid to the right-wing Salvadoran government as part of our 'containment' strategy against Soviet-allied socialist movements. Around the time Márquez would have been a teenager, there were 'murder squads' in operation—the government, which was more or less funded by us, would send out raping-pillaging units to eradicate rural settlements said to be harboring the leftist rebels, which in turn were said to be funded by the Soviets. There was more at work domestically than was understood initially, though—it seemed the 'murder squads' were focused more on the genocide of the native population than on eradication of the rebels."

Laramie was familiar with most of this history. "So the way he tells it," she said, "he survived an attack from one of the U.S.-financed murder squads?"

"You got it," Knowles said. "Apparently he was the only one to make it out of his village."

Laramie nodded. "So, if true," she said, "Márquez's story means he witnessed the wholesale slaughter of his entire village—family, friends, whatever—and blames America for the genocide from which he managed to escape."

Rothgeb leaned in over the table again.

"Yep," he said. "And a recent history of genocidal acts against native encampments is certainly not restricted, in the Americas, to El Salvador—we think there is a high likeli-

hood he used his own experience to recruit similarly disen-
franchised indigenous-culture survivors on a pan-American
basis. He'd have quite a pool to pull from—even if he was
operating solely on the basis of regional genocidal acts per-
petrated by regimes kept afloat in part by U.S. foreign aid."

Knowles made a "who knows" gesture with his palms and
took the baton again.

"Did he discover the biological weapons lab in
Guatemala? Did a scientist who worked there steal some engineered filo and bring it to Márquez? Any number of scenarios would make a great deal of sense on top of what
we've already laid out. It would explain a lot of the variables
here."

"He's your guy," Rothgeb said.

Cole spoke up too.

"Hard to go any other way with it," he said.

Laramie digested what her "cell" had just presented.
Well-oiled machine, indeed—even being the foreign affairs
junkie she was, Laramie was finding difficulty poking a single hole in their theory.

"I'll need a minute or two to soak this up," she said. "Also,
we'll need to get as much intel on him as possible. Can—"

She had been about to summon the man, but watched as
her guide leaned into the doorway as though delivered by
synaptic remote control.

"—we get everything CIA and its brethren have on him
and his regime?" she asked.

"Already in process," her guide said, and retreated behind
the wall.

Laramie decided she ought to arrange to have the man ac-
company her everywhere she went.

Knowles said, "On the topic of the letters 'ICR' and the facility in Guatemala, Eddie and I had an idea." Laramie kind
of turned toward Rothgeb as Knowles spoke, thinking, *Eddie?* "In the course of doing some research for one of my
books, I came across the story of a senior Defense Intelli-

gence Agency attaché who was arrested and sentenced to two consecutive life sentences for treason. Only thing was, they didn't nab him for being a double agent for China, or Russia, or whoever else specifically—instead, he was found to have been in business for himself, a kind of freelance provisioner of all manner of U.S. intelligence committee secrets."

Laramie thought she was familiar with the case, though she didn't remember the spy's name offhand.

"Among what he was caught selling in the Pentagon-FBI sting that snared him," Knowles said, "were certain lists. He generally sold his findings nonexclusively—sometimes selling copies of the same document to six or seven different countries—and the most damaging of the lists he sold revealed hundreds of undercover operatives' true identities. The document I thought might apply to your 'ICR' question, though, was a handwritten list of secret Pentagon file names. Not the files themselves, but their titles and whereabouts."

Rothgeb jumped in.

"Once Wally mentioned the case," the professor said, "I remembered a prosecutor with the Justice Department I'd sat on a panel with, who told me he'd been a part of the investigative team assembled by the prosecution. With some assistance from our friend in the room next door—" —Rothgeb jerked a thumb toward her guide—"I was able to reach him around three this morning and get the necessary approvals to have a look at the document Wally's talking about. Anyway, here it is. One page of it, at least."

Rothgeb turned over the piece of paper he'd been keeping under an elbow on the table and pushed it over to Laramie.

She saw on the page—which appeared to have been faxed—a carefully handwritten, page-long list of what she presumed to be file names, running alphabetically from the last of the *H*s through about twenty *I* listings. A sequence of dates followed most of the file names, with a final entry on each line denoting, from what Rothgeb was telling her, the file's location in the Pentagon.

Nine lines down from the top of the page was the file name *ICRS*, PROJECT, which Laramie took to be the alphabetical listing for something called "Project ICRS."

When Cooper's baritone voice charged into the room through the speakerphone, everyone jumped before remembering he had been listening in.

"Reading aloud," he said, voice distorted by the encryption, "would be helpful."

Laramie explained what Rothgeb had just given her.

When Cooper didn't say anything else, Rothgeb said, " 'ICRS' could stand for just about anything, but we did some brainstorming, and if you consider the notion of R & D relating to the first airborne iteration of a filovirus—in other words, one with wings—it might not be a bad guess to translate 'ICRS' as 'Icarus.' I'm sure you're familiar with the story of Icarus—and if this was a Pentagon-funded lab doing the research, the irony of our military flying too close to the sun for its own good is palpable. Either way, this document specifies the location of a file in the Pentagon—at least the location of the file at the time this attaché was giving away national security secrets—and it looks like a pretty tight match with our operative's three-letter discovery near the lab in Guatemala."

"Might take some juice to dig up the actual file," Knowles said, "but so far, it does seem as though our squad has some serious cider at its disposal."

Laramie looked up from the document.

"We done for now?" she said.

Knowles and Rothgeb said nothing for once—but each man swiveled his head to look over at Cole. Cole, meanwhile, sort of reanimated—Laramie thinking that was the only word for it as, with a slight movement of his jaw, the cop came alive from his place in the chair by the door and said, "We've identified six probable sleepers."

Laramie stared.

"Jesus," she said after a while. "When you guys bury the

lead, you really bury it. You've been holding out on me since last night?"

"Yep," Cole said.

"Good news, huh?" Knowles said.

"Great news—I think," Laramie said. "You said 'proba-ble'—that you've ID'd six 'probable' sleepers. What do you mean by 'probable'?"

"The six probables," Cole said, "are six cases of identity theft. In each case, the assumed identity is that of a person who died young, approximately thirty years ago. In each case, the identity assumed by the sleeper has been in evidence—in other words, there's been documentation of the current version of the identity, for about a decade, give or take. Same as with Achar."

"We also have images of each of them," Knowles said, ap-parently unable to contain his excitement, "in some cases stills, in some cases video, taken at a time that approximates or precedes the assumption of the new identity. Each of the images was captured while its subject was located right at or very near the straight-shot entry points refugees typically take when they're able to make it here by boat from Cuba."

Rothgeb said, "Those routes have mostly dried up, prima-rily due to the increased aggression of U.S. immigration pol-icy, but that was not the case ten years ago."

"Anyway," Cole said, "they're 'probable' because we haven't exactly knocked on their doors and looked around for racks of filovirus serum. It could be there's no connec-tion at all, but in our view that's unlikely. There are too many matches with our criteria."

Christ, Laramie thought, *we may just turn out to be quali-fied for this gig after all.*

She realized as this thought occurred to her that in one sig-nificant way, their job was all but over. They had now accu-mulated enough intel to push things up and out of their reach: she would have to take a closer look at their research, but it was time to offer the whole plate of goods to Lou Ebbers.

Time to take her "cell's" findings to her "control"—presuming her guide hadn't already updated the man top to bottom. Regardless, it seemed to Laramie that Lou Ebbers—and whoever he was working for—was about to have some tough decisions to make.

She took in a breath and let it out slowly, refocusing on the discussion at hand.

"Why don't you show me what you have on these six people," she said. "I assume you've got a working file with the scoop on each."

Cole reached over to the bed, lifted the manila folder he'd been keeping there, and gave it a Frisbee toss to the table. It skidded over to Laramie.

"Scoop enclosed," he said.

44

The spiderphone was in use again.

Laramie's guide had deployed the bizarre-looking contraption on the bedside table in her room. As before, its red indicator light was illuminated.

Laramie sat alone in the room with her guide.

"So where are we?" came the static-ridden and otherwise distorted voice of Lou Ebbers over the spiderphone.

Laramie continued to appreciate the no-nonsense approach of her new boss: *do your job, give me my answers.* Good. She liked it that way.

"Where we are," Laramie said, "is we've reached a decision point."

She'd filled him in earlier on Castro's theme park, so Laramie launched in with the identities of the six probable sleepers. Then, feeling more or less like a teaching assistant to her former professor, she laid out Rothgeb's earlier lecture, providing Ebbers with all criteria, factors, and suppositions her team had incorporated into the "public enemy equation," as they called it afterward, including Cooper's discoveries of the Guatemala facility and its adjoining village of death.

She offered up her "counter-cell's" conclusion that the Salvadoran president and perennial thorn in America's public relations hide was their man. She made sure to cover Raul Márquez's background, which she assumed Ebbers already understood—but even if he did, as the "prosecutor" making her case, Laramie wanted to emphasize the point to her boss that Márquez's genocide-survival story explained the leader's motive. She'd already presented the circumstantial evidence, based mostly on his relationship with Castro, which had granted him the cooperation he'd needed for the Americanization training and that the refugee-dump demanded, in addition to Márquez's potential access to the filo. The motive sealed the case: he had a reason behind his actions, not just the rhetoric he was famous for, and his tale of murder-squad survival gave him the best possible recruiting pitch with fellow victims of regional genocide across the Americas.

"Bottom line, Lou," she said, briefing complete, "is it's definitely a theory based on speculation, but it's educated and informed speculation. When you do the math, he's the guy."

Ebbers took little time digesting.

"The six probable sleepers," he said. "They may be only six of ten, or six of fifty—we still have no way of knowing, at least outside of the apparent enormity of the theme park training operation. Correct?"

"That's right," Laramie said.

"And we've got nothing on timing."

"You mean, when the other sleepers are set to be activated?"

"Yes."

"Nothing there," she said. "Not yet."

A click of electronic static echoed from the speaker.

Then Ebbers spoke up again.

"As usual, Miss Laramie," he said, "you're right—we have, in fact, reached a decision point."

Before setting up the call, Laramie had prepared herself for what she assumed would come next. Starting with the first "job interview," she'd grown familiar with the way

Ebbers preferred to work—meaning she had a pretty good idea he'd ask what strategy *she* recommended they follow.

"I've got my own ideas," Ebbers said, confirming Laramie's suspicion, "but you should take me through the response scenarios as you see them—our choices on what to do now that we know what we know. In other words, what would you do, Miss Laramie," he said, "if Márquez is, in fact, the man?"

Even though she was ready for this, it didn't mean Laramie liked being the one suggesting some of the options she was about to lay out. She counted out a couple of *Mississippi*s in her head, and was about to start in on response strategy number one, when Ebbers spoke again.

"You can assume something else too," he said. "Assume, in making your recommendations, that the president, or some other decision-making entity of equivalent clout, has asked the question. That I am simply posing it for the decision maker, and that the decision maker can act immediately upon reaching a decision."

Laramie hesitated—the way he'd put it, saying "or some other decision-making entity of equivalent clout," struck her as an odd thing for Ebbers to say considering he was comparing such decision-making clout to the commander-in-chief's. Whose clout, of course, was supposed to be unequivocal.

Unless, of course, you consider Congress, and the rest of the checks and balances, as "equivalent." But the way he'd said it gave her pause—she knew Ebbers did not let slip a single word, so there was something to what he'd just revealed. And in her independent study paper, Laramie's recommendation had been for the counter-cell "cubes" to function entirely *outside* the umbrella of government. She found it hard to believe the structure of Ebbers's organization would follow every last one of her recommendations—

There was no more putting it off, so Laramie got to it.

"The alternatives are simple enough to conceive," she said, "but to enact—"

"Get to it, Miss Laramie."

"Fine," she said. "Option one: roll the dice and immediately take out the six deep cover sleeper agents. Remove the pathogen vials from their possession and eradicate the threat they present. Are there ten others? Five? Twenty? Even if there are, we've cut down the threat to American lives by a presumably significant percentage."

"Next."

"Next, possibly executed simultaneously with option one, is to wage war on Márquez's regime. Immediately. I say this because if the action isn't immediate, and immediately effective, it could well cause Márquez to sound the alarm and activate the sleepers faster than he would have without the military action."

The line hissed and clicked dully, Ebbers keeping mum for a minute. Laramie had a pretty good idea he was thinking this one through in precisely the way she'd thought it through before putting it on her list. He spoke up, once again confirming another suspicion of the human lie detector machine.

"War cannot exactly be waged with immediacy," he said, "except, of course, by nuclear strike."

"I had considered and was concerned about that version of the war strategy," Laramie said.

Ebbers dove in on that one.

"You don't think the threat of a virtually unchecked spread of the modern equivalent of the 1918 flu pandemic— and therefore the credible threat to upward of hundreds of thousands of American lives—outweighs the potential damage inflicted on the offending nation by a nuclear strike?"

"If it is, in fact," Laramie said, "an 'offending nation,' and not simply an individual who happens to be the leader of that nation."

Laramie counted to *two-Mississippi* again—mainly to cool herself down.

"Either way, that's a call I'm not qualified to make," she said.

"Well who is?"

Laramie felt the heat pop up through her neck and up past her cheekbones.

"Sir, are you seriously asking my recommendation on whether to authorize a nuclear strike?"

She counted every beat of the voiceless static that followed. She didn't exactly want to have to out-and-out refuse to answer one of her boss's questions, but during the ninety-three seconds of relative silence she confirmed her resolve. *Too bad. I've been known to toss out an opinion or two where it wasn't wanted, but there are plenty of reasons the president and each and every member of the Senate and House of Representatives are elected, and I'm not. This being one of the more extreme examples: it is simply not my call, even in the fucking hypothetical. But considering his words from earlier in the conversation, I'm not so sure it's Ebbers's call either, or the call of anybody he works for . . .*

"What is the next option," Ebbers said.

"As I'm certain I don't need to tell you," Laramie said, jumping in with great relief, "the next option, while less drastic, remains illegal, both domestically and internationally. Nonetheless, particularly considering the complications involved with option two, it must be considered as one of the choices. Option three is to assassinate Márquez. The working theory here is if you cut off the head before the order is sent, the body of sleepers may simply walk away. Assimilate into society, the way it has been theorized the many likely Soviet deep cover sleepers did when the curtain fell. And we do not have evident confirmation that any of the probable sleepers besides Achar have been activated."

"Understood," Ebbers said. "Do you have any additional options?"

Laramie allowed herself to breathe again. "Other than searching for additional sleepers, which I believe we should continue efforting in any case," she said, "no."

"I choose option three," Ebbers said, "conducted in synch with a variation on option one and your continuing effort to identify additional sleepers. The variation: put surveillance on the six probable sleepers and see what they're up to, rather than nabbing them right off the bat."

Laramie realized immediately that Ebbers had just ordered—or at least *chosen*—the assassination of an elected leader of a sovereign nation. An order—or choice, or whatever the hell it had been, she thought—chosen almost entirely as a result of her own analysis, judgment—and *suggestion*. *Could* he have ordered up the nuclear-annihilation option? If so, who else was in on this? Who *wasn't*?

Christ.

Her brain scrambled to sort through the rest of the plan—she'd ask her guide about the logistics, but assumed they'd be provided with private investigators or local law enforcement officers to perform the actual surveillance of the six sleepers. Plus, they'd continue to look for others. Fine.

Still, she hesitated.

Did Ebbers *have* any authority to order an assassination? To order *any* of what was going down? Even in the unlikely scenario that he *did* have some newfound authority to order the assassination of a foreign leader, was he saying she, and her cell, should arrange it? More important, if that *was* what he meant, was she capable of agreeing to it?

When I signed on, I'm not so sure "execution" was on my list of job duties. Maybe it was. Maybe I wasn't paying attention. Maybe I knew it was, and didn't want to think about it. Would we prefer to have taken out Osama bin-Laden in advance, if given the chance?

Of course we would, she thought. *I think.*

Ebbers's next words answered all her questions at once, though not simply.

"Send Cooper to pay a visit on Márquez," he said. "I'll work with you on the rest."

Christ.

"I'll read your silence as a form of shock," Ebbers said, "and offer you some information with which to treat it. In case you didn't know this, your operative has done this before. A different Central American country, and it was a long time ago, but he's done it, and done it well. Despite his subsequent capture, in fact, and the passage of considerable time, one might still call this type of assignment the man's specialty."

Laramie once again experienced the sinking sensation she'd felt in her initial conversations with Ebbers. Not only did it seem Ebbers had picked her partially or solely because of her relationship with Cooper, but now it appeared he may well have been planning all along to give an assassination order, and for Cooper to execute it. And Cooper's long experience in Central America didn't seem like pure happenstance anymore.

All that had been expected of me was to identify the target.

Once an analyst, always an analyst.

Her thoughts of Cooper brought Laramie to the last item she'd wanted to cover with Ebbers.

"Speaking of our operative," she said, "my team would like your help in tracking down a classified document we believe to exist in the Pentagon. As I covered in my briefing, we have reason to believe the discoveries Cooper made in Guatemala point to a connection between the facility that was burned to the ground in that country and the Marburg-2 filo Achar dispersed—and which, of course, we believe Márquez's other sleepers also have in their possession."

Ebbers broke in, speaking flatly.

"The Pentagon," he said, "figures in how."

Laramie chose her next words carefully, and sparingly.

" 'Project ICRS,' possibly a reference to 'Project Icarus,' is the name of a file in the Pentagon. 'ICR' were the three letters Cooper discovered on a charred portion of a crate at the site of the facility that was burned to the ground in Guatemala."

After a short pause, Ebbers said, "Not exactly a precise fit."

He's choosing his words carefully too, Laramie thought. She held no doubt her guide had prepped him on this in advance, but they both understood the stakes, and Laramie wasn't going to back down and give him a way out if Ebbers planned to bury the possible connection *because* of the stakes.

"We know the file location," she said. "At least the location we understand, once, to have been accurate. If there is a connection, sir, we need to understand it. At least you and I do."

She'd planned on using her last phrase from the beginning: it was designed to help him perceive an opportunity to progress and investigate without risk—it was something she, her guide, and Ebbers could bury if they'd need to.

Not that she intended to bury anything. Which he probably understood. But he might nonetheless believe he could impel her to keep quiet—and he might also want to find out the answer for himself.

If he didn't already know it.

Laramie thought back to the CIA man who'd posed the question in the initial task force meeting—the man she'd figured, on sight, to be a Langley spook. His question had sought clarification on how the CDC had obtained documentation of the Guatemala health clinic filo outbreak.

That CIA man knew about the connection, and maybe Ebbers did too.

Maybe she was the only one who hadn't known. Goddammit—had the whole purpose of the task force, and the subsequent transition to her "cell," been to confirm where the organism had come from? Or simply to stomp out the sleepers as quietly as possible, ensuring that the origin of the filo would be kept a secret?

"This isn't going to be easy to get," came Ebbers's voice from the spiderphone. "Presuming it even exists any longer."

Laramie understood Ebbers to have just given himself an out.

He was saying he'd look into it, but she would have to wait and see. Even if he got it, and read it, he could still keep it close to the vest and claim he'd had no luck in the archives.

Either way, she knew this was as far as she could take it.

"I have the file location here," she said, unfolded the page of alphabetical listings of Pentagon files, and read him the details.

"That it?" came Ebbers's electronically distorted voice.

Laramie nodded at the speakerphone.

"Yes," she said. "That's it."

"All right, then," he said, and she heard the line go dead as the red indicator light doused.

45

Following his eavesdropping session by way of a sat phone connection to the Flamingo Inn, Cooper snatched an extra towel from a housekeeping cart in the Naples Beach Hotel and headed, shoeless, for the beach. He'd chosen to hunker down in his preferred four-star digs in Naples while Laramie and her Three Stooges, as he'd begun to think of them, hashed things out at the Flamingo Inn. He'd expected at least some sort of shit to hit the fan following their discovery of the theme-park-for-rent; Cooper, being the dedicated employee that he was—and, mostly, seeing little choice—elected to stay stateside while the shit-fan contact proceeded.

He decided to go easy on his bones today, halving his usual fourteen-mile Naples beach run. He finished in just over an hour—not bad, he thought, for a conch fritter addict.

By the time he trudged back to his towel and sat phone, Cooper found himself to be a heaving ball of sweat, not quite able to find his wind. Running anything faster than fourteen-minute miles now seemed to cause him nothing but physical grief. Used to be he'd log *two* miles in the same stretch on the clock.

So be it.

He strolled off the exhaustion before returning to discover just what he expected: somebody had left a message for him. After confirming the call had come from the Flamingo Inn, Cooper called Laramie back.

"Where have you been?" she said before he said a thing.

Cooper considered the question.

"I've been where I please."

Laramie waited a moment or two, and when she spoke again Cooper thought he detected a notch less tension in her voice.

"We'll need to talk in person," she said.

This didn't surprise him. He checked his watch—12:45.

"How's a late lunch at Paddy Murphy's Irish Pub sound," he said, "great little joint right downtown here."

He expected Laramie to shoot down this idea, and that he'd soon be hoofing it northeast to LaBelle, but Laramie went the other way on him.

"Sounds fine," she said. "See you there at four."

Cooper hung up and tossed the phone back onto its nest in the towel.

He had a pretty good idea what Laramie was going to tell him when they sat down for their late lunch—or early dinner—or whatever the hell it would be. In fact, after listening in on the conversation at the Flamingo Inn, Cooper knew with virtual certainty what was coming. It had only been a matter of time—time enough for Laramie to contact "the people she worked for," and for the decision to be made and sent back down the line.

The "cell's" choice of how to proceed at this point was an easy one—particularly, he thought, when you had someone like me at your disposal. And intelligence agencies always did. Was Laramie's team right about the man at the top of their suspect list? Cooper figured they were. And that was the only real variable—that and the decision-maker's call, but U.S. foreign policy decision makers, Cooper had learned long ago, were predictable. They inevitably thought they could get away with anything, and he imagined the people Laramie was working for would offer no exception.

Considering where Márquez lived, Cooper wasn't exactly looking forward to the task Laramie would be handing him. If he agreed to do what he knew she'd be asking—*ordering*—and fulfill his duty as the Twenty Million Dollar Thug, he mused that his immediate future would resemble the fate of an aging Vietnam vet who's just learned a new war has been declared against the communist regime in Hanoi—and this time, the Army is pleased to inform you, we've decided to draft men in their mid-fifties to go and do the fighting!

Cooper peeled off his tank top—the words LIVE SLOW emblazoned on the front, SAIL FAST on the back—and started down to the ocean. He hit the water and kept walking until it reached his waist, then stopped, planting his hands on his hips, and peered around Naples's white-sand slice of relative paradise.

The beach was almost entirely empty—as might, he thought, be expected on this weekday morning. No boats in sight, no kites hanging in the wind, no fishermen kicked back with their poles dug into the sand near the water's edge.

There's something to the idea of confronting one's past, he thought. You get lucky and maybe you get to taste a distilled form of redemption—something that all the Maker's Mark, painkillers, even the finest Mary Jane in the world would never quite match. Cooper had felt it—maybe he'd even known it was on the way—when he'd looked into the eyes of the rebel soldier guarding the bogus checkpoint in Guatemala.

He'd felt how he craved the confrontation—to peer in at the abyss that was his past. To figure out, by going back, how to establish some kind of comfort level with the hell you knew, and still know. *And maybe, in so doing, to find a way of living with myself without the aid of the charming batch of pharmaceuticals, spirits, and hemp I routinely consume in my busy attempt at distorting the ugly visions of my past and present.*

Of course he knew this was coming.

Hell—taken along with the guaranteed presence of the ever-annoying yet annoyingly ever-pleasant Julie Laramie, he decided he might even have to confess that the job they were about to hand him was the reason he'd agreed to sign on to begin with. *That, and the case it seems I somehow agreed to take as detective-to-the-dead—that priestess statue being my second-ever client.*

You knew they would ask you to go back—and that's why you propositioned them at the all-too-reasonable price of twenty million bucks.

He dove into the shallow waves. After looping down to the bottom, he dolphin-kicked his way around, moving at considerable speed a few inches from the sandy, shell-studded ocean floor. He kept his eyes open, clocking the scenery in the clear water. He swam parallel to the beach for a few dozen yards, heading for the air above only once his lungs were set to burst—at which point he popped into the bright sunlight, breaking the surface in a glittery shimmer of sunshine and foam.

Just because I knew they'd send me back doesn't mean I'm looking forward to it.

He ducked back into the salty silence.

46

Laramie handed him the faxed, heavily blacked-out copy of the two-page memorandum with the words PROJECT ICRS on its subject line. He saw immediately there were seven names on the distribution list, and that the memo had come from an entity called RESEARCH GROUP. Cooper took a swallow from his second pint glass of Bass Ale. Their food orders had yet to arrive, and after the seven-mile run, even he—quasi-retired operative with a liver to match Hemingway's—was already feeling the effects of the brew.

He read the page and a half of text. The document described an amount of funding—blacked out—that had been dedicated to "unconventional counterbioterror research relating to infectious viral pathogens," with a mention that the pathogens subject to "vaccination research" included viral hemorrhagic fever, "aka filoviral strains." The research, it was reiterated, would be "conducted for the purpose of the development of suitable vaccinations or immunizations for strategic national defense use." The author of the memo, speaking on behalf of the "Research Group," wrote that the group "hereby authorizes the establishment of the proposed 'Project Icarus' research facility at which to conduct these operations." The memo was dated "3 August 1979." The location and other details of the facility were either not included in the memo or had been redacted.

Though it was fairly straightforward, Cooper read through the memo a second time before setting it facedown on the clear plastic tabletop, thinking, having followed the grainy words on the pages, that his theory on the place the snuffer-outers worked was becoming uncomfortably incontrovertible.

"Interesting memo," he said.

"Yes. And by the way, I have personally broken six or seven laws in showing that document to you over lunch. But since such egregious security clearance violations seem to be emerging as my specialty, let's stick to the more important reasons behind our lunch meeting."

She plucked a celery stick from the veggie plate the waitress had brought with their drinks and snapped off a bite. As she spoke, Cooper felt another twinge of guilt—now that he'd let the human lie detector machine out of her cage, the snuffer-outers may well get handed to him on a silver platter—but he wondered how well he would do at sparing her from their wrath.

"Obviously the memo speaks for itself," she said. "It is no longer a stretch to connect the dots between an illegal U.S.-funded biological weapons lab, a filovirus outbreak near that lab that managed to erase an entire village of people, a survivor who made it out and paid a visit on a local mission's health clinic—and, somehow, the subsequent appearance of a similar or identical strain of genetically altered filovirus that is about to be used as a weapon of mass destruction within U.S. borders."

Cooper nodded. "Agreed—it's no longer a stretch."

"The other thing about that memo," she said, "the part not included on the page, is that Messrs. Knowles, Cole, and Rothgeb determined while I was making my way to your little kingdom on the bay here that every man on that memo's distribution list is dead."

Cooper raised his eyebrows.

"All of them were murdered," Laramie said. "Separately, and, mostly—actually, in all cases but one—by the method of execution-style beheading."

"They're all dead?"

"Every name on the page," she said.

The snuffer-outers, he thought, have been busy.

But as he thought that through, sipping from the pint of Bass, he considered that it didn't fit. Didn't mean it wasn't the case; it just didn't fit. The names on the distribution list of the memo must, he thought, *all* be on Uncle Sam's payroll—and unless he'd been wrong from the beginning, it was his own status as a CIA hack that had spared his life. So far. It just didn't make sense for the snuffer-outers to have iced the members of the memo's distribution list sometime back, before they'd elected to try to take him out—and on top of it all, he found it unlikely federal government snuffer-outers would use execution-style beheadings anyway. Not exactly one of the top weapons of choice, as he and Riley had discussed near Cap'n Roy's pool, of hired contract killers sent at the behest of U.S. government officials.

Last he checked, for example, he didn't keep a machete under his pillow at Conch Bay.

Cooper decided he would operate under the theory that somebody else had performed the beheadings. This didn't mean there wasn't somebody who knew the details, however, just the way that somebody might have known the details had the snuffer-outers done it.

"It occurs to me," Cooper said, "as I'm sure it does to you, that serial beheadings of people who work at or with the Pentagon probably wouldn't go uninvestigated."

"Yes," she said, "that did occur to me."

"Also occurs to me," he said, "as I imagine it did to you, that this would be a good explanation as to how the people you work for were able to get their hands on a copy of the memo on such short notice."

Laramie nodded absently. "It's certainly unlikely," she said, "that it would have been kept in the same file location after the attaché was busted selling his lists. You're right—it's more likely it would have been top-of-mind for somebody had there been multiple murder investigations under way."

Laramie thought again of the CIA man at the task force meeting.

"The way my skeptic's goggles see it," Cooper said, "it would then follow that the people you work for knew about the memo you were asking to see. And if they knew about the memo, then they probably know what that memo authorized, and probably even what happened in 1983—or whenever it was that the lab sprang a leak and blew out an entire Indian village."

"It also follows," Laramie said, "those same people would have at least a rudimentary understanding of the fact—presuming it's true—that it was the Pentagon lab that developed the filo the sleepers are about to try to kill us with."

Cooper smiled with his lips sealed shut. What he thought, as he offered Laramie the smile, was that *it also follows I'll soon learn who it was who applied the muzzle to the potentially revealing artifact shipment by acing Cap'n Roy, Po Keeler, and a few other relatively undeserving souls. And since it's likely to be the same person or group of people who saw to the slaughter of an entire Indian civilization, I'll soon be in a place where I can seek a little payback for my second-ever client as detective-to-the-dead—that twelve-inch priestess statue and the murdered Indian village she came from.*

"How do you manage to pull this shit off?"

Cooper took a few moments but couldn't figure what it was he might have missed in the conversation that would lead Laramie to ask her question.

"What shit is that?"

"In the ordinary course of events," Laramie said, "leading the life of leisure you prefer to lead, you've managed to uncover the key scrap of evidence indicating the U.S. government's probable culpability in what may be the greatest threat to the country's existence."

"Oh," he said, "that."

The food arrived—for Laramie, tuna and salad; for Cooper, a bacon cheeseburger. Since he had finished his second Bass, he ordered a third. Laramie waved off the waiter's suggestion she select a cocktail from the drinks menu and held tight with her ice water, which they'd refilled three or four times already. This despite Laramie's taking, at most, a pair of quarter-inch sips from her glass between refills.

Cooper took a hefty bite out of the burger. When his beer arrived, Laramie set her fork on the table, crossed her hands together, and rested the weight of her chin on her hands, elbows propped on the table.

"Let's talk about the here and now," Laramie said.

Here it comes, Cooper thought.

"Do you think he's the one?"

"Do I think who," Cooper said, "is the one."

"Márquez."

Cooper nodded.

"Hard to see how it's anyone else," he said. "But you never know."

"I can't believe we've chosen a lively Irish pub," she said, "and are simply sitting out here on the sidewalk for lunch, considering the plan I'm here to tell you about."

He let her get to it at her own pace. He took another bite of his burger.

"We need you to go in and 'eradicate' him," she said after a while—and a little more quietly than she'd been speaking till now.

Cooper chewed his mouthful of bacon, cheese, sirloin, roll, and barbecue sauce, then sipped from the pint glass to wash it all down.

"Márquez, I mean," Laramie said, "of course."

Cooper nodded dully but still didn't say anything.

"I take it this doesn't come as much of a surprise," she said.

"No," he said. "It doesn't."

Laramie told him the options she had presented to the people she worked for and the choices that had been made.

Cooper nodded again, about as dully as before.

"More or less the only choices," he said.

Laramie cleared her throat.

"I was told to tell you a number of things about what happens if you're capt—"

Cooper held up a hand and Laramie stopped midword.

"Nobody knows me, nobody's heard of me, nobody is affiliated with me. Hell, he's not even American, that Cooper character," he said, then gave her another emotionless grin. "Comes with the territory."

They were silent for a bit. Nobody ate anything.

"So are you saying you'll do it?"

Cooper saw the splotchy redness flooding its way up Laramie's neck into her cheeks. He decided he would read the embarrassment as Laramie failing to grasp how to do two things at once—first, to get his confirmation—the ol' "Yes, ma'am"—and second, to express whatever fear or empathy she was feeling about the fact he was about to head into Central America with a ninety-nine percent chance of failing to come out alive. So she came at it from the all-business side, the skin language telling him the rest.

"I'm assuming the people you work for," he said, "can load me up with some intel on our friend with the, ah, possibly short life expectancy."

Laramie reached below the table and touched the shoulder bag she'd brought with her.

"I have a great deal of it here," she said. "But yes. We will get you all that we can. The support issues will of course be handled for you."

"A plane," he said, "not of government affiliation. *Et cetera.*"

Laramie nodded, thinking of the conversation she'd held with her guide just prior to hitting the road.

"There's a man who handles these things for us," she said. "And you're correct, of course—there will be no affiliation or documentation of any kind."

"Famous last words," Cooper said, and held up the memo.

Laramie shook her head. Cooper thought her gesture

looked like the kind of action in which somebody would engage to rid herself of an aggravating flying insect.

"So you'll do it," she said.

Cooper ate some more of his burger without looking at her. Then he polished off most of his beer, looked at then elected to take Laramie's water, and drank some of that too.

"I didn't say I agreed to do it yet," he said.

"I know you didn't *say*—"

"No doubt the Three Stooges believe their theory to be correct, but let me ask you this: are you positive he's the guy? Is he definitely, positively, beyond a reasonable doubt, absolutely good for it?"

Laramie didn't move much or say anything for a minute. Then she said, "The Three Stooges, huh?"

"Your cell."

"No kidding. Look," she said, "I wouldn't put it beyond some doubt. But I will say I find it likely enough for us to take a calculated gamble and make this call."

Cooper nodded. "Not that it matters, but you'll be 'making this call' and taking that calculated gamble on more than one life."

"You mean you? In addition to him? Of course I know—"

"Yeah, me too, but that's not what I mean. I mean others also. Along the way."

"We recognize that too."

"You and your Grand Poobah, you mean," Cooper said.

"Grand—" Laramie shook her head. "Right. Okay—*I*, then. *I* recognize that. But yes, him too. The Grand Poobah as well as the Three Stooges. It should go without saying I don't like risking—"

"Doesn't matter," Cooper said, holding up a hand. "It's just conversation."

"What do you mean?" Laramie said.

He took his time chewing another bite of his burger and swallowing a sip of the beer.

"Since none of you has the luxury of doing the deed," he said, "the decision, of course, rests elsewhere."

"Well certainly, if you're the one pulling the trigger—"

"You may want to keep it down, Laramie, here in this lively Irish pub. Volume aside, what I'm telling you is I'm not going to do it unless I know he's the guy."

Laramie's cheeks popped pink.

Cooper said, "You can feel free to tell the people you work for—if you even know who they are, that is—that these are the only terms under which I'll conduct this mission. Of course, if you, or they, would like to find somebody who takes orders with a bit more verve, then go right ahea—"

"This is the way these things are done, do you understand that?" Laramie said. "There is no way we have of knowing any better that he's the one. This is how it works—you assess the intel, analyze it, determine the probabilities, and make a goddamn decision, whether you like that decision or not. Hundreds of thousands of American lives could be at stake, Mr. Twenty Million Dollar Man. You can't just *elect* to cancel the decisions Lou's mak—"

Cooper interrupted her but didn't miss the slip.

"You can stop with the campaign speech. You'd make a great CIA spymaster. Like our old friend Peter M. Gates, and our other old friend Lou Ebbers. Hell," he said, watching Laramie for a reaction but getting none, "if I were the president, I'd appoint your cute little ass to director of national intelligence in a Caribbean minute. But down here at my lowly level, this here foot soldier—duly assigned the icing of a president of an entire, if annoying, country—has decided he will go ahead and find out for himself from the horse's mouth whether it's the right horse we're talking about. If I'm satisfied he's the 'doer,' then I'll happily do the deed. If not, not. Accordingly, you, the Poobah, and the Stooges can blow this whole thing out your ass, or you can proceed with sending me on my way. Your call."

Laramie didn't say anything, or change expression for a time that felt to Cooper like ten minutes. He decided to keep eating while this inactivity took place. He ordered and began nursing yet another beer while he was at it.

When she finally spoke, Laramie said, "You're not doing this for us. Are you?"

"Ah," Cooper said after swallowing his last morsel of beef. "The return of the lie detector."

"It's not about the threat to American citizens for you at all," she said.

Cooper shook his head in utter nonchalance.

"No," he said.

"It's about you. You're doing this because of your own need to go back. Or," she said, "at least something related to that. To you."

"Why, yes," he said, sounding as though he were about to fall asleep. Which, thanks to the beers, the run on the beach, and the talk of foreign policy decision making, he was.

Laramie's eyes locked on his. She held the stare, and Cooper saw the red splotching creep up past her jawbone before she spoke her next words, so he knew he'd be getting something good. Still, he didn't expect quite what he got.

"In coming here to see you," she said, "I was fully intending, as the commanding officer of this unit, to order you to take me to your hotel room and have your way with me. Because you know what? I don't know whether you're going to make it in, make it out—or make it, period, taking this assignment. But in your inimitable way," she said, "you have managed to infuriate and frustrate me to the point where I almost, but not quite, fail to give a holy shit—"

"And that's because I'm skeptical as to the intentions of the government that put the filo in the hands of Márquez to begin with?"

Laramie kept it zipped, still red in the neck but cooling off a few degrees as she considered his statement. Cooper drained his beer and signaled for the check.

Laramie leaned across the table, almost to where her nose was touching his.

"Maybe that happened," she said. "And maybe Ollie North or one of his pals paid some bills for the genocidal maniacs who killed Márquez's friends and family when he was a twelve-year-old kid. Maybe we've murdered our share of Native Americans directly, in fact, and even used atomic weapons. I'm not disputing those facts."

Cooper stared back at her hard look, but felt himself falling apart again—Laramie the lie detector causing him to feel embarrassment about his rambunctious behavior, logical though it always seemed from the confines of solitude.

"Nonetheless, Mr. Twenty Million Dollar Operative," Laramie said. "This likely victim of our flawed foreign policy intends, it seems, to take more than an eye for an eye. So exactly how much sympathy for the devil do you intend to show?"

Cooper unrolled four twenties on the table, snatched the turned-over memo, and gave Laramie the third version of his unpleasant smile.

"I'll let you know when I reach my limit."

Slowly, Laramie stood, lifted the bag she'd brought, and plopped it on the table.

"Here's the intel on your target. The man I told you about will be in touch to handle your logistics, so be available through the number at your hotel. I'll be in touch also, since, among other reasons, we'll need to sort out the way we communicate during your trip."

Cooper offered his commanding officer a salute from his seat at the table.

Laramie threw back her own unenthusiastic smile.

"Break a leg," she said.

Then Laramie crossed the street to her car and started in on the drive back to the Flamingo Inn.

47

Despite its preponderance of crashes, the MU-2B turboprop cargo plane remained a favorite among drug runners, its high-capacity cargo bay and relatively fast and quiet engines still managing to do the trick for regional dope-transit duties nearly thirty years past its birth date. Plus, the plane also happened to be one of the primary aircraft used by FEMA, the Red Cross, and numerous other international aid organizations—meaning that if you chose your routes carefully, there was a pretty good chance an MU-2B full of cannabis would be ignored by the semiomnipresent U.S. Coast Guard AWACS and P-3 Orion airborne antidrug phalanx.

It also meant that on one particular, startlingly humid night in the moonless skies east of San Salvador, the unmarked, privately owned and cash-leased MU-2B droning by at twelve thousand feet would not have appeared as anything out of the ordinary—just another, technically illegal but government-ignored dope harvest making its way to an equally ignored processing plant along the country's northern border.

Cooper separated from the MU-2B by way of the rear

cargo door. Outfitted and equipped all but identically to the way he'd gone in the last time around, he reflected as the wind slammed him in the face that the only real difference between this dive and the last was that he was doing it solo—that and the fact that he'd aged a century in the nineteen years since that first airborne diplomatic overture to a Central American head of state.

Less than a minute later, he landed—brutally.

Coming into a stand of trees he hadn't seen in the darkness—or maybe he hadn't seen them because his eyesight just plain sucked, and any paratrooper worth his ass would have been capable of avoiding a crash landing with a simple glance downward—Cooper spotted the tall trees a second too late, and plowed right into them while still trying to maneuver away. This caused an instant of confusion—he hesitated in switching from steering to landing mode, and the hesitation resulted in a direct impact with the trunk of the first of the trees in the stand. He struck the tree square, a silent, invisible battering ram that pummeled him in one smack, his body absorbing the crushing blow more or less equally from head to toe. He felt more than heard a muted crunch, thinking it was somewhere near his pelvis, maybe a hip—but there wasn't enough pain for the noise to be that of a broken bone.

Utterly out of air, he tried to grab hold of his straps, and managed to unclip one of the parachute strings in the process. He dropped fifteen feet without any resistance and came to an instant midair halt. Finding, upon regaining his wind, that it seemed he was dangling sideways maybe twenty feet from the floor of the forest—held in place by a single string connecting him to the entangled parachute.

"Jesus fucking Christ," he said.

He considered with grave seriousness that if this was his opening act, then he probably ought to turn his gun on himself now—or maybe make a run for the nearest airport and stow his way into a luggage hold to get the hell out of here.

Once his eyes adjusted, he was able to see some of what

the landing pad below had to offer. It didn't look too painful—mostly low-lying bushes, maybe featuring thorns, maybe not, but certainly looking less deadly than a sidewalk or log. He swung for a minute on the string, orienting his body for a feet-first landing, then went for it, unlatching the clip. He hit the bushes hard but bounced in a kind of rolling corkscrew, the twigs, stickers, leaves and flowers bracing his fall in trampoline fashion as he found himself, when all was said and done, on his back, earthbound and unbroken.

If he'd landed near where he intended to, he knew he could find the road he was looking for about one mile to the west. On the satellite shots provided by Laramie's guide, the road had appeared to be a logging trail—cleared sufficiently for trucks to travel back and forth through the woods with their lumber haul but no more developed than that.

Cooper reached into one of the zippered pouches of his jumpsuit. Laramie's guide had provided him with a portable GPS device of the sort they'd used in Cuba, and he was keeping his satellite phone in the pouch too. Something poked through his skin as he felt around the pouch. He shone his Maglite inside it, only to discover the source of the crunching noise: his collision with the tree had shattered his GPS unit and sat phone.

"Nice work, there, hotshot," he murmured.

He still had at his disposal a fancy-dancy, luminescent-dial wrist compass—also provided by Laramie's guide—and found that on the other wrist, his plain old wristwatch seemed to remain in working order.

He used the compass to pick his direction and set out through the woods, encountering, twenty-six minutes later, twin tracks he figured for the logging road. He headed north, setting out at a jog in the relative blackness along the road. It was mostly downhill, which was good; the path was more overgrown than he'd expected, Cooper needing to high-step it most of the way despite the occasional bald-earth truck tracks underfoot. He timed himself based on a slightly slower pace than what he typically ran on the beach; he had only his watch by which to clock the run, but he'd run varying distances on enough different surfaces to know pretty much what his pace would be. He would run for an hour—five miles, if all went well.

At the end of his hour-long jog, he worked his way around for and found a suitable break in the trees and ducked back into the forest. Naples and Conch Bay beach runs notwithstanding, he found he was already winded, with somewhere near half the trek left.

Not good.

He knew from the satellite photographs he'd reviewed that he was four miles from his destination once he made the turn into the woods, but the last four miles would take him through treacherous terrain—thick jungle sloping up a steep mountain. That, he supposed, was the idea: the residence of President Raul Márquez included, along with various other accoutrements, a security perimeter made up of football field–size lawns surrounded by an eight-foot stone wall. The wall jutted up against the mountain range Cooper was about to climb over—a stretch of land impossible to traverse in any vehicle. You could do it on foot, but it wouldn't be easy.

Something a beach bum should have given more consideration to.

A "source," which Cooper assumed was dubious at best, had provided Márquez's weekly schedule to Laramie's guide. The schedule had apparently been circulated among the various wings of the Salvadoran government. President Márquez had supposedly hosted a Chilean diplomat for dinner at his home five hours ago; he was destined for a session of his cabinet tomorrow, with a press conference to follow, beginning at ten in the morning. The cabinet meeting and press conference were taking place forty-five miles from his residence. Meaning if Cooper was going to nab him under the cover of night, he had until dawn—otherwise he'd be camping in the jungle somewhere near the estate until Márquez returned from his cabinet business and whatever else was on the docket for the day.

It took him three hours to make it over the mountain.

As expected, the perimeter wall was patrolled by an armed military detail. Similar in function and appearance to the exterior fence found at your average prison, the wall included endless coils of razor wire on its crest and a guard tower every two hundred yards or so. The towers were occupied by guards, one man per tower. The men wore brown-paper-bag fatigues and were armed with what looked to be AK-47s. All no surprise. Both the wall itself and the entire stretch of lawn behind it, he saw, were lit like a baseball stadium.

Coming down the last stretch of hill as quietly as he could, Cooper slipped on a mossy boulder and almost crashed headlong into an exterior guard post, which had not been lit on the side that faced the mountain. Even after he caught his balance, he almost walked directly past the open door of the building before realizing there was a light on within, and a pair of guards seated inside.

He peered in from a place a few yards into the trees and observed that the men were playing cards and sipping cups of what might have been coffee. Like the men occupying the towers, these two were armed with AK-47s, plus hip-bound pistols and chunky walkie-talkie units.

Cooper had devised a number of infiltration schemes based on what he'd learned about the facility and its security perimeter, but with these jokers playing cards and probably sipping on spiked coffee while they traded spare change, he thought his life might just get a little easier. He needed the boost, anyway—maybe it had been the ride in the plane, kicking things off with a little airsickness, but he was feeling as though somebody had altered the atmosphere on him and sucked half the available oxygen from the normal mix. He felt like passing out.

The key was to get over the wall. But not here—not where he'd do little but stroll out onto the fucking Best Buy soccer field for all to see. Halfway around the wall, closer to the front of the residence, he knew the sod-moat to be shorter, most notably beside the driveway for the six-car garage, where there was only a few yards of grass behind a series of landscaped foliage beds designed to show visiting dignitaries how immaculate was the home of President Raul Márquez.

The last visible guard tower to the east, he could see—the last one off to his right, where the perimeter wall stretched around the side of the main residence—was close enough to the landscaped driveway to suffice. *If I can get up in that tower,* he thought, *the dash for the shrubs should be easy enough to make without being seen.*

This sounded better to him than his original plan A, which involved pulling the shovel from his backpack and commencing to tunnel beneath the section of wall nearest the landscaped driveway. The tunneling strategy, he thought, being the safer of the two—but if I go that route I may die of oxygen debt before I get knee deep in the dirt.

Let's go, big fella.

He triple-checked his MP5's screw-on silencer and approached as close as the darkness outside the shack would allow—Cooper thinking maybe he ought to lean right into the doorway just to see whether these poker-playing idiots could spot him. Resisting the impulse, he clicked off two rounds with a one-second gap between shots. He came into the shack immediately, doing his best to catch the guards' falling bodies before they, along with their chairs, weapons, radios, and thermos crashed to the floor in the wake of his sniper fire.

It occurred to him as he caught the second man's toppling body that he'd just allowed himself to get caught up in things a bit too fervently. As he'd informed Laramie, he wouldn't be icing President Márquez before determining whether Márquez was definitely the king of the sleepers—but apparently he *was* willing to take out random members of Márquez's guard detail with reckless abandon.

Whatever, he told himself, attempting to buy into his own fairly unconvincing argument: *they're in the military. They get paid to defend their president. They failed.*

Trying to avoid thoughts of the families these guys had just widowed, he propped one of the bodies in its seat, doing his best to shield the flow of blood from the hole in the man's forehead from the view through the open door. He laid the second body on the floor. Then, sequentially dismantling his own array of strapped-on tools and gear, he stripped the guard of his Che Guevara fatigues and stepped into the outfit. He noticed that once he'd buttoned it around his own frame, the guard's uniform stretched embarrassingly tight—*undoubtedly due to the paratrooper suit I'm wearing underneath.*

He took the man's rifle, pistol, and walkie-talkie, reattached his own gear, and got immediately to light-footing his way through the jungle along the exterior of the wall. He managed to traverse the half-mile crescent to the last guard tower without smacking headlong into any other patrol buildings.

The next part, he knew, would get more complicated.

He camped out for a few minutes in the woods near the tower and assessed the feasibility of his scheme. The guard in the tower strolled slowly around his circular platform, eyes active but heavy in the lids. The wall immediately below the tower appeared easily scaled—the stones in the face of the wall were large and held together by mortar or some other substance, the mortared sections full of dugouts that offered plenty of hand- and footholds. Then there was the razor-wire gap: the architects of the perimeter security design hadn't seen the need to stretch the razor wire across the towers themselves, only along the wall leading up to and away from the places where the towers had been built.

He took as much time as his schedule allowed, watching the routine as performed by the guards in all of the towers until he had the hang of things. There was an irregular but continuing cycle each guard followed: walk over to face the mansion, stare that way for a while, rotate to the other side of the tower, take a look out at the woods. Repeat.

He got his silenced assault rifle set, waited until the men

in the two nearest towers reached appropriate and coinciding spots of their observation cycles, then aced the guard in the closest tower with a single, scope-aided shot. As he'd hoped, the guy toppled silently and uneventfully, any sound of his thumping fall, or crashing AK-47, obliterated entirely by the incessant chorus of crickets, frogs, and whatever other creatures were doing their singing from the jungle behind him.

Cooper made sure the guards in the other towers hadn't come around on their loops. When he saw they hadn't, he dashed down the hill from his hiding spot, climbed the wall aided by the momentum of his downhill sprint, and rolled himself over the rail and into the tower. He found that he'd lost the hat he'd taken from the shack-guard, so quickly snatched the cap from the tower guard's body and put it on. He swung the shack-guard's AK-47 strap into the appropriate place on his shoulder, stood, and started in on what he'd observed to be the guard's walk-and-look observation routine.

Slouching as he did it to help hide his face, it occurred to him that this was an occasion on which his tan came in handy—*In my brown-paper-bag fatigues and sun-dried skin, I look positively Salvadoran.*

The guards in the other towers came about as their own routines progressed. He bit his cheek waiting for a problem to arise, but there came no wave, shrug, or other panic-instilling gesture from his newfound comrades.

He realized he'd need to stand the guard's body against the railing and hope it would take a while before the others noticed he was dead in order for his harebrained scheme to work. *Maybe I'm still the homicidal maniac who escaped torture by way of sheer murderous brutality—and chose this option solely because it would require me to kill the most guards possible.*

He had to wait longer than he wanted before making his move, but approximately nine minutes in, the other guards synched up their cycles and appeared to all be looking out at the mountains at once. He got the body propped up, clambered down the tower's interior ladder, and strode across the fifteen yards of grass with as calm a nonchalance as he could muster.

Then he rolled his way into the banana palm beds and crawled quickly away, out of the splash of the lights.

Still no screams, whistles, shots, or sirens.

Per his pre-mission conversations with Laramie and her guide, this was the moment when he was to report in by way of his sat phone. *Made it inside the perimeter,* he might have told Laramie. *Taking a look at the type of video surveillance they've got on the exterior of the house but will need to get in ASAP. You won't hear from me after I get inside.*

Unfortunately, because of the plastic shards in the pouch that had once been his sat phone, there would be no such conversation. He assumed the GPS homing beacon that marked his position on their monitoring equipment would, without battery or logic board, also have failed to work the minute he'd plowed into the tree.

The radio he'd swiped from the shack-guard suddenly made a *chuck-pfft* sound that almost popped him out of his combat boots, but the noise wasn't followed by any dialogue. He turned around and took in a view of the mansion that loomed above him, looking ominously like the Spanish fort it had once been.

Cooper didn't like the look of the place.

He'd read that the fort had originally been built in the late-seventeenth century for the Spanish land baron overseeing the territory. Perhaps—but it looked, for Cooper's tastes, too much like the same kind of seventeenth-century fort where those ruthless, mustached bastards had kept him locked in a subterranean cell almost twenty years ago now.

He knew this place too would contain its own underground labyrinth of dungeon cells and related facilities—after all, no self-respecting Spanish land baron, acting more or less as imperial governor, could manage the savages without his own private chamber of horrors in which to enforce his reign.

Cooper could practically feel the tunnels beneath his

feet—the ghosts of those fucking Mayans, or whatever cousins of the golden princess statue had been tortured and killed beneath him, calling out from six feet under the endless emerald meadow. *Oh, yeah, Cooper,* those pals of the golden priestess screeching to him, *welcome back, old friend. It's been too long a time coming. But there's no salvation waitin' for you here—only pain. Pain and sufferin' enough to last an eternity. Come share in our misery, you tired, drunken fool!*

He shook off the ghost-talk thoughts and checked his watch. It was almost a quarter to five. At best—unless President Márquez was as lazy as he, and preferred to sleep in—he had an hour to get in while Márquez was still asleep, and the sun had yet to rise.

If not less.

"All right, Island Man," he said in a croaking whisper, "Time for the hard part."

His own voice sounded oddly unfamiliar to him.

48

Detective Cole let Laramie into Knowles's room at the Flamingo Inn and closed the door behind her. She held in her hand another Styrofoam cup loaded with bad black coffee, Laramie utterly confused in her caffeine addiction: what had once been a two-cups-per-morning habit seemed to have graduated to a 24/7 unquenchable need that offered no real effect.

They'd summoned her because there had been activity from one of the sleepers, but Laramie asked a different question first.

"What about our operative," she said. "Anything?"

"No," Knowles said, planted in his throne before an array of monitors that had multiplied yet again—the monitors alone now took up one entire wall in the room. "May or may not speak to *his* status, but I'd say that homing-beacon signal is gone for good."

Cole came over to join Laramie alongside Rothgeb and her guide in a loose semicircle behind Knowles and the ever-expanding computer setup. Seven additional monitors had been added; the largest offered a highly detailed but entirely static map of El Salvador. A few hours ago, when Laramie had last been in the room, a blinking set of circles, designed to resemble the outwardly expanding circles made by a rock hitting the surface of a pond, had kept the view on the El Salvador screen fairly entertaining. The graphic had represented Cooper's whereabouts as he approached the drop point in his plane—the homing signal from his GPS device.

Nineteen seconds after the pilot instant-messaged them that he'd "dropped his cargo," the homing signal, and its accompanying on-screen graphic, had vanished.

The other monitors displayed low-resolution digital signals from six separate videophones of the sort made famous by the embedded reporters during the war in Iraq.

Five of the images were of the exterior of a house or apartment; it was dark outside four of the homes, with dawn just breaking on a fifth. The sixth feed looked like something from a tamer portion of an episode of *America's Wildest Police Videos,* a shot captured out the front windshield of a car that appeared to be following another vehicle. The sun had risen already in this image.

Laramie knew this last monitor to represent Scarsdale, New York. The other images were in the central and Pacific time zones, but live, just like the Scarsdale camera. The video was being shot by private investigators, selected jointly by Cole and Laramie's guide. The PIs were working in teams of two outside the homes of each of the six probable sleepers. The last time she'd seen the sixth feed, it had shown the front of a single-story ranch sandwiched between a pair of nearly identical houses. There had been no apparent activity, outside of a strobing blue light they assumed was the man's television.

Knowles turned from the monitor showing the map of El Salvador.

"If our operative's alive," he said, "there's a pretty good chance he could be inside the residence by now. We've been over it, but seven here is six there—be dark or close to it for another half hour based on the Almanac's sunrise schedule."

"Fine," Laramie said.

She'd left the room once Cooper's signal had come up blank for an hour and a half. She hadn't done anything since but sit and stew.

Something was bothering her about all this—the whole scheme as ordered by Ebbers, from the assassination order to the method they were using to perform surveillance on the six potential sleepers—including the plan that would kick into effect once any of the sleepers began to engage in some form of suspicious activity. Laramie hadn't been able to put her finger on what it was that was bothering her, but after thinking things over in frustration in her room, she'd begun to figure it out. Now it seemed one of the sleepers was up to something, perhaps no good, and that meant one of the parts of the plan Laramie was beginning to have a major problem with would need to be put into effect.

She blinked herself back to the situation at hand and jutted her chin at Knowles.

"Let's get on with this," she said. "What's the story here?"

She noted that the car being followed by the camera was an SUV—same as Benjamin Achar. The ultimate assimilation disguise.

"You got it," Knowles said. He spun around in his seat and clicked away with one of his mouses. The moving image on the screen zoomed in a notch. "As you can probably guess from the video feed, our boy in Scarsdale's on the move. Took off around five till seven. In case you've lost track, which we all have more than once, today's Saturday, so he isn't headed for work. Usually leaves at seven-thirty anyway when he does."

Rothgeb chimed in. "Based on what we know from the private investigator about the neighborhood, we've got a pretty good idea where he's headed."

"Ought to see it coming up in a second here," Knowles said.

Laramie saw Knowles was working the mouse again, making circles with the cursor in the upper right of the video image, where Laramie noticed something vague and orange begin to materialize. It started to look like a sign—and then the sign became legible.

"He's going to The Home Depot," she said.

The car—looking to be a Ford Explorer, though Laramie couldn't be completely sure—turned into the massive parking lot. She could see the store's rectangular building, somewhat out of focus, in the background of the shot.

"At seven A.M.," Rothgeb said.

"That'd be the time they open in Scarsdale on Saturdays," Knowles said. "We checked online."

The Explorer pulled to the side of the building that appeared to house the garden supply portion of the store and parked there. Laramie saw the quick flash of the white taillight indicators signaling the driver had thrown the vehicle into Park, and then the door opened and "probable sleeper number six" emerged in jeans and a T-shirt to walk into the store.

Twenty minutes later, the sleeper and his Explorer left the parking lot—his SUV loaded with a heavy cargo of what Laramie counted as twenty-five bags of something that they were all assuming was fertilizer, or some mix of fertilizer and something else like grass seed or topsoil that might help disguise the purpose of the purchase.

He didn't make any other stops—at least not until returning home. They had to watch from a longer-range shot but could still see pretty clearly as he pulled the Explorer into his garage, closed the door behind the SUV, then, seven minutes later, reopened the garage and pulled out again. This time he headed to a gas station—a Citgo—where they watched him fill a number of red canisters with gasoline at the pump. The private investigator's surveillance distance was growing with every stop, presumably to keep from being seen.

"That's about all you need," Cole said, "for a fertilizer bomb of the yield used by Achar."

"Correct," Knowles said. "And we'll have to wait and see,

but I wonder whether the others do the same thing when the sun pops up in their time zones."

"This is not a good thing," Rothgeb said.

"No," Knowles said. "And if there are more than six out there, it'll start to be a much worse thing real quick."

Laramie thought some more about the things she'd been thinking about in her room.

"Either way," she said, "we're going to need to get the tip phoned in."

The major piece of the plan she didn't like was the way Ebbers—through instructions relayed by her guide—had told them they were to "blow the whistle" on the sleepers if they spotted anything like they were seeing from sleeper number six now. Rather than order the FBI or local authorities in to apprehend the sleepers, they'd been instructed to arrange for anonymous tips to be phoned in to both the local FBI office and the local county sheriff's or police department. The tips were to include great detail but would remain anonymous nonetheless.

Cole had expressed his reservations first, and Laramie agreed—it wasn't even certain such tips would be acted upon once phoned in, and if FBI agents and the local cops *did* respond to the tip, who knew how the bust would go down? Would the sleeper panic and set off his bomb?

What *was* certain, Laramie thought, was that neither she, her guide, nor Ebbers were "sending in" anyone directly to apprehend the sleepers. Something was beginning to taste fishy and she didn't like the flavor one bit.

On the monitor, sleeper number six climbed back into his Explorer and, barely visible due to the distance the surveillance man was keeping, simply returned home. Once the sleeper tucked himself away inside his garage he did not reemerge.

"In a minute," Knowles said, "we'll get a text message report from the tail. He'll probably tell us pretty much what we just watched."

Laramie looked over at her guide.

"Call it in," she said.

He nodded and retreated to the other room.

"I take it," Laramie said to the others, "we're stuck at six—that you haven't found any others in the four hours we've been apart."

Cole shook his head.

"We got lucky to get these guys," he said. "It's a pretty safe bet from the images Knowles dug up that most or all of the sleepers, whether it's six, seven, or fifty, got dumped here the way Castro emptied his prisons into the state of Florida. They came by refugee boat. But no way were all of 'em photographed, let alone caught on tape. I think we're tapped out."

"Let's hope it's not fifty," Rothgeb said.

Laramie nodded. She eyed the detailed topography map of El Salvador on the widescreen monitor. There was no sign of Cooper's homing signal.

Decision made, Laramie strode into the room where her guide was on the phone. She didn't like the way things were going at all, and it was time to pull this charade to a close.

She glared down at her guide until he looked up from the call he was making.

"I need to talk to Ebbers," she said.

"This is bullshit, and you know it," Laramie said.

The electronically garbled sound of Lou Ebbers chuckling came from the phone's tinny speaker. Her guide had set up the spiderphone in her room again. She'd asked that he leave her alone this time and he had.

"At least this time around," came Ebbers's voice, "I know you're not asking me whether it's an exercise."

"Oh, I have no doubt it's real," Laramie said. "It's all *too* real. That's why I'm calling you—or calling you *out,* I should say. You've been taking me for a ride, Lou. Answer me this: why aren't we sending in FBI arrest teams directly? By our order? Controlled by us? By you? It doesn't make any sense."

"Ah," came his reply.

"'Ah'? Sir, with all due respect, please quit your *ah*ing and give me an explanation. I just risked the life of a member of my team—a *friend* of mine, I might even say. In fact, I think there's a pretty good chance I just got him killed, considering that he's MIA as of nineteen seconds into his mission. Add to this the fact that the sleepers we've ID'd are kicking into gear. One of them, at any rate. The shit is hitting the fan. And I'm finally realizing you're not being straight with me—about any of it. Please answer my question."

More chuckling ensued.

After the easy chuckling subsided, Ebbers's voice said, "I say 'Ah,' Miss Laramie, because of how well I realize that I know you."

"You think so?"

"Yes. I do. And I'll tell you why: I predicted, even told our mutual friend the guide, that you would put it together quick."

Laramie didn't say anything in the brief pause that followed.

"The answer to your question," Ebbers said, "is, first, that we would not want the FBI to know of our operation—our 'cell'—because we are, as discussed, running a clandestine counterterror unit, one that by its definition must remain clandestine within and without government."

"But there could be mistakes made by the law enforcement teams raiding the sleepers' homes if they're not supervised," Laramie said. "Maintaining the unit's cover is a trivial concern when you consider what's at stake. Among other factors, an anonymous tip does not assure us that the FBI or the local—"

"Part two of the answer is that we do not have the authority," Ebbers said.

As soon as Laramie had digested what Ebbers had just told her, she began nodding slowly, a quiet fury welling up within.

"Let me get this straight," she said. "You *don't* have the authority to tell the FBI to conduct a series of raids—you can only do so by phoning in an anonymous tip—but you *can* order the assassination of a sovereign head of state?"

In Ebbers's silence, the rest of the puzzle came together for Laramie.

"You *can't* order an assassination," she said, answering her own question.

"Whether or not I *can*," came Ebbers's voice, "I *did*. Do you not believe it to be the correct strategy?"

"*You* did. That doesn't mean the people you *work for* did. And *I* may believe it's the correct strategy, but the people you work for may not. So if they haven't been made aware—"

"Don't jump to conclusions."

Laramie took in some air.

"I assure you," Ebbers said, "that the people I work for knew of my decision. And authorized it."

Laramie said, "But it's an illegal tactic, there is no way anyone in the federal government who . . ."

She stopped herself midsentence as the point that Ebbers was trying to express finally dawned on her.

A little too slowly, she thought. Very carefully, she said, "So all this time, you're telling me you—and I—haven't been working for the federal—"

"Some things are better left unsaid," Ebbers said, managing to effectively interrupt her even over the encrypted phone line. "And as I told you, I had every confidence you would come around to this in due course. Now that we understand each other, I'll repeat *my* question to you: do you agree we're taking the appropriate measures?"

Laramie began counting out the *Mississippi*s in her head. She got all the way to eight, rather than her usual three, before she'd sorted through all her potential follow-up questions—namely, *Who the hell is it we're working for then?*—along with the accompanying concern of whether to ask such questions, and what the answers might possibly mean, presuming she'd even get any answers out of Ebbers if she asked. By the time she'd finished thinking these things through—by the time she hit *eight-Mississippi*—Laramie decided the wisest course was to zip it. She'd be better served by storing this knowledge for later. She could then

use it, or make inquiries as she saw fit, to her advantage—
rather than under the stress of the current crisis.

She'd ask her questions later—if and only if, she thought,
they could figure out, down one operative, how in the world
to stop multiple terrorist sleepers from dispersing clouds of
an airborne filovirus certain to kill thousands of Americans,
even with massive quarantining measures put into place.
Which would need to be done *immediately*.

And we're supposed to do all this, she thought, *while
keeping our own role in matters a state secret?*

Or a non-state secret.

She decided to answer Ebbers's question.

"So far, yes," she said, "I believe we're taking the appropriate measures. But we'll need to change the strategy immediately. We haven't identified any other sleepers—so for
all we know there could be ten, or twenty, or fifty more set
to go."

"And you think you've lost your operative?"

"I'm not so sure about that," she said. "Not yet. But even
if he succeeds, this morning's activity from the Scarsdale
sleeper means it's likely the activation command has been
sent to more than one of the bombers. How, by what means,
in what form—as with the rest of this goddamn thing, we
have no idea. Our private party is over, Lou. It's out of our
'cell's' hands, and that's the understatement to top all under-
statements. We need to cause multiple agencies to immediately activate all the avian flu quarantine measures they've
been rehearsing behind the scenes until now. We need to arrest and interrogate the six sleepers we have under surveillance. We need to bring the media up to speed—so that
Mom and Pop in Tulsa can phone in a tip that somebody's
been stockpiling fertilizer in his garage in the house up the
street. There's no more time for this compartmentalized spy
game you recruited me to play."

"All right, Miss Laramie," Ebbers said, "I am hearing you,
and we are not thinking differently from each other." She
heard the measured tone in his delivery, even with the elec-

tronic garble. "But we do, however, have a moment. We're not sure of the progress of your operative yet, if any, and we're also not yet positive any of the other sleepers are being activated. If more than just the Scarsdale sleeper stops by his local Home Depot this morning, then I agree. There won't be any alternative. It'll be time for FEMA, CDC, DHS, FBI, CIA, the media, everybody and their grandmother to board up the windows and hunker down for the storm."

Laramie felt the heat easing back down her neck.

But I'm certainly not prepared to undertake the risk of waiting another day, or two, or more, when the quarantining efforts and the tried-and-true Soviet strategy of impelling your citizens to spy on their neighbors could very well prevent thousands of casualties from turning into hundreds of thousands, or more—

"In the meantime," Ebbers said, "pick up your Scarsdale sleeper, and get up there and interrogate him. See if you can deploy the same charm you did with Janine Achar while you're at it."

It suddenly occurred to Laramie she'd been idiotic not to already have done what Ebbers was telling her to do. Because Achar set off his explosives before anyone was able to speak to him, Laramie had only been able to interview his widow—and now they had the chance to interrogate one of Achar's comrades while the man remained alive and kicking.

"Not sure why I didn't already—"

"The moment one more of them stops by his local nursery or hardware store, we go in and take all of them," Ebbers said. "At which point I'll pull the fire alarm—the leaders of the disbanded task force will be provided the new intel discovered by the 'special investigator' and will immediately, I suspect, activate all the measures you mentioned."

"Right," Laramie said. "The fire alarm."

A moment of static clicked by.

Then Ebbers's electronically distorted voice said, "All right, then," and the red indicator light on the spiderphone flickered out and the line went dead.

Cooper identified what he assumed were most but not all of the video cameras monitoring his side of the mansion. There was also a roving patrol, two guys walking together around the outside of the house, plus a few Secret Service equivalents camped out near a pair of black Chevy Suburbans toward the front of the residence.

There were some weak points in the house's design, mostly the sort related to the historical qualities of the home, including the lead casement windows they'd kept in order to maintain the authentic *hacienda* look. Still, having seen photographs of Márquez's wine cellar—and working from the dread of his sixth sense on the certainty that a sequence of tunnels and rooms originally designed as a prison and torture chamber ran beneath his feet—Cooper decided now, as he had when he'd examined the images provided by Laramie's guide, that the surest way in would be underground.

There were no electrical wires, television cables, or other utility connections visible on the exterior of the home. He looked for and found the mansion's air-conditioner units, which they'd planted in a bed of bark chips alongside some tropical greenery. As he suspected, in a kind of garden of technology, it was in this bed of A/C units that the various utility meters were planted too. Another, larger utility box of some kind stood among the other measuring devices; initially at a loss, he was finally able to identify it as the head end of a cable connection, probably capable of distributing television service across a small city. He learned this by cracking open the lock and peering inside the panel door, where he found labels, printed in Spanish, for the various feeds and splits to forty-three televisions.

Salvadorans' tax dollars, he thought, hard at work.

His theory hit paydirt upon his discovery of a rectangular equivalent of a manhole cover. It was nestled in the bark behind the various meter stands and boxes. With the aid of the knife he'd brought for any hand-to-hand encounters with the security staff, he got the heavy metal lid pried from its roost, exposing beneath a broad band of wires and pipes, held together by an oversize plastic strip of the sort used to secure extension cords and hoses.

The batch of utility connections stretched toward the house in its semiorganized, snaking fashion—running along the side of what looked more or less like a mining tunnel.

Cooper recognized the tunnel for what it was, those old ghosts whispering to him from its walls—there wouldn't be any stains left, not anymore, but he figured it was a good bet that a great deal of blood had been spilled on the floors of these tunnels. If he went long enough without blinking, Cooper knew he'd start seeing the blooms of red, even if he was only imagining it.

He whipped out his Maglite and examined the edge of the access opening for sensors or any other sort of alarm. There was nothing on the rim of the opening itself, but he caught a glimpse of what looked like a motion detector built into the base of the tunnel near where he'd need to jump inside it.

He was deciding whether he ought to just plow a bullet into the motion detector when a bleating, two-tone alarm suddenly tore through the atmosphere, the pealing scream coming at him from all angles, so loud it seemed to be part of the air itself.

Lights as bright as those illuminating the emerald lawn *chunk*ed to life along the exterior of the house, bathing Cooper in sudden bright white. A second, piercingly high-pitched alarm began sounding out over the two-tone blare, all of it so loud it nearly peeled the surface from Cooper's eardrums.

He didn't think he'd set it off with his examination of the utility panel, but it didn't matter—there wasn't much choice on what to do now. He fired a pair of shells into the motion sensor at the base of the tunnel, grabbed the access panel, leaped into the hole, and pulled the heavy panel tight against its stops above as he dropped inside.

No doubt, he thought, the darkness of the subterranean tunnel overtaking him, they found one of the dead guards— *good fucking plan you put together here.*

He clicked on the flashlight and was greeted rudely by the illuminated image of an ancient door about five feet in front of him. The serpentine batch of utility cords disappeared through the doorway by way of a small, square brick of wood that had been cut from the door. The door was made of old wood and iron. It had a round, draping handle that looked like a knocker, along with a modern chain-and-padlock deal holding the door closed. The chain looped snugly around a pole built into the wall.

"Probably gonna hurt," he said, brought his MP5 around, took aim at the older, rusted hinges on the side of the door opposite the padlock, and held the trigger down for ten or fifteen rounds' worth of automatic-weapons fire. He tried to do it in circles around the two hinges, but the muzzle flash blinded him and a couple of ricocheting shells nipped one shoulder and a thigh, so before he completed his intended lines of fire he was ducking, dropping the gun, and covering his head with his arms. When the sound of ricocheting bullets stopped echoing through his skull, he surveyed the door with his flashlight, flipped the rifle strap around to push the weapon to his back, lowered his head, and plowed his full bulk into the door.

The old door broke off its hinges with little resistance and Cooper went flying into the void beyond. Too late, he reconsidered what he'd just done and got quickly to replacing the door, standing it up to approximate its position before he'd mauled the thing. *They'll know I came in here now—at least as long as they're good enough to open the panel and clock the busted-up door.*

Maybe they won't be that good.

On the other hand, maybe they will—he is their president.

That was when the claustrophobia hit.

One instant he was thinking rationally, contemplating his plan—and in the next he could no longer breathe, stand, or think. He fell first to one knee, then the next. He felt as though the weight of the ceiling had fallen on his chest, his lungs collapsing slowly, so that with each successive breath he was capable of bringing in less and less oxygen—until, like an asthmatic, he couldn't find a single cubic inch of air to feed his failing chest. He pushed his hands out against the walls, trying to convince his brain there was plenty of room—plenty of air—but he only felt the walls shrinking in on him. Sweat burst suddenly from his pores, a lukewarm, salty sprinkler sprung to life in a flash of heat.

He wanted to scream, *Fuck!* but he couldn't. He wanted to hear himself say, *It's not real! You're losing your fucking mind!* But he couldn't.

Get up and go now, he heard from some lesser-traumatized corner of his brain, *while you still have the chance. You have to find a place to hide—your past, or the ghosts of these tunnels, or both, are taking away your mind. You'd better get yourself someplace where nobody can find the intruder curled up against the wall in a fetal position, and you'd better do it now.*

He started out on his knees, then rose to one foot, then both, moving deeper into the shrinking tunnel one slow-motion step at a time, unable to breathe—his vision blurry from the sweat dripping into his eyes. He felt as though he had dived into molasses, but he kept on, and in twenty paces came to another door. This door was closed, but not padlocked. He struggled, arms beginning to weaken, but he got it open and a junction of tunnels presented itself to him. He attempted to determine the direction that would take him farthest from the house, and took it.

He lost all focus and impression for the remainder of his meandering journey, Cooper's return to the hell of his past blunted by his accelerating phobias and post-traumatic-stress attack. He didn't know how long it took him, only that he got himself somewhere deep in the labyrinth before deciding almost by default on a hiding place. Unable to fend off the leaking pores, failing lungs, and ringing headache, his weakened mind turned in on itself and he fell to the floor, a sweating, heaving potato sack. He pulled his legs under his arms and lay there, trying to keep warm but caught in a cold-shiver loop of the sort he regularly endured in the course of his recurring nightmares.

He slipped from consciousness, unable even to find a sense of relief.

50

The Three Wise Men—as Laramie preferred to call her team following Cooper's more insulting nickname—decided to recruit a bounty hunter to capture the sleeper and deliver him to Detective Cole's childhood home, a dilapidated ranch in Yonkers the cop said he'd inherited when his mother died eight years back. The peeling old house was a forty-minute drive from the sleeper's home, a drive Laramie understood the bounty hunter, his posse, and bounty to have made in a rented Freightliner Sprinter without incident.

Cole assured them that nobody besides the mailman ever visited the old house. He also claimed to be remodeling it, but Laramie saw no evidence of such as she paid her cab fare in cash and came up the stoop. They had the sleeper, whose current name was Anthony Dalessandro, in the basement. Laramie was greeted in the foyer by a thick-necked member of the bounty hunter's posse; it seemed the seizure team still wore their gear, this guy coming at her with his heavy handshake and a blue flap-down windbreaker of the sort FBI agents wore for public raids. The only difference being the words on the coat—this guy's jacket saying BAIL

ENFORCEMENT AGENT in favor of a more legitimate declaration of authority.

The "bail enforcement agent" escorted Laramie down a set of creaky wooden stairs to the basement. The cellar's floor was made of gravel, which looked wet in places, and its walls appeared to be nothing more than sagging piles of stone laden with leak stains.

Dalessandro was zip-tied to a chair on the far side of the space, hands bound behind the rear of the chair, ankles secured separately to the chair's two front legs. A rectangle of black tape covered his mouth and twin loops of yellow rope secured him around the chest. He was out cold.

A man Laramie knew to be the head bounty hunter—a scrawny, longer-haired version of her escort, standing no taller than Laramie's five-four—came over and shook her hand without introducing himself or asking her name. She noticed that once he'd let go—as compared to the shake of the guard dog who'd brought her down—her fingers seemed less likely to crumble and break off.

"Afternoon," the bounty hunter said. She found his voice almost gentle. "Based on the assignment particulars, we're assuming you'll prefer total privacy during your 'conversation' with the subject. My recommendation, ma'am, is we remove the tape from his mouth so he can speak with you, but otherwise leave him as is. Strapped in. We'll be standing by upstairs for the duration."

"That sounds fine," Laramie said. She thought a little about how unwilling to talk the sleeper might turn out to be while strapped to the chair, but she wasn't figuring on getting much out of him anyway and wasn't about to risk her life for zero intel. Better, she decided, to stay on the safe side, particularly if she wouldn't have one of the guard dogs with her. Which she wouldn't regardless—the bounty hunter was right. Neither he nor the members of his squad would be permitted to listen to the interrogation.

"If you prefer, we can hang tight in the van," he said. "But

I'm always more comfortable sticking to what I like to call 'bumrush range.' "

Laramie nodded, needing no explanation.

"Agreed," she said.

The bounty hunter came around behind her, lifted the folding plastic-top table he'd been keeping there, and placed it in front of the sleeper. He repeated the circuit and brought a second chair over to where Laramie could sit and face Dalessandro from across the table.

Then he nodded and smiled.

"Use the word 'help' or just make a lot of noise," he said. "We'll be right down."

"From bumrush range," Laramie said.

"Yes, ma'am."

"Thank you."

"Oh," the bounty hunter said. "Almost forgot."

He headed to the storage post against the wall one last time, carried a heavy bucket over to Dalessandro's side, reared back, then doused the comatose sleeper with a full bucket of what Laramie assumed from the reaction to be very cold water.

Dalessandro came suddenly awake, wide-eyed, sucking frantically for air through his nostrils, searching in a panic around the dim basement for some clue as to his whereabouts and circumstances. The bounty hunter assisted Dalessandro in his effort to breathe, ripping off the rectangle of tape in a quick swipe that looked to Laramie as though it hurt like hell.

Dalessandro heaved in a few breaths of air.

"There you go," the bounty hunter said to Laramie. He walked upstairs and shut the basement door behind himself.

Laramie waited, standing, until the sleeper got his bearings and settled down. Once she could see he'd realized that a fairly unthreatening woman was all who stood before him, she approached the table, flipped the file she'd brought onto it, took a seat, and pulled her chair nice and close to the table.

"Hi, Tony," she said.

Dalessandro blew some dripping water off the edge of his nose. He took the opportunity to peer around the basement again. After a while his dark eyes settled on Laramie, where they stayed for a confused couple of minutes.

"Who the hell are you?" he said.

She noticed there wasn't any particular accent to his speech—maybe a slight East Coast edge as was appropriate to his assumed identity, but otherwise pretty much neutral, like a news anchor.

"More to the point," Laramie said, "who are you?"

"What are you talking about? What's going on here? One minute I'm having a beer on my couch, the next thing I know these goons bust in and throw me on the floor and I wake up in this fucking basement."

"I can answer part of my question for you," Laramie said. "One person we know for certain you're *not* is Anthony Dalessandro. Unless, that is, you died from leukemia at age six and were subsequently resurrected in full health."

Laramie might have seen the first spark of something besides confusion or anger in his eyes—but if so, the spark lasted about as long as a spark normally does.

"My name is Tony Dalessandro," he said, "and I still have no idea what you're talking about."

"You're pretty good at this," Laramie said. "You know the first thing they teach at CIA? 'Never go belly-up.' Even when caught red-handed, there's always the chance they'll have some doubt you're good for whatever they're accusing you of, as long as you never actually admit your guilt. You're familiar with the Central Intelligence Agency—I'm sure they taught you all about them in your classes under the hill in San Cristóbal."

There was the slight flash of rage—Laramie reading it as *how the hell could anybody know these things, I'll kill you*— but that look too, real or imagined, left the basement as quickly as it came.

Laramie knew Dalessandro, or the man who called himself that, to be single, thirty-six years of age, living in a rented two-bedroom, two-bath townhouse, working as a site foreman for a major rural housing contractor, up to his ears in debt, and blessed with one hell of a handsome appearance. He'd been putting this appearance to work with a different woman almost every night since they'd been watching him—belying the source of the majority of his methodically built debt. According to his many credit card statements, Tony had spent a great deal of money on dinners, weekend getaways, sports events, private-room cash-outs at numerous strip joints, and virtually every other form of foreplay invented to date.

Not quite Benjamin Achar, Laramie thought. But in a way, very similar: both seemed to be soaking up the life they preferred to lead with great relish. The problem, as Laramie saw it, was there seemed nothing to threaten him with. Unlike Achar, he had no family, and he'd already bought the fertilizer, so was obviously fully resigned to fulfilling his assigned mission. How do you convince a guy like that to reveal whatever secrets Márquez, Fidel, or anybody else on the public enemy team had vested him with?

She went straight to the only strategy she'd been able to devise, sorting through the options on the Jet Blue flight from Fort Myers to JFK.

"I thought I'd skip the part where we beat around the bush," she said. "We've been watching you, Tony. You and your colleagues. We've seized the fertilizer and the diesel fuel you bought this morning. We searched your home and found the filovirus vials, so we took that too. We know where you trained. We know who sent you, when, and how. But you know why I'm being blunt and getting right to it?"

He watched her with lukewarm interest. She'd earned a portion of his attention—as to whether that would get her anywhere was anybody's guess.

"The reason I'm skipping the pleasantries is for your own benefit. The organization that has captured you is not the Central Intelligence Agency. This is relevant to your situation because CIA, or any other arm of the American government, frequently has to concern itself with pesky little things like international law. Things like civil rights and trials. At least most of the time."

She shrugged.

"The people I work for—the people who brought you here—don't have to answer to any of that. Plus, Tony, you don't really exist to begin with. Therefore I'd say the simple solution to this filovirus-dispersal scheme, at least as far as your involvement with it goes, is pretty simple: after our conversation, you vanish. I think that in the place you come from, it's probably called 'disappeared'—you'll be 'disappeared.' No trial, no sentencing. One bullet. Two, if necessary."

She stood in the way a person would when she'd come to say all she'd come to say.

"If you're interested," she said, "I'll give you an alternate scenario. If not, you'll die an anonymous failure within the hour. Goodnight."

She offered him a courteous smile and turned to go.

About the time she was halfway up the rickety old stairwell, she heard a phlegmy kind of grunt that might have been Anthony Dalessandro clearing his throat. Then again it might have been something with the plumbing, so she continued to the door and had it open before Dalessandro said, "Just a second, lady."

The bounty hunter and a different but also large cohort were seated at the table in the kitchen consuming a couple boxes of pizza and Diet Cokes out of the can.

"Be another few minutes," she said, then closed the door again and retreated down the stairs.

When she'd retaken the chair across from Dalessandro, he shook his head.

"You've got the wrong guy. I don't have anything to do with what you're talking about."

In Laramie's experience, anybody who used the phrase "You've got the wrong guy" had, in stating it, for all intents and purposes, admitted his guilt. She decided she'd play his game and let him stick with whatever he was trying to convince himself he'd convince her of.

"There's something else," Dalessandro said, his voice congested. He cleared his throat again, the same sound she'd heard climbing the stairs. "There's something else I hear they teach you about interrogations in the CIA. Or at least I've seen it on *CSI* and *Law & Order*. It's that if the cops haul your ass in, you should tell them what they want to hear. If you do, they'll let you out of it. Make a plea-bargain deal. Or let you go. So what does that organization of yours want to hear? Tell me and I'll give it to you, and you can let me go back to fertilizing my lawn."

As nonchalant as he was being about this, Laramie continued to believe what she'd thought would be the case before coming here—that he wasn't going to tell her much, but that he might, nonetheless, show some of the same tendencies as Achar. Maybe, she thought, he likes his "deep cover" life and, if caused to believe he might have a shot at getting back to some form of it—via witness protection or some such route—he'd give them *something*.

"You're a smart cookie, Tony," she said. "I've got some influence with the people I work for, and that's exactly what I'm talking about: if I put a word in, you'll be spared immediate execution. So yeah, you tell me what I want to hear—even if you've got nothing to do with any of this suicide-bombing business—and maybe it'll work out for you."

He shifted in his chair, waiting.

"I'm skeptical you can even help me with any of this, Tony. I think you're a compartmentalized drone, busy with nothing but assimilating until the order comes in for you to wipe your useless self off the face of the planet."

. . . but I'll bet your fellow San Cristóbal alumni have followed whatever course you were told to take, and I'd like to hear a little more about it . . .

"But whatever," she said. "If you'd like to walk me

through how it is you knew to go out and buy the ingredients for your SUV bomb, I'll consider putting that good word in. What was the signal?"

Dalessandro grunted, or maybe chuckled, or was just clearing his throat again, Laramie wasn't sure. Then the noise progressed into a well-defined chuckle, and finally to a level-toned, mean-spirited sort of laugh.

He kept at it, Dalessandro utterly pleased with himself, until the laugh slowed, then subsided back to the phlegmy throat-clearing noise. At that point Dalessandro lowered his head and glared at her with eyes that looked, set behind his dripping-wet skin as they were, flat, black, and long since dead.

When his next words came, they streamed forth in an un-abashed, thick, odd-sounding accent Laramie couldn't place and could barely understand.

"Good luck, bitch," he said. "Good luck finding any of us. Good luck stopping us. All one hundred and seventeen of us."

Laramie felt ice water trickle down her spine.

"You didn't know that, did you, bitch? That's right—you have no fucking idea—*no fucking idea* what is about to happen. You'll never find the others. No matter what I tell you. And I won't be telling you *shit*. So just get it over with. Kill me, bitch—do it. Do it!"

He made a game attempt at leaping from his chair to attack her, but only succeeded in stretching the ropes and tipping himself forward an inch or two. Veins popping in his neck, eyes bugged and frantic, Laramie saw in his otherwise useless lunge an undistilled rage—the kind, she supposed, from which terrorist plots are hatched.

In catching her glimpse of this, Laramie came to two realizations instantaneously: first, they could torture this guy with every technique known to man, and no way in hell would he tell them a thing. Second—though she supposed it should have been obvious—one doesn't train, hide for more than a decade under an alternate identity, then mobilize to execute a mass killing without being driven by the kind of anger that no threat, law, or preventive strategy has much chance at all of stopping.

Benjamin Achar and the love he'd found in himself for Janine and Carter notwithstanding—true love, she thought, being a one-in-a-million score anyway, or at least far worse odds than one-in-six—Laramie now understood with a concrete certainty that there would be no turning this army.

For the first time since her meeting with Lou Ebbers in the Library of Congress, it occurred to her she was probably going to die. A lot of people were—however they'd done it, Márquez's army of sleepers were now immersed in the American fabric, and whatever it was they were pissed off about—genocide, murder squads, whatever—it was painful and sure enough for these people to seek only the destruction of every last one of us.

And who the hell was going to stop them?

Me?

Something on her hip vibrated—the GPS unit her guide had provided her. It doubled as a cell phone and her team had the number. The thing had surprised her because she hadn't used it yet.

Laramie rose, climbed the stairs without another word to Dalessandro, and found a room bereft of bounty hunters in which to talk on the phone.

"Yes," she said.

"Laramie."

It was Rothgeb.

"The other sleepers are on the move," he said. "Not all of them—only two of the other five. But each of them just drove to a home and garden store of one kind or another and bought pretty much the same quantity of fertilizer as your Scarsdale pal."

"Crap," she said. She fought against asking whether they'd seen any activity on the screen that was tracking Cooper's homing device.

She knew he'd have told her if they had.

Laramie asked Rothgeb to put her guide on the phone,

and once he'd announced his presence on the line, Laramie said, "Even if you've already updated him, call Ebbers immediately."

"No problem," he said.

"Tell him it's time," she said, "to pull the fire alarm. Tell him it's time—as he put it on his call with me—for the federal government, the media, and everybody and their grandmother to board up the windows and hunker down for the storm."

51

When Cooper came to, he discovered his body to have recovered from its toxic bout with post-traumatic stress, or whatever the fuck, he thought, turned me into a puddle of hyperventilating mush. *But maybe that's what you get when you pay a visit on the worst episode of your past— you wind up throwing it in reverse for real, your body decid- ing it's time to curl up and see whether there're any available wombs interested in taking you back.*

Coming around, the first thing that occurred to him was that he was screwed. Even if the security squad managing the presidential residence believed the intruder to have fled through the woods rather than into the belly of the beast, he held no doubt they'd keep the facility canvassed 24/7 for at least the next few days. And until some slice of evidence turned up proving he was no longer around, they'd be forced to maintain an elevated security presence.

Cooper knew they'd also need to operate under the as- sumption this raid was an attempt on Márquez's life, aborted though it might have been. Point being, he wasn't going to have much of a shot at getting home, let alone taking down

Márquez. At the moment, the fact that he'd escaped capture and torture was satisfaction enough—at least now, having calmed his dysfunctional body toward something approaching normalcy, he had the freedom to mull things over. *Could be there's even a plan C, or a plan D, that could get you in front of the man.*

He sat up in the dank, humid tunnel.

As much as he enjoyed playing whatever games with Laramie that would irritate her the most, there remained the issue of his mission—which, even as the most obstinate member of Laramie's team, he had nonetheless come to believe to hold probable significance.

Having read Laramie's documents from the terror book, examining the San Cristóbal theme park up close and personal, and seeing that fucking Pentagon memo . . . hell, even before dropping from the MU-2B, Cooper concluded that the U.S. populace was, in fact, up to its ears in some very deep shit. And were the U.S.-government-employed snuffer-outers who'd taken out the likes of Cap'n Roy also ultimately responsible for putting their own nation's populace in the deep shit in which it currently found itself? Probably— make that definitively yes.

But it didn't matter now—when it came to the suicide-filo threat, too many somewhat innocent lives were at stake. *Which Laramie had been trying to point out to you during her huff at Paddy Murphy's lively Irish pub.*

Possessed of too much firsthand experience staring at the ass end of U.S. foreign policy, Cooper couldn't discount the danger of the products the Guatemala research lab might well have turned out—meaning that whoever had been culpable to begin with, even if they were trying to silence that culpability now, the fact remained that if Márquez had got his hands on the filo that fucking lab had pumped out, and was now planning on using it in a wholesale bomb-dispersal scheme, then somebody had to stop him.

And why wouldn't the bastard stepchild of the government that had empowered Márquez to begin with be the right man for the job?

Yet here you sit, an emissary of the Great Developer of Weapons and Hate, sent to dispose of public enemy number one—

And you've failed miserably.

In fact, you failed *pathetically*: all that you've managed to do is kill a couple of twenty-year-old soldiers and suffer a panic attack.

Flicking on his Maglite, Cooper picked a direction and started carefully down the tunnel. It wasn't long before he grew comfortable—cozy, even—experiencing that feeling of pulling on an old sock, wrapped around you in a way you're accustomed to, but not without a hole or two. Like a paroled convict finding solace in the stupidity of returning to the joint.

Apparently one fort's maze of passageways weren't much different from another's—Cooper occasionally wondering whether he'd turned a corner into the same labyrinth of his imprisonment. Ducking down the short tunnels and into rooms, some featuring prison bars, some with decrepit storage racks, it occurred to him that these passages hadn't been built entirely by Spanish land barons.

No historian I, he thought, *but some of these are older.*

He decided the more likely scenario would have seen the conquistadors discovering the subterranean tunnel work, razing whatever the natives had put atop it, then constructing palatial forts in which to hunker down while the pillaging continued apace.

He thought for a moment of Ernesto Borrego, a thought that made him curious how deeply Márquez's contractors had explored the meandering rabbit runs he was caught in now, and whether there might be any number of buried chambers loaded with some good old-fashioned antiquities the Polar Bear wouldn't mind snatching.

If so, maybe a new wave of violence would follow that stash wherever it headed too.

Márquez's mansion, it seemed, was positioned at one end of a vast network of passages and rooms. Cooper spent a few hours poking around, and had almost convinced himself he'd seen all there was to see when he encountered something odd.

He'd made a few mistakes, been through the same tunnels a few times, but the door he now stood before was a new door. Not just a new sight for him on his exploration of the tunnels, but literally *new*—of recent construction, assembled with materials mimicking the authentic style of the arched, shoulder-high doorways that came with the place, but lacking rot and rust.

He thought suddenly that he heard a noise, and switched off his flashlight. In a few minutes—when there came no subsequent sound—he wondered how disoriented he'd become, and whether this section of the grid was too close to the main house for comfort. *Congratulations—perhaps you've discovered Márquez's wine cellar, including the armed security detail standing at attention beside the Bordeaux.*

He kept the Maglite doused and his eyes soon adjusted somewhat to the darkness. He couldn't detect any residual light from the tunnel, and it seemed no lights were on behind the door. Satisfied he remained alone, Cooper flipped the flashlight back to life, turned the door handle as silently as he could, and pushed open the door.

It hit him immediately—an oddly familiar, distinctly sour scent.

He thought immediately of Eugene Little, the malpracticing former plastic surgeon and current medical examiner for the U.S. Virgin Islands. Little always reeked of the scent Cooper had just taken in, mainly because the place the medical examiner worked reeked of it too. Which made sense for Eugene Little and his place of work—but not, Cooper thought, down in these tunnels.

The bouquet of vinegar and lime he'd just caught was unmistakable: it was the fragrance of formaldehyde.

He was half expecting *some* kind of surprise—a bullet or a punch, perhaps—but when he lifted the flashlight to pass its beam across the contents of the room, he found himself caught completely off guard by the unexpected sight before him.

Cooper had just seen a ghost.

52

Her body lay in repose, more or less the way children's books depicted the fate of Sleeping Beauty, placed on a gilded coffin in the center of the room. Preserved to perfection not ten feet from him, Cooper found himself staring at the real-life version of the priestess depicted by the golden statue from his bungalow—the only clue to her inanimate state the moonlike pallor of her skin, exposed as it was by the beam of the Maglite. Otherwise, the woman looked as though she'd simply nodded off.

If this wasn't the real-life person represented by the golden statue—which Cooper gauged to be all but impossible—she presented as close a match as you'd find. Cooper had to assume that Sleeping Beauty here was a descendant of the tribe from the Guatemala rain forest crater, massacred by the Pentagon lab spill.

But the resemblance seemed even too uncanny for that.

Oh, yeah, Cooper, came a caustic, hollow whisper he recognized immediately as the voice of the golden priestess. *Make no mistake—it's me you've found. Been callin' you here, and now I'm found. Only you're too fucking late, old*

*man. And ain't that too bad? But it doesn't matter . . . and it
never did. You were the one calling yourself back—*

Cooper shook off his latest flirtation with insanity and
closed himself in the room. He turned, steeled himself
against the reek, and came back around with the flashlight.
Time, he thought, to conduct a more rational examination of
the mausoleum you've just stumbled into—*maybe I can
even determine whether I'm hallucinating, or I've managed
to stumble into a new phase of my nightmares.*

He came in and took a look around.

Like its new door, the room too had been updated with recent construction. Peering at the ceiling, corners, and walls,
Cooper thought for a moment he was feeling some kind of
déjà vu aftershock, a residual rhyming vibe put out by Sleeping Beauty or her golden priestess statue counterpart—but
then snapped out of the dream state and realized where he'd
seen this place before. Almost to the inch, it matched the main
room of the subterranean crypt he and Borrego had found beneath the rain forest village. The key difference being the
decor: the crypt in Guatemala, when they'd found it, had already been pillaged by Borrego's intrepid grave robbers;
here, the sort of gold artifacts found in Cap'n Roy's lost stash
of goodies remained fully intact and on glorious display.

The treasures had been kept, or installed, or meticulously
re-created—however they were put here, Cooper thought,
this place is loaded. Designed as some kind of honorable
burial for the woman.

He walked a circuit around the room, finding a series of
pedestals between the walls and the elevated coffin, some
holding candles that appeared recently burned, some propping up statues or other gold loot. Along the walls, designed
with indentations similar to those in the Guatemala crypt,
stood more artifacts—mostly statues depicting Sleeping
Beauty in one pose or another, sculpted in identical tradition
to the golden statue in his bungalow.

He'd heard that statue call out to him for help—calling

him to Guatemala and now here, where he'd seen what he was meant to see. But Cooper knew it hadn't been the statue, or Sleeping Beauty, who'd really been calling. He knew he hadn't been called here by a ghost, or statue, or Julie Laramie and the people she worked for.

He'd called himself here—or, he thought, the ghost of your MIA-POW self had. That long-abandoned chunk of your soul, gone missing, replaced, in your everyday existence, by pain and medication, but still alive and well here in these dungeon hallways. Haunting the chambers beneath the mansions and forts—calling you back for an assist.

Fine. I'm here—I've heeded your call. Some fucking good it's done the both of us—trapped right back where we started. You happy?

He passed a tapestry and came to a marble slab embedded in the wall. Upon closer examination, the slab appeared to represent some kind of memorial: a long list of names had been carved into the slab. It felt to him a little like the Vietnam Memorial in Washington—only the marble on the wall here was of a lighter hue, and all of the memorialized names were either Spanish or, well, *native* sounding, he thought, that odd, almost vowel-free spelling of Mayan people and places. Cooper ran his fingers across some of the names before continuing with the remainder of his once-over mausoleum survey.

Then he stopped and came back to the marble slab.

He counted the names, then counted them again. The number of names on the slab, both times he'd counted, came to one hundred and seventeen. This number didn't mean anything to him particularly, but the feeling he'd just got about what he was looking at did.

He turned and looked over at Sleeping Beauty.

"Jesus Christ," he said.

He knew it could have been any of a number of duties for which the names on the marble plaque had been honored. And he knew there wasn't anything pointing specifically to what had just occurred to him. But sometimes you just had a feeling—a bad feeling—and you goddamn well knew the feeling was right.

He thought of the terror book, and the scenarios the CDC had laid out for the potential spread of the filo epidemic. He remembered a reference in one of the reports to "ten, or twelve, or twenty" suicide bombers, and the potential spread of hemorrhagic fever that could result.

Ten, or twelve, or twenty, the report had said. Too bad, though, he thought: it isn't twenty—or even fifty.

If my sense of what this memorial is all about is right, then it's one hundred and seventeen.

He reflected that most of what he'd just encountered—everything he'd encountered during the past month, in fact—defied explanation. He knew he wouldn't necessarily get all the answers. Maybe, he thought, you'll get none of the answers. But last time he was here, he'd been sent on a fool's mission—dispatched to accomplish nothing, a pawn in some political chess match that ended in a useless draw. And despite the relative success of his assassination effort, he'd been ruined for his trouble.

Maybe this time, his trip could actually turn out to be worthwhile.

He found among the crushed implements in the pouches of his paratrooper suit a scrap of paper and something with which to write. Propping the Maglite between his left arm and rib cage, he copied all one hundred and seventeen names, reading and writing carefully, getting the spelling of every man and woman precisely right.

If his instincts proved correct, then Laramie and her Three Stooges could probably do something with this goddamn list—*trouble being how I'm going to get it out of here.*

That was when he heard another noise.

This one had definitely come from the hall. He killed the Maglite and kneeled down to hide behind Sleeping Beauty; the sound, which he interpreted as footsteps and the opening and closing of another door, came again. He guessed it had come from slightly above and very nearby. He considered again that this section of the subterranean labyrinth must be close to the house—at least *some* part of the house.

Another door opened and closed and the sound of footsteps grew louder, coming now from somewhere just outside the door.

Cooper drew his pistol, knowing he'd be better off using it in the tight quarters of the crypt than the MP5. He rotated the strap of the assault rifle so the gun draped from his back, out of the way but still handy.

He heard the metallic clink of the handle as it was engaged from out in the hall. Iron scraped against stone, the edge of the door brushing the floor of the room as it pushed open.

Then somebody came into the room.

53

Cooper heard the flare of a match, and kept his knee to the ground as an orange glow overtook the room. He slid around the coffin, listening to the scuff of footsteps to keep track of where the visitor stood in the room, Cooper keeping himself hidden. When the room was fully aglow with candlelight, he heard the visitor retreat to the door and close it. For a moment Cooper wondered whether the visitor had only come to light the candles, then departed, but another foot-scuff from the opposite side of the coffin answered that question.

Considering the visitor sounded as though he or she was alone, Cooper decided he may as well find out who'd come to say hello. He held the FN Browning tight against his palm, feeling its cool comfort, and stood.

There wasn't as much shock as he might have expected to encounter on the face of Raul Márquez. It looked more as though the man was insulted that one of his staff would be allowed in here—but then Cooper could see the gradual interpretation of things in the man's eyes and, soon, a kind of hardening of his expression.

Fear did not appear to be a component of the man's reaction.

"Buenas noches, Señor Presidente," Cooper said flatly. "It is nighttime, isn't it? I've more or less lost track."

There came less and less expression on Márquez's face.

"The trespasser," he said in English. That was all he said.

"Sí," Cooper said.

Márquez adjusted his line of sight to take in Sleeping Beauty. Judging from where Márquez stood, Cooper assumed him to have already been looking at the corpse, before the odd sight of the beach bum in the paratrooper gear had popped up behind the coffin.

"Beautiful, isn't she," Márquez said.

Cooper took a careful, sideways sort of look at the embalmed woman beneath them.

"Statuesque," he said.

Márquez looked at Cooper again.

"You're here to assassinate me," he said.

In surveying the photographs provided by Laramie's guide, Cooper had noted a resemblance in Márquez to the statues in Borrego's antiquities stash, and in person it was the same—he looked distinctly Native American. From the rich brown color of his skin to the high cheekbones and black hair, Márquez fit right in with the faces depicted in the artifacts in this strange room—including the face of Sleeping Beauty.

"Maybe," Cooper said.

"I suppose I expected a more . . . *militaristic* response," Márquez said.

"Such as?"

"An air strike, perhaps. Missiles launched from a drone. Who knows."

"Well," Cooper said, "you got me."

Márquez shrugged.

"Appropriate that it should happen here," he said.

"My assassinating you, you mean."

"Yes."

Cooper waited. Márquez seemed to have an idea in mind

he was looking to express, and Cooper saw no reason to slow the head of state from taking the path.

"My own vengeance is wrought," Márquez said, "or will be, in short order, thanks in significant part to the selfless contributions of those honored in this room. And now you're here—meaning, I'm sure, to exact *your* vengeance. It is a circle of violence—or cycle, perhaps. I did not begin the cycle, but I've long expected my demise would become a part of it. I'm relieved. Relieved my painful journey is concluding; relieved my conclusion comes now. Now that I have set in motion what I was meant to do."

"So you've told your deep-cover jihad to combust themselves, then," Cooper said.

"Yes. They've been activated."

"All one hundred and seventeen of them?"

Márquez's eyes twinkled behind his otherwise sullen visage.

"If you say so," he said.

"Depending on when you carved the plaque, of course," Cooper said, "they wouldn't all have made it this far."

"No," Márquez said, "they wouldn't."

"But probably more than six of them, I'll bet," Cooper said.

"I'll bet you're right."

"How?"

"Sorry?"

"The people I work for," Cooper said, almost cringing at the words his mouth had chosen, "would want me to ask how it is you activated them."

Márquez chuckled unemotionally.

"How else to inform an army to engage its capitalist enemy," he said, "than through the most capitalist of acts?"

"Sorry," Cooper said, "but I'm a little rusty on my Marxist dogma."

"You should bone up," Márquez said. "Comes in handy from time to time. The answer is through a very expensive broadcast television media campaign."

Cooper digested the business speak.

"Containing some phrase or other," he said.

"Or other," Márquez said. "Yes."

"Care to provide some of your army's assumed identities? Lessen your sentence at the pearly gates?"

Márquez almost let a smile crease his lips.

"My dear assassin," he said, "please go fuck yourself."

Cooper nodded, then jutted his chin at his captive.

"Who is she," Cooper said. "Sleeping Beauty, here."

Márquez then offered a clamp-lipped smile—not appreciating the joke, it seemed.

"My lover and partner."

"The king and queen of the suicide sleepers," Cooper said. "How nice."

The thin-lipped smile held, serving as Márquez's response to Cooper's wiseass commentary. In a moment, the smile evaporated.

"Ironic, isn't it," Márquez said, "that in life, her blood may have yielded a vaccine."

Cooper blinked.

"For the 'filo'?"

"Yes. She survived it."

"Christ," Cooper said. "The girl from the clinic?"

Márquez looked at him and sort of shrugged—the expression meant to convey, Cooper figured, that Márquez didn't really care to understand, but had no idea what Cooper was talking about.

Cooper thought about the story from Márquez's childhood, as relayed by Laramie's Three Stooges during the "cell's" powwow at the Flamingo Inn. Then he thought about the village he and Borrego had found in the rain forest crater.

"The bride and groom of pain," he said. "Birds of a feather, eh, Raul? She made it out of the village that took the brunt of the Pentagon lab's little error, and you made it out of another Pentagon-funded genocidal strike?"

Márquez looked at Cooper about the way Cooper would expect a man to look at somebody as certifiably loony as himself—or the way he'd look at somebody who couldn't possibly know all these things—but then spoke up again.

"You could put it that way," he said.

"The irony you mentioned," Cooper said. "It's ironic because she held the key to surviving the 'filo' in her bloodstream but brought you the weapon in the first place?"

Márquez just kind of dead-eyed him.

"How did she do it? Come on, by the time you're through with your end of that cycle you were talking about, I'm sure you'll have exacted a few thousand American lives as your toll. Why don't you come clean—maybe it'll give you some extra credit when you visit the big man upstairs."

"You know," Márquez said, "you're a strange sort of assassin."

"You don't know the half of it, *Señor Presidente.*"

"She studied science. Earned a Ph.D. from Johns Hopkins—her specialty was pathology. Came to me with an idea following my first election. And a few other things."

"Such as some fine rapture, I'll bet," Cooper said.

"Yes, that too," Márquez said.

"And among the other things—a crate or two of goodies?"

Márquez gave him the same dead-eye stare.

"Left behind," Cooper said, "by the lab people when they tried to burn the evidence to the ground. But she lived up there, so she knew where to look. And maybe she found a stockpile the idiots with the napalm missed. How am I doing?"

Márquez had apparently decided to clam up.

"What happened to her?" Cooper said.

"I killed her," *el presidente* said.

"Why?"

"It became necessary."

"For what reason?"

Márquez eyed him, then shrugged. "I think she would have killed me next. Lot of rage in that woman."

Cooper nodded at this. It partially confirmed the last piece of the crypt-puzzle he'd been assembling.

"By 'next,'" Cooper said, "you mean she'd have be-headed you too?"

Márquez looked at him again but didn't offer a reply.

"I'm curious how she would have found the Pentagon memo," Cooper said, "but then again maybe she had access to that kind of thing through the university."

Either way, he thought, it seems the Indian girl from the village has sought and found her vengeance—both on the people who authorized the lab and, depending, an unhealthy dose of citizens from the country who funded it.

Too bad the swing of her machete missed the neck of a couple last souls—the snuffer-outers, the last survivors of the vengeance she hoped to exact on the architects of the filo lab.

Enter me.

He coaxed his thoughts back to the topic of the names on the memorial slab of marble. Despite the fact that they'd need to work in reverse, and track the current identity of the sleepers from their original, local names, Cooper figured Laramie, the Three Stooges, and the Grand Poobah could still make use of the list of names he'd just transcribed.

And aside from the fact that he'd been sent to "eradicate" the man, he'd now have some use for the continued survival of Raul Márquez—the King of the Sleepers.

He straightened his elbow and held the Browning tight, taking aim at Márquez's head. Márquez almost seemed to sigh in relief—even pleasure.

"The assassin," Márquez said, closing his eyes, "taking the assassin."

Yeah, Cooper thought, *I've wanted to die plenty of times too after what happened to me.*

"Not quite," Cooper said.

Márquez opened his eyes.

"I thought you were here to kill me," he said.

"I was," Cooper said. "And I am. But too bad—you'll need to wallow in your misery for a little while longer."

Keeping the Browning trained on Márquez, Cooper came

around Sleeping Beauty's coffin and—making sure to maintain a few feet between himself and Márquez's watchful eyes—grasped the handle of the door.

"Let's take a walk," he said.

54

Upon her return to the Flamingo Inn, Laramie found herself greeted by a strange call from Lou Ebbers.

Not unexpected, but strange nonetheless.

He told her he had pulled the fire alarm—how, he hadn't clarified further than before, but he said he'd pulled it nonetheless. He mentioned that emergency quarantine preparations were now in process; the identity and location of the sleepers Laramie's cell had found had been revealed to the FBI, CIA, and other relevant agencies, and busts made immediately. "Other cells," as he'd put it on the call, had also identified additional sleepers on the same approximate time line as her team, and those sleepers had been rounded up too—fifteen total captures. He indicated that in the past hour, the media had just been given a great deal of advance intel, something Laramie already knew from the coverage of the "credible terror threat" she watched on CNN from the DirecTV-equipped seat on her Jet Blue flight back down south from JFK.

This much she'd expected; these measures, among others, were the idea behind pulling the fire alarm in the first place. She had even expected to hear, at some point, that there were "other cells" doing what she and her team had been doing, parallel to them.

The part she found strange, though also not unexpected, was the warning Ebbers mentioned next.

"Just a quick reminder, Miss Laramie," he'd said to her over the spiderphone. "You haven't been doing what you've been doing. None of the intelligence you or your cell has generated, in doing the things you haven't been doing, is to be revealed to anyone."

When it seemed he was waiting for an acknowledgment of his order, Laramie went ahead and gave him one.

"I've always understood that to be the case," she said.

"I mention this not because of what you will now see in the media coverage of the 'credible threat' to the nation's security—but because of what you *won't* see."

Laramie had a pretty good idea what was coming.

"In the media, as well as in the government circles that have now been exposed to your findings," he said, "you will find no mention of Guatemala. You will hear nothing about a research lab there, or a hemorrhagic fever outbreak that occurred in the same region as documented in a journal found by the CDC. You will hear nothing about Cuba, Fidel Castro, or an underground theme-park-for-rent under a hill in San Cristóbal. And finally, Miss Laramie, you will hear nothing about Raul Márquez, nor any operations related to his assassination."

From the moment she'd logged her request, through Lou Ebbers, to see the Pentagon memo referencing the "Project ICRS" research lab, Laramie had assumed these pieces of the puzzle would be left out of any official government inquiry into the suicide-sleeper situation. It didn't mean she liked it, but she knew she wasn't going to be given any say about whether the omissions should remain omitted, or not. She also knew this piece of the puzzle didn't need to be addressed immediately.

"Thank you for keeping me in the loop on that," she'd said, and Ebbers told her she was welcome and broke the connection.

In the twenty hours since she'd taken the call, her guide had instructed Laramie to keep the Three Wise Men doing their work; also in the meantime, the shit had hit the fan.

The Krups brewer in her room made its exasperated sounds announcing the end of its percolation and Laramie rose to refill her Flamingo Inn–issue Styrofoam cup. The television blared as she walked past it for the refill, and kept on blaring on her way back.

Laramie had left the war room to brew a fresh cup of coffee, but now that she was here, she realized she hadn't sat through a full coverage cycle from any of the news bureaus, and that she should probably take the chance to watch one now.

She sat at the table and watched the news.

The Fox News Channel had its usual BREAKING NEWS banner at the bottom of the screen, punctuated by the words TERROR ALERT: RED, both of which circulated with the freshly devised label for the crisis ruling the day: BIOTERROR BOMBS: AMERICA UNDER FIRE.

Various updates rotated through their cycle beneath the banners at the base of the screen, most of the headlines related to a pair of suicide bombings that had taken place in the past six hours. The first had been set off around five P.M. in an Illinois suburb near Lake Michigan; the second, in Yakima, Washington, along the Columbia River, two hours later. News on such matters as the quarantine measures officials had enacted following the blasts were also being covered by the headline prose.

The first pair of suicide blasts had come from sleepers they hadn't known about.

On-screen, Brit Hume was busy discussing with a terrorism expert Laramie didn't recognize the likelihood that "additional bombings may be planned," something the Homeland Security secretary had stated in a press conference thirty minutes following the Illinois blast. Concluding his grilling of this first expert, the news anchor turned in his chair and moved on to the next authority, an official from the

Centers for Disease Control to whom he was connected live via satellite. As they dove into a discussion on the topic of the potential filovirus outbreaks—along with such statistics as the quantity of Tamiflu and other antivirals the CDC kept on hand, and various measures individual citizens could take to avoid infection—Laramie swallowed a few sips of the sour coffee.

The quarantining efforts, she knew, would remain productive only if a sufficiently low number of filo bombs were set off. If more than a handful of the suicide sleepers were able to succeed in launching localized animal-and-human breakouts, the quarantine barriers would be breached and the casualties would mount horrifically.

The conclusion she drew from all this was that she and her "counter-cell cell" had failed.

Miserably.

They'd failed to stop the sleepers. They'd failed to find the Illinois and Yakima bombers, and who knew how many others—regardless of the presence of other "cells." Her team had managed to identify public enemy number one in Raul Márquez—or at least engage in educated speculation to that end—but they'd obviously made their determination, and launched their assassination operation, too late to stop the activation order from being issued.

Plus, in gauging his identity as late as we did, we managed to send our "operative" on a fruitless mission—what good did it do to assassinate the opposing army's leader if he's already sent his troops into battle?

Meaning that for all she knew, she had personally ordered Cooper to his death.

Brit Hume continued his presentation of BIOTERROR BOMBS: AMERICA UNDER FIRE, confirming what Ebbers had told her about the news coverage on his call: there was not a single angle in the coverage that featured Márquez, Cuba, Guatemala, Castro, the source of the engineered filo used in the "bioterror bombs," or any ramifications thereof.

Laramie poured herself another cup of coffee, clicked off the television with the remote, and opened her door—fully intending to return to the room that was now completely overtaken by Wally Knowles's computer system.

55

Cooper found the first-aid kit in his jumpsuit and located an Ace bandage.

He tackled Márquez and pinned him to the mucky floor of the cavern—thinking, as he did it, of his episode with Jesus Madrid in the velociraptor's Manchester United–inspired workout room. He held Márquez down so he couldn't squirm away, wrapping the Ace bandage around the leader's mouth, winding it tightly behind his head and securing it with a few strips of the adhesive tape that came along with the bandage in the kit. He used the tape to "cuff" Márquez's hands behind his back.

Then he pulled Márquez to his feet. He swung his assault rifle around to the front—figuring the MP5 would put on a better show than a handgun—and pocketed the Browning where he could quickly snatch it with his off hand.

"After you, *Señor Presidente*."

He offered Márquez a hard kick in the ass to emphasize his point.

"Take us back in the way you came out. And don't worry," he said, "you've made your point that you don't give two shits about dying. Rest assured I'm skilled at causing great pain with my choice of where to plug you full of holes. One at a time."

He knew it was a mostly idle threat.

Márquez led him around enough corners to get Cooper feeling dizzy. He worked at keeping the ideal distance between them, close enough to grab Márquez the minute a guard came into view, but far enough away to prevent the guy from elbowing him in the chin. He learned the best way of using his flashlight was to pin it between his left arm and rib cage, the way he had while copying the names from the marble slab. He kept the beam trained past Márquez so he could see—and use the beam to blind, if necessary—the first security man to make an appearance.

A set of musty stairs appeared, and Cooper could see a bud of hesitation in Márquez's step. The president hadn't meant to reveal it and Cooper would take and use the error to his advantage. Another door, recently constructed like the one guarding the entrance to the crypt, stood at the top of the stairs.

Cooper poked Márquez in the shoulder with the end of his assault rifle.

"Open the fucking door," he said in a caustic whisper.

He felt the temperature and humidity conditions shift the instant Márquez opened the door—this door led into the house.

Cooper closed the gap as the door swung over its jamb, shoving himself quickly against Márquez and propelling them both into and through the doorway faster than his quarry expected. This kept Márquez from doing any yelling or screaming—

And before the two guards, positioned on opposing sides of the wine cellar door, were even able to figure out what the hell the president was doing with an Ace bandage around his head, Cooper processed the scene—

Guard to the left. Guard to the right—slightly behind the opening door. You're in the wine cellar—walls full of racks. Door opposite him—closed. Nobody else in the room—

The first bullet down the silenced barrel of his MP5 caught the edge of the first guard's eyebrow and sent a chunk of his skull, and some of the brain behind it, into a row of Syrah. As he pivoted, Cooper delivered a savage kick with his combat boot into Márquez's shin to keep him at bay. The second guard couldn't decide between radioing in this disturbance and defending himself, walkie-talkie wrist rising from waist to mouth, gun arm reaching to take aim—neither act making sufficient headway before Cooper's second bullet tore through the bridge of his nose and plastered an airborne mist of red, white, and gray across a pane of glass protecting a cooled section of Sauvignon Blanc.

He repeated the cycle of gunshots, ensuring that neither man, as he fell, would find enough remaining consciousness to sound an alarm. Then he reached out and picked up Márquez by the collar and set him back on his feet. He jammed the hot barrel of the assault rifle into Márquez's spine and listened.

He wondered how much racket he'd made. He saw that the Maglite had fallen from beneath his underarm, that the armor-piercing shrapnel, or skull fragments, or whatever, had broken a few bottles of the Syrah. Plus, Márquez had crumpled from the kick to the shin and the guards had fallen like redwoods.

He stood, waiting—listening for another pealing two-tone shrill, or the crackle of radio static, or the shuffle of hustling footsteps. There came no sound but the whirring of some climate-control device doing its thing in the cellar.

I need a fucking fax machine.

Time was running out—it wouldn't be long before his usual half-ass sort of plan caved in on itself.

"Let's go, King," he said, and shoved him toward the door that would take them into the house.

The phone on Laramie's bedside table jangled noisily.

She came over to the table, fumbled the phone in her first

attempt to answer, then finally managed to lift the receiver to her ear—at which point Julie Laramie encountered the second strange call to greet her in the same twelve-hour span.

"Yeah—"

The screeching blare of a fax tone assaulted her ear before stopping abruptly. A rattle-and-bang sound was followed by a harsh, almost unrecognizable whisper, spoken so closely into the microphone on the other end of the line it was difficult to tell it was a human being doing the talking.

But Laramie could still tell who it was.

"Goddammit, I didn't even think—I need a fax machine, what the fuck is the fax number at your hotel?"

The words from Cooper's noisy whisper were bundled together like a ball of yarn. A rocket science degree was not necessary for Laramie to understand that she would need to hustle.

"Um, Christ, fax, ah, room Fourteen," she said, "dial the same number and hit fourteen instead of—"

The line was already dead.

Laramie ran from her room, down the sidewalk outside the row of rooms, and banged on her guide's door. The numeral **14** was affixed in cheap plastic to its exterior.

She barged in when he opened the door, heading for the fax machine she knew him to keep on his side of the two-room suite setup.

"It ring yet?" she asked her guide, to no reply—but then the fax machine answered her question, bleating out a gurgling ring, then going silent.

Then it rang again.

"Christ," she said, "how many rings do we have this set for—"

The machine picked up and she could hear the screeching data-feed noise again, followed by silence, and then the machine's status screen told her it was RECEIVING.

"Our operative," she said, "has surfaced," and she and her guide stood over the machine as it began printing page one, announced it was receiving the second page, and repeated the cycle for a third time before declaring with a *bleep* that the data feed had been halted, at which point Laramie heard Cooper's whisper on the machine's speaker.

"Goddamn this thing, how does it work—"

She snatched the machine's receiver from its cradle. She could see the long list of names on the fax printouts, all seemingly Central American native in their spelling, hastily scribbled on a smaller sheet of paper highlighted by darker shading outside its rim on the pages—

"You're alive," Laramie said.

"Not for long. I sent three pages, you get 'em all?"

"Got 'em. Wait a minute, are you telling me—"

"Those are your sleepers. All one hundred and seventeen of them."

"What? How could you—"

"These are their original names, obviously. So you'll need to track 'em backward—or whatever way you analyst types and the Three Stooges you have working for you track those sorts of things."

"My God," Laramie said, looking at her guide, who offered her a shrug. She handed him the list and he went immediately over to the seat in front of his laptop and jumped on his telephone.

Laramie thought through what this meant as quickly as she could. It would be a challenge working backward against the clock, with only the original names and no places of original residence, let alone photographs to work from—but Cooper had just put them ninety-nine names closer than where they'd been a minute ago—one-seventeen minus Achar, the fifteen captured sleepers identified by them and the "other cell," and the Illinois and Yakima bombers. Local records with photographs would be the first, and hardest step, depending on whether Márquez had recruited from multiple Central and South American nations—

"He sent the activation by television ad," Cooper said,

"and that's all I've got, except for the fact that I've got our pal Raul here in a headlock. One question—just in case, against every probability imaginable, I make it out."

"A headlock—what? What is it?"

"Yes or no answer. No maybes."

"Fine. What is it?"

"You agree?"

"Fine!"

"Mr. Grand Poobah," Cooper's whisper said.

"What?"

"You let half of it slip—only once, but I need to know. For my own reasons, and don't ask. Is Lou Ebbers your boss?"

Despite the evident circumstances in motion on the other end of the line, Laramie hesitated. *What in the hell is he going to do with—*

"No fucking maybes, Laramie. And have some goddamn faith."

One-Mississippi—

"Yes," she said. "Yes."

She flicked her eyes in the direction of her guide, who was busy at his workstation.

Then she said, "I'm glad you've made it—so far, I mean."

" 'So far' being the key phrase," he said. "I wouldn't be throwing me any parties anytime soon."

A few snaps of static came.

"See you around," he said.

Then the fax machine announced with another *bleep* that the line had gone dead.

56

Cooper released the headlock, grasped both his guns, and rewrapped himself around Márquez like an Ace bandage in his own right. With his left arm, he got Márquez into a half nelson—elbow jammed against the man's underarm, forearm mashed against his neck. Taking the Browning, he held it backward and jammed the barrel against Márquez's temple. His thumb served as the trigger finger: any slight, unexpected jostle, and Cooper knew his beefy thumb would engage the weapon—something he hoped the security people would immediately grasp. He pressed the front of his body against Márquez's back and wrapped his right arm snugly around the front of him, MP5 in hand. He'd need to walk sideways to his left—like a crab—but he'd be protected by his quarry in the front, and could pivot and shoot with the MP5 by turning them both in a circle.

He crab-walked his hostage up a stairwell to a door—a door leading, Cooper was sure, to the main body of the house.

"Open the door, King," he said.

When Márquez did, Cooper whacked his forehead against the softer backside of the president's skull—a head-butt he hoped would stun the man but not drop him. He heard an *umph* from behind the Ace bandage and felt Márquez go slightly limp.

Then he crab-dashed through the door.

He immediately clocked three security men in the room as he and Márquez, joined at the hip, flew into the library.

Then he went nuts.

"*¡Lo tengo! Tranquilizate, no haga nada! Lo mato, lo juro que lo mato!* Back the fuck off!"

He kept moving, picking out the archway at the other end of the room and heading there, Cooper and Márquez a four-hundred-pound exit-seeking bundle waddling its way outta town. As he crab-shuffled along, he tried to keep all three men in sight. Their weapons were drawn; two of them were soldiers, Cooper seeing AK-47s, while the other wore a suit and came armed with a pistol. The man in the suit started talking, trying to get his words in over Cooper's screams—

"*¡Tranquilo, tranquilo!*"

Cooper hearing muffled grunts from behind the Ace bandage, knowing his precious few seconds of advantage were wasting away. *Keep moving, you useless old hack—another twenty feet and you'll be through that fucking archway . . .*

Cooper ready to guarantee he'd find windows, and maybe even a door, when he reached the room beyond the arch. He saw a fountain there, heard the *clack* of approaching shoes on tile.

"*¡Tengo una bomba para matarnos!* You move too fast, I'll kill this motherfucker!"

He crossed beneath the threshold of the arch in his slow waddle, picked a direction, and turned immediately out from under the arch, pressing his back against a wall, so that the wall blocked the library goons' view of him. The *clack*ers appeared around a corner—*two soldiers and two suits*—and then Cooper saw the tall windows behind them and, beyond, the *driveway*.

He swiveled the barrel of the MP5 to point it in the direction of the approaching guards, coming to a sorry realization as he did it. *You turned the wrong way—you'll need to cross the archway again to get to the window.*

Too bad—carpe diem *time.*

He let loose with the MP5 on the four newcomers, none of the men more than twenty-five feet from the mouth of his gun. The automatic fire from the rifle sounded oddly silent, Cooper first thinking the gun had jammed, then understanding the silencer at the tip of the barrel was doing its thing, a function he no longer required but seemed to fortify his jump on the guards.

Releasing his grip on Márquez, he plowed a knee into his back and sent him sprawling across the tile. Regretting he'd never taken the chance to practice such things with video games, Cooper rotated the Browning to a normal trigger hold and put half a dozen rounds into the King of the Sleepers while he kept at the four soldiers with the MP5.

He couldn't be sure he'd taken down Márquez with his half-ass potshots, but he doubted he'd gone worse than four-for-six. Cooper wasn't sure it would make a difference anyway. The King of the Sleepers' memorialized army was already doing its thing.

Maybe Laramie, the Stooges, and the Poobah would stop them; maybe not.

He lowered his head and started a sprint for the window, turning as he ran across the open archway to fire blindly into the darker library and the three guards within—guards he knew would now be lighting him up without hesitation.

A bullet punched into his right leg below the knee and he almost stumbled into a heap when he felt a wrecking ball bury itself in his shoulder, but then he was past the open archway and realized he was in for a hard collision with the window—and with the window coming up on him, he let loose with the MP5, feeling the clip go empty as he drained its shells into the thick pane of glass—

And then he lowered his good shoulder and smashed headlong into the heavy wall of glass. He felt and heard a dull *crunch,* experienced an odd, fraction-of-a-second delay, but then the resistance was gone, a crystalline symbol crash enveloped him, and he felt the unforgiving asphalt plant itself across his cheekbone and jaw before it dawned on him he'd broken through.

He rolled to his feet and started running again, hoping his forward momentum would go to battle against his new crop of injuries. The two-tone peal was blaring across the compound and the lights had flared on again as he hauled his battered body down the driveway; the clatter of automatic-weapons fire echoed along the drive.

He turned sharply and ducked off the road.

Coming in, I had to do it the back way. But going out . . .

Past the trees that lined the drive, across a bed of bark chips and strip of sod—and then he reached the wall.

They'll take me back down to the chamber of horrors if I let them catch me. They'll put me in the fucking chair and strafe my balls—they'll whip, knife, and pummel me, take me for a ride on the electric roller coaster with their fucking car battery—I'll be left for dead in my cell, chewing on crusty tortillas—

Get a hold of yourself—you've been here before, and last time, you had fifty miles to go, or farther.

This time, you've only got one steep hill.

Clear it and vanish. Like a Mayan ducking the conquerors in a subterranean tunnel, like the Vietcong in the jungle. Get yourself over that hill, and you're free.

Both of you—the guy you left here twenty years ago and the one who came after.

He tugged his sleeves out over his naked hands and hit the wall running, leaping from earth to stone and cranking his legs like a cyclist. He used his sleeves like gloves, Cooper grabbing the razor wire to pull his body the rest of the way up the wall, feeling the blades tear through to his skin, and then he'd reached the top of the wall and planted his good leg and pushed off—

The eight-foot drop hurt, but he managed to land mostly on the cushion of flesh provided by his aging ass, and then he thought—

I'll be goddamned if anybody's catching me now—

And Cooper, with his twenty-year MIA-POW soul in tow—blistered, cut, broken, bruised, and shot—hauled tail into the woods.

57

Laramie came into the Weston Reading Room—
vacant, as before, save for the solitary, seated figure of Lou
Ebbers. From out in the stacks, she'd caught wind of the
same scent as before: it seemed he'd brought along another
grande Starbucks and commissary-issue breakfast sandwich.

She took the seat that coincided with the placement of
coffee and food.

Just like the first time around.

"Thanks for the coffee," she said, "but I'm surprised:
when we began this process you knew my every routine. A
week ago I decided it was high time I broke my addiction.
I'm working on shaking my java habit."

"Nectar of the gods," Ebbers said. "Your loss."

Eyeing him head-on, Laramie decided Lou Ebbers looked
fifteen years older than when she'd seen him at this table
only a month ago. His skin appeared jaundiced, the man's
fatigue punctuated by deep, sorrowful bags beneath his
eyes. This was probably better than she could say for herself, and much, much better, she considered, than the 11,246
victims, according to the latest Homeland Security press re-

lease, of the six filo-dispersal bombings successfully detonated to date.

Most of the credit, in limiting the casualties, was being given to the relentless, multijurisdictional quarantine efforts. Laramie knew there to have been sixty sleeper arrests; only ten of these had been publicized, the judgment having been made that the real number was too big for America's public relations palate.

She knew the other basics too: in addition to issuing a ban on all television commercials, the federal government had temporarily restricted commercial air travel to cases of documented emergencies only. In affected cities, only essential services were being conducted, and numerous anti-infection measures were being carried out under the martial-law-type command of numerous federal and local agencies and law enforcement organizations, including the National Guard and multiple wings of the active military. Trading had been suspended "until further notice" in all major financial markets.

There had not yet been a documented case of the fever in Virginia or the District of Columbia—nor a detonation—but Laramie hadn't spotted more than a few dozen people out and about on her drive to the Library of Congress. Life in the U.S. of A. was one big ghost town, but there was the general impression, Laramie thought, that the government had things under control.

Ebbers busied himself reading a sheet of paper he held between table and waist.

"Numbers are leveling out," he said. "As of this morning, it's crossed twenty-four thousand. We'll grow the publicly disseminated figures gradually, so that their impact can be mitigated with stories of successful quarantines, arrests, and so forth. We had two additional arrests since you and I spoke last. The total accounted-for sleeper count is therefore eighty-five of the hundred-and-seventeen total: Benjamin Achar, the probables your team identified, the six successful blasters, and the rest, as you know, found through investigations based on the list from the Márquez memorial."

Laramie nodded. Both her cell and much of the rest of the federal government had worked around the clock on the names from Cooper's list, investigating backward from the sleepers' original names, tracking a family photograph here, a government identification card there—some of which they'd been able to match with photos taken under the sleepers' new American identities. As Ebbers had just covered in his count, they'd failed to apprehend Márquez's entire roster.

"Of the thirty-two remaining names," Ebbers said, "we think it's safe to assume ten percent of the total, meaning of the full one-seventeen, fell out—died in training, were eaten by sharks en route from Cuba, failed to establish an identity, maybe 'went native,' as you put it, like Achar. That puts us around fifteen active but un-ID'd sleepers, assuming our ten percent 'churn rate' is reasonable. As you know, we've had no detonations for eleven days now. We believe the threat has been mitigated for the time being."

"At this point the remaining sleepers would be better off waiting it out anyway," Laramie said.

"If they choose to think for themselves, yes."

Ebbers inclined his chin.

"You heard from your operative?"

Laramie held his gaze for a moment. A story had run in the midst of the suicide-bomb crisis covering the assassination of the president of El Salvador by "rebel insurgents." Laramie had assumed from this news that the "headlock" Cooper mentioned he'd held on Márquez when they'd last spoken had graduated to his assigned eradication. As to whether Cooper had made it out alive—that was another question.

"No," she said. "No word."

"Overall," he said, "how you holding up?"

"Me? Better than most. We didn't exactly save the day."

"No?"

"Far from it."

"I say we did," Ebbers said. "I say *you* did."

"Twenty-four thousand casualties? That's a lot of people."

"The task force," he said, "was in the process of dismantling itself—a total failure—when we assigned you the case. There were one hundred and seventeen sleepers. Not ten, or twelve, or whatever was suspected by the eighteen-some-odd agencies examining the antics of Benny Achar. Twenty-four K is a boatload of people, I will agree with you, but what you did was save the other three hundred million. That is a larger boatload."

Laramie examined the grain on the tabletop.

"We've arranged for your return to work," Ebbers said.

Laramie looked at him.

"Malcolm Rader is expecting you back on Monday. Nobody there knows what you and your team have been doing. In fact, nobody anywhere does. Besides me, of course, your cell, and your guide."

"Along with the people you work for," Laramie said.

Ebbers looked at her—*into* me more than *at* me, she thought. She didn't like the look one bit.

"I suppose you're right," he said. "Either way, we will need to maintain radio silence on the issues we covered by phone after your interrogation of the Scarsdale sleeper. The radio silence will need to extend further: any and everything you and your team did, thought, or spoke about during this matter shall never surface. We don't want anyone in the federal government to know about it. We don't want anyone in the media to know about it; we don't want Congress to know about it. This includes whether you are someday subpoenaed to testify on these topics under oath."

There it was again—the *we*. The *we* that she assumed would never be fully revealed or explained.

"As far as anyone involved with the task force is concerned," he said, "the White House sent a special investigator. You were never named. As the unidentified special investigator, you generated some intel for the task force, and the task force and other federal and local agencies and law enforcement organizations reacted as effectively as possible to the gravest of threats to our nation's security. The real you, meanwhile, has been gainfully and separately employed by the Central Intelligence Agency throughout this ordeal."

As much as it bothered her, Laramie had to admit that the pieces of the suicide-sleeper puzzle that involved the Pentagon, its biological weapons research, and the origin of the Marburg-2 filo were better dealt with later. The only problem was that with this form of acquiescence, the chance these facts would ever see the light of day would decline in an accelerated manner as time progressed. Documents would be shredded; people would be bought; all that would remain in a few months' time was hearsay from the likes of her, Detective Cole, Wally Knowles, Eddie Rothgeb, and Cooper. And numerous measures were probably already teed up that would discredit any such accounts.

Laramie had a pretty good idea how it had worked. Whatever authority Ebbers possessed—if any—waging a battle against another wing of the federal government wasn't a part of that mandate. A judgment call had been made—and while she might well be capable of raising a stink in the media, or elsewhere, she decided to agree with the call. For the moment.

There wasn't much choice.

"On a going-forward basis," Ebbers said, "the people I work for will retain the right to utilize the services of you and your team. This right will be exercised in a case-by-case manner."

Laramie noted the form of Ebbers's comment. Since it had not been a request, she saw no need to provide an answer.

"In keeping these services available to us, however," he said, "there will, and must necessarily, involve a single, logical, and, frankly, ruthless caveat. The caveat, of course, is that every member of your team must remain utterly silent on the matters of which he or she has recently partaken. Any violation of this caveat . . . well, Miss Laramie, don't allow anyone on your team to violate the caveat."

Ebbers said this with a dark twinkle in his eye, Laramie struggling to return the gesture with a comparable expression, considering she'd just been told that if she or any member of her hastily assembled squad were to say a word about the operation they'd just conducted, the indiscretion would be punishable by death—or something close to it.

They warned me about this during my training at The Farm. That in taking a position in the intelligence ranks, your successes may never be trumpeted—and your failures, almost certainly exposed.

Not that I appear to be working for the Central Intelligence Agency any longer. At least not solely . . .

Resigning herself to matters, she thought of her moment with Cooper on the boat, motoring over to Cuba on the flat, dark sea.

Live slow, mon, he'd said, and she let those words roll around her brain now.

"Report to your office on Monday," Ebbers said. "Malcolm Rader knows one thing only—and he is the only one who knows. He knows it is not true that you fell ill and required surgery, plus a one-month recovery at a specialized facility, as the rest of the personnel in your department, as well as those in your private life, have been told. You were not permitted to take any visitors, of course," he said, "due to your condition."

"Fine," Laramie said, her first word of the last few minutes sounding loud and annoying to her as she spoke it.

"And look," Ebbers said, standing, "you've made a full recovery. Congratulations and here's to your health. Now if you'll excuse me."

On autopilot, Laramie took his cue and stood. She shook his hand as he extended it.

"Though it may seem difficult to grasp at the moment," he said, "your performance in this investigation has been exemplary."

Handshake concluded, Laramie nodded her thanks, started to say something, then decided to leave it. She also decided to leave her untouched coffee and sandwich on the table, Laramie simply adjusting the strap of her shoulder bag until it hung comfortably as she steered her way out.

58

When Ebbers reached the street and his waiting Lincoln Town Car, the engine was already running, its rear door unlocked, per the routine. The car featured heavily tinted windows, which normally kept people from seeing Ebbers within—but today, kept Ebbers from noticing that the deeply tanned individual behind the wheel of the car was not the man who usually did his driving. As Ebbers closed his door, the locks did a four-door stereophonic *chunk*—prompting Ebbers to examine the man behind the wheel. Realizing he'd made a mistake, Ebbers discovered, upon attempting to exit the vehicle, that the door handle didn't do him any good.

Cooper turned and had a look at the initially nervous but gradually calming former head of the Central Intelligence Agency. Having discovered the Lincoln to include a handy child's lock on each of the rear doors, he'd activated the feature shortly after offering the driver a brief nap.

Ebbers spoke first.

"Appears our operative has made it out alive," he said.

Cooper smiled with little to no cheer.

"So it does," he said.

Ebbers looked around the interior of the car, then out its windows onto the virtually abandoned street.

"What'd you do with my driver?" he said.

"He'll be fine," Cooper said. "So Lou?"

Ebbers crossed his arms.

"Yes," he said, shooting for indifferent impatience.

"I've been watching the media onslaught documenting every facet of this terrifying crisis for two and a half weeks now," Cooper said.

"Have you," Ebbers said.

"Yep. And you know, it's interesting—there's been nothing, anywhere, on how, where, and by whom this M-2 filo was created."

After a digestive moment, Ebbers said, "Now that you mention it, I don't recall seeing any such coverage, either."

Cooper nodded.

"Probably," he said, "if a story were run a few months from now, mentioning that the biological weapons of mass destruction deployed by the sleepers had been created in a lab funded by the Pentagon—that would be, well, bad for the image of the good ol' U.S. of A."

Ebbers looked at him for a while.

"Probably," he said, "but then again I'm sure the administration would discover and then point out the lack of double-sourcing by the reporter breaking the story, or expose some other questionable ways the reporter generally goes about doing his business, and the way he investigated this story in particular." Ebbers held Cooper's eyes. "Even so—yes, such a report would potentially do some damage."

"Be tougher," Cooper said, "for the government's spin to take effect if, say, the reporter had documentation, double-eyewitness testimony, artifacts, and other hard evidence backing his piece. Come to think of it, it'd be even tougher if more than one reporter broke the same story on the same day."

Ebbers looked at him for another little while, then said, "Yes. Tougher still."

Cooper nodded again, appearing marginally more cheery in doing so.

"So there are two issues for us to tackle here today, Lou."

"Two issues."

"Right. Issue number one," Cooper said. "Starting yesterday, if Laramie, myself, or any of the Three Stooges should step into harm's way—for any reason, you understand, anything outside of expiration from old age, which only I am in danger of experiencing—then on the day of that harm, six prominent journalists will be provided all the documentation we just discussed. Laramie and the Stooges, by the way, are unaware we are having this conversation. In fact I am certain she, at least, would be highly ticked off to learn that I've added her to my little self-preservation scheme."

Cooper shifted in his seat, wincing at the discomfort of the full slate of injuries from which he was recovering.

"But Lou, I foresee at least *some* scenario by which you, or the people you work for, will someday conclude the personnel you recruited to work this suicide-sleeper case know just a little too much about the wrong things. I doubt, however, that you or the people you work for would like to see the Pentagon's funding of biological-weapons research debated *ad nauseum* by the likes of *Hannity & Colmes*. I'm sure you had nothing to do with it in the first place, but you and your gang seem to be charged, if nothing else, with the preservation of this lovely status quo you've got going. Wouldn't want to disturb that, now would you?"

"Go on to number two," Ebbers said.

"Number two is quite simple. A single request."

Ebbers did and said nothing.

"You or the people you work for were highly instrumental in acquiring a copy of the 'Research Group' memo authorizing funding for 'Project Icarus,' or however else the Pentagon referred to the lab in Guatemala."

"You're welcome."

"Why, thank you," Cooper said. "However, due to the efficiency with which you obtained the document, I would like you to deploy your ingenuity and wherewithal once more. I'll say again: it's a simple task. I'll just need you to tell me who *wrote* it."

Cooper shifted again in his seat.

"I want to know who worked for the 'Research Group' during the period in question—1979 or thereabouts, or in other words, the time when the lab was funded. Mostly, I'd like to know who made the call. I'm sure it shouldn't be too difficult—hell, Lou, based on the efficient way most of the findings unearthed by the 'cell' that reported to you were kept utterly quiet, I'd guess you're probably fast friends with some or all of the relevant parties anyway."

Cooper tapped the steering wheel a couple times.

"Once you track down the names, you can leave the list, however long it might be, under my name at the front desk of the Jefferson Hotel. I'll need it by eight A.M. tomorrow."

Ebbers said, "Under your real name, or your assumed one?"

Cooper chuckled.

"Not bad, Lou," he said. "Tell you what—take your pick. And just in case there are one or more names on the list with considerable clout—which I suspect there are—it goes without saying that once I get it, well, I didn't get the list from you. Not, of course, unless I step into that aforementioned harm's way."

Cooper unlocked his door, opened it, and climbed out. He leaned in and tossed Lou Ebbers the car keys.

"Your driver's in the trunk," he said. "Slap him once or twice and he oughta come around."

Cooper grinned.

"Live slow, mon," he said.

Then he shut the door and strolled around the empty corner, Ebbers seeing the awkward fits and starts in his walk as Cooper limped his way out of view.

The alarm box in the building's basement had taken some highly technical fiddling, but once he'd disarmed the window sensors, Cooper had been able to climb into the Georgetown brownstone undetected—and now sat in a very expensive leather reading chair in the brownstone's library.

Besides the glow from a couple of safety lights in the hall—lights that hadn't managed to keep the place safe from trespassing beach bums—the room was dark. Alone for the moment, Cooper pondered the concluding act of his "snuffer-outer" theory from his throne of darkness.

The snuffer-outers, which Cooper now believed to be a snuffer-outer, singular, had sought to eliminate all traces of the shipment of gold artifacts seized by the late Cap'n Roy. The snuffer-outer had caught wind of the artifacts' existence upon the Coast Guard's discovery of Po Keeler's cargo in the hold of the *Seahawk*. The snuffer-outer had applied the muzzle to the tale of the pillaged artifacts because he knew where the artifacts had come from, and what had happened there: the snuffing out of an entire indigenous civilization. Said genocide occurring due to an accident, leak, or spill from the Pentagon-funded biological weapons laboratory operating, until then, under a shroud of secrecy a couple miles east of the village in the same rain forest crater.

And while the snuffer-outer had, until now, kept Cooper—CIA employee that he technically remained—out of the dead pool, Cooper figured the exclusion would now be rescinded. Particularly since Cooper, and the "cell" for which he worked, had found enough to connect the dots between the late Raul Márquez, his army of bio-bombers, their genetically engineered strain of filovirus, and the lab that had developed the strain.

The crayon that connected the dots, oddly enough, coming in the form of the sole survivor of the accidental genocide—a woman immortalized, at least temporarily, in a mausoleum beneath some very fine wine. And she'd had her revenge—she'd taken more American lives than the American filo lab had taken from her brethren. Including a sequential beheading of the full roster of names from the "Research Group" memo.

But in the end, she and Raul had been a little off target: they'd missed the actual author of the memo—the one to authorize the funding of the lab in the first place.

In the sealed envelope delivered to the Jefferson Hotel came a list of four names. The envelope had been addressed to Cooper's real name, rather than his current, made-up identity. Though already fully aware of how Ebbers knew, Cooper still enjoyed the joke.

Four men had run the "Research Group" from 1976 to 1979, or so the new document retrieved by Ebbers revealed. Following a Langley database check of the three names he didn't recognize, Cooper confirmed what he'd assumed to be true on his first read: only one of the four former Pentagon staffers on Ebbers's list now held the kind of position that would have allowed him to learn of the Coast Guard's seizure of the good ship *Seahawk*—and only one of the former staffers, the same man, possessed the power to engineer the snuff-out whose wrath Cooper had thus far managed to avoid.

He now sat in the man's library—the personal study of the Snuffer-Outer-in-Chief.

When he came, Cooper knew the man would be arriving in a Lincoln Town Car, same as Lou Ebbers always did.

Henry Curlwood removed his coat and came into his brownstone.

"Hennie," as he was called, had been *Lieutenant* Curlwood during his days at the helm of the Pentagon's Research Group, but was now known—by Cooper and just about everyone else who read a newspaper—as *White House Deputy Chief of Staff* Curlwood.

Curlwood wore a holier-than-thou expression everywhere he went, including in the privacy of his own home—a fact to which Cooper was able to attest as the safety light in the vestibule illuminated the man's face from the angle Cooper had on him from the library.

Cooper knew there would be a Secret Service detail accompanying Curlwood, but he didn't much care. He was betting on a reaction from Curlwood, the Snuffer-Outer-in-Chief, that would preclude the need for the bodyguard to come to his rescue. Cooper assumed the deputy chief of staff's famously brilliant mind would quickly estimate the meaning and ramifications of Cooper's presence in his study.

Presuming, of course, Curlwood was the snuffer-outer.

"Hennie, my boy!" Cooper said. "How about a fire?"

He'd considered lighting up the fireplace earlier but reconsidered—might have brought the Secret Service man in the door first.

Curlwood poked his irritable face into the opening that connected the hall and library as Cooper flicked on the light beside the leather chair—Cooper's peeling hull of a tan popping to life in the splash of the lamp. The expression on Curlwood's face popped to life too, as it registered first confusion and surprise, but next, a calming sort of recognition—Curlwood giving Cooper all the confirmation he needed in that one look.

There's no reason he would recognize me except as the man he decided not to snuff out.

The Secret Service man was good. In one swift motion, he shouldered Curlwood behind the wall, drew his gun, took one and one-half steps across the study, and smothered Cooper with a diving tackle, the barrel of his pistol digging into Cooper's rib cage as Cooper toppled backward in the chair and let the bodyguard spin him to the floor and cuff him, knee-to-head and gun-to-back, with relatively little resistance.

"Nice work," Cooper said.

"Shut up," the Secret Service man said with a thrust of the gun, hard, into the space between two of Cooper's ribs.

He'd begun to radio for backup—by way of the usual communication device secured to his wrist—when Curlwood reemerged in the hall.

"Let him up," he said to his bodyguard. "I know him."

"You sure about this?" the Secret Service man said, shifting all his weight to the knee planted on Cooper's head. Cooper thinking the guy must have wanted to add, *He seems like a fucking wiseass—I wouldn't trust him if I were you,* but knowing as well as the bodyguard did that these guys didn't get paid to offer their opinions to the people they guarded.

"Let him up."

When he had, and the Browning had been carefully removed from its spot in the small of Cooper's back, the Secret Service man said, "Cuffs on or off?"

"Off," Curlwood said. "Leave us alone here for a minute, please."

"I'll be in the next room if you need me," the bodyguard said. He picked up the fallen chair and lamp and set them in their original places. Then the cuffs came off, and the Secret Service man canceled his call for backup and began explaining to his wrist what had happened as he turned down the hall. Cooper noticed the man didn't holster either firearm—Secret Service–issue Sig Sauer nor CIA-issue Browning.

The deputy chief of staff hadn't suggested he return to his place in the chair, but Cooper did so anyway. Curlwood remained standing despite the available clone of a chair two steps behind him.

When the guard had passed out of earshot, Curlwood spoke. "What do you want?"

Grinning like a kid in a candy store for the duration, Cooper dictated arrangements to Curlwood as he saw them proceeding, giving the deputy chief the same basic fuck-with-me-and-Project-Icarus-goes-public threat he'd used with Ebbers. This time, he mentioned Ernesto Borrego and Lieutenant Riley of the Royal Virgin Islands Police Force as the other individuals who, were they to step into harm, would also trigger the release of the documentation on the lab and the various and sundry roles its genetically engineered "filo" had played.

"Including," Cooper said, "the name of the lieutenant who allocated the funding for the lab in the first place."

"Fine," Curlwood said.

He didn't ask for explanation or clarification.

Cooper hunkered down in the chair, staring up at Curlwood for a long, silent while. Curlwood didn't say anything to fill the void. He didn't particularly hold Cooper's gaze either.

"You've got some kind of faith, Hennie," he said. "Misplaced though it is."

Curlwood the crackerjack advisor digested and interpreted in two seconds flat.

"I suppose," the deputy chief of staff said, "I could say something like, 'I spared you, and therefore assumed you'd spare me,' but in actuality I had you checked out. Quite early in the process. Top to bottom."

"That so," Cooper said.

"You're known for your extortion schemes. You show up in my library—logic completes the equation."

"You ought to exercise a little more caution with your profiling, there, Hennie," Cooper said. "Normally, your assessment might prove correct, but Cap'n Roy Gillespie was a good man. And though I didn't know them, the Mayans in the fucking rain forest crater probably weren't bad folks either."

"Perhaps he was. And perhaps they were. Are we through?"

Cooper breathed in a long, slow volume of air and let it out the way a slow leak might result in the deflation of an inner tube. He'd given this a lot of thought—short of establishing a scholarship fund for other, as-yet-alive Mayan Indian villagers, what the hell was left to be done? Sleeping Beauty's fellow villagers were dead and gone. Lying in a hospital bed in São Paulo for the few weeks of recovery his wounds had required, Cooper had ultimately decided that unless he decided to make his appearance at the snuffer-outer's home armed with a machete—prepared to behead the final target on Sleeping Beauty's vengeance list—there existed few options beyond the usual self-preservation extortion scheme, albeit loaded with a shot at protecting a few others in the process.

Seated before him now, however, Cooper found he had to physically tamp down the temptation to throw his São Paulo thinking to the wind, reach up, and strangle Curlwood with his bare hands.

Hennie, it's your lucky goddamn day: after two trips down the hatch, my murderous streak seems to have been replaced by a stronger than normal desire for self-preservation—as though for the first time in twenty years I've got something to live for, and somehow it turns out that an institutionalized, murderous powermonger like you gets the honor of being the first to be spared.

Cooper stood. He stepped up to the shorter Curlwood, leaned his face down until their noses nearly touched, and grabbed hold of Curlwood's head, feeling the man's fleshy ears and cheeks against his palms. Then he slapped the deputy chief of staff on his left cheek—twice, extremely hard.

"For now," he said. "We're through for now."

He released Curlwood from his grip.

Curlwood didn't do anything but stand in place as Cooper

limped into the hall and said, "My gun," speaking in the direction he'd seen the Secret Service man go.

When no reply came, Curlwood yelled, "Give it to him!"

The Secret Service man came into the hall and flipped Cooper his Browning, which Cooper noticed, upon snatching the weapon, felt considerably lighter than before.

He returned the bulletless gun to the waistband at the small of his back and headed for the hills.

Laramie hadn't told anybody but her supervisor that she was back in town, so the knock at the door concerned her. There hadn't been word of any new bombings—not that she had heard, at any rate. But once the filo was found to spread into fresh territory—it was happening in small pockets throughout most regions of the country—Laramie understood part of the quarantine process to involve door-to-door visits by the National Guard.

This city is now under lockdown, she expected her visitor to announce. *You are not to leave your home; not even to stand in your yard. Violators are subject to immediate arrest.*

The visitor she spied through the peekhole in the front door of her condo was not, however, a member of the National Guard. She watched as Cooper lifted a thermos and two full-figured cocktail glasses so she could see them through the peephole.

It occurred to Laramie she was wearing only her panties and Lakers nightshirt. She considered ducking into her bedroom to pull on a pair of jeans, then thought *what the hell* and opened the door.

Cooper slid in and Laramie noticed he was wearing an oddly conformist selection of clothes—a sweater with a beefy collar-and-button arrangement, khaki slacks that actually reached below the knee, and even *shoes*. Laramie couldn't remember the last time she'd seen Cooper out of uniform. Taking it in reverse order, it was always—*always*—flip-flops or sandals, *almost* always shorts, and usually a tropical-pattern short-sleeved silk shirt.

Cooper raised the thermos and cocktail glasses.

"Would have preferred to hold this little reunion on the beach near San Cristóbal," he said, "but with air travel restrictions being what they are, I'm figuring genuine Cuban *mojitos* will serve as the next best thing."

Laramie shut the door and stood facing him with hands on hips.

"You look different," she said.

"You don't," he said.

Laramie hadn't moved from her place near the door, and Cooper noted that Laramie, in keeping with the manners of other government employees, hadn't suggested he make himself comfortable on one of the available surfaces that surrounded them.

Therefore he, too, stood his ground.

"Was that a compliment?" Laramie said.

"Probably," Cooper said.

Laramie nodded this time.

"What are you doing here," she said.

"Saying hello," Cooper said, "and, while I'm at it, congratulating my commanding officer on her relative success in defusing the 'bioterror' crisis—"

"Probably there was some other business you were here to attend to," Laramie said, "but as the human lie detector machine, I'm going to posit the theory that you're also here in an effort to impress me."

"What gives you that idea?"

"When was the last time you swung by my actual home?"

Cooper said, "That would be never."

"When did you last wear clothes a normal person would wear?" Laramie said.

"Tough question," he said.

"These almost appear as gestures of the sort that would lead one to conclude there's no longer an ultimatum in effect," Laramie said, "requiring that I return to the islands to hop from resort to beach to spa and back again—or incur the wrath of zero phone calls."

Cooper said, "Well, strangely, you seem to prefer living where people bomb you with filoviruses just for living here. But eventually one comes to accept such eccentricities."

They kept standing in their places.

"What's in a *mojito?*" Laramie said.

"A lot of very good rum," Cooper said, "a few crushed mint leaves, some sugar, and very little soda water. Over ice."

"Sounds pretty good."

"Celebrated yet traditional Cuban cocktail," Cooper said. "Speaking of tradition, by the way, this would be my first booze since departing on that Central American cruise you sent me on."

Laramie stood firm but almost cracked a smile.

"Funny," she said.

"What's funny about recovering from massive and lengthy liquor abuse?" he said.

"I'm a few days in on the caffeine-withdrawal headaches myself," she said.

"Ah," Cooper said.

After a moment, Laramie said, "We don't get along very well."

Cooper considered this.

"Probably about as well as an old married couple," he said.

Laramie looked at him.

"Except," she said, "by comparison, we'll probably see each other once every month. Or every two months—instead of every day. And yet, we will probably still get along just as poorly."

Cooper shrugged.

"I've got a reputation to uphold," he said.

"As a grouch, you mean."

"Yeah," he said. "As a grouch."

Laramie let one hand drop from her waist.

"You said you haven't had a drink since you pulled that skydiving stunt of yours?"

Then she thought of something.

"And what happened, by the way? Did you drop your portable electronics out the window of the plane? Next time, would you care to update any of us a little faster, maybe?"

"I hit a tree," he said, "but why don't you come back to what you said before you started in on the interrogation."

Laramie felt the heat pop from her shoulders into her neck.

She said, "You mean the part about your not having a drink since then?"

"Yeah," he said. "That part."

Cooper felt as though he were leaning forward—as if Laramie were some sort of magnet, and he, a slab of steel.

"Oh," she said. "That."

"Where were you going with that," he said.

"Who's the lie detector now?"

"Where were you going," Cooper said.

Laramie sighed.

"Fine," she said. "If you must know, I was going to say something in the order of, 'Well, why start now,' and, well . . ."

Great, she thought: *from bold to shy in thirty seconds or less . . .*

"If you walk in there," Cooper said, "and I set these drinks down and follow you into your room, then you won't have to say what it was you were going to say before you started to think a little too much about—"

"Quiet," she said, dropped her other hand from her waist, and touched his shoulder as she walked past him and on through the darkened doorway to her bedroom.

Cooper bent down and set the thermos and glasses on the floor.

Quiet it is, he thought, and followed her in.

ACKNOWLEDGMENTS

It is unlikely this book would exist anywhere but the hard drive on my PowerBook were it not for the efforts, generosity, and excellence of Marc H. Glick and Stephen F. Breimer, Matthew Guma and Richard Pine, Jess Taylor, Michael Morrison, Lisa Gallagher, and Sarah Durand. I'm also grateful for the effort that Rachel Bressler, Lynn Grady, and Eryn Wade—along with the many other talented people at HarperCollins—constantly put forth on Cooper's behalf.

I'd also like to mention my gratitude to Mark Shapiro, Ron Semiao, George Bodenheimer, Mike Antinoro, Fred Christenson, Crowley Sullivan, Ron Wechsler, and the long roster of my former and current colleagues at ESPN.

The world of fiction-writing and -selling includes some very kind souls, and for their kind words about *Painkiller*, I'd like to thank Michael Connelly, Clive Cussler, James Patterson, James Rollins, James Siegel, David Morrell, Christopher Reich, and last but not least, Gregg Hurwitz, who actually saw fit to introduce me to most of the people in the top paragraph above. I'm also way in debt to every bookseller—independent bookstore owners and staff, as well as everyone at the bigger stores too—willing to put Cooper and Laramie on shelves.

Finally, novels don't get written—at least not by me—without boundless support and patience from the home front. In that sense I'm the most fortunate person on the planet. Nadine, Sophie, Brick, Mystery Kid #3—this happens because of you guys. Mom, Dad, and Bart: thanks for always being there, and for putting this stuff in me.

As before, a salute to you all: *live slow, mon.*

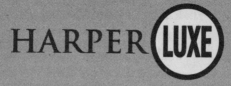